TO REMEMBER WHAT YOU'VE READ,
WRITE YOUR INITIALS IN A SQUARE.

WOMAN No. 17

WOMAN No. 17

A NOVEL

EDAN LEPUCKI

HOGARTH

LONDON/NEW YORK

Copyright © 2017 by Edan Lepucki

All rights reserved.
Published in the United States by Hogarth, an imprint of the
Crown Publishing Group, a division of Penguin Random House LLC, New York.
hogarthbooks.com

HOGARTH is a trademark of the Random House Group Limited, and the
H colophon is a trademark of Penguin Random House LLC.

Library of Congress Cataloging-in-Publication Data has been applied for.

ISBN 978-1-101-90425-1
Ebook ISBN 978-1-101-90426-8

Printed in the United States of America

Book design by Lauren Dong
Jacket design by Elena Giavaldi
Jacket photographs: Francesco Sambati (woman);
Space Images/Blend Images/Getty Images (pool)

10 9 8 7 6 5 4 3 2 1

First Edition

To my mother, Margaret High Guzik, who always says,
"If you're bored, read a book."

WOMAN No. 17

LADY

1.

I T WAS SUMMER. THE HEAT HAD ARRIVED HARSH AND BRIGHT, bleaching the sidewalks and choking the flowers before they had a chance to wilt. The freeways shimmered, any hotter and they might crack, might explode, and the poor cars would confetti into the air. People were complaining, they were moving slowly. They were swarming the beaches like tiny bugs upon the backs of dead animals. I preferred to stay home: ice cubes in the dog bowl, Riesling in the freezer. The air conditioner was broken. I had taken to sitting in the living room with the curtains drawn, my body edged with sweat like frosting on a cake, daring to see how hot it could get. I ate salad for dinner every night and had almost checked myself and the boys into a hotel. I'd refrained because of the babysitter search. What would applicants think if I requested they meet me poolside at the Roosevelt?

Instead I waited. It didn't take long for the job hunters to come calling.

The doorbell rang eight minutes ahead of schedule and I jumped. This was the first interview. I'd been fluffing and re-fluffing the couch pillows, adjusting my ponytail.

When I opened the front door, a gust of gritty air came rushing at me and I felt its particulates dirtying my lungs. A young woman stood on the welcome mat, smiling so wide I could see where her gums webbed into her mouth.

I'd expected her to be pretty, almost all young women in L.A. are, especially those raised here, the beauty's in the tap water, but she was plain-looking, her wide, hazel eyes too far apart, her dark blond hair thin and flat.

"Esther?" I finally said.

I knew she didn't go by her full name, but "S" felt so pretentious, as if she'd rebranded herself at sleep-away camp.

"Please," she said. "Call me S."

I admired her assertiveness. "S it is then. Come in."

She was wearing a cheap floral-print dress and leather sandals. The dress was loose where it should have been fitted and it accentuated her wide hips. As my mother might have said, the poor girl doesn't know how to dress her own body. Know thy size and shape. Being female is a lifelong lesson that starts with how to wipe (front to back), and ends only with death, graceless always. Clearly, this young woman hadn't been properly instructed.

With another gummy smile she stepped into the house. There was no hesitation.

"Sorry it's so stuffy in here," I said. "The air conditioning isn't working—something's wrong with the ventilation system. It needs to be completely rehabbed. I keep hoping the heat will break, but it just gets hotter and hotter. I'm sure there's a wildfire or two in our future. Maybe the whole city will just burst into flames. That might be kind of fun, actually."

I realized I was babbling and shut my mouth. S still hadn't said anything, she was too busy taking in the high-beamed ceiling of the living room and the framed prints on the wall: the antique circus poster, the black-and-white photograph of a Pizza Hut that my sister-in-law Kit had taken and given to me and Karl as a wedding gift. I wondered if she'd ask for it back.

S walked closer to the photo and I recalled that she had graduated with a minor (a minor!) in art. In an email she'd written that she loved the Pre-Raphaelites.

"Was there traffic coming up the hill?" I said.

"Not too bad," she replied, not looking away from the photo. And then, "This is rad."

When she finally turned back to me with her big, pretty eyes I said, "Thank you," as if I'd taken it.

S looked so young standing there. She *was* young, she couldn't have been older than twenty-two. I remembered myself at that age: my pure, unlined face; my brain-dead roommates and our giant glass ashtray; my potential—that feeling I could apply to graduate school whenever I was ready and all would be solved. I'd been beautiful. The past tense was like a shove to the chest.

"Did you study photography in any of your classes?" I asked.

"Nah. Mostly your standard paintings by Dead Guys."

In the photograph a man leaned sullenly against the glass doors of the Pizza Hut. Big clouds ballooned across the sky.

S finally turned from the picture. Beyond the ghost of gloss on her lips she wasn't wearing any makeup. She hadn't even put on mascara for this interview.

"My mom calls it Pizza Slut," she said, and laughed.

I laughed too, mostly out of confusion. S didn't seem nervous enough—or at all. Maybe she didn't really want the job.

"Shall we go into the kitchen to talk?" I asked. "We can discuss your qualifications."

She nodded and smiled again. "Sure thing."

"Devin's asleep," I said as I led her through the dining room. "In case you're wondering."

"I was, actually." She widened her eyes, goofy. "What if you'd lied about having a kid? What if you were really a murderer? Wasn't there a Craigslist killer?"

This time I laughed for real. Who was this girl?

"Don't worry," I said. "Killers don't post for nannies. They want personal assistants, and they would definitely ask to see a photo first."

S looked down at herself. "So much for that," she said.

I laughed again. She was so easy with me, as if we'd met dozens of times before. Of course, I'd never heard of her until she answered my ad, LIVE-IN NANNY WANTED FOR BRIGHT AND ADORABLE TODDLER (HOLLYWOOD HILLS ADJACENT), with a sweet email that advised me to "please peruse the attached curriculum vitae." Her mother must have ghostwritten that.

"Dev should wake in about fifteen minutes," I said.

I'd planned it this way. I had to make sure S wasn't a weirdo before introducing her to my child. But I knew she'd be normal. She was a recent Berkeley grad, for God's sake, and had been raised right down the hill. She may have dabbled in the Pre-Raphaelites but her senior honors thesis was on early childhood education.

We walked into the kitchen, which Karl and I had redone. The sink was wide as a pig's trough and the chrome fridge hummed. Milkshake, our old Maltese, lay in the corner, panting.

"He didn't come running when the bell rang?" S asked, bending down to pet him.

"He's so old he's forgotten how to be a dog," I said. "Would you like some water, or maybe some iced tea?"

I expected her to say no, but she took me up on the iced tea. I watched as she drank it down in one long gulp.

"The AC in the Camry's busted," she said when the glass was empty, as if we were sharing the car. She wiped her mouth with the back of her arm.

Karl, who had moved out just a few weeks before, would have said that S lacked self-awareness, but that wasn't it. It wasn't a deficit. S was comfortable with herself, with her average looks, her unflattering clothing, her interest in art. *Take it or leave it,* she seemed to say. I only wished I had that kind of confidence. The bravado of someone younger, twenty years younger, cuts deep. And yet, I didn't resent S. In fact, I liked her.

"You said you're living with your mother?" I asked.

"Staying, not living," she replied. "On the couch."

All this time I'd been imagining her mother in a condo in Westwood. She'd keep the treadmill in the guest room, next to a bed outfitted with brocade shams, and, in the corner, a big bag of wrapping-paper supplies. But apparently there was no guest room.

S held up her glass and gestured with her chin to the sink. She wanted to wash it, I realized.

"Go for it," I said.

"I'm looking to get my own place as soon as possible," she said, turning on the water. "It's why this position is ideal. I also love the age Devin is—two, three years old is when a kid's imagination really soars. If you take language development into consideration, you're—"

"What did you say your thesis was on again?" I passed her a towel and we sat at the kitchen's center island. Her résumé—her curriculum vitae—was printed out on the counter.

"Thesis is too strong a word," she said. "It was my senior project. I wrote about the benefits of play for children aged eighteen months to four. How they use it to make sense of the world and themselves, to test limits and face their fears. It's incredible, really."

I nodded. This was the poised, studious S.

"Have you ever given Devin a big cardboard box to play with?"

"I put him in one when he's been bad," I said.

She squinted at me.

"I'm kidding."

"Oh. Ha. Sorry. I've just read about stuff like that happening."

"Between that and the Internet murderers—what are you reading?"

"Mostly erotica."

This time, I squinted.

"Kidding." She smiled. "Anyway, if you give Devin a big empty cardboard box you'd be amazed by the things he comes up with. In two minutes it'll be a car, or a spaceship."

"Or a coffin."

"Are you sure you're a mother?" she said.

"Maybe, maybe not." I winked. "Follow me."

On the back deck, the sun was so strong I closed my eyes. Even my lids were perspiring. A bead of sweat slid between my breasts. The sounds of wood sanders, buzz saws, and jackhammers rang out across the hill. Someone was always knocking down something old to build something new.

I opened my eyes and led S down the deck stairs.

"Devin still sleeps for over two hours every afternoon, thank goodness," I was explaining. "And when he wakes up I try to get him to use the potty, even though he usually refuses."

S was looking at the pool, glittering in the sunlight and circled with a border of Astroturf. (Karl's idea—the drought and all that.) Behind it towered a steep wall of canyon landscaped with chaparral and sage scrub. A line of houses looked down on us from above: one dilapidated shack, a couple of tasteful mansions, and a modern thing, all concrete, like a parking garage. Karl called these houses the Eavesdroppers.

"I didn't mention the pool in the ad."

"Freeloaders need not apply?"

"Exactly. I also didn't mention that I'm separated from Devin's dad."

S nodded.

"And . . ." I turned around and pointed at Seth's window on the second floor. "I have another son, from a previous relationship. He's eighteen. Seth. That's his room."

It had only taken me twenty minutes to come clean: Seth was holed up in his room, and Devin was asleep in his new big-boy bed, and I was a soon-to-be divorcee like so many other women in the neighbor-hood. That my sons were fathered by two different men, almost two decades apart, made me slightly more interesting. That was my theory anyway. Before this interview, I thought my situation might impress or intimidate a young woman who wanted a job in childcare. At the very least, it might give me an excuse to offer her less money. But it all seemed so silly now. S couldn't be ruffled.

"He's nonverbal," I said finally.

"Who?"

"Seth. He doesn't speak, never has."

"Has he—"

"Is he autistic? No. Is that what you were going to ask? He's also not deaf." I lowered my voice. "And he isn't a genius either."

This was what I always said to people. My script. My shtick. It made it easier.

"No," she said. "I was going to ask if he'd ever had speech therapy. I've read about children with language disabilities."

She'd *read* about them?

"He was treated by quite a few doctors when he was younger," I said.

We were steps from the pool and I imagined pushing S into the deep end. Her horrible dress would bunch around her waist and I'd see her blurry cream-cheese-white thighs. I was diligent about cleaning the pool every morning, for myself and for the Eavesdroppers, and so there'd be no plant debris or floating bees to wreck my view of a submerged S. She most definitely wore sensible underwear.

Instead I said, "I couldn't send him to speech therapy because he couldn't speak."

"I'm so sorry! I didn't mean to offend you," she said. For a second I'd shaken her up. But if she was worried that the interview had gone south, she didn't show it. She seemed concerned only for my feelings.

I smiled at her and put a hand on her arm. Just a nudge and she'd be in the pool. "It's totally fine," I said. I cocked my ear. "I think Devin's awake."

As we headed into the house, I wondered whether she was still thinking about Seth. People were always curious about him. Eager, even, as though he were a rare animal you could pet.

I thought of the Hottentot Venus. Seth and I had read about her: sold into slavery over two centuries earlier and made into an attraction, to be ogled and inspected, laughed and gasped at. It was no doubt what the Man in the Yellow Hat had initially planned to do with Curious George: lock him up, make money off of him. That was Devin's hero—the man, not the monkey. Just the other day, Seth had typed to me on his iPad: Doesnt he know the guys an animal poacher? I told him to give Devin a break, he wasn't even three yet.

For his final high school paper, Seth had written about the Hottentot Venus. I've forgotten her real name, though I'm sure Seth remembers it.

"Mommy! Mommy!" Devin yelled from his room. He'd say it until I came to rescue him.

He was sitting up in his little toddler bed when we got to his room, and when he saw we had a visitor he grinned and then covered his face with Bucky, his stuffed rabbit.

"Did you sleep well, baby?" I asked.

I took his hand and helped him out of bed. S was already kneeling down to his level.

AFTER I'D INTRODUCED them, I stepped back. Devin didn't care where I was; he wanted to show S his truck collection. I watched from the doorway as they pushed them back and forth across the rug, talking about the colors, both of them making engine noises with their mouths. When Devin moved to sit on her lap, S didn't make note of it, as another adult might. She taught him a song about fish, and together they sang it, my son's big blue eyes widening with delight. His cheeks were still pillow-creased from his nap, and his hair, knotted and sweaty, stuck up in tufts. Placed thusly in this nanny tableau, Devin looked perfect.

He *was* perfect. A billion traumas would be upon him someday. But not yet. And if they didn't come to him, he'd seek them out. We all do—look for pain I mean. Until then, my baby was a beloved fool, not a mark on him.

Then Devin did the unthinkable. He looked up at S and said, "I need water."

I gasped, I couldn't help it.

S looked up at me, puzzled.

"The prince usually doesn't let anyone else but me wait on him."

S bowed her head to Devin. "I'd be honored to be your servant."

"Uh-oh," I told her, "now you're in trouble. He's very literal."

"Please?" Devin said. "Please!"

I hired her. Someone else, someone like Karl, would have checked S's references first, but the thought only flitted across my brain before I dismissed it. Devin had chosen this girl, in his way, and I liked her too. I could fictionalize a background check for Karl. If I said, "I had a good feeling about her," he'd insist on vetting S himself, and that would take forever.

She would move into the Cottage the following Monday. She'd work four days and one evening a week.

When I handed her the key, she hugged me and Devin, who was slung on my hip. S really came in for a squeeze, and as she pulled away, a sharp hint of body odor, metallic and musky, took root in my nostrils. I wanted to remember it.

As soon as S had driven away in "the Camry," Devin and I went upstairs to find Seth. I knocked on his door twice, and then, together,

Devin and I counted slowly to ten. Only after that did I turn the knob.
I'd done this ever since Seth was thirteen and I'd accidentally walked
in on him naked.

"Seth?"

He was sitting at his computer wearing only swim trunks and a
Lakers jersey. The room, as usual, smelled dank. Today Seth had
lugged the fan from my bedroom so that he had two going, their heads
rotating back and forth like land surveyors. He sat between them and
every few seconds his hair lifted in the breeze. He was playing a video
game. I hated the video games, but Karl had argued on their behalf,
saying I shouldn't be suspicious of new forms of storytelling. As if a
stupid *New York Times* article could possibly justify the Fallout mara-
thons he and Seth played, but I'd let it go. Before Karl moved out, Seth
and I referred to him as "College Boy," because he dropped big words
in his emails and referenced articles from the *Times Literary Supplement*
to bank tellers, and got up before sunrise the day the Booker Prize
nominees were announced, even though he wasn't British or a writer.
He was a television producer.

Seth glanced up and I smiled; for once he wasn't rolling his eyes.
He hadn't cut me any slack since Karl had moved out.

"How's it going?" I asked.

Seth looked more and more like Marco as he got older: black hair,
olive skin, long eyelashes. Swarthy as a swashbuckler. He hadn't been
a cute kid; he'd been too skinny, too haunted-seeming, his nose too
big and adult for his face. But he was growing into his looks. Karl had
joked that, pretty soon, women would start lining up. "The strong,
silent type," he'd quipped.

Seth paused his game and gave Devin a high five. To some strangers, Seth's silence was awkward and difficult to handle, a barrier they
couldn't surmount. But if you knew him, Seth was just Seth. To
Devin, Seth was his amazing big brother.

"Seff! Seff!" Devin yelled.

"Inside voice, baby."

"Seff! I have a new friend."

"The nanny came," I said. "S. She's moving in Monday, so you
need to vacuum the Cottage for her. You promised."

I waited for Seth to grab his iPad and type out a message. It had taken years for me to expect, to demand, some response, even if it was merely a shake of his head. I hated waiting and waiting and getting nothing from him.

"Seth," I said again.

This time, he nodded at the computer screen. On it, an image of a castle, shot from above, was cloaked in mist. For all I knew, it was supposed to be from a dragon's perspective.

"Only one more hour," I said. "I mean it. And no more snarky tweets about the gazpacho I made, okay?"

Every day I checked his account, @sethconscious. His tweets were clever and wise, and the #GazpachoFail series had been retweeted two dozen times at least. I just looked at his feed, I didn't have my own account. Seth said I couldn't, and Karl said it was like dancing at a wedding. "If you really want to, go ahead," he'd said, "but you'll regret those moves the next morning."

Now, Seth made one of our old signs: *You got it, Ninja Mama.*

Thanks, Burrito Flower, I signed.

Love times a million, he signed.

"What him doing?" Devin asked.

"Seth's playing video games. You know that's for bigger kids, right?"

Devin shook his head violently. "With his hands! What him doing?"

Seth grinned. He held his two hands in a prayer position and then clapped the lower halves together three times. That was our sign for *Mambo time,* which meant, basically: You're busted!

"It's just something Seth and I do," I explained. Devin had learned a little ASL, but none of the special signs. "Instead of talking. You know that."

Devin sucked on a finger contemplatively and Seth crossed his eyes until his brother laughed.

"Come on, Devy-Dev," I said, hitching him higher onto my waist. "Let's go draw a picture for S. Isn't she the best?"

2.

I WASN'T BORN WITH THE NAME LADY. MY BIRTH CERTIFICATE reads Pearl, and I was called that for the first year of my life until one evening, as my mother was getting ready for a party, I stepped into her shoes. They were so big, the heels so high, that I couldn't lift my feet. I had to ski across the room to her.

"Look, Mommy," I said.

My mother glanced up from her jewelry box or her address book or her vodka soda and said, "What a lady." Like that, I had a new name. Like that, I became someone else.

It would be a sweet little story if my mother weren't so damaged. She didn't talk to anyone in her family, wouldn't say why, and she rarely let me see my dad until it was too late and he was in the hospital with the stroke that would kill him. For as long as I could remember, it had always been just my mother and me, marooned on our pathetic female island. If she forgot to pick me up from school—which was more often than I want to admit—I'd have to walk the three miles home. Once I took the bus and my mother was appalled. "We do not take public transportation!" she cried. In the eighth grade, I hitched a ride from a woman who said I looked like an orphan, shivering like I was, my hair a mess.

"There's something to that," I told her.

When I was a girl, my mother would sing me "Happy Birthday" at night as a lullaby. If that sounds cute, it wasn't. Even now I equate the song with darkness, with the long toss-and-turn to dawn, and on my birthday, I still ask for something else. "Sing me Elton John or what-ever," I'll say, because I don't know his songs, not really. Marco once refused me this request, and I wouldn't blow out the candles. They burned down to little eraser-tops, the wax pooling into the white frosting until Marco intercepted, pulling the candles out in a mad rush, extinguishing the flames between his fingers. I wish I could say that was our last birthday together, but then I got pregnant with Seth so we dragged things out for another year or so.

Did you know that if you bite on a real pearl, it should feel gritty against your teeth? I learned that when I was in my twenties, and ever since I've wished for my old name back. But I'm Lady now, for better or for worse, and people love the name, or they say they do.

Marco told me all the time. He'd sing *"Lady, lady, my fair lady,"* when we were drunk, the two of us staggering home from one neighborhood watering hole or another. "How ladylike," he'd say whenever I got dressed up. On the back of the only photo I still have of the two of us, the one I hide in an old cigar box in my bedside table drawer, Marco scribbled "Lady and the Tramp, 1997." In it, we're in the deep armpit of the Valley, outside the dialysis center where his mother went for treatment. Marco is leaning against a wall, wearing the vintage mechanic's shirt he cherished because his name was embroidered in cursive across the front badge. He's smoking a cigarette and I'm standing next to him, looking at him with a mixture of admiration and irritation. I'm twenty-two and you can see my nipples through my too-small VIRGINIA IS FOR LOVERS shirt. Even now I can conjure Marco next to me—or, not him, but how he felt. How he smelled. We would make love and for the next few hours I thought I could smell the nicotine every time I went to pee.

His mother was dying when she took that picture. "Smile," she said, and because we were young and didn't like being told what to do, we didn't.

I COULDN'T TELL Karl that I'd hired S because she seemed natural with Devin in a way that I wasn't with Seth when I was her age. He'd claim I had issues about being maternal.

"That's because I'm not," I'd said once. This was right after Devin was born.

"Would you please just look at yourself? Your baby is sucking milk right out of your body."

"I realize my argument is shaky."

"It sure is. Look at Seth! You've been a natural. Always."

But Karl hadn't known me always.

3.

I WAS DIFFERENT WITH SETH. AS SOON AS I FOUND OUT I WAS pregnant with him, I drove to Planned Parenthood on Vermont in my beat-up hatchback. I wanted to pee in a cup, have it confirmed by a doctor, or at least a nurse, I didn't care whether their clinic was in a mini-mall. I'd forgotten how long the wait could be without an appointment, and by the time the beleaguered Filipina woman told me I was indeed carrying a child, I was so hungry I could barely think.

She held up a plastic wheel with numbers on it. "When did you say your last period was?" I told her, and she bit her bottom lip as she turned the disk. It was like some ancient device. I imagined Cleopatra owning one.

"You're about ten weeks along." She glanced at the disk once more and told me my due date.

"What are my options?" I asked.

She was waiting for me to elaborate, so I did: "I want to terminate the pregnancy."

I'd said those words before, it wasn't a procedure I was unfamiliar with. I'd already fallen from grace four years before, when I was eighteen. Not that the words rolled off my tongue.

"Do you have some almonds or something?" I asked.

"Excuse me?"

"I'm, just, really hungry. . . ."

And that's when I pitched forward, off the exam table. My nose hit the linoleum. When I came to, there was blood all over the nurse's hands and chest. Edwina, that was her name. "I'm gonna need some help in here," Edwina was yelling, like we were on a medical drama and I was dying of heart failure.

They got me back on the exam table and gave me some Gatorade and, weirdly, a fig. This was before every woman carried an energy bar in her purse. Now I never faint.

They called Marco. He took three hours, who knows what he was doing, probably helping some guy do a thing. That night he told me to move into his studio apartment in Koreatown. "Have my baby," he whispered.

Of all the stupid decisions I've ever made in my life. A mother isn't supposed to regret her child, so I won't. What I will regret is my belief in Marco—because, even now, I can't regret Marco. That night, I let him hold a bag of frozen broccoli to my face with one hand as he undid my jeans with the other. I let him say "I hope it's a boy" as he pulled my jeans and then my underwear down my legs and off my ankles, the bag of broccoli balanced across my whole face so that I could neither see nor breathe very well. I let him yank off the bag and pull me on top of him as he said, "I guess we don't have to be careful anymore."

I wanted to believe that Marco and I could make a family. It didn't matter that he only worked once a week at the Bagel Broker, plus odd jobs in his pickup truck, claiming that making money was a waste of a life. Or that he wrote spec scripts that no one ever read, or would read. Or that he sometimes didn't call me for days at a time, or that he'd introduced me to his coworkers as his *friend*. So what? The baby would change him, and us. Had I known that Marco's one and only wish was to give his mother a grandchild before her kidneys failed her for good, I might have stopped to reconsider. I wasn't a genie in a bottle, I was a twenty-two-year-old woman. I should have known that he was doing it for his mother because he called her that same night. I heard them talking when I emerged from the bathroom.

"No, Mom. Lady." A long pause. "A baby! Can you believe it?"

At the time, I was working as a personal assistant to an older actress. She was an actress in name only; she hadn't worked in over a decade. Not that it mattered; she lived off her dead husband's money and had the dubious honor of playing, in 1972, a woman slashed to death in some it's-so-bad-it's-good cult horror movie. She very seldomly traveled to conventions to sign autographs, and I'd tag along to make sure she had a functioning pen and a hot mug of ginger-lemon tea. When we weren't traveling, it was my duty to book her doctor's appointments, take her cat to the vet, and pick up her dry cleaning. Occasionally, I'd have to shoo away a schlubby fan who rang the doorbell, the scary-movie-themed star map clenched in his fist. It was an easy job, and the Actress's damask curtains and self-playing piano comforted me. They were the sorts of things my mother might buy if she had a mansion on Benedict Canyon Drive. My mother and I hadn't spoken since I began dating Marco, and I wasn't so dumb that I didn't see my job for what it was: the Actress paid me to be her best friend, and because I needed a mommy, I allowed the Actress to kiss my cheek as she handed me my paycheck.

The stability was nice too; back then everything felt a little precarious. My three roommates and I made just enough money to cover rent, food, and booze. It was a questionable lifestyle: the shower mold, the stolen cable, and a gangster neighbor who came over with his bong every now and again. I thought I was all right with it, but when I decided to have Marco's baby a great relief sputtered through me like an undone balloon. I'd been a middling student of English in college, and I had no clue what I wanted to do with my life. I was in love with a man my mother had called a "pathetic loser." Now that I was having his baby, I had a plan, a purpose. "I'm moving out," I announced to my roommates at the next house meeting. "I'm going to be a mom." I didn't try to hide the triumph in my voice.

If I could have been pregnant forever, I would have. I loved watching my body change, it was like puberty but without the emotional trauma, and I loved being doted on. The Actress gave me a bloomer set from Neiman's and a check for $5,000. Now that I was carrying his baby, Marco called me his girlfriend and always returned my calls. We painted a wall of his studio a bright yellow. The crib would be pushed against it.

I didn't tell my mother. I imagined one of her friends seeing me at the supermarket and reporting the news, shocked. That I hadn't broken our stalemate to tell her myself would wound her, and I knew she'd pretend to already know. She was like that: a liar.

Instead, when Marco's mother asked me to call her Mom, I complied. And when she left our apartment I let Marco fuck me until I neighed and kicked like a horse. Afterward, naked and slick with sweat, my belly so large I couldn't bend over to tie my own shoes, I let Marco feed me: he knew how to poach eggs, and I loved poached eggs. The yolk would slime down my chin and I'd lick it back into my mouth. I was going to be a mother and for the first time in maybe forever I was happy.

For those thirty-some weeks, Marco and I were in love. I finally held his attention, which was what I'd wanted all along. Did Seth, in his amniotic chamber, intuit all that was happening? Some parents-to-be are too disturbed to have sex during pregnancy. It didn't bother me, I understand the basics of anatomy, and I felt that if my unborn child were somehow witnessing my congress with his father, it would be a privilege. His papa loved his mama.

But I must have known that Marco's attention was temporary. That made me want it all the more badly.

Seth has always been a keen observer, watching at the edge of a scene without offering a single line of dialogue. I bet he came to know the sounds of traffic on Normandie, where we lived, and the tension born of too little residential parking. He must have recognized the coos of his grandmother, Marco's mother, and felt my annoyance at having to raise the volume on our TV for her. He would have heard the sound of the needle hitting whatever record Marco wanted to play, no matter what time of day or night it was, and the rasp of the Actress's voice when she called for me from her bedroom. When Seth smelled potpourri and Tiger Balm, he no doubt knew we were in her large dark mansion. I bet he could feel my heart cartwheeling each time I opened the Actress's front door to see those wide, carpeted stairs, how they split into two at the second floor, like a giant letter *T*. "A staircase fit for Fred and Ginger," I said to Marco once. Marco didn't get it, he didn't watch old movies, but Seth would.

If Seth came to recognize what was present in his world to come, he must have also sensed what was absent. My mother, for one: her voice, and her hand on my stomach (not that she would have wanted to touch a pregnant belly, but I would have made her). Also: my father and Marco's father. Both men were dead, which meant that the only male Seth heard regularly was Marco, and Marco didn't have much use for conversation. I hate to confer magical powers on a mute, but even now I wonder whether my son decided in the womb that he wouldn't speak. He'd keep it all inside.

Did Seth know what he was being born into? Maybe he intuited that the love between his parents was circumstantial, and that most of the time his father shuffled between lust and apathy. I am sure he knew that for all my happiness, I was lost and afraid. Sometimes at night I prayed that my pregnancy would last forever. I never spoke these prayers aloud, and I don't have much belief in God, so who was I talking to? Seth was my only listener.

When I pushed him out of me, he didn't cry. I tried to describe the moment to Karl on one of our early dates. "I'm pretty sure that's normal," he said, trying to comfort me. "They had to suck the mucus or what-have-you out of his throat first, didn't they?" But it wasn't just that, I said. Seth's cry was hoarse when he finally let it out, and the look on his tiny wrinkled face told me that making the sound pained him. I think it did.

I should have felt protective of my baby at that moment, but instead I was disgusted. They placed his writhing body atop my chest and I almost asked them to remove him. It's not that I wanted him to be taken away, it's that I wanted him back inside.

Even in my weakest moments, even when we were having our big fight, I never told Karl that.

4.

KARL INSISTED WE MEET FOR DINNER EVERY WEEK DESPITE our separation. "Kit thinks it's a good idea," he said. Kit was his photographer sister. I hated almost everything about her, starting with every piece of advice she gave Karl and ending with the essential oils she rubbed on the soles of her feet whenever she was feeling stressed. I'd been calling her Pizza Slut in my mind ever since S had come over.

"We're taking advice from Kit now?" I said. "She's hardly objective."

"*No one* is objective. Ever," he replied.

I rolled my eyes.

"I can hear that, you know," he said.

"Hear what?"

"You loathing me."

"I don't loathe you, Karl."

"Listen up, we're meeting at Paul Feldman's at six."

I sighed. "Which one? Galleria? The one at the Bev Cent closed."

"You betcha." He hung up.

PAUL FELDMAN'S WAS our name for P. F. Chang's. Karl had read somewhere (he was always reading somewhere) that the Chinese restaurant was actually owned by a Jewish guy with the initials "P. F."; the Chang was total fakery. Karl couldn't remember the name of the actual restaurant mogul so we called him Paul Feldman, Karl's old friend from Hebrew school.

We were only a week into dating when I took him there for the first time. Seth was with his tutor all afternoon and Karl needed a new belt, so I suggested we go to the Beverly Center.

"Beverly Center?" Karl said, his eyes twinkling. "I think I went to college with her . . . Bev! What a gal!"

I laughed. These were the pre–eye rolling days.

At the Beverly Center, we wandered into one store and then another until Karl finally said he was starving. A few blocks away there was a café he loved. "Great coffee," he said, "in cups as big as your face."

I knew the place. It was favored by rich Hollywood types and out-of-work actresses, flawless in yoga pants. I wrinkled my nose and said, "Let's do a mall restaurant."

Even then I was testing Karl's willingness to give me what I wanted. That he gave and gave and gave, and with humor, was one of the reasons I fell in love with him. And out.

Karl shrugged and looked around. "When in Rome . . ."

"I don't mean the food court," I said, and led him to the escalators.

As we passed the huge stone horses that flanked the restaurant's front door, Karl said, "These are like the horses outside China's original Forbidden City."

He described how an insane emperor had built a city-sized mau-

soleum for himself with hundreds of terra-cotta horses and soldiers
guarding its gates.

"So we're entering a giant tomb?" I said.

"Which makes this the most romantic date I've ever been on," he
replied.

Inside the dark restaurant, a ponytailed blonde, no doubt a recent
transplant from Iowa or Fresno, greeted us with a big smile. She was
dressed in head-to-toe black polyester.

"Table for two," I said.

As he slipped into the booth Karl kept his gaze on the Chinese
scroll hanging above the bar.

"God, it's so offensive in here!" he said gleefully.

"You should order a specialty cocktail," I said.

"Something with lychee, I presume." Karl held the menu far from
his face, squinting.

I put a hand on his arm. "Hey, silly. I like you in your glasses." He
was over a decade older than I was, and trying not to draw attention
to it. As though I didn't notice.

Once he had his little granny glasses on, Karl crowed. "Gluten-
free! Did you see this?"

He couldn't stop laughing, and neither could I. With Karl the
world was a delight.

We were married six weeks later, at his friend's house in Malibu,
and in our whirlwind courtship we had tried every Paul Feldman's
in the Southern California region. In record time, Karl had become
a scholar of P. F. Chang's, and of the other establishments we frequented: California Pizza Kitchen (CPK), Yogurtland (Yogalandia),
Cheesecake Factory (Cheesecock Perfunctory), et al. Karl drew the
line at Domino's, but before that line he reveled in what he called
Chain Tourism. He told all his friends about it. "You can experience
the restaurant ironically, and yet, when you bite into a slab of Oreo
cheesecake, it's almost impossible not to slip into an earnest, unmiti-
gated mode of pleasure."

Before I met Karl my critical gaze was flabby, practically atrophied;
one date with him and I felt like I was back at CSUN, except that instead of studying literature I was taking classes on everything from

the politics of traffic to the societal pressures of eating Swiss chard. His interest in the world, combined with his interest in me, eradicated my boredom.

Never mind that Seth and I actually liked the chain restaurants Karl so loved to analyze, irony notwithstanding, and that we frequented them on special occasions. Karl would never admit it, but his Chain Tourism was a variant on Lady Tourism. My life and rituals were exotic to him: I was the person who watched the shows he produced—not because I wanted to, but because I couldn't afford cable. I was a single mother who lived in a one-bedroom apartment with her teenage son. That I hadn't been raised poor myself made the country of Lady even more fascinating. Karl wanted access to my world: as stunning, amusing, and tragic as a third-world island.

WHEN I ARRIVED at Paul Feldman's, I saw that the booths were full; everyone wanted to get out of the heat, even if for only an hour. They'd stuck Karl at a table in the center of the room. There was already a high chair set up across from him, a kids' menu and crayons in place of a plate.

He stood as soon as he saw me. "Where's Dev?"

"I got a sitter."

I was still getting used to how much attention Devin required at restaurants. He'd throw food, drop a glass of water, request a sip of my wine. I knew if Karl and I tried to have our own conversation, Devin would interrupt us, saying stuff like, "No talking, Daddy!" Or, "Lions have sharp teeth! Lions have sharp teeth!" He would not, could not, be ignored.

"You knew I wanted to see him," Karl said, standing to hug me. I let him even though I was still a little sticky with sweat. He was freshly shaved and wearing a nice white shirt I didn't recognize. But he'd gone overboard with the Kiehl's and smelled like a grove of eucalyptus trees.

"You'll have him all weekend," I said, pulling away. "We have a lot to discuss and if he's here that won't happen."

A smiling waitress came over with two frosted martini glasses, halfway filled with something magenta-colored.

"It's something with açaí berries," Karl said, beaming at the waitress. He asked her for the salt-and-pepper calamari, my favorite, and after a brisk nod she was gone.

The drink tasted like a blended Fruit Roll-Up.

"Now you're ordering for me?" I said.

"You said I was too nice, so I'm trying to be an asshole."

"Karl," I said.

"Lady," he said. "I want to come home."

I took another sip. "You said you'd give me time."

"Time," he echoed. He looked exhausted. Kit was letting him stay in her guesthouse, and I wondered if the bed there was firm enough.

"I hired a nanny," I said. "Her name is S." I drew the letter in the air between us and punctuated it with a jab of my index finger. I described how well she and Devin got on, and her recent degree. "I know you'd prefer a Stanford grad."

"Is she certified in CPR?"

"Of course," I said, though I didn't know. Then I said, "She's live-in."

I wasn't surprised by his anger. "What? You said *nanny*, Lady. You never said *au pair.*"

"She moved from Berkeley, not Paris. I told you, I need the help."

"You need the help because I'm not there!" He picked up his glass and downed the whole sickly drink. "Is there even alcohol in this?"

The waitress was suddenly between us, plate of calamari in hand. "Why, yes sir, there is! You'd be surprised how much," she said.

"Give us a minute?" I asked. "And also—the pot stickers."

Before the waitress could ask, Karl said, "Pork, please. Steamed."

When we were alone again, neither of us spoke. I rolled a piece of calamari in the cup of salt, and popped it into my mouth.

"This is a *trial* separation," Karl said, his hands flat on the table. He was calm now, but I could tell the news of S was bothering him, because he wasn't eating. "I am giving you time, and that is all."

"I need a nanny's help. It's more affordable for her to live in."

"I won't let you go," he whispered.

"I hired her because I'm on contract. You know that."

"You'll write the book. You already have two chapters and the proposal."

"And it's been three months and I still haven't written a word."

With the help of Karl's friend Joyce, I'd published an essay in *Real Simple* about raising Seth, which had landed me an agent, and then a deal to write a book about my experience. "Our experience," I told Seth when I got the news. He'd smirked, and I hugged him fiercely. After we pulled apart he tapped his right elbow with his left hand, three times fast. This meant *Big-time!* Karl had looked on, confused. He was better at ASL than I was, and maybe for that reason I'd refused to teach him the special signs.

"You'll get into the book now that you have Est. I'll need to meet her, immediately."

"Her name isn't Est. It's S."

"Just the letter?"

"Just the letter."

"Jesus, Lady, where did you find this girl?"

"Devin loves her."

That seemed to hurt him, but it also, thankfully, distracted him from any further questioning.

I turned my attention to the menu. "Beef or chicken?" I said.

"To be or not to be?" Karl replied, which was what he always said.

As we ate, I told him we needed to come up with a regular custody schedule.

"I want to see him every day," Karl said.

"You work every day. And you can't come over in the evening."

"Why not?"

"Look, I'll give you every weekend if you want. Friday evening, afternoon even, to Monday morning."

"Really?"

What I didn't say was that S would be around the other days to take care of Devin. That I was effectively never going to have to watch my son.

"Maybe if I have time away from Devin," I said, "I'll be able to write. I can take the weekends to focus, and Seth and I will do stuff together that Devin's too young for."

I took a bite of beef something-or-other (gluten-free, because we could), and imagined writing. Just picturing myself in front of my laptop, the cursor blinking like a well-behaved narcoleptic, was enough to make me wish I'd never met Joyce for tacos to go over "my incredible story" as she called it. Joyce was connected to everyone in the magazine world, and she wanted to help me. ("She's obsessed with you," Karl had said.)

Over one afternoon I told her a couple of what she called "key vignettes," which she recorded on her phone before hiring someone to transcribe. Together we worked over the transcription, discarding what didn't fit, elaborating on dramatic moments, and then she crafted a through-line, which was, basically: We are all God's creatures, the agnostic version. But now Joyce was back in Manhattan, working for an online magazine about day trading, and she couldn't help me.

"I hate Joyce," I said now.

"Joyce believes in you. I believe in you. Devin's getting older and this is an excellent career path for you. Everyone always says you tell the best stories."

"This isn't a *story*, Karl, it's my *life*." My fork slipped into a swamp of brown sauce. "This food is so fucking garlicky. Garlic should not be the dominant flavor in every single dish! I can already feel it seeping out of my pores!"

Karl leaned forward and put two fingertips against my sternum. "You aren't breathing, sweetie." He pushed against the bone as if he were trying to find a secret passageway. "Open up. You need to open up."

I reared back. "Stop it!"

He removed his hand. "What?"

"Don't tell me what to do."

"Fine. Don't breathe." He looked around for the waitress, and I knew he was going to ask for the bill.

"You're so paternalistic." It was one of his words, only he didn't apply it to people but to things like the government and foie gras bans.

Karl already had his wallet open. The black AmEx. " 'Paternalistic'?" he echoed. "You know not what you speak."

"Kill the Shakespeare. You're not my dad."

This time, he rolled his eyes. "Lady, you have no clue what it's like to have a dad. And if I do remind you of your father, it's obvious why." He held up two fingers, and counted off: "One, I love you, and two, I am a man. You can't handle a man loving you." He sighed. "Sometimes I want to find your mother and yell at her for fucking you up."

"What about all the other times?" I asked.

But Karl was already standing. "I'm going to find that waitress."

While his back was turned, I slipped the drawing Devin had made for him onto the table. Devin had used the brown crayon and so instead of a drawing it looked like he'd squatted over the picture and taken a messy shit.

5.

I N ALL OUR CORRESPONDENCE, S HAD HARDLY ASKED A THING about me. I get it: I wasn't the kid she would be taking care of. To her credit, she did ask about Devin's sleep schedule and eating habits, whether he was up to date on his vaccines and even whether he was afraid of loud noises, like blenders and vacuums. It was as if she was putting together a dossier on my child. When she asked how many teeth he had, I said, "When you get here, you can ask him to open wide."

After that remark, the questions stopped.

S never once asked me why I needed to hire her. She must have assumed I didn't work, and that I merely needed help so I could attend to self-care: my hair needed to be dyed, my spine realigned, my chi centered. Lord smite down the stay-at-home mother who doesn't actually mother. S had probably turned onto our steep street, cataloging the luxury German vehicles parked along the curb, the Latinas dusting the mailboxes, and once she'd seen our house, she decided I was wealthy enough not to need an occupation. It was true. After Karl and I married, I quit my office-management job because his salary had turned it into a cute little hobby. Once Devin was born, it didn't seem like I'd

ever work again. It had been only a few months since Joyce had engi-
neered not just a job for me but a career, and I was still in shock.

And so when S rang the doorbell for the second time in seven
days, I thought I might keep the Lady-who-lunches ruse going. I'd
wear drawstring linen pants and pretend I was going for a Reiki session when really I was headed to the Coffee Bean on Sunset to suffer
sentence-making and pick through the memoirs Karl had bought me.
If I needed to call my editor with some inane question about how close
the manuscript had to adhere to the proposal, I'd sneak into my car.
Because once S knew what I was up to, she'd hold me accountable.
That was partly why I'd hired her.

I was still ruminating on this as I opened the door. There she stood
as before, but this time, an enormous backpack hovered over her shoulders. I was reminded of Richard Scarry's hitchhiker, the raccoon with
the backpack larger than his own body, the one who can't get a ride.

"Don't you love my backpack?" She rolled her eyes upward.

"It's large."

"My mother gave it to me. Some graduates get a ticket to backpack
around Europe. I just got the backpack."

I smiled. "It's useful, at least." I stepped aside and she gave a stiff
little twirl into the foyer. The backpack was reflective and mesh, and
stuffed full with clothes.

"Seth took Devin to see some construction down the block," I said.
"They'll be back in a few." What I didn't say was that Seth and I'd had
an argument, or as close to one as you can have when one party can't
speak. Devin had been throwing a tantrum, flinging himself across
the living-room couch, his face pink with effort, and Seth had typed,
See? Needs Karl. As if Karl could cure a toddler of being a toddler.

But Seth had a point. Since his father had moved out, Devin was
quicker to cry, less sure of himself. Suddenly he was afraid of the
howling wind outside and, oddly, of rats, which he was convinced
would come squeaking out of the closet after nightfall. The day Karl
packed up his Audi, Seth had stayed out for hours. He'd gone to Kit's
for dinner, and would have spent the night had Karl not made him
come home to me. I knew he and Karl emailed daily, and that sometimes they met for lunch. Seth didn't tell me, Karl did. Hoarding

information was a by-product of my son's silence, and so I pretended this withholding was simply more of the same.

S drooped a shoulder and unhooked the backpack.

"Did you notice the construction?" I asked. "Not that you would, since it seems like one in every three houses is being renovated up here."

She smiled politely. She hadn't been listening.

"I hope you don't mind me asking," she said after a moment, "but I wondered how they—Seth and Devin—communicate."

I waited for her to blush, but she didn't.

"I don't mind," I said, which is what I always said, because people asked that all the time. "They sign some. Not much. Little kids are enormously adaptable. Devin just talks to his big brother, and doesn't really expect an answer."

S nodded thoughtfully.

"Seth may not be able to talk, but he's capable of so much. If he wanted to take care of Devin all the time, I'd let him. But Seth has school. He's at SMC. He wants to transfer to UCLA."

"I guess it's good for both of you that I'm here." She looked as grave as a priest arriving just in time for last rites.

I led her outside and showed her the side gate, where she could come and go as she pleased. "Within reason," I said. "The latch wakes Devin, so if you're really into clubbing, we'll have to figure out an alternate plan."

I'd expected her to make a joke of some kind, how she was queen of the discotheque, but all she said was, "Don't worry, I prefer to stay in most nights."

Was this the same woman I'd interviewed the other day? Her face was still plain, and her dress was as unfortunate as the last one, its wide horizontal stripes like an exterminator's tent. It looked like she'd used a plastic newspaper string to tie up her hair; she smelled of sweat and Lubriderm lotion. But there was a new hesitance to her, as if the professional S were trying to conquer the other, unkempt one.

As I helped her unpack her car, she explained that she'd brought a bunch of old textbooks with her in case I wanted to see the studies on play she'd mentioned. "And I have a copy of my senior project if you're in the mood for typos." Her modesty sounded rehearsed, and I pictured only one tiny error in her paper, a homonym problem, or an unnecessary space between two words. And yet, there was also a hint of shame on her face: this typo needled her, haunted her.

I must have been silent for a beat too long because S asked, "What? What's wrong?"

I answered, without thinking. "You seem different." We were standing on opposite sides of the car, and a crate of books S had rested on the roof blocked my face. Maybe that's why I'd said it.

"I do?"

The intense heat wave had passed, but it was still very warm, and the car's roof glowed in the glare of the sun.

I didn't think I'd actually speak, and now I didn't know how to respond. What could I say, that she'd been less uptight last time around?

I was about to laugh it off when she said, "Karl called me."

"He did?" After our dinner, I had forwarded S's résumé to Karl. I'd assured him that we'd set up a time for them to meet. I hadn't expected him to call her, though I should have.

"He went ahead and enrolled me in a CPR class," she said. "It shouldn't be a scheduling conflict." She pushed the crate away so that I could see her face, and she, mine. "Sorry, I didn't know you'd—"

"No need to apologize. I'm the one who lied about it. Did he call your references?"

She nodded. "But he thinks you did as well."

"Thanks for covering for me," I said. "Why *didn't* I call your references?" I crossed my eyes and shrugged; this was exactly what Seth had done when Devin and I caught him smoking a cigarette last year.

S laughed. "I'm very trustworthy," she said. Then: "It's cool you're writing a book."

"So he told you that too." So much for my ruse; now S would have to keep me in line.

"Is it a secret?" she asked.

"It is until I actually start writing. I'm blocked. I'm worse than blocked, I'm constipated. No, I'm paralyzed."

"My mom read the article you wrote."

"Wow, you know about that? You and Karl really covered it all."

"Usually my mom doesn't remember anything." S blushed, I wasn't sure why.

"It was the magazine's most popular piece for a while," I said. "It got tons of letters and there were all these intense posts on the mommy blogs." I realized I was bragging, and stopped talking.

"I love mommy blogs."

"You do?"

"Another girl in the Psych Department was writing her senior project on them, about how they simultaneously inspire and create anxiety for other mothers. I kind of got sucked in. What a bunch of freaks, right? Wait—you don't have a blog, do you?"

"No, but my agent wishes I did." I lifted the crate from the car's roof. It was heavier than I imagined.

"I'll get that one," she said, coming around the car.

"So your mother reads *Real Simple,* huh? Does she have a good system for organizing Tupperware too, because I could use some guidance." I imagined the woman who had raised S. She attended past-life regression therapy workshops in saffron-colored tunics. Or she played tennis and stocked the fridge with dozens of plastic water bottles.

S shook her head. "She doesn't have a subscription."

"Why bother, right? If you get it delivered, you're always the last to receive it. First, it's on the Internet, then it's on the newsstand, and then, *finally,* it's at your door." I was mimicking Karl, who had made this very speech a few months before about *The New Yorker.*

"My mother shoplifts magazines from drugstores," S said.

"Ha—uh, that's not what I was expecting."

"I wish I were kidding. She thinks it's funny."

S was already lifting the crate of books; she was quite toned, actually, beneath that droopy dress of hers. She began to carry the books toward the house, the graveled asphalt crunching under her thin-soled sandals, and I could tell by her efficient movements that she'd told me the truth, and maybe wished she hadn't.

"My mom once seduced my high school principal," I called out.

S turned around and grinned. "I need to hear the rest of that story."

I remembered what I'd told Karl the other night—*This isn't a* story.

"No, you don't," I said.

I'd been fifteen, and it was right after the fainting had begun, when I was going to the nurse's office once or twice a week to lie on a firm cot in a small back room. Sometimes the nurse would come in and give me a Ritz cracker, put her papery, cool hands across my forehead and cheek. She was married to the principal.

"We should set our mothers up. They can play tennis together. Steal stuff." S had lifted a bent leg to balance the crate on her thigh. She looked like a demented flamingo.

I was about to tell her that I didn't know where my mother lived when Seth and Devin came up the hill. Crested, really—Devin was on Seth's shoulders, and Seth was running. Devin drummed on his brother's head, calling out, "Moo! Moo!"

"The two-headed cow has arrived," I said, and I watched as Seth slowed down, walking as if stepping through syrup. Devin giggled.

Seth was wearing his TALK WITH THE HAND shirt, which his deaf friend Mitch had given him before leaving for boarding school, subsequently rejecting anyone who could hear. The shirt was getting small, and as Seth reached up to steady Devin, it lifted to expose his stomach. He was hairy for a young man, hairier even than Marco; from here I could see the dark fur spreading across his stomach. It made me think of his days as a newborn, when he was covered like a leaf in tiny fine hairs, and I'd wondered if I'd given birth to a marmoset.

Seth was so skinny that his jeans hung loose off his hip bones, revealing the waistband of his underwear. Although I was too far away to make out the words across the elastic, I knew they read HANES HANES HANES. Karl had tried to convince him to switch to Calvin Klein because the fabric was softer, but Seth remained a staunch defender of cheap clothing. He'd purchased his jeans for a dollar at the Salvation Army, and now their chewed-up hems dragged along the concrete. Once again, he'd gone walking barefoot. I imagined the bottoms of his feet: black with dirt. Maybe they sparkled like the sidewalks of Hollywood Boulevard.

I turned to S. I wanted to watch her watching my boys. She must have noted Seth's disgusting feet, compared his orphan getup to Devin's striped romper, which Kit had purchased in Paris not too long ago. "For your dauphin," she'd said as she handed it to me.

Did S see the joy between Seth and Devin, or was she merely seeking out their differences? People were always comparing one to the other. Seth was thin and dark, while Devin was chubby and blond as a Barbie doll. Seth didn't speak, and Devin was a chatterbox. People assumed I was grateful that my second son could speak. Ostensibly, he was the improved upon model: son 2.0. But that wasn't the case; one wasn't any better than the other. "And that's an essential truth!" Joyce had cried, triumphant, during our work together. I didn't tell her that sometimes I wanted to shove all of Devin's language back inside of him, just as I'd wanted to unbirth Seth so many years ago.

S's expression was neutral. I couldn't discern what she was thinking, and that was a relief.

As soon as Seth saw us standing there, he stopped to pull Devin off his shoulders. Devin signed, *Up!* but Seth couldn't see him.

"Mommy!" Devin cried, his eyes meeting mine. Then he made a hissing sound and I realized he was saying S's name.

Seth laughed. Though he can't speak, Seth can laugh, and it has a sound, unexpectedly deep and husky.

S had already put down the crate to talk to Devin, who was telling her all about the excavator he and Seth had seen.

"You and me go drive it someday!" he yelled, directly into her ear.

"Sounds fun," she said, but she was already looking up.

"Seth, this is S," I said. "S, Seth."

Seth nodded curtly, and I wondered whether he was still upset about our argument. Now he was looking behind and above S, at the roof. It was as if he'd laid out some tarot cards there, and was trying to read them.

Here we go again, I thought. The spectrum.

Over the years, I had discussed and debated with doctors an autism diagnosis for Seth. Like many autistic children, he didn't speak. But unlike them, he didn't suffer from sensory overload or daven madly when uneasy. He didn't exactly like to snuggle, but he didn't flinch when touched; he could express and accept affection. He was typical except for his silence.

But my son could be on the spectrum, couldn't he? Seth was nonverbal, and it wasn't because he had social anxiety. If I wasn't vigilant he'd get obsessive, listening to the same song for three hours straight, or finish an entire book of crosswords in one day. And although he was funny and charming with people he knew well, when he met someone for the first time he was someone else entirely: distant, awkward, almost dismissive.

Still, I'd rejected the diagnosis, which not a single doctor had been confident about anyway. The word "spectrum" is useful until you realize that said spectrum can stretch on and on, and in both directions.

"Seth," I said now. I turned to S. "He's a little shy." I knew what she was thinking: Hello, Asperger's!

Seth rolled his eyes at me in his big, dramatic silent-movie-actor way. He signed, *Looking for the soccer ball,* and nodded at the roof.

I felt his words like a migraine. His behavior wasn't proof there was something wrong; once again I had presumed impairment where there wasn't one. And even if he had avoided eye contact with S, that was just Seth being Seth, as Karl might say. Joyce claimed that the central theme of my memoir was acceptance, but if that were the case, I shouldn't be the one writing it.

I was so deep in thought that I almost missed what happened next. Seth was signing, *I'm good, thanks for asking,* but not to me. To S. She was poking her head forward like a turtle, struggling to understand. Seth has always been a flamboyant and colorful user of ASL, and he moves his hands quickly.

"You sign?" I asked her.

Her neck turned pink. "I took one semester at Cal, but it wrecked my GPA."

Cool, Seth signed, and by S's smile I knew she understood him.

"Well," I said. "If you want to tutor S, you can. She now lives in your backyard."

"You make it sound like I'll be sleeping in the bushes," S said, laughing a little.

Devin was pawing at her thighs. "I want some uppy," he said. "Just a little uppy."

She looked to me like he'd asked for a sip of wine.

"You can pick him up," I said.

I'm too busy with school, Seth signed. By the way he shaped the words, I knew he was being apologetic. He was flattered that she'd tried to sign with him. Hardly anyone knew how, and the deaf friends he'd made as a child had since distanced themselves from him. Being deaf was a thing, a scene. If the rejection hurt Seth, he never showed it.

"He's got school," I translated.

She hitched Devin onto her hip. "I'm pretty sure I'm a lost cause anyway."

Seth pulled his iPhone out of his pocket and was about to type something. Before he could, Devin grabbed it from his hands.

"No, Devin," I said.

"Are you screen-free?" S slipped the phone from Devin's chubby little hands and passed it back to Seth.

"Screen-*what*?" I said. Then I shook my head. "Devin watches TV."

"Please I watch *Dora*?" Devin asked.

"Sorry, honey, not right now."

Devin let out a sob and squeezed S's arm. "Dora!" he yelled, his face crumpling at the injustice. First the phone had been taken from him, and now I wouldn't let him watch TV. And why not? Sometimes it felt like all I did was take from my son, refuse him whatever he wanted.

I eyed S, who had furrowed her brow but said nothing. She was letting me be the parent, which I appreciated but also resented. I was paying her, after all.

"I can hang with him," she said finally, giving him a little bounce. Devin kept crying.

"That would be great. You guys could watch *Dora* together."

Devin stopped weeping as abruptly as he'd begun, and I turned to Seth, who looked like he was getting ready to type something on his phone. I waited for him to show me or S the screen, and when he didn't, I assumed he was about to tweet, probably turning this moment to comedy gold: Do you think Dora the Explorer uses a flat iron to get those bangs? #NotThatImJealous

Sometimes I suggested tweets to Seth. He never used them.

>>>

ONCE WE WERE back inside, and Seth had retreated to his room, my shoulders dropped. This happened sometimes, when I witnessed someone meeting him. I got tense. Now I felt Karl's phantom fingers at my sternum.

"If it's cool with you, I'm going to go write," I said.

"Totally," S said. "I hate unpacking anyway." Devin was already leading her to the couch. He was sucking in air and laughing, which he did when he was totally pleased by life. Maybe it wasn't Karl he missed, I thought. Maybe we just needed another grown-up to keep the scary sounds and the rats away. Maybe Devin knew I couldn't do it alone, or at all.

After I showed S how to work the remotes, I made a big show of looking for my computer cable and my canvas tote of books. I felt no urgency to write, I never did, but as Joyce had said, I needed to make it a habit, a practice.

"If he gets hungry, you can give him raisins or an English muffin with jelly," I told S. Clearly, I was lingering.

"Muffin buffin!" Devin cheered.

"Got it," S said.

I shuffled toward the front door.

"Write like the wind!" she called out as I left.

I GOT DOWN the hill faster than I would have liked, and before I knew it I was sitting at a wobbly round table, slurping iced caffeine, staring at my unopened laptop.

I'd left the books in my car. I was sick of memoirs and the swagger of survivors, the way they mounted the past above the mantel for all to ooh and aah over.

I opened my laptop and went straight to the Internet. Early on, Karl had suggested getting me a computer without a wireless card and I'd almost spit in his face.

Seth's timeline hadn't been updated since yesterday at 11:29 p.m.: Im going to get a really big purse and carry a Great Dane in it. If he had tweeted something before I left the house, maybe he'd deleted it. I'd caught him doing that once before, when he'd tweeted about his lack of speech, Just because Im not talking doesnt mean Im listening, only to delete it a few minutes later. Seth may be nonverbal, but @sethconscious wasn't.

On the left side of the screen, a box urged me to join the site. All it asked for were my full name, my phone number or email address, and a password. What if, what if . . . ? I'd loitered my cursor over these fields before, but this time, something felt different. This time, Karl had moved out, and at night before falling asleep I scissored my legs across his side of the bed, the sheets cold and slippery. It was and wasn't space I'd craved when I asked him for a separation. S was currently sitting with Devin on the couch, or feeding him, or getting him to step into an unsoiled pair of underwear. I was liberated, at least for a while. Karl would no doubt be calling after work to ask why I'd been so reckless with our son; until then, I was free. This place stunk with bitter coffee, and the young baristas were slamming their espresso clubs (*It's called a portafilter,* Karl said in my head) against those tiny rubbish bins (*It's the knock box*), and the man at the next table over was reading a pink copy of the *Financial Times,* his legs crossed. An American paper would never be pink. There was probably some reason—Karl would know—but at that moment the color choice felt frivolous, and frivolity was what I craved. What if, what if . . . ?

In the required field, I typed Pearl Financial, my pulse quick in my wrists. I used a nearly abandoned email address, my graveyard site for online shopping.

I went with @muffinbuffin41 because @muffinbuffin was already taken. I wouldn't use my real name. No one would follow me. I wouldn't follow anyone.

I could have made my profile private, but where was the risk in that? This was an era of hypotheticals.

Dora the Explorer's fat belly looks post-menopausal, I tweeted, and laughed aloud.

The Briton looked away from his pink paper, but only for a moment. I was nothing to him, and that was everything to me.

6.

THERE WAS A TIME WHEN EVERYTHING MATTERED TO ME, when life was grave, when I required that gravity to survive. Seth had just been born. I was getting up every hour or two to feed him, heating up his bottles in Marco's dark galley kitchen. I still thought of it as Marco's kitchen, even though I'd been living there for almost a year. The only thing in the apartment I considered mine was Seth—in the middle of the night I'd hold him close and mouth the words *I love you* against his still-soft skull. (*Fontanel,* Karl had explained to me when Devin was a day old, and suddenly those long-ago nights with Seth felt so close that the past version of me could have been sitting in the next room.)

Seth was all mine, but I didn't breastfeed him because I was afraid of what it would do to my breasts, which belonged to me and also to Marco. Not that Marco was touching them in those months. His mother had been moved into hospice and he came home only to shower and change. He didn't want to talk about it, and he didn't want me to bring the baby to see his mother. Immediately after Seth was born, Marco realized what a muck of shit he'd gotten himself into, becoming a father. A grandchild was his mother's dying wish, but in the back of his lizard brain Marco must have believed that a child would keep his mother alive. When Seth couldn't do that, he failed his father's only request.

The money was running out, and six weeks after Seth's birth, I returned to the Actress. In those days, I'd strap Seth onto my chest to walk the Actress's new Havanese (had she gotten Angela to replace me?), and during Seth's naps I answered the Actress's mail and booked her travel. The Actress loved Seth, and gave me a small raise. I could keep this going, I thought. The fear that I couldn't, that my whole universe might collapse at any moment, was near-constant, but this same fear gave me the strength to get dressed in the morning when I felt too tired to move. I'd leave notes for Marco to find when he got home, and I thought I could tell when he'd read them, as if his gaze would alter the shape of my handwriting. It was my unspoken, shameful wish that

Marco's mother would finally die. Only then would Marco recognize his progeny as family, only then would he recognize me, period. We could be motherless together.

My mother, my mother. "It's relevant, sure," my editor, Anya, told me in a phone conversation a week before I hired S, "but remember, your fraught relationship with her is not the center of this story. This book is about your son." I imagined the manuscripts piled on her desk, all the memoirs about fucked-up mothers. Poor Mom. People were always trying to peddle that story.

"But—" I said.

She sighed. "If you must write it, Lady, then write it. We can always see how to fit it in later."

Anya wanted the origin story of Seth's disability, as if my realizing he didn't speak was akin to being exiled from the Garden of Eden. And "origin story" isn't the right phrase anyway, because I don't know why Seth doesn't speak, only that he doesn't. How to tell her too, that a single moment of revelation never happened, that it was instead a series of moments, which led, if not to his silence, then at least to my recognition of it? I would have to travel back, and farther back than that, long before speech was even expected of Seth, to understand it.

The first moment, then. Or an early one at least.

I'm at the Actress's house, waiting for the pool man to arrive as I remove the deceased contacts from her giant Rolodex. Seth's asleep in the bassinet I keep in the maid's quarters, a room otherwise empty of furniture. The Actress is upstairs, napping with her cold cream smeared across her face so she looks like the Wicked Witch of the West. I wish I were asleep, I want to cry I'm so tired, but I'm only on the letter *G,* and the doorbell will ring at any moment. Besides, I can't sleep on the job.

On the stove, an egg is set to boil. When it's ready, I plan to unpeel this egg and then roll it in salt and bite into it like an apple as I stand over the sink. (Was the egg the serpent's fruit, then?) Marco hasn't poached an egg for me in months, and I know a hard-boiled one is a poor substitute, that instead of the drippy yolks of yore I'll be left with a crumbly gray and yellow ball that will stick in my throat. I know too that a year before I had a tiny egg inside of my body and that it found Marco's sperm and became Seth. Egg to bird to standing by a stove, hungry and exhausted. The water is slow to boil and I sit back down, Rolodex before me.

The pool man arrives and I lead him to the backyard, explaining the clogged filter in the deep end. Then I go get Seth, who stirred at the sound of the doorbell. He's lying on his back in the crib, gazing up at me with his dark eyes. Like Marco's, they are spaced wide apart, but the effect is exacerbated because his head is so small. He reminds me of a dinosaur, something prehistoric. Even so, I like looking at him, and I do so every chance I get; it's as if there is a magnet pulling me toward his tiny body.

He is only four months old. If he had spoken then, it would have scared me.

I decide to take him into the den to feed him his bottle. We will sit on the glider. I know I shouldn't, it's too comfortable for someone as tired as I am, and yet I can't resist, it's like a giant hand that will cup and rock me.

Seth sucks down his bottle, and as I burp him, my mouth saying a soundless *I love you* into his skull, I slide into a deeper part of my brain, its sunless basement. It's not that I'm sleeping, my eyes are open. But I'm not seeing.

Something is beginning to smell at the back of the house, it has a chemical singe to it, but from the basement of my mind I assume it's a chemical the pool man is using to clear the filtration system. I am thinking of the plastic flap of the pool filter, how it opens and closes like a mouth, water in, water out, just as the glider moves back and forth, back and forth. To the left of the pool filter, right above the line of the water, shiny black tiles spell 6 FT.

Did the doorbell ring before I noticed the stink, or right after? At the time, the stink and the sound nudged at my consciousness simultaneously. At the sound, or maybe it was the smell, Seth lifts his head from my shoulder, pulling me out of my reverie.

"Coming," I call out, my voice full of phlegm. The smell seems to be getting worse, and now there's a new sound too. A crackling.

I don't look to see who it is before I open the door. Why not? It's a question that will needle me for a long time. Had I known who was on the other side, I wouldn't have opened it. Or I would have put Seth down. I would have hidden him.

It's her. ("It is *she*," I can imagine her saying. See also: Karl.)

She stands on the wide steps of the Actress's mansion, hands on her hips. The gate is still open for the pool man. It used to close automatically; it's on my to-do list to call Ernesto to come fix it. The Actress calls Ernesto "the groundskeeper," as if we're inside an episode of *Scooby-Doo*.

It has been almost two years since I've seen my mother. She looks the same: same halo of honey-colored curls, same painted lips, same eyebrows, thicker than the fashion of the times, but groomed by a professional. I don't recognize her gray shift dress, but I do recognize the pumps, vaginal pink. They're her post-office shoes: expensive, but comfortable, ideal for errands.

"I see," I say, looking at her shoes. I hold Seth to my chest; I hold in my breath.

"Mark gave me the address," she says.

"His name is Marco."

"Of course it is."

"His grandfather was born in Belgrade," I say.

I imagine my mother talking to Marco. But how? She doesn't have our phone number. She must have tracked him down at the Bagel Broker. And when she found him, he hadn't withheld a single thing. He probably thought she would give us money.

I feel myself start to cry, and I put my hand on the heavy doorknob. The acrid smell asserts itself once more. It seems like it's coming from the back of the house, but perhaps it's the stench of my mother's soul. She is a spiritual landfill in heels.

"You have to go," I say. "I'm working."

"I'm here to meet my grandson." When he leans forward I cover Seth's face with my hand.

"Lady, don't suffocate him." She wants this to be mean, but concern creeps into her voice.

"How did you find out?"

"I told you. Marc-*oh*."

"But how did you know about Seth?"

"Seth. So that's his name," she says. Marco hadn't revealed that, he'd left it to me to botch things.

I wait for the criticism, but before it comes, I hear the Actress scream from the kitchen. She must have gone down the back staircase, the servant stairs, she calls them.

"Lady!"

I turn away from the door. "Coming!" I call out, running with Seth toward the kitchen.

My mother is behind me.

I turn around to hiss, "I didn't invite you in!" I keep moving, leaving her in the dark hallway.

I push open the swinging door, my other hand on Seth's tiny back.

The large room is filled with smoke, and the Actress stands over the sink, running the faucet over whatever has been on fire, smoke rising. The Actress has cleaned the cold cream off her face, but I know if I get close enough, I will see some of it trapped in the wrinkles by her ears.

The egg. I forgot about the egg.

"I was cooking—"

"Well, you almost burned the house down! The water must have boiled away long ago. The pan is scorched and you can forget about the egg!"

I hear the door swing open behind me. "It sure is smoky, isn't it?" my mother says. Her voice is singsongy, and I realize she is addressing Seth.

The Actress doesn't like to be seen without due notice, and she looks up, alarmed. Her hand goes to the nude stocking cap stretched over her almost bald head.

"I'm sorry to intrude," my mother says. "I'm Simone, Lady's mother. She wasn't expecting me."

"We shouldn't be in here," I say, and lean over to open the window. The egg sits black and charred in the drain.

I know the Actress is stunned. She turns to me, speaking softly. "Lady, I thought you said your mother died when you were in junior high."

"That was Royce," my mother says, shaking her head. "Her father."

It never occurs to my mother that I pretended she was dead. She chalks up the mistake to the Actress's age. My mother hates old people. The Actress is sharp enough to realize I've lied, and plays it beautifully.

"Oh but how wonderful," she says, "to still have your mother."

I lead them out of the kitchen. And then, because I know how much it will hurt my mother, I ask the Actress to hold Seth. "While I walk her out," I say.

My mother isn't savvy enough to overstay her welcome with grace, so she lets me take her moisturized elbow, and walk her outside.

"I'm frankly surprised you didn't get fired for that," she says once we're standing by her car.

"She cares about me."

"She's your employer."

"Marco and I don't want to hear from you," I say.

She sighs and adjusts her dress. "Let's be adults for once. I am sorry you were upset by what I said about Marco. But that was months ago."

"But you aren't sorry you said it."

"Honey, he sells bagels."

"He's a screenwriter."

"He's never sold a script! And the tags on that truck are expired."

"His mother is dying."

"And yours is long gone, apparently. Besides, he's short."

"Marco's just under six feet!" I think of the Actress's pool: 6 FT. "He's taller than Royce."

"And look how that turned out."

"I'm alive," I say.

"Barely," she says. "Look at how thin you've gotten." But I know by her look that she's jealous of my thin arms and my stomach, concave as a contact lens.

"I just don't know, Lady . . ." she says softly, and trails off.

I remember I leaned in then, as if she might say something kind to me. That Seth was cute, even if he wasn't.

"You don't know what?"

"Can you really do it? Take care of a person?"

>>>

THE ACTRESS WAS waiting for me when I went back inside. "Your mother is so pretty," she said. Everyone said that.

"She used to be a catalog model," I replied, taking Seth from her.

"When Seth's older, you'll understand."

"Understand what?"

"All parents fail their kids."

"Just because she's pretty doesn't mean she isn't a witch."

"Did she molest you?"

"No!" (Later, Anya will pose the same question, as if this were the litmus test for parental cruelty.)

"Then you must forgive her," she said. "For Seth's sake. A grand-mother's love is so pure."

And then she leaned forward and kissed me on the cheek. "Let's take the day off and get lunch. You need it. Think we can get a table at Kate Mantilini?"

I TRIED TO tell this story to my agent. "So—what?" she said. "You think Seth inhaled the burnt egg smoke and it impaired him?"

"What? No—you don't understand."

"So help me then."

"It was my mother . . ." I said.

She laughed so long I had to wait for her to finish. "I'm sorry, Lady, but you are bat-shit crazy. You think your mother's visit is somehow responsible for this?"

"Not exactly, no. It's not the whole story. It's the first in a series of—"

"Let's keep 'the witch did it' out of the proposal for now. This isn't a ghost story."

ESTHER

7.

EXCEPT FOR THE FOG, I DIDN'T MISS MUCH ABOUT THE BAY. My dad was still living up there but I could call him whenever I wanted. He picked up 99.9 percent of the time and texted almost every day to report what kind of pizza they were serving at the Cheese Board, which he called his pied-à-terre even though it's a restaurant ("And fromagerie!") a mile from his house. He wrote on my Facebook wall so often that I threatened twice to block him. Right after I moved back to L.A., he sent me (and, by proxy, my mom, aka his ex-wife) a bouquet made of strawberries and chunks of pineapple. It was called an Edible Arrangement but on the card he'd written, "Here's your Oedipal Arrangement!" which my mom thought was gross. I just laughed and texted him a picture of me with the basket balanced on my head. No less than ten seconds later he texted back: Selfie!!!!!!! which, by the way, on a circa-2006 flip phone, is no afternoon nap.

My argument is that my dad was available, even with more than three hundred miles between us. The fog wasn't. The marine layer in L.A. is pantyhose compared to the heavy white shawl that hangs over the Berkeley Hills. And don't even get me started on the fog across the water in San Francisco; that shit is so dense you could open your mouth and take a bite out of it. And chew. It's the gnocchi of weather. Everett, my old boyfriend, or *whatever*-he-was, said that.

Before we broke up, Everett and I would drive up to my dad and Maria's place off Grizzly Peak to walk their dog. On foggy days we wouldn't be able to see anything beyond Ritz's dark fur. I loved it; it felt like my very limbs were disappearing in the heavy white mist. "Amputation by fog," I said once, and Ev laughed. I said that I loved painting it, and he laughed again.

Too bad the fog was the only thing I missed about the Bay; otherwise, I might have stayed. Why not? I could have found a job; maybe not one that covered both my rent and my student-loan payments, but a job nonetheless, one I liked, and I could defer and defer on the college debt. Plus Everett was long gone; he was headed to the Yale art program, middle fingers pointed to the sky. But I couldn't make myself stay. Even if I'd fallen in love with Berkeley, which I certainly had not, I had to return to L.A. It was home. It was where my mom was. And, more important, it was where Esther Shapiro wasn't.

Ugh, Esther *anything*—I did away with that name altogether. When I returned to L.A., I started using my mother's name, Fowler, and became known as S. I'd always hated the name Esther and shortening it to a single letter felt like sloughing off so much dead skin. A psychic facial.

S Fowler was done with all the frivolous shit that Esther Shapiro had gotten herself into. Including, and especially, her art.

My last project had come to me the same day I concocted a flimsy plan to get a master's in psych. Everett had already left for Connecticut and we hadn't been talking for weeks anyway. I was subletting a studio apartment in West Berkeley and temping at one soul-sucking office or another in the city, usually as a receptionist. I felt like I'd never paint again. What was the point? There was a reason I'd majored in something other than studio art: I didn't want to be an artist.

But then, I was walking down Shattuck with one of those obvious GRE practice bibles under my arm, ready to tackle trigonometry, when it hit me: I would never open the book. I couldn't. I didn't want to be a therapist.

A few feet in front of me stood a woman in her late fifties, maybe early sixties. Between her thumb and index finger she held a bank receipt as if it were precious. Or rotten. She wore a sun hat, typical for the neighborhood: waterproof, reflective, breathable, and with a strap under the chin like a fucking baby's bonnet. She was only a little older than my mom, but she was unlike my mom in almost every other way.

This stranger was careful, whereas my mom was carefree. Or careless. I hadn't seen my mom in a few months; instead I had to see this
woman.

Maybe because of that, she pissed me off. Or maybe it was just her
bad hat. I squeezed my GRE book and kept watching. *You,* I thought.
You are probably a therapist. At the very least she'd been to one that day.
I bet she had original art in her California Craftsman bungalow. An
unremarkable landscape over the fireplace.

I knew I had to channel my rage, turn my reaction into something
productive, something funny yet meaningful. "Artist-as-translator,"
as Everett liked to say.

This woman walked her bank receipt to her Subaru, which had a
bike rack on the roof and a license-plate holder that read BERKELEY:
DECIDEDLY DIFFERENT. I turned away. What could I do with this
feeling? Definitely couldn't take it to graduate school. I'd painted my
way into an art minor, but painting wouldn't work this time.

Enter, stage left, my Give Us Your Tevas program by Esther Shapiro.

Give Us Your Tevas was modeled after the programs introduced
in inner cities all across the US of A that asked people to turn in their
black-market guns, no questions asked. Except Berkeley doesn't have a
widespread gun-violence problem, it has an eye violence one. I could
have asked people to return their sun hats (like my muse was wearing
that fateful day), their COEXIST bumper stickers (undeniable proof that
you're a meek and shitty driver), their walking sticks (Solano Avenue
is not the French Alps!), or any variation on waterproof hiking wear,
or, or—I thought about it for weeks as I worked and commuted and
cleaned my grimy sublet. The possibilities were endless. I decided, finally, that Tevas, and every other Franken-sneaker-sandal on the market, were the worst offenders. It didn't matter if it was cold, because
people just paired the things with nubby socks, and it didn't matter
that the shoes were ugly, because ugliness was powerless against comfort. To be comfortable: that's the fashion ethos of Berkeley. I wondered at how my mom, who didn't care about clothes, had never put
these on her own feet. It seemed miraculous.

To my dad, I explained that Tevas were part of the baby boomer uniform. (Sun hat? Check. Gray hair? Check. Khaki shorts for men, quirky museum gift shop earrings for women? Check and check.) All of these Berkeleyites looked the same, I told him, which suggested that it wasn't only their clothes that were identical, but their beliefs, their families, their diets, their thoughts, their *everything*. While they were enjoying their retirement plans and succulent gardens, my generation was facing underemployment and debt. Despite what they wanted to believe, the boomers hadn't changed shit about the world. The artist Esther Shapiro, I told my dad, saw it as her duty to give voice to the young and fight these automatons, one pair of Tevas at a time.

I couldn't tell him that I'd been thinking about my mom too. He wouldn't understand. Katherine Mary Fowler didn't have the life he had, that these boomers had. It was something she and I shared, wasn't it?

The campaign began on a Monday night in July, three hours before sunrise. In darkness I slapped two hundred silkscreened posters across the city. I left large drop-off barrels in front of markets, banks, and community centers. A week before, I'd commissioned a welder to make me metal signs to post at Berkeley's city limits; on the night in question I nailed them directly below the infamous NUCLEAR-FREE ZONE signs. My dad wouldn't help because what I was doing could be illegal, but because Maria was afraid I'd hurt myself lifting the barrels, he did hire a guy named Clay to transport them for me. (I'd had the idea myself but I'd already maxed out one of my two credit cards to fund the project, and if I had fifty bucks to slip to anyone I would have given it to myself.)

At 5:00 that morning, the website went live (the first FAQ: *What should I wear instead?*) and I sent a press release to various media outlets. Then I passed out facedown on my futon, my hands still icky with wheat paste.

First there was the irate but witty blogger who came along three days later. He was probably right, I was a Banksy wannabe. I wasn't an artist but a hoax-puller. Or, worse, I was an artist, but a mediocre and derivative one. Then the *Oakland Tribune* picked up the story. Some guy from the North Berkeley neighborhood association, his long white ponytail greasy as an old shoelace, declared my metal posters vandalism, saying they perverted Berkeley's spirit of safety and public good. He organized a group of outraged citizens one Saturday afternoon. "We recycled the signs," he told the reporter. Ponytail Man was also a guest on a local radio program, during which a few people called in to harangue me. "What some might find funny," one woman warbled, "others find offensive." I could just see her frizzy gray hair, tucked under a purple velvet cloche, the kind of hat that reminded me of chemo patients. And maybe she *had* survived cancer, making her all the more smug as she loaded half a dozen Seckel pears into her reusable mesh produce bag at Berkeley Bowl (organic, of course. Big whoop, lady, no one cares, etc.).

THE PEOPLE'S REPUBLIC of Berkeley had acknowledged my work and swiftly reached a verdict. That is: Esther Shapiro wasn't an artist, she was a shallow *beeotch*. Not that they used those words to describe me. No, they said it was unfortunate I focused on the superficial. They lamented that I hadn't directed my talents to issues of global importance, thus wasting said talents.

Oh, Esther Shapiro! If I'd taken a moment to predict what might happen, I might not have felt so dejected about how the project actually turned out. But what had I wanted? To get away from my boring future? To try something sexier than painting, something that Everett would actually respect? To connect with my mom in some bogus, indirect way? I hadn't even told her about it.

My dad, at least, said the attention I received proved the project's success. I wouldn't go that far—but it's true, at least my work had been noticed. By the time he was giving me this pep talk, people were tweeting and Instagramming pictures of my project and posting quips about running in heels, about knockin' da boots. It wasn't a trending topic, but the numbers weren't anything to sneeze at either.

A few days later, a local footwear brand came forward to applaud my sentiment; they started the campaign #SoulSole, urging people to take pictures of their shoes and post them online for all the world to see. "What we put on our feet is an expression of our identity!" read their website, and I nearly spit my Cheerios all over my laptop.

A single pair of abandoned Tevas showed up at the bottom of the only barrel that hadn't been removed. (God bless the Whole Foods on Gilman!) I found a photo of the donation on Instagram: it was tagged #SoleSoul, #SoStupid, and #ArtSux.

My dad said I should be proud: people were reacting. But I didn't feel proud. I was dead out of money and the project had been happily endorsed by a lame shoe company, for fuck's sake. Most people had probably assumed it was corporate from the start. Nobody was laughing. Even my father didn't seem to get it: he bought some mustard-colored brogues and asked me if I approved. Maria was convinced I was upset that my dad had married her and was settling for good in Berkeley.

"My clothes okay to you?" She pointed at her cashmere sweater, concerned.

No one seemed to notice the way I adapted the fallout shelter symbol so that the three triangles looked like feet. Or that I had bound the drop-off barrels in rubber to mimic the Tevas running sole. Or that the website included fake banner ads for handwoven espadrilles from Brazil and clown shoes made of children's tongues, with links that clicked to nowhere. People wondered who Esther Shapiro was, but not because they thought she was so smart and original, but because they wanted to have her tarred and feathered and thrown into the cold, cold Bay.

Then Rivka Browne called. Her voice was like maple syrup sliding across a pancake. "Esther Shapiro," her voice poured. She said she was a spokeswoman from Teva. "Some people don't realize the brand name isn't officially pluralized."

"How did you get this number?" I asked.

"Clayton Barnes."

The barrel guy. Fucking snitch.

"How'd you find him?"

"He's my cousin." I heard her take a sip of something and I imagined a hot latte freshly deposited on her desk. "Have you visited our website?" she asked. "I think you would enjoy seeing the full array of our products. Some of our line is quite fashion-forward, actually."

"What can I do for you?" I asked.

"Well, primarily, we wanted to thank you," she said. "For making Teva part of the conversation."

I said nothing.

"We'd love to meet with you, talk next steps. I think we could cultivate a really interesting partnership."

I admit, I considered it for a split second. There was my not-insignificant debt, and the fact that I had to be out of the cheap sublet by the end of July. My dad said that I could stay with him and Maria, and that she would certainly help me pay my credit-card balance. She wouldn't charge interest either. But I didn't want that, didn't want to take her money. With Rivka's help, I didn't have to. I could do this: become a corporate shill.

I rejected the idea as soon as it came to me. I was an artist, no matter how bad (#ArtSux #IHaveASoul).

Rivka Browne continued: "Guerrilla marketing is the new frontier—but I guess I don't have to tell you that, do I, Esther?"

"Gorilla marketing?" I cried. I knew she wouldn't hear the difference between the two words but it felt good to say it wrong. Everett, who used to wear a baseball cap that read TAKE ME FOR GRANITE, would have appreciated the joke. "Go to hell, Rivka Browne," I said, and hung up. My hands, long scrubbed of wheat paste, were shaking.

I had to get out of Berkeley (I'd use the phrase *NorCal* if it didn't instigate my gag reflex), and I started making plans to return home. The world was probably right: Esther Shapiro didn't care about conformity or intergenerational strife, she was just a fashion snob. Or it was Maria who was right: I was just a little girl, trying to process her daddy's new identity.

Whatever it was, I have my dad to thank for hatching the next project in my brain. As he helped load my car, he said, "Give Us Your Tevas was just too comedic for this town." He laughed. "It's almost something your mom would do, if she ever did art." I knew he was remembering some goofy shared joke, two decades old. I would've asked him to spill it had my brain not been spinning like a rainbow-striped top. Was my dad right? Was the project something my mom would have come up with?

I was already barreling down the 5 into a cloud of cow shit when my dad called to tell me about an article in the *New York Times* Style section about sporty footwear.

"I'm surprised they didn't reference Esther Shapiro," he said.

"I'm relieved they didn't," I said. "Anyway, I'm the artist formerly known as Esther Shapiro. I'm trying on Fowler. S Fowler, actually, not Esther. S, like the letter."

"S Fowler," he repeated. "But what's wrong with Shapiro?" He would never admit that it rankled him that I was aligning myself with his ex-wife, but I knew it did.

"I swear it's nothing personal, Dad," I said. "It just sounds classier." I couldn't tell him more.

His voice turned serious, "Waterbug, be careful down there."

"No one wears Tevas in L.A."

"It's not that. I mean . . . Kathy may not be—"

"I can handle Mom. Besides, I won't be staying at her place forever. I think I'll look for a nanny job."

"A babysitter? You've got a degree from Cal!"

"It's not a forever thing. And you know I love kids."

"I do. And, hey, you can use what you learned from writing your senior project. Just don't abandon your art, okay?"

"Sheesh, guilt trip."

"You know what, honey?"

"What?"

"This is the first time in your twenty-two years that you and I will be apart for more than a week."

"It was bound to happen. This is what you get for following me to college."

"And hey, it worked out, didn't it? I met Maria."

"You met Maria. Too bad she lives in the worst place ever."

"There are probably a few war-torn countries that would win that distinction before Berzerkeley."

"I'm kidding."

"Just don't let that humor get S Fowler in trouble."

"You know it will."

"That's my girl."

What I didn't tell my dad was that I wasn't abandoning my art. As

I reached the Grapevine, the smell of cow shit behind me and Magic Mountain's spooky horizon of roller coasters still ahead, my new project glowed in my imagination. I could feel its potential. I squeezed the steering wheel and sped forward.

I would try to become my mother.

8.

KATHERINE MARY FOWLER. I KNOW IT'S PHENOMENALLY SCREWED up (and I know because Everett told me so), but if given the chance to raise my mother as my child, I'd do it. I don't mean some *Freaky Friday* scenario where we switch bodies because of a spell cast from a magic fortune cookie or whatever. I mean I'd take Katherine Mary from scratch, and raise her to be a fine, stable woman. Because I believe, I have to believe, that Katherine Mary's raw ingredients were sound: it's the barely remembered mother who died when she was a baby, and the vodka-pickled father who never said I love you, and the junior high school music teacher with the roaming hands, and the . . . on and on and on, that ruined my mom. By the time Steven Shapiro tried to save her she was already shipwrecked. And husbands who double as life rafts don't last very long. Who loves a life raft?

I knew my mom moved to L.A. from New Jersey when she was twenty-four, and that she worked as a nanny. The year was 1985. Thankfully she is both sentimental and vain, lugging along a few boxes of photos and keepsakes from apartment to apartment, storing them under her old mattress. My mom has had the same bed my whole life; she got it in the divorce (she got a lot in the divorce but she's since pissed the rest away), and won't let it go even though every night she says, "I'm putting myself on the rack," which means she's going to lie down. That is, she says this if she hasn't already blacked out.

It's from staring at these photos when I was in high school that I know my mom wore her hair long and parted down the middle, flat, flat, flat. And that she never wore pants, only dresses, which looked a lot like the cheap ones they sell downtown: polyester, poorly sewn, almost cool until you realize that some Bangladeshi child was instructed to cut off a sleeve in the name of some outdated trend. My mom is prettier than I am, or the younger version of her was, but you would never know it. With some lip gloss, some foundation under her eyes, my mom could have been a knockout—but she was pretty enough without all of that, and she couldn't be bothered to care. Meanwhile, I'm lint in a troll's armpit if I don't spend forty-five minutes on my hair and makeup. ("Hair and makeup!" Maria once repeated after me. "What? Like an actress in her trailer?" But Maria would look pretty after an all-nighter and a root canal. Only women from Spain can put olive oil on their scalp and call it shampoo. No, Maria, I can't just rub it in a *leetle beet* and leave for work. I am not a salad.) Everett confessed he'd never dated a girlie girl before. He thought intellectual women didn't care about that stuff. I told him I must not be an intellectual.

As soon as I got to L.A. I went to a hair salon where an old high school friend worked and asked her to make me as mousy as possible. She stripped out the blond, made it ashy. She cut it shorter too, so that it cowlicked in all the worst places. As payment I gave her all my cosmetics. It was like a makeover in reverse: After and Before.

And then I took my mom to Melrose (she refused to go downtown because of traffic) to pick out dresses. For me.

"I don't understand this," she said. "You're pretending to be a younger version of me? Why?"

"For fun," I said. I didn't say "For art," because, one, she would have made fun of me and, two, she had no idea I did that anymore. It wasn't just the Give Us Your Tevas program; she didn't know about my landscapes, or my art minor. Withholding stuff from my mom is key: compartmentalize that woman or perish. She has boundary issues.

I did admit that I planned to photograph some of my role-playing experiments. I hadn't decided what other forms the project would take. I was thinking out loud. I was also trying the role on for size. My mom blurts everything out.

"Kind of Cindy Sherman–esque?" she asked.

I was so shocked I almost toppled a mannequin in hooker boots.

"Don't get too excited, Esther," she said. "Someone on set had a book of hers."

My mother was a wardrobe assistant on a successful network comedy. Jules, her boss, was competent and well connected, and she made sure my mom followed her from show to show. At first I thought it was a charity-case thing, and then I visited the set and saw how much everyone loved my mom. Also, the woman can hold about a zillion pins in her mouth while saying, "Get yourself a sandwich! You are too thin!" which is what every size-frail actress wants to hear.

"I'm not a photographer," I said. "I told you, it's just for fun."

She squinted at me. "Did you change your hair?" And then she gasped. "This is like *Single White Female*!" She threw her head back and cackled.

Later I took sixteen Polaroids of my own laughing face. From the lips down I looked just like my mom. I angled the camera to capture only that: my mouth open wide; my unsure-of-itself chin; my skin, sad-white; and my lips, cracked and flaking since I'd stopped moisturizing them. I felt something jolt awake in me, becoming Katherine Mary. It was a relief and a responsibility.

In those shots, the resemblance was uncanny. I was Katherine Mary's ghost.

9.

I'D BEEN DEVIN'S NANNY FOR THREE DAYS BEFORE I MADE MY bed. And I don't mean I failed to pull up the duvet and fluff the pillows, I mean I didn't even unpack my sheets. In Lady's cavelike guesthouse, which she called the Cottage, with its dorm-room mini-fridge and hot plate, and the overhead light fixture that looked like a nipple, I slept on a bare mattress, my body wrapped in a dingy white sheet. I was a corpse ready for my own burial at sea, dreaming I was a tiny hotel soap.

My mom would have slept like this and not cared. Her housekeeping is just barely acceptable now, and that's because my dad and I trained her like a dog. *No, Kath, you don't wash a dish with the same sponge you scrubbed the bathroom floor with. No, Mommy, I can't wear my underwear inside out and call it clean.* The first time my dad came to my mom's place, date number three, she stuck a marshmallow onto a bent wire hanger and roasted it for him over the stove. "I was appalled," he told me. "But also, wow, what an adventure!" Sometimes I pity young Steven Shapiro, walking willingly into my mom's arms, believing he could tame her. (My dad wept when Roy got mauled by that tiger. Not that Roy's misfortune was the particular issue. He'd have cried if it had been Siegfried too. A little too close to home, Stevie?)

I was trying my best to be Katherine Mary: the bad hair, the sloppy clothes and nonchalance, the drinking not long after the sun set. But I also had Devin to watch; art project or not, I was being paid to keep him safe. One of my professors liked to say that babies and toddlers aren't as helpless as adults think, which is true, but Devin was still a few months shy of his third birthday: he bent over after using the toilet so that I could wipe his butthole, he kept asking for a gun so he could shoot *aminals,* and he also seriously believed that he was qualified to operate heavy machinery—if only someone would let him drive a front-loading garbage truck! What I'm saying is this: with Devin in the room, there were limits to how thoroughly I could inhabit Katherine Mary. If Lady wasn't vigilant, well, Karl would be. Plus: babysitting with a hangover? Torture.

I also couldn't hold my liquor like my mom could. It was something I needed to work on, and not only because I could barely focus the camera after one drink. I'd had two beers before meeting Lady for the first time, just as a little experiment, and by the time I was driving up her street, everything felt unreal, like I was in a diorama of my own life. When Lady opened the door I almost said, "Yes, yes, y'all!" like a white kid loitering outside a suburban 7-Eleven. Thank goodness I didn't, Lady wouldn't have hired me. Or maybe she would have: it seemed like I could have said anything during that first meeting.

Lady was pretty but not beautiful, with light-blue eyes, sharp cheekbones, and impeccable eyebrows. She wore her hair in a long blond ponytail that looked effortless but totally required mousse. If

I had to name her lipstick, I'd call it coral. Her outfit was probably 100 percent organic, including her jeans. For some reason I'd expected her to be younger; she was in her early forties. Of course she's older, I thought. The rich start making babies late. All those Brentwood twins start in petri dishes.

It was so hot, I wouldn't have minded another beer. Lady might have offered me one too. That day, she seemed both wonderful and completely bonkers, like my mother, actually, alternately wooing and alarming the world. Lady wanted to hire me so quickly—but why? I'd nearly shrieked with glee when I saw the Kit Daniels photograph on the wall—*Kit Flippin' Daniels! She's the sister-in-law?!*—and I tried to make up for it by spouting random child-psych facts like an insufferable know-it-all. Lady seemed more interested in showing me her glorious swimming pool than discussing her kid's development. I got the sense that she occasionally forgot Devin existed.

And then Lady, almost embarrassed, definitely defensive, told me about Seth, and I knew this life in the Hills was her second act. I was much more interested now. In high school, I used to watch VH1's *Behind the Music* with my mom. Whenever I tried to get out of it, she would whine, "Don't do your homework, Esther!" until I came to sit with her on the couch. If there's one thing I learned from that show, it's that life always offers you a second—if not third!—act. (Also: that for every female pop star there's a homely blonde wearing an ankh choker who claims to be her childhood best friend.) Lady was now married to a rich guy who adored his stepson, disability be damned, and she and this guy had a cute little boy and they all lived happily in a multimillion-dollar house high above the city, every sunset a sky of spilled Kool-Aid. Lady said she and Karl were separated, but something about how she explained it made it feel fake: like she too had downed a couple bottles of Stella and was skimming through her life as if it were a Choose Your Own Adventure book, like if it didn't work out she could just flip back a few pages and start the story over. Ha, Lady. Just, ha.

Clearly, her first act had been rough: silver fillings dotted her back molars and everything nice in the house belonged to Karl, from the Eames chair in the living room to the daguerreotypes on the wall along the staircase. She might as well have said, "The only thing I contributed to this house is Seth." It was obvious she was defensive about her son not being able to speak, but it was only because she was in love with him. That's normal for a single parent. (Trust me, even after my dad married Maria, he continued to write me florid, sentimental cards on Valentine's Day.)

I was stone-cold sober when Karl called two days later. And that's lucky because our conversation was thorough, a real interview, not the witty banter I'd traded with his wife. By the end of the conversation, I'd agreed to enroll in a CPR class and get fingerprinted. I felt sort of bad for Lady. Why had she been so brazen with her own child?

"She can be kind of prickly about Seth," Karl said, before hanging up.

"What do you mean?"

"She doesn't want you to treat him differently." He laughed. "And don't go on and on about how wonderful Devin is. He is, trust me. I know, and so does Lady. But it offends her." I heard a phone ring—he was calling from his office—and he said he had to go. "You'll be fine as long as you don't play favorites with anyone in that house," he said before he hung up. "Not even the dog."

10.

BY NOW DEVIN WAS CALLING ME "S FOR SNAKE," AND HE kissed me on the lips every morning, gasping as if bowled over by my existence. I'm not gonna lie, his enthusiasm did wonders for my self-esteem. The night before I'd ordered a Breathalyzer online and as soon as it arrived I planned to start the Katherine Mary Project in earnest, tracking my alcohol intake each evening and recording the sounds of my breath blooming into the machine. The Polaroids were piling up, but I wasn't sure what I would do with them.

It was our fourth day together, and Devin and I were bobbing on the shallow steps of the pool. Since I'd started working, I'd only seen Seth in passing; he was doing the summer session at school, Lady said.

"And he's been seeing Karl a lot," she added. Tonight was my evening with Devin—Lady was going to a party—and then I'd have the next three days off. But I didn't want the free time: not as S or as Katherine Mary. I sort of missed Esther Shapiro, who felt like a Peter Pan–style shadow I'd left up north, maybe in Everett's bedroom.

Devin was walking up the shallow steps of the pool to grab his beach ball when he squealed.

I looked up. Karl stood on the back deck, grinning, arms akimbo. How long had he been there?

"Daddy!" Devin skipped to him, his legs slick with water. I watched as his father swung him into his arms. Karl's linen shirt was soon imprinted with the shape of Devin's tiny wet torso.

"Hey, kiddo!" he bellowed.

I recognized Karl from the photo in Devin's room, except he was better-looking in person. His hair was as white as Santa Claus's beard and cut close to his head. It seemed to glow in the sunlight, exactly like Milkshake's fur did whenever he trotted outside to pee. Karl's hairline was receding slightly, and the skin at his forehead and scalp was tanned to a rich, I-summer-on-Lake-Como olive. He was tall—six foot three, easy—and thin, but not macrobiotic-thin like so many of the bike-riding boomers in Berkeley. Karl probably took fish oil every morning and pasted his under-eyes with avocado cream every night. He probably went to an H_2O Boot Camp class at the local JCC, and drank red wine with dinner. He was hale, as my dad might say. ("Good crossword-puzzle word!")

Karl's sunglasses were tortoiseshell and he actually took them off when he waved to me. I wondered if he was the kind of dude who said "Eyes are the windows to the soul." He couldn't be: he was a producer and was probably over fifty, the type of guy who throws a snow globe at his assistant on Christmas Eve. But even though Karl was dressed the part of Older Hollywood Asshole, he wasn't one. I just knew it. He sweated the word "nice."

Karl looked away from me to kiss his son, basically hickeying the water off of him. I was relieved. As Katherine Mary, I'd stopped my regular wax appointments, and I didn't want Karl to see the five-o'-clock shadow that had become my bikini line, or the poof of hair that made a Lycra dome out of my bikini bottoms. In poor conditions, it looked like I was wearing a codpiece.

I pulled myself out of the water without using the steps, just like my mom would, and wrapped one of Lady's gigantic towels around my body. She also had a green Beverly Hills Hotel towel, so threadbare you couldn't put it in the dryer. The way she folded it, into the tiniest parcel, gave me the feeling she'd stolen it in her pre-Karl days, and didn't want anyone else using it.

"Good to meet you," I said, approaching him with a big smile. I'd been practicing this quality of my mom's—she was outgoing, she loved to meet people, talk up strangers.

Karl reached out to shake my hand while simultaneously trying to keep a giggling Devin from grabbing the sunglasses off his head.

"S!" he said. "I'm thrilled to meet you in person."

The glass door behind him squeaked open. Seth nodded at me as he stepped outside; he had on the same clothes as the day we met, but this time he was also wearing a pair of old red Converse.

A woman around Karl's age followed close behind, a glass of pink Champagne in her hand.

She looked vaguely familiar but I couldn't figure out why. Her hair was long and dark and celebrity-perfect; she probably called it frizzy like so many women with great hair did, but it wasn't, only had been maybe once in her life when she went to Florida for a summer wedding. Her eyes were large and green and rimmed with eyeliner. Blue feathers dangled from her ears. Her dress resembled a potato sack, or a uniform for postapocalyptic factory workers, but she was thin enough to pull it off. Her slip-ons looked like they were made of crinkled tissue paper yet somehow still worked as shoes. Already I was drafting the text I'd send my dad: She was wearing these eccentric booties!

The woman took a sip of the pink Champagne and said, "At least she's kept the pool clean."

Was this Karl's new girlfriend? No, I thought. No way.

I must have looked suspicious, because Karl said quickly, "S, this is Kit. My sister."

Kit Flippin' Daniels!

"I love your work," I said. I couldn't help it.

"You do?" Karl's eyes twinkled.

"I'm sure Lady hates that," Kit said, downing the rest of her drink.

"Lady doesn't know," I said.

Karl raised an eyebrow.

"You said not to play favorites." I was having fun, saying whatever I felt.

Seth snorted and signed something I couldn't make out. Karl shook his head curtly.

"I love the photograph by the front door," I said to Kit.

"Thank you."

"My sister's playing it cool, but she loves that you're a fan. Don't you, Kit?" His sister didn't answer, only took a sip of her Champagne, and he added, "For Pete's sake, it's amazing!"

"Pete skate!" Devin yelled, squirming out of his dad's arms. "Skate on my penis! Penis crane!" He giggled and Karl put him down, shaking his head.

"What a poet," he said.

Seth laughed. It was a hearty, surprising baritone. He'd lifted Devin into the air and was stomping toward the pool as if he were going to throw him in.

"So everything's okay here?" Karl asked.

"It's great," I said. We were all watching the brothers.

"Where's the boss lady?" Kit asked me.

"Writing."

"Good one," Kit said.

"No," I said, "she really is. I think she turned a corner."

Karl was grinning again. He looked so proud of Lady. If she'd been there to see his face, she'd hate it.

"See, Kit? I told you." He took the Champagne flute from her, carrying it carefully by the stem. Unlike me, Kit and Karl had been raised to hold crystal correctly. But I was a quick study; Everett only had to correct me once.

"Where're you guys coming from?" I asked.

"Lunch," Karl said.

"And . . . ?" Kit said. When Karl didn't answer, she continued,

"We went to a screening of the short film Seth made for school. A midterm thing. It, the film, was fabulous."

"Oh? Lady didn't mention—"

"She probably has no idea," Kit said, and this time Karl didn't argue.

"Make sure Lady remembers I'm coming at nine a.m. to pick up Devin," he said. "She agreed I could come as early as I wanted."

"I'll make sure she knows."

"I can't wait for the slumber party," Kit said. For once she sounded as enthusiastic as her brother. Clearly, she was wild about her nephew, who was now skipping up to her as if he'd only just noticed her presence.

"Kit," he said.

"Devin," she said.

"I come over your house tomorrow?"

"You bet, kid."

Devin hopped around. "And S for Snake come too!"

"I have to stay here, Dev," I said. "But I'll see you Monday morning, okay?"

He began to cry.

"See that?" Kit said to Karl, so quiet I had to lean forward to hear. "Notice who he *isn't* crying for."

Karl was stone-faced. "Give it a rest, Kitty."

I knew, from her LACMA show, that Kitty was her real name.

AFTER I CHANGED Devin out of his wet swim trunks, I put him down for his afternoon nap. I went back downstairs to clean up the pool toys, the towel still wrapped around me like rice on a California roll. My bathing suit underneath was clammy-wet (*Come on in, yeast infection*), but I wouldn't take it off just yet. The afternoon sun was high in the sky, baking the back deck, and I wanted to go for another swim.

Seth lay on one of the chaise lounges with a T-shirt spread across his face. I looked away from his bare chest, narrow and covered in hair from practically his collarbone down. Then I looked again. The T-shirt lifted at his nose, and dented at his open mouth, and moved up and down with his breath. He had a hand on his furry stomach.

A year ago I probably would've been disgusted by the sight of Seth's body. All that hair. But a year ago, I hadn't yet met Everett, who is as hairless as a little boy, and I hadn't yet had my heart chewed to meat gristle by said boy. I used to be really into Everett's smooth body. It reminded me of an ancient sculpture. But now? Those sculptures weren't always white, their paint faded over time so what we see now isn't what we would have seen back then. That day by the pool, I decided that Seth's body was somehow more complete than Everett's. It was authentic. A man should have grit, I decided, and like my mom always did, I cannonballed into the pool.

Seth was sitting up when I swam to the surface. He had the stomach rolls of the very skinny: like wide-wale corduroy.

"Sorry," I called out, and swam closer. It struck me that I was waiting for a reply. The expectation was habitual and automatic, like flipping a light switch during a power outage.

He shook his head, as if to say *No worries*.

I reached the edge. Was I supposed to say something, keep a one-sided conversation going? I probably wouldn't, but I knew my mother would. Katherine Mary would kill to chat with a mute.

"Congratulations on your film," I said. "Kit said it was really good."

He rolled his eyes and shook his head, but his expression was more nuanced than those two gestures alone. He had learned to communicate with a single look. Maybe Lady was wrong and Seth was a genius.

Then he held out his hand, palm down, and wiggled it from side to side. *So-so.*

"So, so, suck your toe, all the way to Mexico," I chanted, and pushed off the edge of the pool. It was total Katherine Mary in one of her goofball moods.

Seth laughed and I knew I'd said what I said so that I'd get that reaction. That sound again, I wanted to elicit it over and over again.

"Is the film a secret from your mom?" I asked.

He nodded, and I pushed back to tread water for a minute, my legs pumping hard through the silky water. He couldn't elaborate—of course he couldn't. I had to figure out how to get answers. My mom would think of it as a game, even though it wasn't, Seth was a person. Not that that would matter to Katherine Mary.

I stopped treading and floated closer to him.

"Why don't you tell her about it?" I asked.

He shrugged but not sullenly. He really wasn't sure.

"I can't believe your aunt is Kit Daniels. This guy I used to date, Everett, he, like, worships her." I stopped. Just because someone can't speak doesn't mean they want you to go on and on.

Seth reached for his iPhone on the table next to him. My stomach fizzed like soda as he typed. What would he tell me? I pulled myself to the edge and lifted myself up to read the screen he was turning to me.

Shes famous I know

"Do you like her work?"

Sometimes

"Sometimes?" I wondered if Seth was more forthcoming because he didn't have to speak. His life was one long Gchat, which had to be liberating.

Sometimes I think she exploits ppl

"Wow, really?" But I'd heard this before. In my Contemporary American Photography seminar we'd read a recently published article called "A Love Affair with Poverty: The Kit Daniels Effect," and another: "Holding the Camera, Controlling the Narrative: Kit Daniels and the Politics of the Body." A kid in class had claimed she photographed women like a man would, that her gaze was deliberately masculine. The class had gotten into an argument about whether this was a critique of sexism, or the propagation of it.

"I guess I could see that," I said now.

I like it 2. I like her Females.

"Pervert." It sounded flirtatious but Seth just kept looking at me. I kicked off the edge of the pool, my ears hot in the cold water. I wished I could unsay it.

By the time Lady returned, Seth was holed up in his room and I was wiping down the kitchen counters, my hair wet and knotted like seaweed against my neck.

"I wrote!" she said, slamming her laptop bag onto the kitchen island.

"That's great!" I remembered Karl's face, his pride.

"My editor will probably say it's totally off-topic, but I don't care!
I wrote five whole pages!"

"Congratulations!" And then, "Devin's napping."

She didn't seem to hear. "You want some sparkling rosé? Just a
glass won't hurt."

"Really?"

She already had her head in the fridge. "He'll be asleep for a while."
And then, "Who the fuck opened my—"

"Kit Daniels was here," I said quickly.

She slung her head out of the fridge, her forehead furrowed into
dozens of deep lines. At least she'd withstood the peer pressure to get
Botox.

"She was with Karl," I said. "They were dropping off Seth."

"I see. And she took the liberty of opening my bubbly. Classic."
She shut the fridge, without the wine, as if her sister-in-law had in-
fected the bottle.

"You know what I call her?" she said.

"Who?"

"Cunt Daniels."

"Cunt Daniels!" I repeated, applauding. My interaction with Seth
had put a little Katherine Mary in me, and it was easy to tap into my
mother's forwardness, no alcohol needed.

"Cunt with a C or a K?" I asked.

Lady laughed. "I love you, S for Snake."

"Oh my God," I said. "You. Are. Drunk."

She smiled. "I wrote at a bar. Not some dive, don't worry. It was
a bar-café—call it a bistro. I had two Kir Royales. Okay, three. I ordered a Caesar salad too, but it came with tomatoes and not a single
anchovy so I sent it back in a huff. Which is what Cunt Daniels would
do, by the way. I learned how to be a pill from her. Karl is the good
twin, for sure."

"They're twins?"

"Yep. There's always an evil one."

"In fairy tales, maybe."

"And their mother, Nance, was either a vicious witch or an elegant queen, depending on who's telling the story. She was probably both—she died before I could meet her. Apparently, Nance doted on Karl but was hard on Kit. He always felt like he had to protect his sister, so he's the one who had more issues with her." She stopped. "Someday I'll tell you about how I met Kit. Right now I'm calling Pink Dot and getting them to send me some more rosé and a loaf of bread, the healthy kind with the seeds. God, I'm starving."

She ran off to find her phone and I took the baby monitor into the Cottage. Didn't matter what time of day it was, the light was milky inside that space. There was something off about it: creepy, lonelier than a dorm during spring break. From the door two steps led down into the room, and each time I entered I felt like I was descending into something unknown, something muddy. I could age cheese in there.

I considered getting drunk and asking a Ouija board what the deal was with this Cottage—that was pure Katherine Mary, for sure—but I was still a little too creeped out to try it.

I texted my dad about meeting Kit. I really wanted to tell Everett, but I wouldn't. Anyway, the good twin inside me had erased his number weeks ago.

11.

EVERETT FOREVER JAMES. I SWEAR THAT'S HIS MIDDLE NAME. His mom added it to the birth certificate the day after he was born; his dad was in the hospital cafeteria, slurping down some orange Jell-O. Or so goes the myth. Everett didn't tell me the story; his mom, Hannah, did when she drove up from Los Gatos to visit. Everett blushed as she talked. His blush was one of my favorite things about him.

How could I not fall in love with a guy whose middle name is Forever?

"And even if he isn't immortal," Hannah had said, "his art will definitely live on."

"Mama," Everett said. Mama! How could I not?

But Hannah was right. I swear Everett is one gallery show away from wowing everyone at the Whitney Biennial and being profiled in *The New Yorker*. I'll probably impress my grandkids someday by telling them I used to be his lover. "Everett Forever James?" one will say, and another, the fuck-up (there's always a fuck-up), will ask, "Who's that?" (But even the fuck-up will know Everett's work once someone describes it.)

Everett and I used to live in the same decrepit two-story clapboard on Ashby. It was an intentional community; I still don't fully understand what that means. I was only in it for the cheap rent and the view of the magnolia tree from my bedroom window. I was right down the hall from Everett, who liked to sleep with his door open a sliver. On windy nights, it tapped against the jamb, open, closed, open, closed, waking me. There was a SHIT HAPPENS bumper sticker on his door. The nights I crept to his room, I'd press on the letter *I* with an index finger. Everett would do the same with my clit five minutes later.

I'd met him in Art Studio. At the time I was living alone in Clark Kerr, on a quiet floor, and I was complaining about it to the girl next to me. I thought the quiet policy would make me feel peaceful but instead I felt anxious all the time, imagining the computer science nerds behind their closed doors, writing code in all that silence. I spent half my nights at my dad's. "Which is fine," I was telling the girl. "But not great."

Then Everett leaned over and offered me a room. A girl named Hippo (don't worry, she was lithe and beautiful) was going to move out of the house he shared at the end of the semester; her anemia had resurfaced and her doctor told her she needed to eat beef and other animal products. To become a roommate, all I had to do was abstain from eating or cooking meat at home, and pay $350 a month. The rent was so much cheaper than what the dorm was costing, I would've agreed to eat, or not eat, anything demanded of me.

And I had to attend their monthly happenings.

"Happenings?" I asked.

Everett nodded. By this point we were standing at the large sink in the corner of the studio, and he was washing his paint-covered hands and arms like a surgeon. "We play music and cook food," he said. "Over dinner we discuss books, politics, art, sex." Here, he blushed. "We get drunk. All of us are artists."

I handed him a paper towel. "That's the intentional part?"

"Hardy har-har," he said, I swear to God. "You're funny, Esther."

I hadn't been making a joke, I'd truly wanted to understand what an intentional community was, but I didn't push it. This was my fourth year at Cal and I still didn't have many—or any—close friends. I often hung out with my dad and Maria on the weekends. I studied a lot too, sometimes I painted, and if I was lonely I'd ask someone from one of my psych classes if they wanted to meet at the library to prep for the exam. I'd always been a loner; chalk it up to having a cool dad and a fuck-up for a mom: I was either hanging out with him or taking care of her. Anyway, I didn't want to mess up my chances with Everett and his intentional roommates.

"When I first saw you," Everett said, "I wondered why you were so dressed up. Who wears nice clothes to paint?" I knew he was judging me like all the other arty kids did. I painted, but to them I didn't look like I did—their practice required a certain level of grubbiness that I just couldn't go for.

He continued: "But you're cool. The other roommates have to vote but it's just a formality; they'll want you."

That line: *they'll want you*.

I came to the next happening, read some Spanish poetry Maria had foisted upon me, and *bam,* I was intentional. I would move out of the dorm after finals and start my final semester in the house.

"But I'm only an art minor. I'm not really an artist," I said to Everett. "Not like you."

By then, he had already begun work on his senior show and he'd already applied to Yale with work that everyone in the department drooled over. This studio painting course was the last class I needed to fulfill my minor. I was painting the views from my father's house—Maria's house, really, earned with her attorney's salary. The money my dad made from insurance sales would have purchased him a decent place in Reno or Kansas, but not in California, no way. The view from their living room, perched above Berkeley and overlooking the Bay, was almost sickening it was so picturesque, no smog or sprawl to besmirch it. My mom had no idea her ex-husband's new life was so great. She'd never see this view. I'd never show her the paintings either.

Everyone in class thought they were ironic. Apparently no one but old biddies did straight landscapes. I didn't correct them.

"You're an artist," Everett told me. "You make art, don't you?"

I did, but only for class. I wasn't like Everett. He woke every morning and drew his reflection in the mirror. These were painstaking pencil drawings, almost as small as matchbooks, and he wouldn't even let himself pee until he finished one. I mean, honestly, he usually had morning wood during the entire process, which maybe was the point. He went to galleries and museums every weekend, and he not only subscribed to, but read, art magazines. One of his professors was letting him use her back garage as a studio. I asked him what was wrong with the studio they gave him at school and he told me he needed more space. Then he solicited my opinion about encaustic paints, as if I would have one.

"Art is my life," he told me after the first time we made out. Our lips were stained purple from the house happening, my second. "I seriously don't care about anything else," he said.

That should have been the end, my dad said later.

At the time, Everett was building a bunch of small cameras. He had embedded one in the eye of a lion Beanie Baby, which he attached to the strap of a tiny purple backpack a girl in kindergarten might carry.

The cameras were part of his senior project. On two different occasions, Everett Forever James wore an old T-shirt of his father's that pictured Barack Obama in a turban, the words "Allahu Akbar" in a cartoon talk bubble above him. Everett hated when his father wore this shirt and so he'd stolen it over Christmas break. "Out of rage, but also, even then, I knew I'd do something with it," he said. The shirt was an XXL, and it hung off Everett like a nightgown; it made me think of the narrator in "The Night Before Christmas."

While I was setting up an easel in my dad's house and painting at

my leisure, Everett was wearing this incendiary shirt around Berkeley, Oakland, and San Francisco, secretly recording the responses of
people who passed him. The sneers! The wrinkled noses! Even slurs.
A drunk woman laughed. Only one person, a heavyset white guy in a
golf shirt, a liberal's dream of a Republican, nodded and smiled. Everett's tiny camera recorded it all.

He printed out and enlarged stills from this footage, and mounted
them in ornate gold frames. The faces of these people were awful:
there was so much cruelty in them, so much unrestrained judgment.

For the show, Everett also displayed the T-shirt, backpack, and
camera in a rectangular Lucite box. He screened a video in which he
puts on and takes off the T-shirt; in the footage you can see a blush
spreading across his neck. He's aware of the camera in a way that his
subjects weren't. He has betrayed them in order to display their intol-
erance. On one wall, a single silkscreen poster read BUT WHAT WILL
MY DAD THINK?

My own dad thought my descriptions of the show made it sound
mean. But the moment Steve Shapiro walked into the gallery, he
loved it.

12.

I'S LIKE AN OLD MAP, THE KIND MY DAD CONTINUES TO USE,
even in the digital age: you turn it to match the direction you're
facing in order to see more clearly where you're going. By the time I
moved back to L.A., Everett was behind me. I saw everything differently.

The first time he and I had sex he'd closed his bedroom door. He
actually got up from his bed and walked butt naked to close it, his
dick pointing so straight and hard from his body he could have hung
a small-town sign from it that read EVERETT JAMES, DDS. No one
ever talks about the diversity of erections in the male species: some
stick straight out, others diagonally, some flip so flat against a man's

stomach you have to pull it like a lever to make anything happen. I
remember thinking it was information my mom would get out of me
about Everett if I wasn't careful.

His door had made an impressive click when he shut it, bank vault–
style. It made me feel special. In the moment it didn't occur to me that
Everett might want everyone else in the house to hear the sound of his
door shutting. Maybe he got off on the assumed audience. Just because
someone blushes doesn't mean they don't enjoy the heat of that shame.

Our first time, Everett didn't have a condom and I went to get one
from the stash I kept in my old Sanrio pencil case. I didn't bother with
clothes for the journey from Everett's room to my own, and with every
step my thighs swished together and my bare feet picked up all kinds
of gnarly dirt from the crooked wooden floor. If someone caught me,
I planned to say "It's intentional," and keep walking.

When I returned to his room, Everett said, "If I could have, I
would've recorded you running naked back to my bed."

"You couldn't do that." I peeled open the Trojan wrapper. "Ever."

At the time, and for months afterward, I thought that was the right
answer. But it wasn't, not for Everett. If I had agreed to let him film
me, would he have decided I was interesting enough to keep dating?
Would he have texted me from Yale?

For a long time, I thought Everett's lack of condoms meant he was
innocent and pure. What kind of attractive male at a top-tier univer-
sity doesn't have a prophylactic hanging around? One who hesitates
before going all the way, that's who. One with discerning taste, a gour-
mand who won't eat at just any restaurant. I had only slept with four
other guys my whole time at Cal, and even with that small sample size
I knew enough to know that Everett was the exception. Exceptional.

But since I'd started working for Lady, I understood something
new. In that haunted-seeming Cottage, with only my own fingers to
keep my body company, I realized that Everett inviting me into his
room for sex even though he didn't have a condom meant either that
he was afraid to have sex with me, despite overtures to the contrary,
or that he presumed I'd handle it, that I would go ahead and solve our
problem, plan the picnic, book the flights, do whatever women have

been doing for men since the dawn of time. Or it meant that he was hoping I'd shrug and fuck him anyway, too turned on to worry about pregnancy and STIs. Nope.

Not long after I slept with Everett for the first time, I overheard a girl on Telegraph tell her friend, "I'm not a condoms girl." I should have leaned over and told her about a guy she had to meet. There's a chance Everett wouldn't have gotten tired of her.

When I started the Tevas project I hoped Everett would catch wind of it. I wondered if he'd see echoes of his own stuff in mine, the way we both investigated modes of judgment and censure within a distinctly delineated community, or whatever bullshit we used to volley back and forth during crit, and call me up to discuss it. I'd come a long way from painting. Everett didn't even have to call—I'd settle for a Facebook message. But there was nothing.

Later I was happy to imagine that he'd never heard of the project, which, let's tell it like it is, I'd conceived out of heartbreak, or at least partly. It was a way to stop thinking about Everett, but also a way to think like him, a way to see if he was right. Could one live and breathe art? Could I?

Everett would say no. The semester was ending, and everyone was moving out of the intentional community. Standing in his packed-up room, he told me he couldn't see me anymore. "We're just too different." He went on to say that he needed to focus on his art.

"Seriously?" I said. "You're only here for a few more weeks."

"You don't get it, Es." S, I thought.

"What is there to get?" I asked.

"You were right, you're not really an artist. And hey! That's okay!"

He tried to step forward to squeeze my arm, or hug me, and I stepped backward. In that moment, I wanted nothing more than to get away from him.

Later, though, I missed him. Okay, he was insufferable, okay, he was a jerk, but he was also talented, he was interesting. I loved him.

13.

A COUPLE OF HOURS AFTER I MET KARL AND KIT, LADY GOT ready for a housewarming party in Brentwood. By seven she was gone, and by eight, Devin was fed and bathed and lullabied to sleep in his tiny bed, and I felt the evening growing plump ahead of me; there was so much time left. Before returning to the Cottage, baby monitor in hand, I waved good night to Seth. He was headed to his room to play Grand Theft Auto. (Till dawn, he typed on his phone.)

On the video monitor, Devin slept with both arms over his head, his stuffed bunny straddling his chest. The screen was green, it made me think of drone-strike footage on the TV dramas my dad watched with Maria. It was Thursday—what shows would be whirring their DVR tonight? I texted my dad something about how I was post-TV, and a second later my phone chirruped. I'm disowning you. And then: JK LOLZ!

I smiled and headed for the tiny fridge. The small bottle of vodka lay flat on the freezer shelf, covered in what looked like shaved ice.

I thought about calling my mom, but she'd yack on for over an hour.

I checked the small window that faced the pool. The coast was clear. I pulled a juice glass from the cupboard, then unscrewed the bottle. The liquor smelled antiseptic. I wished I had olives, but my mother liked her vodka pure and unadulterated. When she was in a mood, even ice cubes bothered her.

I knew it was wrong to be drinking, but the baby monitor didn't lie, Devin was deep in dreamland, and, anyway, if anything happened, Seth was home.

Here's a question I'd had since middle school: What did it feel like to black out? Katherine Mary fell down the well enough to know its mossy insides like a best friend, but it had never happened to me. I hadn't let it.

The liquor made my throat burn and a snarky blogger appeared in my head: *She calls it art, but really she just wants to wear alcoholism like a Barbie doll wears plastic heels.* My imaginary blogger was clever.

I poured another. If I was going to do this project, I had to really do it.

As the liquor warmed my belly, I felt Katherine Mary arriving apparition-style. She stepped into my body as a bride steps into a hoop dress. Here we are, I thought.

I circled my wrists like my mom sometimes does before tucking in to a big meal. I pushed the hair from my eyes as she would, even when she'd tied her hair into that pernicious purple scrunchie and there was nothing to brush away. I took in the room with a distracted nod as if I didn't notice the bare walls or the yellow pool noodle in the far corner. My mom could be as blind as a bachelor to her surroundings. I would be too.

I was becoming Happy Kathy—that's what she called herself after a drink or two. *"Happy Kathday to me,"* she liked to sing. *"Happy Kathday to me."* I sang the song now and the voice I heard was deeper than my own, deep as a bassoon. I waved my arms above my head and swayed; it was a dance my mom thought was sexy even though she looked like a demonic sea anemone.

I shuffled over to my camera. It was a hand-me-down from Maria, digital, not adequate for an artist like Everett, but nice enough for a sometime photographer like me.

As I clicked photos of my empty glass and my wrists, a love for Katherine Mary soared through me. Mom! I danced between each click. My ass cheeks quivered. I brought the vodka bottle to my face and the frost on the glass cackled. I kept dancing, mock-gasping at the cold. It was a sweet duet and my eyes were watering. This was what my dad had been seduced by: Happy Kathy's utopian urge.

I decided to go into the Manse.

I was tilting as I crept up the stairs, the evening glistening with promise and mystery. My body felt loose. Novocained.

I'd told myself Devin was stirring and that I should check on him. That's the line I'd give Seth if he caught me, and I held my breath as I passed his door. When he didn't open it, I kept on. I didn't even poke my head into Dev's room. Katherine Mary wouldn't, she'd go right for Lady's door: to the boss lady's quarters, to her boudoir. She'd want to check out the master bedroom in this house. My mom was a private eye in a past life—she says that sometimes.

I wondered if Karl's stuff still covered one of the bedside tables. Maybe he had a jar of collar stays on top of the dresser or a tube of gross hemorrhoid cream in the medicine cabinet, incriminating chest hairs in the shower. Or had Lady taken over the room completely? The rest of the house was so nice, I wondered if their room was a wreck. Maybe that's why Lady kept the door shut.

But no. The room looked like something out of a movie about rich people. There were two huge windows that overlooked the backyard. The king-sized bed was dressed in all white, and there were reading lamps built into the wall. Minimal clutter. Above the bed hung a wreath of succulents: velvety, spiky, alien. The only sign that Lady lived here was her computer bag against one wall and a pair of flip-flops by the door. Next to the bed, on a small table that looked like a giant sugar cube, was a folded up issue of *Variety*. Karl.

On my dad and Maria's favorite TV dramas, terrorists would film their hostages with the newspaper under their chins, as a kind of time stamp. I picked up the issue; four weeks old, but Lady couldn't toss it into the recycling bin. Why had she kicked him out? I felt a sudden ping of despair for her, for this ineffectual hoarding. And for Karl, who might come up here, see his stuff untouched, and feel hopeful.

Oh, who cares? Katherine Mary wouldn't. I flung myself on the bed and flapped my arms up and down like I was making snow angels, which I've never done in real life. I wished I were naked, or wearing a flapper-style dress and black pantyhose, the kind with the lines up the back.

The thought of that outfit carried me to the closet and I opened its door, felt up the wall for the light switch.

Once the light was on, I was standing in a room about half as big as the Cottage; it was like a closet on a reality TV show: soft lighting and soft carpeting, built-in shelving, two tiers of hanging space on each side. His and hers.

Karl's side was just a bunch of shirts and garment bags. Lady's side was packed, coordinated by color rather than type of clothing (which was lunacy—how did she find anything?). On one shelf a big basket held a dozen scarves. I wound one around my neck and checked out my reflection in the full-length mirror that hung on the far wall. Blue was my color. Katherine Mary would've pocketed it, but I held back. I needed to commit to being my mom, but if I got fired I'd be nowhere. And, besides, what would I do with the scarf—use it for a mixed-media collage? I dropped it back into the basket.

Lady had hung a few kid drawings next to the mirror. There was a photo of Seth at the beach, maybe at age twelve or thirteen, posing by a sagging sandcastle, and, next to it, one of her with a just-born Devin.

I turned to face Karl's stuff. I hoped it would smell like a man, like shoehorns and wool sweaters, like a park statue plaque: metal and weather. I leaned in and breathed into a row of Oxford shirts, the hangers swinging and settling back on the rod. Katherine Mary would probably put her face into the clothes and hug them to her, but Karl might be OCD about his shirts.

I needed more vodka.

I moved to Karl's dresser, which was covered in receipts and a pile of hardcovers. A small tower of quarters waited next to a parking ticket like they were having a conversation.

Hanging on the wall above the coin tower was a framed black-and-white photo. It was one of Kit's, from her Women series, and my heart stuttered as I leaned forward to get a better look. I recognized the style right off: the tight shot, the domestic details—in this one, a paisley-printed shower curtain; a curling iron propped on the edge of a sink; two ratty towels on the rack, the word SEA on one, and WORLD on the other. And a woman.

She sat on the edge of the tub in a bra and stockings. Her stomach sagged over the waistband. The stocking seam was like a scar bisecting the lower half of her torso. One dark nipple peeked from the top of her demi-cup, but it wasn't sexy, it was embarrassing, like she'd been caught with a booger in her nose.

I was looking at her body first, as Kit intended, or so a classmate had said. When I got to the woman's face, I stepped back.

"Holy fucking shit."

It was Lady.

Someone put a hand on my shoulder and I shrieked.

Seth was standing a foot away from me. He was holding up his hands, as if to say, *It's okay, calm down.*

"Fuck, Seth! You scared me!"

Now he smiled.

"I thought I heard Devin and I came up here. I . . . Your mom's at a party. For someone who used to live on this street? I guess they moved . . . ?"

He was waiting—or no, I reminded myself, yet again, he just couldn't talk. I was drunk enough for him to notice. Could he smell it on me?

"I have a sore throat so I took some cough syrup. I think it's making me kind of loopy. Oh my God, Seth, please don't tell Lady."

He just stood there.

I was going to say sorry but instead I made my hand into a fist and held it to my chest.

Sorry, I signed.

He signed something back. Judging by his smile, it meant something like, *I would never tattle.*

"This is your mom," I said, and nodded at the photo.

Seth took two steps back with his hand on his chest, pretending to be surprised.

"With your acting skills, who needs dialogue," I said. I'd meant it as a joke but Seth shot me a serious look that said, *Do you really want to go there?*

Unnerved, I turned back to the photo on the wall.

"Does Lady hate it?" I asked.

He nodded.

"I bet Karl loves it."

He nodded and then shook his head. It was complicated.

I had so many questions, but Seth wasn't about to write me an essay on the topic. I wished I could remember anything from my ASL class.

Where's the library? I signed.

He laughed. Again, sound. He could make sound.

"See? I'm practically fluent," I said.

He stepped past me and I smelled the minty tang of his shaving cream. He had on a different T-shirt than earlier. He'd bathed. He'd shaved. My ears felt hot.

Seth grabbed a pen from Karl's dresser. On the back of the parking ticket, he wrote something and handed it to me. *Santa Monica at Rexford.*

"What does this mean?" I asked. And then I knew. "Ha. The Beverly Hills Library, I get it."

Seth looked very pleased with himself. But now what? We were standing in his mom's closet and I was drunk.

"Can I ask you something?"

He didn't nod, but he didn't shake his head either.

"There's something I've wondered about."

For a second, Seth's face fell slack, annoyed. He thought I wanted to know about being mute.

"Not about you," I said quickly.

He made a face like he didn't believe me.

"I don't give a shit about that," I said. There was a meanness in my voice; it was my mom's when drinking took her down a scary, potholed road.

Seth looked startled and I felt powerful. He nodded, as if to say *Go ahead.*

"Did your mom feel exploited by Kit?"

Seth obviously hadn't expected me to ask that. He turned to the picture, as if considering it for the first time.

When he grabbed the ticket from me, our fingers touched.

He wrote something else and handed it back.

ASK HER.

LADY

14.

THE PARTY WAS A CLUSTERFUCK. NOT MY WORDS—I OVER-
heard one of the caterers murmur them as she slipped into the
kitchen, her tray still half-full of unloved endive. I don't think she understood what the phrase meant because there weren't that many people at the party. The hostess kept eyeing the front door as if expecting
some magical guest of honor to walk through it; meanwhile, her husband had gone to show a colleague the grapefruit tree he'd planted in
the yard, never to return. Between serving drinks, the bartender was
not-so-discreetly reading something on his phone. I wondered with a
thrill whether he was on Twitter. Since becoming @muffinbuffin41,
I'd tapped out a few more tweets, though I didn't dare follow anyone,
for fear they'd see them. After my Dora cleverness, the next had been
useless:

It's hot. This has been a tweet.

But after that, I tried:

There's a secret delight to farting after getting a Brazilian. The gas
travels! Physics!

I'd tweeted this one just before getting out of the car and heading
to the party. It still had me giggling; it was the only thing keeping me
vertical. Otherwise, I might have found a room to lie down in. The
catering girl had been right, except it wasn't the party that was the
clusterfuck. It was me.

I kept picturing Kit walking through my house just a few hours
earlier: her Maoist couture, her stink-eye. She had opened the spar-

kling rosé that I'd been saving to celebrate a good writing day. Of course she would take that triumph away from me.

Why had she come over? Karl knew I wouldn't want his sister around snooping; once upon a time he'd been protective of our life together. Now, maybe, he'd given up on that—maybe he'd given up on me, as I had him. The hostess of the party certainly thought that's what I had done. "I'm sorry to hear about you and Karl," she said when I arrived, but instead of empathy in her eyes, there was only judgment. "I imagine you have your reasons," she added.

"So imagine them," I said, and shuttled myself to the sofa. I'd come because I thought it would be good to get out and socialize, and because I was already paying S for the privilege. But never again, or at least not here. Now that the hostess no longer lived on our street it would be easy to pretend she didn't exist.

I didn't recognize this sofa. It must have been purchased with the housewarming party in mind. It was a sleek midcentury piece, which meant I wasn't supposed to actually sit on it. I wanted to stand up and lift it over my head. Throw it across the room. Maybe I could aim for the stereo, which was playing cabaret covers of Leonard Cohen songs—they'd probably bought the CD at Starbucks. I forced an asparagus spear down my throat, counted to three hundred, and slinked out the door.

I WAS STILL upset when Karl rang the doorbell the next morning. I kissed Devin and sent him downstairs with Seth; I waited in my room until they were gone. I had to, otherwise I'd be compelled to talk to Karl about his visit the day before. He'd be contrite. He'd insist on running down the hill for a new bottle of bubbly, likely a more expensive vintage than the one I'd chosen, and he would present it to me with yet another apology. He wouldn't let me stay mad.

Or would he? I didn't want Karl to grovel, but I also didn't want the opposite: he might pshaw my concerns, let me stew. Not out of unkindness, but apathy.

It was Friday. Karl would be wearing the linen shirt I loved: charcoal-gray, the buttons tiny and wooden but somehow breathtak-

ingly masculine. It was one of the few items of clothing he'd packed
upon moving out; he always wore it on pickup days and I never com-
plained about the ritual because the shirt looked so good on him. If
I'd asked him to leave it in the closet, just so I could gaze at it every
now and again, on my own terms, he would have complied. It's why I
didn't say a thing as he'd carefully folded it into his suitcase.

An hour later, Seth left for his morning film class and I crept downstairs, the house quiet except for the thrum of the dishwasher. Sometimes I wanted to crawl in there, let the water wash over me, toss and
scrub me clean.

Instead I checked my phone. I went first to Seth's timeline; his
newest tweet time-stamped twenty minutes prior: My stepdad picked
up my brother & it felt like a drug deal. #LegalizeToddlers.

I heard myself shriek-laugh even as I wanted to cry. If @muffin
buffin41 followed @sethconscious, she might reply. But how? Instead
I typed to no one:

Clusterfucks should be named, like hurricanes.

From the window I could see S doing laps in the pool. Her hair
would turn green from all the swimming. Upstairs I kept a drawer of
bathing caps; I'd offer to lend her one.

I walked outside and kneeled at the edge of the pool. S was swimming toward me from the other side, and her skin looked as pale and
quivery as I'd imagined.

"I'm worried," I said when she reached me.

She grabbed the concrete edge and looked up at me, stricken.

"Your hair," I said. "Also, you need goggles."

She treaded away from the edge, her chin dipping in and out of the
water's surface. "I don't care." The words took her some effort.

"One day," I said, "you'll look at yourself in the mirror and wish
you'd started the anti-aging creams early, that you'd never gone outside without SPF. And that you'd used a deep conditioner on your
hair, at least monthly. Also: never stop doing squats."

"Squats?"

I grinned and stood up. I pretended to sit on an invisible park
bench, ass out. "Squats, S. S is for squats. Otherwise, your butt will
fall."

We both laughed.

"Seth told me something," she said. "Well, he didn't *tell* me, obviously . . ."

I couldn't help but be annoyed. "You can still say 'tell.' "

"Kit took a photo of you. Seth said you were one of her Women?"

My blood turned cold as the pool water. *One of her Women.*

To Kit, I'd always be Woman Number Seventeen, whose Sea World towels she loved for reasons she couldn't quite articulate. (The day after she came over to photograph me, I drove those towels to the Goodwill and shoved them at the blue-vested employee, refusing a receipt. There is always someone less fortunate.)

"It's true," I said. I let my voice drop a few octaves: "I am Woman Number Seventeen."

"Okay, Darth Vader." S was now floating on her back. I was surprised how decent her body looked; she was curvy but thin, her breasts small but buoyant. "Don't squander your good looks," my mother had once said to me when I dared wear a mock turtleneck. I felt like telling that to S.

Instead I said, "Why were you and Seth talking about Kit?"

"I guess because she stopped by."

"I wasn't aware you knew Kit's work."

"Only a little. From school." Her body faced the sky and she squinted in the sun. "Did you meet her through Karl?"

"It was the other way around." I headed back to the house. "It's too bright out here, come inside if you want to talk."

She jumped out of the pool and in moments was right at my heels like a puppy.

"Jesus," I said. "Eager, are we?"

"I like stories," she said lamely. She'd wrapped her towel under her armpits.

"You should wear it slung on your hips," I said.

"Wear what?"

I nodded at her towel, and she looked pleased. "I would, but . . ."

"But what? You've got a nice midriff."

"My mom taught me to do it like this."

"Don't listen to your mom." I thought of the pink bubbly going flat in the fridge. It was the same brand my mother drank and I hated myself for liking it. The day my dad died, she'd opened a bottle and proposed a toast to extramarital cheaters everywhere.

"I have an idea!" I said. "Let's get drunk tonight and share stories about our fucked-up mothers!" I hooted as I stepped into the house. S was quiet. "Sorry, sorry," I said. "I've just been out of sorts since Kit showed up here yesterday."

"You hate her photo."

"What's your obsession with the photo? The photo is okay. It's mildly exploitative and I look flabby and depressing in it even though I am neither, and certainly wasn't before I had Devin—flabby, I mean. But it's just a photo."

"And it's anonymous."

"Kit made thousands upon thousands of dollars off those photos, but every time she and I meet for lunch she insists on reviewing the bill, calculating exactly who owes what."

"But the photo itself. What do you think?"

"Did you know she wouldn't tell me when she was coming over to photograph me? She gave me a two-week window like some awful cable guy—she did that with all the women. She wanted us unprepared, and she wanted our apartments dirty. Next time you see her, ask her about YouTube videos. She loves when people do dance routines in front of dressers covered in junk. If there's a kitchen counter in the background with a stick of deodorant on it, or, I don't know, a car battery, she goes wild. I'm serious, clutter and grime turn her on."

That was actually something Karl had said when he took me to coffee for the first time; his crudeness, I realized later, was an act, a way for him to show me he was on my side.

I had refused a dinner date with him. He was the artist's brother, it was too weird. Besides, Kit had given him my personal information, which felt like a violation. In his email, Karl admitted the creep factor. He couldn't help it, he said; he'd fallen for my image. "I purchased the photo before Kit's show opened," he wrote. "But that makes it worse, doesn't it?" It did, and yet, I replied to his email, and four days and a string of correspondence later, I agreed to at least meet for coffee. I was conspiring to get the photo back; I hadn't planned on falling for him.

"Lady?" S said.

"Sorry. Just thinking." And then, because I saw that she was standing there, waiting as if for a compliment, I said, "I won't show you the photo."

Seth had been at school when Kit had taken it. And thank God, because it wasn't until I started dressing for work that she even brought that big camera to her eye. She didn't care about me watering my plants or how carefully I marinated the chicken for dinner. She wanted nudity and beauty rituals. She liked my pantyhose. "Those are great!" she cried when I pulled them from the dresser.

"It's in Kit's book," S said.

"I realize that. I still won't show it to you."

"No, I mean . . . I own that book. I've already seen it."

"You have?"

She nodded.

"And out of all those photos, you remember mine?"

"Not specifically," she said quickly.

When Seth found out I'd given away his favorite Sea World towel set, he freaked out. I told him I had to get rid of the towels, that the towels had been cursed by that stupid photographer. But nothing I said helped; he was hurt, it was my fault.

"So, later on?" I asked S. "It's your day off, so if you don't want to spend time with me, you don't have to."

"You really meant it? You want to hang out later?"

"Unless you're going back to your mom's place. You should probably go see her."

She shook her head. "She expects me to come, she's hopeful."

"But you aren't going."

"When I was a freshman at Cal, she badgered me for weeks to visit for spring break, and when I got here, she wasn't there. She'd left with Frank—that's her on-and-off-again boyfriend—for San Luis Obispo."

"What's in San Luis Obispo?"

"I don't know, but I can tell you that I wasn't."

"When I was little, before my dad died, my mom would purpose-
fully give him the wrong time to meet me, and when he didn't show
up I'd have to call her from a pay phone to pick me up."

"She left you somewhere alone?"

I nodded. "At the Hamburger Hamlet—the one that used to be on
Sunset?"

"Why didn't he pick you up at your house?"

"My mother didn't trust his driving."

"Why not?"

"Because he used to sleep with other women in that car." I let out
a bark, which is the laugh of jaded women everywhere. "So anyway.
Stay here this weekend. As revenge."

She squinted. There was the promise of a wrinkle, its prequel,
forming between her eyes, and I felt the urge to warn her. "Maybe,"
she said.

15.

WHEN I MET KIT, SETH WAS FIFTEEN AND ATTENDING A PRI-
vate school called Greenhouse geared toward "alternative
learners." He was on scholarship. No one else was nonverbal, but there
were a number of students who either couldn't write (dysgraphia), or
couldn't stop writing (graphomania), and there was one girl who spoke
in a squeaky Martian voice and was obsessed with ancient Egypt. She
was otherwise normal; meaning, I suppose, that aside from the voice
and the King Tut thing, she worried about her training bra and could
write perfectly coherent essays about *To Kill a Mockingbird*. She and
Seth hung out a lot, actually.

I'd spent the day before writing about Greenhouse; Anya had suggested I draft out of order and follow whatever inspired me. "We can
organize it chronologically later," she said. "Why not start with that
amazing school of his?" So that's what I did, and to my surprise it was
easy to describe the principal's office, with its beanbag chairs; a round
table in lieu of a desk; and the young teachers from places like New

Hampshire and Hawaii, who encouraged Seth to get into filmmaking and creative writing. They didn't push math on him like so many experts of yore had. As if numbers were the consolation prize for those who couldn't communicate. As if Seth couldn't communicate.

And yet, even as I described all this and the pages piled up, I knew I was avoiding the more important stuff: the beginning, the painful parts. At the end of my first meeting with Joyce, she'd put her hands on my shoulders and said, "Don't worry, Lady, you're up for this. You'll be able to capture the pain." At that, I imagined a great big net, my pain caught inside of it like a shark, two hard cysts for eyes, and I nodded vigorously. But the truth was, I could write about Greenhouse until I died (graphomania indeed), and I wouldn't even be touching that pain, let alone the net.

I needed to start from the beginning and write what my editor had asked for. That would get me closer to the pain, and I knew it. "Why is he silent?" Anya had asked. "When did you realize he wouldn't speak?" I murmured like she'd posed something profound, when in fact those two questions were the most common. They were also unanswerable. How could I tell her that all I had were a few measly memories that I connected, however indirectly, however illogically, to my son's silence? They were part of the gnarled web of his disability, but they didn't untie it. If anything, they tangled it further. My pain was just that: pain. It wouldn't explain or solve anything.

THAT FIRST YEAR. Seth ended it with just four teeth, two on top and two on the bottom, and for all of it, he didn't sleep. Sometimes he lay awake in his crib, slapping the air at the mobile I had fashioned for him out of tinfoil, sea shells, and a wire hanger. Sometimes he sprawled on my stomach, sucking my knuckles, an empty bottle between his thighs. Devin cooed constantly his first year, but I don't remember if Seth did; I wasn't looking for a lack.

If I slept at all in those first twelve months it was wearily, my dreams flimsy and half-lucid, and almost always anxious: Seth falling into a campfire; Seth crawling into the road; Marco changing the locks and forgetting to tell us; Marco forgetting Seth's name and mine.

I often awoke abruptly on the couch next to Seth's crib, my back com-
pressed into a series of knots, Marco snoring from the bed across the
room. Wherever Seth was, on me or in the crib, those big dark eyes of
his were always open.

Seth was nine months old when Marco's mother died. For the funeral I strapped the gingham carrier to my chest and bounced Seth up
and down as they lowered his grandmother into the earth, my mouth
on his head, hushing him quiet. A few of Marco's mother's friends
made moony eyes at the two of us, but Marco didn't bother to make
introductions. He shuttled me and Seth into the car as soon as the service ended. I didn't realize we weren't driving to the reception until
we were halfway home. "But Seth eats now," I said, as if that had anything to do with Marco's decision.

At ten months, Seth was already ambling across the apartment like
a drunk. Perhaps he walked early to make up for other, nonathletic,
deficiencies. At the time, I thought he might be ahead of schedule on
everything: he'd been born a week early; he was tall for his age; and
now, look, he'd gone from tadpole to ape to human in no time. Talking, I presumed, was the next frontier, waiting to be conquered. It's
my presumptions that are most painful to recall.

Back then, Marco was still shutting himself into the bathroom
to cry—or to vomit, that's what it sounded like. Whenever Marco
retched behind the closed door, Seth would cock his ear, listening.
As I said, I was still expecting Seth to talk, and soon: if not in a few
months, then within a year; soon he'd be speaking in complete sentences. If he could have spoken then, he might have said, *Why Daddy
still sad?* I guess I was assuming his questions because I always said, "He
just needs time, baby. More time."

When Marco opened the bathroom door, his face waxen and ashy,
Seth toddled toward him, arms up.

"Lady," Marco would say, and I'd rush in to swoop Seth under my
arm like a football.

Seth never cried over his dad's subtle gesture of neglect, and neither did I. Marco was doing enough crying for everyone, and, anyway, grief was still a powerful excuse. Not just for his crying in the
bathroom, or for his lack of interest in Seth, but also for his long trips

to Vegas, not a single phone call, and for the time he told me my rust-colored blouse "looks like your period." If I had laughed, he would have gotten angry, and so I smiled. Grief made him angry too.

Seth had been walking for just over a month when Marco quit working at the Bagel Broker. In the last year he'd increased his hours there, had even become a shift manager, but he said he just couldn't do it anymore, couldn't stand smiling at the customers or picking cornmeal out of his fingernails every night, the funk of lox like a wicked cologne on his skin. That was all true, sure, but the real reason was that Marco expected to sell his mother's house and live off the money.

I can imagine my own mother saying, "A smarter man would have investigated the state of her finances before depending on them," and she would have been correct. Marco walked out in the middle of a shift, and the next day found out that his mother had been about to lose her Chatsworth shack to the bank when she died, her medical debt a mushroom cloud over the backyard's straw-colored lawn and termite-infested garage. There'd be no money, only a house to clean out and papers to file. Upon learning the news, Marco punched a hole in the wall above our bed.

We needed money, and not only for rent. Now that Seth was walking, it was becoming difficult to bring him to the Actress's house. She loved Seth, but she also loved her glass figurines.

The memory that's stuck in my mind, and won't let go, even seventeen years later, is from the day she and I catch Seth gnawing on her crystal candy bowl.

"Why don't you look into getting a nanny?" she says, and I agree.

It's been a long afternoon, filled with phone calls and door-answering, all the while shadowing Seth to make sure he doesn't bother the Actress. Her colonoscopy is scheduled for the next morning, and her nerves are, as she says, "fringed like an Indian's moccasins." At five, I kiss the Actress on the cheek and hurry with Seth to the car, eager to be home, to be done with it all.

By the time I find a parking spot three blocks from our building, I'm so hungry my stomach is sucking itself like a straw. My eyes burn with lack of sleep. If I could eat a hoagie in bed, I would. But I can't do that: Seth must be fed and bathed and rocked and hushed before I can even fantasize about a sandwich. And a fantasy it will remain because there's never any bread in the house.

I am holding Seth on my hip because if I let him walk from the car to the apartment, he might decide suddenly to run in the opposite direction, and I don't have the energy to chase him. On the walk into our building, I accidentally pinch him in my attempt to keep him from wriggling out of my arms, and he cries into my shoulder. "Baby, baby," I say, over and over again as I let him into the building.

Now we're in its long hallway, which always smells of hair spray and fried food. Someone is yelling in Armenian.

Even from here, I can hear the music playing from our apartment, loud and raucous; it's "I Wanna Be Your Dog." By the time we reach our door, I can make out Marco singing along; the sound of his voice, scratchy and vulnerable, makes me smile. I am still in love with Marco, despite his meanness and the way he fails to acknowledge Seth. I can't help it. The night before, Marco pulled me from the couch and into our bed, and after going down on me until I whispered *Good, good, good,* he sighed his pussy-stink breath into my face and said "Good night" so sweetly my eyes got hot with tears. I love him. I consider tattooing *I want to be your dog* on my wrist.

"Do you hear Daddy?" I say to Seth, and he nods.

I unlock the door. The music is so loud it feels as if we've stepped inside a chainsaw. Seth's squirming in my arms, his hands are on his ears now, and he's wrinkling his face, in disgust or discomfort, I don't know. But when Marco walks into the room from the kitchen, Seth drops his hands, straightens his posture. Is he trying to be brave for his father? Maybe just tolerant.

"Hey," Marco yells.

I put Seth down and he runs into the bathroom.

Marco looks confused.

"The music," I call out. I walk over to the record player and lift the needle. All at once the apartment drops into silence.

"Really?"

"Sorry," I say.

Seth's standing in the bathroom doorway with a cloud of toilet paper in his arms.

"Fuck!" Marco yells.

"Marco," I whisper.

"That was our last roll. Fuck."

I gently remove the toilet paper from Seth's arms and begin to wind it around my palm. "We can still use it," I say.

Marco lets out a big whoosh of air and runs a hand through his hair. "Okay, yeah. That's true." And then he winces. "Are your hands clean?"

Instead of replying, I carefully remove the toilet paper and step into the bathroom to set it down. "Come on, Seth," I say, heading toward the kitchen, "let's eat a sweet potato." (I too will eat a sweet potato for dinner.)

"Lady," Marco says, and grabs for my hand as I pass.

"If you require more pristine toilet paper," I say, "you'll have to go out and buy it. With whatever money is left in your bank account."

"Wow, aren't you being a bitch." He releases my hand. I look at Seth to see if he's listening. He is; his eyes are on his father.

"You're going to have to stay with Seth tomorrow while I'm at work," I say. "I can't bring him with me anymore."

"So that's what's got you in a pissy mood."

"Can you do it?"

He pauses. "Sure. Yeah."

And then he leans forward and puts a hand on Seth's cheek. He hasn't done that since the day Seth was born. "Right, Seth?" he says. "Us boys are gonna hang?"

It's supposed to feel good, this moment when my lover claims my child as his. And it does, it does. I think: We are finally a family. I think: Grief hasn't swallowed Marco. Or: Grief did swallow him, but he was spit back out again as a better man.

But then Seth points to the kitchen. And then he opens his mouth. And he speaks.

"There," he says.

There, there, there, there. I say that word to myself sometimes.

I let out a shriek. "His first word! Yay, Seth! Yay!"

"Really?" Marco says. "He hasn't done that before?"

I shake my head, and we both look at Seth, who has gone silent again. It's like he lifted the record player needle inside of himself.

"There!" I say. "There is where dinner is! Right, Sethy, right!"

I whisk him into the kitchen. Already I am imagining what other words he might say, and even, how he might say them the next day, when he's with Marco. With his daddy. With his daddy's hand resting on his cheek.

Before I fall asleep that night, I curl into Marco and whisper, "Everything's going to be all right," and Marco says, "Yep." The headlights from a passing car slide across the ceiling and disappear.

This memory is mostly good. It ends happily, even if it showcases my presumptions about Seth, and emphasizes my naïveté, my willing suspension of disbelief, regarding Marco. I really thought Seth had started talking, and I really thought Marco had turned tender.

It hurts because nothing turned out the way I thought it would. You think you know how a story begins, or how it's going to turn out, especially when it's your own. You don't.

There, there. So there.

16.

SETH TEXTED TO SAY HE WAS GOING TO KIT'S AND WOULDN'T be home until late. I didn't reply for an hour, and when I did all I wrote was the letter *K*. I imagined them roasting marshmallows over Kit's backyard fire pit, Devin bouncing on Karl's lap and Seth leaning into the flames until Kit yelled at him to be careful. Devin would ask for one more marshmallow, and then another. Karl would give him five, maybe six, before restraining himself.

I was surprised by how much I missed Devin. I ached for him in the way I used to ache for Seth when he was a baby. I imagined Devin's wispy blond hair and his chubby legs, the way the toilet imprinted arcs across his thighs after a good effort to poop on the potty like a big boy. The space between his chin and his neck smelled like the inside of a cereal box and I loved the way he kissed me: openmouthed, slobbery as a dog. His lips were the color of raspberries. I wanted him back.

Maybe this was why I'd let Karl take our kid for the weekend, so that I could remember what longing felt like.

When the sun began to descend, I heard the back door slide open and S calling my name.

"Be right down," I yelled. I'd been going over my pages, as if rereading them would do any good. I'd also showered and put on the long white linen dress I'd worn on my honeymoon. It had been the three of us in Hawaii: Karl, Seth, and me—or four of us if you count Devin's cells already multiplying inside of me. We'd spent our days on the beach, building elaborate sand castles and running in and out of the water. The dress still smelled like that trip, like ocean and sunscreen. I never washed it.

S was sitting on the living-room couch with her hands folded across her lap. She had on the dress she wore when we'd met, her black bikini dark beneath it.

"Twiddling your thumbs in the Cottage?" I said.

"My toes too. Actually, I fell asleep outside and now look." She stood and showed me the backs of her thighs, which were pig-pink.

"Ouch! I have some aloe upstairs. Or, better yet, let me get you a drink."

In the kitchen we toasted to sunburns and drank the rest of the sparkling wine. At least Kit had the decency to put in the Champagne bottle stopper.

We'd only each had a glass when S said, "Can I ask you something?" Her voice had the manic quality of all tipsy women everywhere.

"Drunk already?" I asked.

She shrugged and cocked an eyebrow mischievously. We were still standing at the counter.

"My question is . . ."

In that pause it seemed like she had a billion questions to choose from. But then she grabbed the bottle and poured the rest into her glass. "Why did you ask Karl to move out?"

I considered my empty glass and walked to the fridge, where a new, unopened bottle waited. I would need to drink fast or S would lap me.

"Let me guess," I said. "You think he's such a great guy."

"And you don't?"

I popped the cork with my bare hands and a curl of smoke snaked out of the bottle's mouth.

"I do. Karl *is* a good guy. But does someone have to be a bad person to want to leave him? Men leave women for all kinds of reasons." I stopped. "Look, we did have a fight, but the fight wasn't why I told him I needed space. Not the only reason anyway."

"My mom asked for a divorce because she liked this skateboarder who was always outside of Erewhon. She wanted to see where it could go. He was, like, nineteen."

"What happened?"

"They were together for almost a year."

"My mother never had any boyfriends."

"What about the high school principal?"

I tipped the bottle into my glass. The foam threatened to overflow and then receded, and the glass wasn't even half full. "Surprisingly, things with Mr. Hall didn't really work out. The nurse left him, but he didn't date my mom or anything." We were both watching the foam spit and twinkle in my glass. "My mom pours sparkling wine perfectly." I topped my glass off.

"So does my dad. But only recently, after going to Napa. I think he and his wife literally took a class on how to pour wine." She pulled her phone out of her pocket and aimed it at our flutes sparkling pink on the marble countertop.

"Instagram?" I asked as her phone clicked.

"I'm texting it to my dad." She smiled and pressed a few buttons. "He's sort of like Karl, I think. Really dorky."

"That makes me your mother."

She looked startled. I could tell she'd been deep in her drunk-mind, momentarily unaware of me. "I guess, yeah, it does." Then she laughed. "Crazy. She's everywhere."

I didn't know what she was talking about, and I didn't want to ask.

"Let's go outside," I said, and she said okay without looking up from her phone.

THE SKY WAS still bright, but there was a loneliness to the air that said dusk. It would be cool as soon as the sun went down; according to Karl, this was one of the reasons people come to California and never leave.

I lowered myself onto one of the chaise lounges, careful not to spill my drink. I could feel the Cottage behind me, radiating ugliness, and I turned. The bougainvillea we'd planted along the front wall looked garish in its bright-pink finery; what should have improved the flat, putty-colored exterior only made it worse. There was something off, something wrong, about the place.

"Is the Cottage . . . okay?" I asked.

"It's great," S said. "Except for the vibes."

"The vibes?" But I knew what she was talking about. Karl never wanted to discuss what had happened, but maybe S would.

"It feels like someone died in there," she said.

I laughed even though it wasn't funny.

"It's haunted," I said, "but not by a dead person."

S took a sip of her wine; she was surprisingly sanguine. "What do you mean?"

"Do you really want to know?"

"Ha—don't put this on me. You obviously want to tell me."

Was that true? I sighed, as if cheerfully dismayed. Usually my mannerisms felt natural, or if not natural, then at least comfortable, but now the wine was starting to do its work and I sensed a deliberateness to everything I did: the way I held my glass, the way I smiled at the pool, as if it were part of the conversation. It all required effort. It was all affectation.

"Seth was fifteen when we moved in here," I said. "That's not really a great age for anyone. He was having some . . . troubles."

"Troubles? Sounds sort of 1950s."

"That's what Karl called them. Seth missed the apartment he and

I had lived in for almost his whole life, the commute to school was longer than ever, and we had this new family dynamic to get used to. It was a difficult time."

S had her eyes on the Cottage door. "Was he really *bad*? A rebel?"

"Until then, no, not at all. Karl and I thought he was mature enough to have his room in there. Let's just say we were wrong."

"Did he get into drugs or something?"

"No"—I remembered the cloudy bong—"or, yeah, but that wasn't the real problem."

S picked up the bottle and refilled my glass.

"He kind of disappeared," I said. "Into the Cottage. Days would go by and I'd realize I'd hardly seen him. He was eating his meals in there, even. Don't ask me why I let him. First I was hugely pregnant, overseeing the renovations inside, and then I had Devin. Plus I really wanted Seth to be independent—I was happy to see how far he'd come." I thought of Seth as a kid in our tiny apartment, creeping into the living room and onto my futon, scared from a nightmare or some raccoon chortling outside the bedroom window. Sometimes I'd wake in the morning with our backs touching, and feign sleep until he stirred and moved away from me with a jolt. Seth was sleeping in my bed pretty regularly until Karl came around. It ended after that. I didn't tell this to S; I knew it would sound worse than its reality, which had been comforting and close, his gentle snore a song I'd always hum along to.

"Finally I went into the Cottage when Seth wasn't home. I was horrified. It was full of all kinds of crazy shit he'd picked up off the street, like traffic cones and even a broken shopping basket from a supermarket. There were dirty plates and laundry everywhere. He'd been brushing his teeth with a tree branch, I'm not kidding."

"Honestly, it doesn't sound so terrible."

"I wish it ended there. A mother from Seth's school showed up not long after that, said her daughter Tanya had stayed at our place the night before—and they didn't just sleep, apparently. She wanted to know who the fuck I was to let that happen. The truth was, I'd had no idea. Karl did though. He met Tanya in the morning and offered to drive her home. They stopped at the Coffee Bean on the way. I'd slept through everything, I was totally clueless."

"Did the mother scratch your eyes out?"

"Just about. The girl has a sensory sensitivity, doesn't like to be touched, that kind of thing. I think the mom was jealous of Seth for getting to feel her."

"That must have been hard," S said.

"Really?"

"What if you'd found out Seth had talked to someone?"

The sun had sunk lower, the sky turning gray and smoke-colored. S looked pretty in this light, and I could see how someone might fall in love with her. Plus she was funny, which Karl had once told me was what good men looked for in a wife.

"If Seth talked to someone else . . ." I said, my voice wobbly. "I can't even go there. It hurts too much."

"Totally," S said. If she noticed the emotion in my voice, she didn't let on. "If it was me, like if my daughter wouldn't let me touch her and then I found out she'd spent all night in some guy's arms, I'd want to . . . I don't know. I'd probably go postal. Or bring it inward—get a little suicidal."

I downed the rest of the wine, a metallic taste at the back of my throat.

"You should probably go call your mother," I said. "She's probably really missing you."

"Maybe." She stood up. "Thanks for talking to me."

"Anytime." Before she turned away, I said, "That's what the fight was about, by the way. It was about Seth and that girl. Tanya."

"The fight with Karl, you mean? But I thought you said Seth wasn't even sixteen when he lived in the Cottage—that was, like, three years ago."

"It was. But I didn't know Karl had driven Tanya home. I found that out recently."

"And it still bothered you? After all this time?"

"Karl told me in passing, as if I wouldn't get mad. But there's more to it. . . ." I suddenly felt overwhelmed by the details, tired of thinking about Karl. And I didn't want to talk about Seth and the Cottage any more than I had to. "It's boring," I said. "Never mind."

S didn't ask me to elaborate. She shrugged and called out good night as she headed for the Cottage. Her ass was flat and wide at this angle, and I looked away.

I WONDERED WHETHER I should have told her more. Not about the stupid fight, but about how, those years ago, I moved Seth back into the house on my own. Karl was filming in the desert, it was his first production since Devin's birth, and when he returned, the Cottage was empty of furniture, any proof of my son's transgressions eradicated first by the housekeeper, and then by the men I hired to repaint the walls and hang new window shades. I required Seth to eat ten meals a week with me, which I tallied on a dry-erase board in the kitchen. I would have taken away his iPhone, but since that was his main way of communicating, it seemed inhumane.

I should have told S that Karl had been upset by what I'd done. It wasn't my decision that rankled him, but that I didn't seek his input first.

His protests struck me as preposterous. He didn't get it. He didn't realize how worried I'd been. What did Seth do when he had a nightmare?

"We need to teach him independence," Karl said during one of our arguments. He thought the dining quota was a little much, but it took me six months to budge from that rule.

I knew Karl wasn't trying to come between me and Seth; he was respectful of our relationship, and often encouraged us to do "bonding activities" like hiking and baking. Once, he sent us to Color Me Mine to paint plates and then had them displayed in his office.

"You're such a good mom," he'd sometimes say.

But he had opinions. He had the money. Ways of doing things. And, as I found out later, he had Tanya's phone number, and her mother's too. He encouraged that relationship.

17.

THE FIRST TIME I WENT TO WORK WITHOUT SETH, I CALLED home only once; the phone rang seven times and with each trill I pictured worse and worse fates, all of them ending with Seth dead. When Marco finally answered I asked brightly, "Everything okay?" I was in the sitting room, at the mahogany secretary, and the Actress had just entered, her index finger up, which meant she had a new task for me.

"Where are the diapers?" Marco asked. I could hear Seth in the background, whimpering.

"Should be a new box in the linen closet." I'd been gone for four hours, and Marco still hadn't changed his diaper? Seth was very regular, which meant he'd been sitting in shit for—I checked my watch—two hours. His rash would be red and painful.

I smiled at the Actress and rolled my eyes, pointing at the phone.

"Thanks." Marco hung up.

The Actress smiled. "Everything okay with Papa and Baby?"

"I think so! They're going to check out the story time at the library."

I had pointed to the flyer on the fridge on my way out that morning. I was pretty sure Marco wouldn't bother, but still I'd urged him to go. "Activities," I said. "They'll rescue you."

I wonder, if Marco had taken Seth for a few outings then maybe he wouldn't have given up so easily. But he hated the stroller, said the wheels got stuck on every sidewalk crack, and the car seat eluded him—he said he couldn't get it to lock into place. That first night, he admitted to being afraid to drive with Seth.

"Why? Have you been drinking?"

He smiled sheepishly. I must have looked so aghast that he gave me a pitying glance. "That's a joke, Lady. It's called a sense of humor."

The truth is, Marco lasted only two days alone with Seth before he told me he couldn't do it.

"I'm miserable, he's miserable," he confessed. "I'd rather get my old job back. I love the kid, but I'm not cut out for this."

Because I didn't want to ask him what *this* meant, I said, "You know I can't bring him to work anymore. And until we've saved some money we can't afford a nanny . . . or even day care."

"Trust me, you don't want me doing this. If I could get a job that pays okay you could quit yours and stay home with Seth. Too bad that old woman throws so much money at you. It'd be a shame to give that up."

"It would." Marco was under the impression that I didn't do anything for the Actress but keep her company. To him, it was free money.

"I did have one idea," he said.

That's how I began speaking to my mother again. I called her that evening and the next morning, per our agreement, I drove Seth to her place in Beverlywood. My childhood home: ranch-style and un-assuming, the pool in the back drained because my mother couldn't swim, the front door as black and as lacquered as a jewelry box. I hadn't set foot in it since our argument about Marco. The time before that, there'd been an argument about something else, I couldn't re-member what. It seemed every time I went to visit her, we fought so bitterly that we didn't speak again until the next fight.

But now I had Seth, and I needed her to watch him. There would not be an argument. She could be horrible to me, but Seth was a baby, and I knew she would take good care of him—to spite me, or to prove me wrong, or make me jealous. Or maybe, simply, because her love for him was still uncomplicated, without reservations. I could tell she already loved him, and fiercely. If she didn't, she would have made me beg her to babysit. On the phone she'd been quick to offer help. "I'd love to," she'd said, and it was pure.

Seth had still only said that one word, *there*.

I carried Seth toward the door, so dark it made me feel woozy, and my mother answered before I could ring the bell. She wore a long navy-colored dress, cinched at the waist with a thin white belt. She was barefoot, as she always was at home, even on cold days, her hair pulled into an elegant yet practical chignon. She looked as if she had stepped off the deck of her private yacht.

"Seth!" she said.

He was immediately interested in her, specifically her necklace, which looked like a thick bicycle chain, but white as porcelain.

"Simone," I said.

"Simone? Do you want me to call you Pearl?" She was smiling, though, and so I smiled too.

"Thank you for agreeing to this," I said.

"Thank you for asking me." She reached out for Seth, saying, "I'm your nana! Nana Simone!"

He went to her willingly and I followed them into the house.

The foyer was dark and hushed as always, a low vase of pink roses on the end table like always. No matter how little money she had, my mother never went without flowers. When funds were low, she put them on her credit card; the day I turned nine, she'd handed me the kitchen shears and told me to find something in the neighborhood: no stingy buds, she instructed, but nothing that had completely bloomed yet either. After that, she successfully volleyed for more money from my father, who funded much of our life even though he wasn't in it.

Now that the house was paid for, my mother needed only a modest income. For as long as I could remember, she made her living by selling antiques and paintings to a network of wealthy people across Los Angeles. Some, she said, were old contacts from her modeling days, another had been a colleague of my father's, years ago. One client begot another and another.

I asked her how sales were going.

"Fantastic—just sold this armoire for . . . well, to mention the figure aloud would be almost uncouth. And I've also started doing voiceover work." Seth was squirming out of her arms. "Shall I put him down to crawl?" she asked.

"He walks," I said.

"No!" she cried in disbelief, and we both watched as Seth wandered across the foyer and into the living room. He was headed straight for the remotes on the coffee table.

"Sethy," I warned, and he pretended not to hear me.

"It's fine. Don't worry, I won't let him watch TV. Today we're going to walk all over the neighborhood. And we'll go to the park!"

Seth grinned at her.

"He's smart," she said.

"He's just starting to talk, so listen out for any first words."

My mother nodded, and then turned to me. "You're looking a little haggard."

"He still doesn't sleep through the night."

"It's not just that."

"Mom, please."

"You're so thin."

"Thank you."

I thought that would shut her up, but she said, "You're on the un-happiness diet."

I inhaled, exhaled. Marco had coached me on this. I was not to take the bait. We needed my mother to watch Seth, at least until Marco found lucrative work and we could hire someone. I could stomach a few months of this. I had to.

I passed my mother the diaper bag and explained its contents. "And maybe he'll nap in the stroller," I said.

"I bought a crib."

"You did? Last night?"

"Months ago." She wouldn't look at me, and I felt the guilt like a knife to the gut. But my mother was a master at this. If I let her she would use my guilt against me, at a later, unforeseen date. I couldn't let that happen.

I kissed Seth goodbye. He cried a little, which felt like a victory. See, Mom, I wanted to say, I'm doing fine, I've bonded with my child. He loves me.

FOR A WHILE, it seemed Marco's plan would work. I could go to the Actress's unencumbered, and Marco could look for work, and my mother could take care of Seth. Seth liked his grandmother. The first day, I retrieved him twenty minutes early, without warning. I found them in the backyard, gardening. Seth was wearing a tiny apron, and he was digging into her garden bed with a tiny shovel, his brow furrowed in concentration. My mother had changed into khakis and a men's shirt.

"You look like Walt Whitman," I said, rounding the pool, its bottom now lined with black gravel.

"Don't you like his little getup? We bought it today at a consignment shop. I also got him a sweet little bonnet. But he threw it off."

I laughed. "Sounds about right. Did he say anything?"

"Didn't even babble."

I cocked my head at this piece of news. "Really?"

Seth walked toward me and I was about to pick him up when my mother swooped in to wipe him down with a washcloth. There it was, the whole Cleansing Station behind her on the table: one bucket filled with clean water, one with soapy water, and one for rinsing. Beside all that, a neat pile of washcloths made of Turkish linen, which she special-ordered.

I didn't say anything as she cleaned his hands and arms, wiping even under the sleeves of his onesie. My son didn't wrest away from her; she had trained him so quickly.

Apart from that, things seemed all right. The Actress was thrilled that "Simone the Gorgeous" had stepped in to help; Marco knew someone who was hiring PAs on a film, and the pay was decent. His grief too had tapered, or at least the sobbing had. He told me he'd left a picture of Seth at his mom's gravesite. I was surprised: not that he'd done it, but that he'd told me about it. Here, again, I thought, was his newfound tenderness. Seth had begun to sleep for four hours straight, and I was having more than fleeting, anxious dreams. I couldn't remember details, only that they had happened. I recalled flares of color, stories I couldn't catch.

It was going so well I didn't think anything of my mother asking about Marco. What kind of work was he looking for, and how much had he hoped to sell the Chatsworth place for, and what was his schedule nowadays, and did he go out a lot at night. Her questions, collected like this, sound prying, but spaced apart over a week or two as they were made her seem interested and invested. She was not writing Marco off anymore; after all, her grandson looked just like this man, and perhaps was developing his same disposition: exuberant until moody. On the second or third day, she mentioned having us all over for brunch. I waited for her to bring it up again, but she didn't.

"Marco's doing a lot better," I said one day. "About his mom's death, I mean. And we're getting along great."

She waited a moment before she replied, "Have you ever noticed, Lady, how defensive you are about Marco?"

Inhale, exhale.

"Is it really worth it?" she said.

I dared to ask, "Worth what?"

She smiled at me, almost kindly. "Pretending he's a good man. You don't honestly believe this is going to work out, do you?"

THE NEXT NIGHT, I knew something was wrong as soon as I approached the apartment door. Seth knew it too, because he put his tongue to the doorknob, as if to taste the rot.

"Stop that," I said.

He kept licking until I moved him out of the way to unlock the door. It was too quiet: desolate, depleted. But of what?

"Marco?" I called out, though it was obvious he wasn't there.

I saw the empty card table. Marco's computer was gone, as were his piles of papers, and the little graveyards of tangerine peels he never cleaned up. The record player was also missing, and the box of records.

With an intake of air, I turned on the TV for Seth and walked to the closet. *Stay calm,* I told myself.

I opened it. Marco's clothes had been removed, as well as his duffel bag. He had left one pair of shoes, the brown Oxfords, but they pinched his toes and he had vowed to never wear them again. At least he could keep one promise. He had never promised me anything, ever. I shouldn't have been surprised by his exit.

Barney the dinosaur, purple and benign, sang from the TV. Seth stood an inch from the screen. He was pretending not to notice the change, the loss, but he must have. His father had left us.

The note was on the fridge:

Lady,

I have to get my head right. Someday youll be happy I did this.
Your better off without me. And sweat Seth is too. I'm sorry. –M.

I turned over the paper. He'd written it on the back of the library story time flyer. He couldn't even be bothered to find a clean sheet of paper. With hands trembling, I turned on the stove and waited for the burst of blue flame.

I burned the note. I didn't want my mother to see it, or a well-meaning friend, or Seth, when he became literate.

Sweat Seth?

I turned and vomited into the sink until there was nothing left to expel, my stomach acidic and clawing. Now I understood Marco's impulse to purge his grief, to heave it out of the body all at once.

I TOLD MY mother the next day. I had to get it over with. If I hid the truth, and she discovered it, she'd never stop dwelling on my duplicity. "Stop gilding the dog shit," she'd said in our previous argument. So I wouldn't. Seth's father was a piece of shit, and, yes, okay, she'd been right. Now she should have nothing else to say. Happy now, Mom?

I pulled her into the kitchen while Seth was playing in the living room with a toy phone she'd bought him. Quickly, her place was filling with toys, primary-colored and beeping.

"Marco's left," I said.

"That fast?"

"I don't know where he went. He moved out while I was at work."

"He's a coward," she said.

"He's just insensitive." Was that somehow better? And why was I defending him again?

"He's a coward," she repeated. "But I'm not."

Here is the memory I keep coming back to, the moment I can't let go of. It occurred only a few weeks after Seth spoke his first word, but it feels like decades separates these two memories. I'd gone from hopeful to hopeless in such a short span of time; at first I was ever vigilant for more language from Seth, and then it all went to hell, and it was like I'd plugged my ears with cotton. I wanted to keep the world out.

I'm standing against the kitchen counter, the yellow tiles that always remind me of pats of butter. The fridge hums and a dying fly flings himself desultorily against the window. My mother is wiping down the sink with a sponge. It's pink. I can hear Seth's new phone in the other room, the piercing ring, and then the mechanical rendition of "Itsy-Bitsy Spider." Then the piercing ring once more.

I don't hear Seth, he is silent, as he's been since my mom started watching him. Even after Marco's abandonment, my ears remain open: at least for my son. In my head I list all the words he might say next: *Mama, go, no, yes, truck, baby, milk, me, you.*

"Who said you were a coward?" I ask.

"Remember the armoire I mentioned selling? Well, I called Marco and told him about it."

"You did? When? Why?"

"Seth and I called him, a few days ago. To say hello. And to invite him over."

"You what? He came over here?"

She nodded. "For only a few minutes. Yesterday."

It takes me two steps to cross the kitchen. I grab the sponge from her hand.

"What the fuck did you do?" I ask.

"Lower your voice, Lady."

"Answer me."

"I asked him how much he needed."

"Needed for what?"

"I was curious about what he'd hoped to get from the sale of his mother's house." She sighs and takes back the sponge, runs it under the water for a moment. "I wasn't surprised that he didn't have an answer. It's like he can't imagine a sum beyond what you can fit into a piggy bank."

She tosses the sponge into the sink. In my memory, I hear it land on the porcelain with a whisper. Then she turns off the water and faces me. "I gave him nine thousand dollars."

"You what? Nine *thousand* dollars? Why?" I can't breathe, I realize, and I stop to bend over. When I stand, I say, "He took that money and ran, Mom. He split."

"From his visit, I got the sense that he resents you. For denigrating his grief. Oh, honey, I'm sure that's not what you intended. He's a child, that's clear. But you shouldn't have asked so much of him. He lost his mother. You don't just get over that. Maybe not ever."

"You're changing the subject, Mom. Tell me about what you did. He took your money?"

"That's right."

"He's gone, Mom. Should we press charges?" Even as I said it I knew it sounded absurd.

"Lady, you don't understand me. I wouldn't give him the money *unless* he left."

"Excuse me?"

"I'd have given it to you, but you would have taken it and kept him on. He's a leech. A magpie. Something larval and speck-brained. I had to lure him away." She craned her neck over my shoulder. "Seth shouldn't be around that."

"Do you understand what you've done? Do you even have any idea?"

"I realize it sounds bad."

"It doesn't *sound* bad, Mom—it *is* bad. It's evil. You lured a father away from his son—his baby son! I can't even look at you!" I am yelling now, and my mom's eyes grow wide, her face hardening into a mask of stony panic as it always does when I get upset. She can't stand to see me angry even though she's the cause. It's as if she returns to plunder my rage, again and again, with the hope that one day it will run out for good.

"Look, he came to pick up the check and left. He only hugged Seth for a second before handing him back to me. Good riddance."

My mother moves around me to open a cabinet. She's pulling out the tea, and any minute now she'll be filling the kettle. As if I could sit down and drink it with her.

"How could you do this to me?" I ask.

"The question you should ask, Lady, is how you could do this to yourself. Why you would have a child with a man who could be bought for nine thousand dollars. Children do not need their fathers."

She slams the cabinet shut. We both flinch.

I was so eager to get away from my mother, I got in my car and headed to the Actress's house as if it were any other day.

It wasn't that I assumed Marco and I would be together forever. I simply didn't think in those terms. Lately, things had been good between us; if they weren't, I figured we'd work on it, as if our relationship were a sewer project. Love was arduous. Wasn't it?

But now. Our demise had been designed by someone else and the powerlessness made me tremble. I was a dupe. I could accept that I was worth less than nine thousand dollars. But Seth? That hurt the most. The trauma was abrupt and blunt, and it belonged not just to me, but to my son as well. I had to get him away from my mother before she caused us any more harm.

That day, I began to make changes.

I looked for a new job right away, one with benefits. I was hired to be the office manager of a doctor's practice, located on an unnoticeable stretch of Pico sandwiched between a Yeshiva and an auto-body shop. A week later I found a one-bedroom nearby, cheaper than the studio; the landlord, who was a new father and took pity on me and Seth, offered us a deal.

Seth's day care was run by a Guatemalan woman named Alma who barely spoke English. She was warm and kind and hugged me the first time we met. She ran the operation illegally from her home; her prices were criminally low, and included a hot lunch for Seth.

The Actress cried when I gave my notice and as a parting gift wrote me a check for five hundred dollars. It smelled of baby powder and I cashed it immediately. Then I drove to my mother's house and retrieved Seth. Without a word I packed up his stuff, and before leaving, said we would not be back.

"This is what you deserve," I explained. "You went too far this time. He was Seth's father, for God's sake!"

For once, Simone looked scared. "I was only protecting you, Lady," she said. "Please. You can't do this!"

"I can and I am."

That was the last time I saw my mother.

AS THE MONTHS and years wore on, and Seth still didn't talk, not in English or Spanish (as I'd hoped, after three years with Alma), I kept returning to what my mother had said: *He came to pick up the check and left. He only hugged Seth for a second.*

My son had been present for this bribe, this dirty deal. He wasn't even a year old and he was forced to witness it. To receive one stingy hug. I don't care how young he was, he understood. He knew before I did that his father was leaving, that he had left. My mother forced Seth's complicity, which is its own kind of trauma.

This is what I knew: Seth had started to talk before I brought him to my mother. Before she paid his father to leave. And then he stopped.

ESTHER

18.

I COULDN'T KICK THAT TREE BRANCH OUT OF MY MIND. SETH had brushed his teeth with it. What kind of tree had it come from? Did it leave splinters?

After Lady repaired to her bedroom, I went into the Cottage and kept drinking. I wanted to black out, crash into the dark like my mom did whenever she didn't have plans the next day. And I wanted to get drunk enough that I stopped thinking about Seth, so that I stopped thinking, period.

I drank until I barfed all over myself. I had to do a top-secret load of laundry just so that the Cottage didn't smell like a corpse in a heat wave. Katherine Mary probably wouldn't have bothered for another day or two, not until the vomit had turned to suede, but there's only so much I can withstand. I'm not pretentious enough to call debauch-ery art.

By the time I was back with Devin on Monday morning, it was like the universe's operating system had rebooted itself. I felt grateful and shaken. Sober felt good. I would have to ask my mom if she liked this as much as I did: the feeling of being wrung out, battered but whole. I'd drink hard again if it meant another chance to recover.

Devin and I swam for hours that day, the water so comforting it was practically amniotic. After lunch we made smoothies, adding experimental ingredients to the blender every few pulses: a sprig of lavender, a dash of salt, and even a single macaroni elbow. It was something my mom and I used to do; it's how we discovered the versatility of barbecue sauce.

Seth walked into the living room while Devin and I were building a fort with bedsheets and couch cushions. I hadn't seen him since Lady's story. The way he appeared and disappeared felt like a magic act. That boy could cut me in half if he wanted to, I thought, and then shuddered. It was the kind of thing my mom would say, like, if an ad came on for a Vegas magician, the fake-sexy kind who wears rings and eyeliner and a leather vest. My mom is powerless to her bad taste. It's a miracle my father wasn't a creep who lives on a houseboat with his pet ferret.

Seth just stood in the doorway, phone in hand. He had on a plain white T-shirt, his chest hair a shadow beneath its fabric, and the same old ratty jeans. White athletic socks gone gray. I was pink from the sun, my hair crunchy from the pool, and I was wearing the most heinous khaki shorts. I smelled like sweat and chlorine.

Devin was too busy adjusting the couch cushions to notice his big brother, and when I opened my mouth to say something, Seth put an index finger to his lips to stop me.

I mouthed the word *hello* with wide eyes, and he nodded. I realized he never mouthed words, or not to me at least. Did he even know how to? Katherine Mary perked up inside of me. Like a little kid, my mom was curious, unembarrassed. Had his disability left those muscles to atrophy? Could he kiss with his tongue? I thought of Seth taking that girl into the Cottage, pushing aside the dirty plates on his spare pillow. And then I thought of the tree branch again, its knuckled edge. Did he put toothpaste on it?

"Seff!" Devin cried out suddenly. "Come play with us!"

"We're building a fort," I explained.

Devin had his fists under his chin like a Christmas caroler singing "Silent Night."

"We gonna do a show," he explained.

"With flashlights," I said. "We'll shine them onto the ceiling of the fort."

"Her daddy taught her!" Devin said, and I smiled.

Seth typed something on his phone and handed it to me.

Wheres my mom?

"She went writing this morning but then she had a hair appointment."

I waited to see if Seth would type more, but he didn't.

"She was kind of distracted after today's session." I didn't want to say too much. Lady might be afraid that Seth would tell Karl, or worse: Kit.

But he seemed to be waiting for me to continue. Was he? I hated that I couldn't tell, and I wondered if it was easy for Lady, and for Karl and Devin, to read him.

"She was on her phone a lot. I bet she was emailing her editor or something?"

Before Lady had left for the hair salon I'd asked how she thought the writing had gone. Without looking up from her phone she'd said, "Great! Also, terrible!"

Part of me, the Esther Shapiro part, wanted to ask her more about it, offer her advice or commiserate, swap stories about artistic process like I used to do with Everett as we sharpened his pencils. (I can't believe I actually helped him shave his pencils down to sharp points.) But Katherine Mary wouldn't give two fucks about Lady's book, or at least not about her failure to write it, she'd just want to read the thing when it was done, and so I kept my lips zipped.

"Play with us, Seff!" Devin yelled.

Seth looked at me and signed, *Can I?*

I nodded, pleased that I'd understood.

I assumed he would make the fort's architecture more complicated (as Everett would) or its foundation more secure (per the Steve Shapiro Method), but Seth grabbed one of the flashlights and crawled inside.

"It's done?" Devin asked. "We ready?"

"I guess," I said, and let him crawl inside.

A real-estate agent would have called the fort cozy, charming. I wasn't sure we'd all fit. Seth kept nodding and gesturing for me to join them, and every moment I didn't raised Devin's begging another decibel. "Please, S. Please!" he yelled until I gave in.

It took us a few minutes to get settled, Devin elbowing me in the stomach and then in the face. It was like Tetris, with pain. When we finally found a configuration that worked, it actually felt comfortable. Hibernation has its perks. Seth and I lay on our backs with our legs bent, and Devin sprawled across us, his head on my shoulder and his legs across his brother's chest. My left knee grazed Seth's right thigh, but when I tried to move it, Devin squeaked in protest. I let it be.

Our makeshift roof was a slate-gray, king-sized sheet. It darkened our den, clouded it over, and the light-blue couch cushions surrounding us worked against the overcast. There were lines in the sheet, creases from where it had been folded, and if Devin and I had been alone, I might have told him to pretend they were hieroglyphics, or contrails from an airplane. With Seth there, I didn't say anything. Devin babbled between us. He was already playing with the other flashlight, throwing its beam across the ceiling, making a *pew-pew-pew* noise.

"We aren't shooting," I said. "This is a show for our eyes."

I heard Seth make a noise that was almost a laugh, and then the click of the other flashlight. The beam was smaller than Devin's. It was a nickel of light. Seth dragged it slowly across the sheet, back and forth, back and forth.

"No!" Devin yelled and snatched the flashlight from his brother's hand.

Seth made a flurry of signs. He spelled Devin's name, and then signed the word *no,* but I couldn't follow the rest.

Devin was now tapping the flashlights against each other like they were drumsticks and this was an arena rock show.

"Devin," I warned.

Seth tapped Devin on the shin until the boy looked at him. Seth carefully held up one fist and wrapped his other hand around it.

Paper beats rock, I thought.

I held up my hands and did the same.

Devin stopped. "Seff! She also knows *Stop Drop Dead*?" He let go of the flashlights and the larger one knocked me in the chin before rolling away.

Seth propped himself on his elbows to see if I was okay. I waved him off.

"You did it wrong," Devin told me, sitting up. "The other hand does the punch." He lifted his left hand and made a fist.

"You can tell your left from your right?" I asked. "Wow."

"It's Mommy's signs. The special signs! She and Seff do them. I have my voice, so I don't need to."

"But you know them."

Seth sat up too and his head hit the sheet. Devin cringed for a moment and I said, "It doesn't hurt because it's soft."

Seth typed something on his phone and passed it to me.

Dont tell her I taught you a special sign

"You didn't teach me. Devin did."

Devin was crawling over me to get out. "I want to play LEGOs," he said.

Seth didn't move and neither did I. Devin was already galloping out of the room. I felt short of breath as I passed Seth his phone. He typed something and passed it to me.

She doesnt want Dev doing the signs

"Why not?"

He gave me a look that suggested the answer was too complicated to type, but then he was writing something anyway.

Its our thing I guess. Me and my mom.

"If that's true, how does Devin know . . . *Stop Drop Dead*?" I handed Seth his phone and did the sign once more.

With the phone in his hand, Seth drew something in the air between us. The letter *K*.

I told myself to let it go—You aren't a detective, Esther—but I knew Katherine Mary wouldn't.

"K. Karl?" I said. "Lady taught the special signs to Karl?"

He shook his head. He pointed to himself.

"You taught them to Karl. And Karl taught them to Devin."

So Lady had no idea. Or she had found out.

"Oh shit," I whispered.

Seth's smile turned wicked. I remembered how Lady had described his few months in the Cottage. He'd had *troubles*.

The doorbell rang.

>>>

IT WAS THE BREATHALYZER. As I signed for the package, Devin asked the UPS dude a dozen questions, including "Can I drive your truck tomorrow?" Seth had gone kaput in that magical way of his, taking whatever we'd shared in the fort along with him. By the time I carried the box into the kitchen, I was shocked to see he had materialized there, eating a banana at the counter as if he'd never been anywhere else. He lifted his chin at the box.

"It's nothing. . . ."

He waited. Or, no: he was just standing there. This wasn't a calculated move—the guy couldn't speak even if he wanted to. I bet everyone assumed he wanted to. I wouldn't.

Devin was tugging on my shirt. "Open it! Open it!"

"It's private," I said.

"Is it an ax?" Devin asked. "Is it a gun? It's a gun!"

Seth laughed: that deep sound.

"It's not an ax or a gun. I'm doing a project. An art project."

Seth looked surprised but I didn't explain further.

"Don't tell," I said.

THAT NIGHT I locked the Cottage door and drank a beer as fast as I could, its ocean foam tickling my nose. Unpacked, the Breathalyzer looked smaller than I expected, like a digital camera with a little tube sticking out of one end. It had cost me almost $250—more like half a grand if I counted the interest my credit card would charge me by the time I paid it off. And if it didn't work . . . I couldn't even fathom how that would feel.

I had another beer and then I blew into the Breathalyzer's tube. I tried to record the sound with my phone, but it didn't pick up anything except for the beep of the digital readout. Light-headed, I leaned in to read the screen: .06.

I recorded the number in my notebook. I'd also been keeping a catalog of alcohol consumed, as if I owned a liquor store and this was my inventory. Beneath the date, I scribbled *Amstel Light, 2 bottles*. So far, I had zero clue what I would do with these figures, or how they related to the Polaroids, or to my extended performance: the bad hair, the ugly clothes, the blunt questions I asked Lady, like I didn't care what she thought of me. The way I'd stayed in the fort with Seth after Devin had left.

I just had to keep going with the project. I remembered something Everett had told me: "The process will elucidate the intention, Es." We'd been driving to San Francisco, crossing the new bridge, the old one beside us, getting dismantled rail by rail, the water so pretty I could barely stand it. We were talking about his show. Again. Always about his show.

Alone in the Cottage, I brought my left fist into the air and enclosed it in my right palm. *Stop Drop Dead*. Seth had taught Karl the special signs, and Karl had taught at least one of them to Devin. And now I knew it too.

I shoved the Breathalyzer under the bed. Seth had fucked that girl here, that didn't seem to be in question. She'd let him touch her and he'd done it.

I pictured him teaching the girl one special sign, and another, and one more after that, as Lady slept soundly in the house above them.

19.

FRIDAY NIGHT.

I fixed myself a vodka gimlet and boiled a hot dog to eat sans bun, as my mother preferred it. She ate like a toddler but was still thin and straight as a pole.

It was time to get serious, to not only elucidate my intentions but to decide if I had any to begin with. I was going to see my mom the next day and I already felt anxious. I'd been avoiding her because I was too busy trying to become her. Her sitcom would be on hiatus soon, meaning she'd be broke and then antsy and then clingy. She'd let go of her cleaning lady the same day I moved into the Cottage and

I didn't want to imagine her kitchen sink. From a housekeeping perspective, Katherine Mary's utopian urge was dystopian.

The vodka was already warm in my wrists by the time I conquered the hot dog. It was so salty I had to drink more, almost ravenously. Was that why my mom ate so many hot dogs?

By the end of the drink, my alcohol level read .10. I wrote it down in my notebook, whose pages were beginning to resemble an Ellis Island ledger. I wanted to drown it in the Manse pool. The record wasn't a story, it wasn't a person, it told me nada. Katherine Mary would never have cataloged anything.

I poured myself a third gimlet and went to dig up my sketchpad and charcoals. I needed to make something. The Polaroids didn't feel like enough. They were languishing in the dark of my dresser, Miss Havisham–style, until I could figure out what they meant.

With my charcoal pencils, I drew the tube of the Breathalyzer. First, up close, just its plastic ridges, ribbed like a screw, and then again as if from far away, as if the tube had been detached from the machine and was lying discarded in an empty lot.

By now I was very drunk, and so my hand was looser. The drawings were sloppy but intriguing; they didn't have much in common with my cautious little landscapes of yore. One prof had called my work "as well behaved as a lap dog" and I sadly agreed. These drawings were nastier. I drew another: this time, the tube's opening, with its cobweb of spittle.

I drew, and drank, and felt exhilarated. Like Happy Kathy. And like myself too. My mother was bringing the grit but I had the skill.

This wasn't the first time I'd split apart. My parents broke up when I turned five and the world was sliced in two. My mom didn't ask for full custody, probably because the skateboarder was still in the picture and they liked the privacy. After he left her but before she foreclosed on the house, she said she just needed time to let loose. That's privacy too.

My dad gladly agreed to the every-other-week agreement; Steve Shapiro would never keep a daughter from her mother. He was still in love with my mom and he probably hoped I'd bring back a little of her each time I returned to him. As if I could.

Until I went to college, I migrated from one parent to the other every Monday, schlepping to school whatever I couldn't stand to be away from: a specific pair of shoes, a certain sweater, my change purse of jewelry, my makeup. Otherwise, I had two of everything: two bedrooms, two favorite stuffed animals, two computers. There were also two Esthers: the one my dad took care of, and the one who took care of my mom.

As I finished my fourth drawing and my third drink, I saw how my life had trained me perfectly for this project.

20.

THE SECRET TO VISITING MY MOM IS TO GET THERE EARLY, BE-fore Kathday festivities are under way. I was down the hill by nine the next morning and I didn't bother calling. It wasn't like she'd bake muffins or fan out a bevy of women's magazines next to a box of aloe-softened tissues like my dad did. Besides, Katherine Mary gets a kick out of surprises.

I knew she was awake because I smelled coffee and the TV was on. A stick of incense burned on the coffee table, its gray ash dusting a soy-sauce packet.

"Mommy?" I called. As soon as I said the word, I became Esther again, the ruse of Katherine Mary becoming just that: a ruse.

My mom walked into the living room with a dish towel in her hand. Her T-shirt pictured a marshmallow with wide eyes. It read: STOP INTERRUPTING ME WHILE I'M TRYING TO ANNOY YOU! I'd won it in a school raffle when I was eleven.

"Baby!" she said. "You're here!"

She let go of the dish towel, just let it drop to the floor as if some butler (i.e., me) would ferry over shortly to pick it up, and came to give me a hug, bending down so that her head fit under my chin.

"Mommy," I said. "That shirt?"

She let go. "It makes me think of you."

"I never wore it. Not once."

"But you look like the marshmallow." Now she stepped back to take me in. "Looking cute as always, Waterbug." She grinned. "God, did I actually dress like that when I was your age?"

"Sadly, you haven't improved."

She shrugged and headed back into the kitchen. "Want a Siggy?"

"You're having a hot dog now? It's not even nine thirty."

My mom favored the Costco hot dogs, the Kirkland Signature brand. Siggys.

"I swear I haven't had one for a week," she said. "I need the protein."

I followed her into the kitchen, expecting a mini apocalypse: a pile of greasy pizza boxes and empty wine bottles; maybe a handle or two of vodka, also empty; pasta sauce splattered on a wall, probably the ceiling too. Human hair clogging the sink. A zillion dishes crusted over with multiple meals, the sponge a living thing. The overhead would be burned out and she'd have brought in a reading light. Or hadn't and tonight it would be as dark as pupils in there.

But everything looked decent. There was a full trash bag on the linoleum, waiting for someone to take it out, and some mugs scattered on the counter. That was it.

"I thought you said you fired the cleaning lady."

"I did. I felt like a shit for doing it, I mean, taking that paycheck from her, but the show stops filming next week and then I'll be poor again." She dropped a hot dog into the boiling water on the stove. "Want some coffee?"

"Frank's here, isn't he?" I said.

"Want some coffee?"

"Don't pretend you didn't hear me."

"He's asleep."

"When did you guys get back together?"

"I'm not sure we're together." She wiggled her nose. "Or, no, maybe it's that we never broke up. I can't keep track of our . . . what's the word? Our status? This is why I'm not on Facebook."

"They actually have a box for that: 'It's complicated.' "

But she wasn't listening. "So what's shaking in the Hills? Anything new with the dumb kid?"

"Mommy."

"What? I'm talking about the two-year-old."

"Sure you are. It's really disrespectful."

My mom speared her hot dog with a fork and lifted it, steaming, out of the pot. "You were in Berkeley for too long."

"Devin's great. He knows his left from his right, isn't that amazing?"

"And the one who doesn't talk?"

"Seth's eighteen, Mom. I don't watch him."

"Doesn't the mother worry about you two being in the same house together?"

"I have the Cottage, I told you."

"Ah, yes," she said in a nasally British accent. "The Cottage."

"Stop."

"How is the duchess, by the way?"

"Her name is Lady," I said. "She's fine."

"Except that she's worried you're going to take her son's virginity. The mute's, I mean."

"Mom!"

"What? You're playing at being me, aren't you?" She winked and took a bite of her Siggy. With her mouth full, she said: "Relax, Miss Square. I'm just teasing you."

I told her I had to use the bathroom.

My mom had moved into this place after I'd left for school. She had no need for a two-bedroom anymore, and without my dad helping her with the rent she couldn't afford one. This new apartment was a guest-house above a garage. The place shook each time her landlord, Brian Fairbanks, opened the garage door below to back out his BMW, and then again when the door shuddered closed. The bedroom was separated by flimsy drywall, the kind artists build themselves in an afternoon. You had to walk through the bedroom to get to the bathroom, which was so small there was no room for a plunger or toilet brush.

The bedroom was dark, but I could make out the big lump of Frank in the bed. He lay on his side and the comforter didn't cover his meaty white shoulder, whiskered with hair. I may have thrown up in my mouth a little as I rounded the mattress.

Frank. He and my mom couldn't seem to stay away from each other, even though a year before she'd scratched his face so hard she drew blood and he vowed never to talk to her again. They'd met on set; Frank was one of the transportation guys, or he had been—he was on disability now, who knew why or how. His mother, who lived in Boca Raton, had woven the basket hanging like a picture above the bed. My mom had attached it with yellow thumbtacks and string. The basket was the only thing Frank had ever given her. Okay, so he cleaned her house. But he helped her be a pig in it first. He had a snout face.

On the milk crate next to the bed, I noticed an ashtray with two cigarette butts in it. I leaned down, and sniffed. They smelled fresh.

I hurried to the bathroom. Toilet paper floated like jellyfish in the bowl, the water the color of apple juice. Too bad it didn't smell like that.

"Mommy," I said when I emerged from the bedroom.

She was sitting on the couch, with two mugs in her hands. "That was fast," she said.

"Brian Fairbanks said if he catches you smoking in here again, that's it."

"I wasn't smoking," she said.

"Do you want to get evicted?"

"I told you, I wasn't smoking. Maybe Frank had one before bed, but I'm sure he blew it out the window."

"There are two butts in that ashtray. Brian Fairbanks won't care if it was you or someone else."

My mother handed me one of the mugs. "Thank you for reading my lease, Esther, but I can handle it."

She made room for me next to her on the couch. We left one side empty, and huddled next to each other, my legs atop hers. We called it "Siamese-ing." For all my mom's flaws, she had a warmth. I wanted that. I needed to emulate that too.

"I brought you one of my new dresses," I said. "It already has a hole in it."

A few minutes later she had her sewing box out and her glasses on, and she was hunched over the coffee table, needle and dress in hand.

"It's so cheap," I said. "It hasn't even been washed yet."

"I know—it's got that hamper stink." She looked at me over her glasses. "What are you up to, Esther Shapiro?"

"What do you mean?"

"I mean with your getup . . . and your face. When was the last time I saw you without lip gloss on? Are you seriously doing this—pretending . . . ?"

"I told you, it's for fun."

"It's too intense to be for fun. It's bizarre."

"Didn't you have fun when you were my age? Tell me about the family you nannied for."

"What do you want to know?"

"Whatever you remember."

"They lived in Nichols Canyon. Their house was built on stilts. I thought it would fall down at any moment, I bet it did eventually. The little girl was four or five, I think."

"You don't know?"

"Is there a difference between four and five?"

"Loads. Did you drink then?"

My mother pierced the fabric with the needle and sighed. "Esther."

"What?"

"You're fixated," she said. "Did I ask you over here to hold back my hair while I threw up? Or to clean my apartment? No. I'm enjoying my Saturday morning."

"Sorry," I said. "I just came to get a book."

I'd brought my art books back to L.A. with me, and my mom had asked if I could leave them with her, that she'd take care of them. She said she liked looking at them, and that she wanted something of mine to keep her company.

The Kit Daniels monograph was on the bottom of her bookshelf.

"She's Devin's aunt," I said.

"Who?" My mom pointed to the woman on the cover, who was lying across her bed in underwear and a camisole, talking on the phone. The drapes were closed, but sunlight seeped in at the edges.

"The photographer," I said.

I was thinking how Kit would love my mom's apartment, especially if what Lady had said about her having a thing for clutter was true. On top of the TV, a stapler sat next to a juice glass. A Priority Mail sticker was stuck to the door, right next to the peephole.

My mom began looking through the book. I leaned forward, hoping to get a glimpse of Lady, but the pages flipped by too quickly.

She said, "Remember, in high school when you painted freeway exit signs, but you changed the words?"

I remembered. Instead of Robertson or Fairfax, the signs read stuff like Heaven or Hell.

"Ugh, so cheesy," I said.

Everett and I had enjoyed a good, postcoital laugh about that one. If I'd told him about the drawings before we had sex, he wouldn't have fucked me.

"They weren't cheesy! They were fantastic! I loved your art. Steve has all that, doesn't he?"

I nodded; they were in one of the many boxes marked with my name in his garage.

"Bastard," she said.

"Good morning to you too," Frank said from the bedroom doorway. He'd put on a rumpled Hawaiian shirt and a pair of jeans, praise Jesus. I tried not to look at his toenails.

"Hi, Frank," I said.

"Hey there. Nice haircut." He came over and patted first my head and then my mom's, like he was playing a game of Duck-Duck-Goose. "I was thinking of going to get some cake."

I'd forgotten about Frank's sweet tooth.

"What kind of cake do you like?" he asked.

I shrugged. "All kinds, I guess."

"How about urinal cakes? They serve those in the bathroom at Dodger Stadium."

My mother held her head back and laughed.

"Don't get any for me," I said. "I can't stay long."

"How about chocolate?"

"You have to stay!" my mom cried. "Don't you want to sleep over?"

"I told Lady I'd watch Devin tonight," I lied.

"Stop it," my mom said.

"Stop what?"

"If you want to be me, even me at twenty-two or whatever, you can't lie. I never lie."

"Is this the Cindy Sherman thing?" Frank said, nodding at me. He was putting on a newsboy cap. He would slip into his sneakers, not bothering with socks, and be on his way.

"Is this Kim Daniels involved?" my mom asked, flipping to the front of the book.

"Kit," I said.

"She is then."

"No! There's nothing to be involved in."

"You've always been an artist," my mom said.

"Thank you," I said.

Frank opened the closet door and my mother screamed.

"What?" I asked.

There was a white bunny with red eyes, twitching its nose like it was about to sneeze. It ran under the coffee table.

"What the fuck?" I yelled.

"Peter Rabbit!" my mom called out.

Frank was peering into the closet. "This cage needs to be cleaned, Kathy."

"That's not a cage, it's a pen," my mother said.

"That's not a pen, it's a closet!" I said.

"There's a pen inside the closet," she explained.

"What's going on?"

"I didn't want Peter Rabbit to poop all over the place," my mom said. "It's my understanding that I can actually train him to poop in a bin, like a cat goes in a litter box? But I haven't yet." She had the bunny in her arms now, and she was stroking it ears to butt.

"Mommy, you can't have pets here."

"It's only temporary. Cheryl gave him to me." That was one of the actresses on the sitcom. "Did you know Cheryl's an amateur bunny breeder, out on her ranch in Malibu?"

"Brian Fairbanks said no animals under any circumstances. Do you know how high rents have gone up since you moved in here?"

"This *pen* reeks, Kathy," Frank said.

"I couldn't say no to Cheryl. She's desperate in this way that's hard to describe." She lifted Peter Rabbit. "Wanna hold him?"

I shook my head. "Mom. Your credit is horrible. Brian Fairbanks will kick you out because of this, and then you'll be in real trouble. You know this animal isn't worth that."

"Please don't monetize my bunny," she said, but she didn't protest when I pulled out the pen and began cleaning it. I said nothing when she switched from coffee to beer, perhaps willing Happy Kathday to commence despite what I was doing.

"Do you have to take him?" she asked when she kissed the bunny goodbye. His pen was already in my trunk.

"You know I do," I said, and ushered Peter Rabbit into the travel carrier my mother had, after some urging, pulled out from the bedroom.

Ten minutes later, I was driving back up the hill with a bunny in the passenger seat.

WHEN I GOT back to Lady's, Milkshake came trotting up to me, sniffing. I wondered if he could smell the Esther on me.

"S?" Lady called out. "We're in here."

She sat at the dining room table with a half-played Scrabble board in front of her. She was in a pair of men's pajamas, rearranging tiles on her easel.

"I've got all vowels," she said distractedly. And then, looking up, "Where'd you go?"

"Just a few errands."

Seth walked into the room with his hand up in a peace sign, bending his fingers. So he'd seen Peter Rabbit.

"What happened?" Lady asked. Her voice had gone cold and I wondered if my mom had been right; maybe Lady did worry there was something between me and her son.

"I have a rabbit with me," I said, sitting. I explained the situation. "I know I should have asked you first, but it seemed necessary that I remove the animal from the apartment."

"Is it your habit of rescuing your mother from eviction?"

"Actually, yes."

"Well, bring it in here," she said. "As long as he doesn't make a big mess, I don't mind. What about you, Sethy? Do you mind?"

Seth shook his head. He was gesturing with his chin toward the front of the house. He wanted to get the bunny. I nodded.

"So . . . Scrabble," I said, when he was gone.

"I make him play with me." Her voice sounded distant again. Had she found out that I'd learned *Stop Drop Dead*? Or that I'd been in that fort alone with Seth? He could have tattled on me, which meant she knew I'd been snooping in her closet.

"Are you upset with me?" I asked. "I don't have to keep the rabbit. I really don't."

She flicked her fingers at the pen and score pad. "Not at all. I'm just losing."

Seth returned with the bunny. Now he really was a magician, I thought. Like Lady, he was wearing pajamas. Not a set like hers, just some plaid pants and a T-shirt with a hole at the collarbone. I thought of my mom; she'd have mended that hole by now, pajamas or not.

"His name is Peter," I said. "Peter Rabbit."

Lady looked up from the board where she was placing some tiles. "Peter Rabbit! Better make sure he doesn't sneak into Mr. McGregor's garden. Do you have a little outfit for him to wear? The real Peter Rabbit wears a waistcoat and loafers, doesn't he?"

I said I didn't know, and Seth handed me Peter.

Lady was looking at her son. "Karl probably won't like that we've let her keep a rabbit here. He'll be afraid Peter might bite Devin. Or that Devin might squeeze Peter to death. Oh my God, can you imagine?"

I covered Peter's ears. "Devin would never do that," I said. Neither looked at me and I realized my mistake. As we used to say in elementary school: "This is an A-B conversation, C your way out."

Seth was flashing his hands like he was performing "Twinkle, Twinkle Little Star." A special sign! I felt my body go hot.

Lady shook her head. "Don't be so dramatic."

He switched to ASL, his hands moving so quickly that I recognized nothing. He was flinging the words at her.

"You're going too fast," Lady said. "I can't understand you."

He picked up the pen and began writing something on the notepad.

"Not there," Lady said. "We need the room to keep score."

He shoved the notepad at her.

I couldn't help but lean over too, to see what he'd written.

Learn it already.

I expected Seth to rush out of the room, angry, but he didn't move. I held my breath and held tighter to Peter Rabbit. I admired how Lady maintained normalcy. She was so used to her son not talking that this argument wasn't any different from one with spoken words.

Finally, Lady said, "I've tried to learn ASL, you know that. I just can't get my brain to work like that." Her voice was gentle, apologetic. "Your turn. I got nine points. What a joke."

Seth took back the notebook and added the score.

"I had this boyfriend," I said. I don't know why I spoke, except that I felt invisible. Or I wanted to give something away, confess random shit like my mom sometimes did.

Lady turned to me. "A boyfriend?"

Seth was looking at me too.

"Everett. In high school he went to two big-box stores with the vacuum sealer his mom used for her raw food snacks. He unwrapped the Scrabble boxes, stole some letters, and then sealed the boxes back up again."

"Didn't anyone see him?"

"Somehow, no."

"Let me guess," Lady said. "He stole the tiles to spell out 'Will you go to prom with me?'" She raised an eyebrow. "And you said yes and it was magic."

"What? No, this was before my time—before our time, I guess." *Our time*—the words caught in my throat. I tried to play it off by snuggling with the bunny, who smelled like tortilla chips; my mother had probably eaten with him on her lap. I wished I could give him a bath, or vacuum him. "The tiles didn't spell anything," I said, "or maybe they did by accident. Everett took whatever ones he grabbed first. It was a chance thing."

"He sounds like a real asshole," Lady said.

"He's an artist."

"That's what I said."

21.

NIGHT FELL. A RAGER WAS HAPPENING SOMEWHERE IN THE Hills and as the music reverberated across the canyon a girl squealed and a guy said, probably not to her, "I get it, man." Someone jumped into a pool. An owl hooted, then stopped, and later, when a coyote sent out its shrieking bark, another coyote answered. I put Peter Rabbit in his pen and covered it with a blanket. I didn't want him to be afraid.

I'd planned to draw the Breathalyzer again, and then sketch a few of my outfits. I liked the seam my mother had fixed for me because the thread was a slightly different shade of blue and you couldn't see it unless you were looking. I'd look.

But first I sat with Kit's book. I remembered the photographs, but now that I knew Kit and Lady, they felt different. The woman leaning over her washing machine: the one with the hairy upper lip and her hamper full of stuffed animals, for instance. She looked like a hunter now, not the hunted. Especially compared to the woman on the next page, who was half-naked and very pretty as she put on her lipstick in a full-length mirror. There was a stain on her underwear; I'd never noticed it before. It was right at the crotch, a tiny splatter of what I assumed was menstrual blood. The calendar on the wall behind her said DECEMBER and I wondered if she was getting ready to go to a Christmas party. It made me want to cry, she was so real. Or she seemed real.

I was making myself wait until the ice in my margarita melted before I flipped to *Woman No. 17*. I drank and checked my glass, drank and checked.

Finally, I flipped to the page. There it was: the Sea World towels and the bathtub, and Lady sitting on its edge with her stockings pinching her waist, her face like a deer's: beautiful and useless.

But there was something different. I leaned forward. My index finger traced the objects in the shot, including Lady's body: her legs and belly button, her arms. I stopped at her chest. There it was. In this version, Lady's nipple wasn't sticking out of her bra cup. She looked tasteful and sexy. Confident. Another hunter.

Who had changed it? Which was the original?

I was downing the rest of my drink when someone knocked on the door. I pushed the book under the bed and went to open it.

"Lady?" I said. I was a little drunk but it was my day off, she couldn't get mad.

I opened the door but no one was there. The pool looked like a sheet of obsidian.

I was about to close the door until I saw the Scrabble tiles on my welcome mat. Two of them. I picked them up—one said I, the other, H. Five points, total.

I thought of Seth in the fort drawing the letter *K* with his finger, how it had seemed to float in the air between us until it sparkled out like a firework.

I and H.

Hi.

LADY

22.

ALLOWED S TO KEEP THE BUNNY EVEN THOUGH I FOUND THE circumstances under which she had procured it a little troubling. To remove it from her mother's house—like a social worker removes a child in danger. Considering my own mom-hatred, perhaps I could relate. Either way, I said yes because Seth had always loved rabbits and I hoped this one in particular might calm him down. Appease him. He'd been touchy; I couldn't say a thing about Karl without getting reprimanded and he never wanted to hang out. He'd even signed *stop honking* right in front of S. We came up with *stop honking* after seeing some geese at a state fair. It meant quit talking and saying nothing, you silly bird.

If Seth saw my Twitter, he'd be signing that all the time.

Cheek implants: for when you want to look wealthy and insecure.

My dog's eye boogers smell like the saltiest egg rolls.

My dog looks like a bunny with dreadlocks. #RastaMaltese

The bunny had been S's roommate for a week now, but Seth was testier than ever. I had to ask him three times to take out the trash (that had once been Karl's purview), and every time he left the house he either slammed the door or snuck out without a goodbye.

I'd taken to hiding in my room with my phone. I liked to check it in my closet, lights off, and one morning, after S and Devin had left for a walk to the nearest construction site, that's where I headed. I told myself I would get writing in a minute or two.

With a reassuring click, the phone came to life, its extraterrestrial glow brightening the dark closet and no doubt my sallow face. I tapped on the cheery white bird icon and let it expand across the screen.

As always I searched Seth's timeline first, but there was nothing new. I'd already seen his most recent tweet, posted days before:

My greatest fear is that someday i will forget the titans

I wanted to tweet something about how my teenage son was a clever little jerk when I saw it. Someone was following me.

She called herself @CarolGardens55: Brooklyn dweller with an interest in roses. She tweeted photos of sunsets and musings on the tea she was drinking. Who knows how she found me but I suppose I wanted her to because I hadn't designated my account private. I didn't follow her back, but I didn't block her either.

Then I tweeted, If my knuckle hair is blond does it count? and set down the phone slowly, as if it were a bomb.

When I checked six minutes later, Carol had retweeted it. I panicked at the thought of her thirty-nine followers reading what I'd written, but then I imagined Carol pruning flowers before going into the bathroom to shave her fingers one by one and it made me feel a little less alone.

The next morning I had two more followers. They were bots, their desire for me so unequivocal there was no way they weren't machines. I considered blocking them but I couldn't bear it because their pouty-lipped avatars had to be real women . . . somewhere.

My fourth follower was @MichaelRLafferty of Sioux City, South Dakota: environmental lawyer and popcorn eater, unapologetic bed hogger. "All tweets are my own," he'd added, as if anyone would ever assume his firm had forced him to broadcast such inanities as I hate traffic!

A day after Michael began following me, I ventured a tweet from the front lines of my bathroom: Why does it feel so good to tweeze my nipples? Within a minute, he had liked it. The South Dakotan lawyer, that leering bed hogger: what a lecher. He had imagined my nipples and their wiry black hairs and then he had liked them with that little red heart icon. He'd turned me into a bot. I dropped my phone in disgust, sending it bouncing across the floor

Before I put on my clothes I blocked him from seeing any more of my tweets and, once dressed, I went downstairs to ask S if I could cradle her bunny for a few minutes. She must have thought writing had me down, and I guess, in a way, that was true.

I hadn't worked on my book in days, not since Kit had stolen my bubbly. I tried not to think about how much I was paying S to look after Devin while I did nothing but tweet and wander the aisles of Bristol Farms, aghast at their high prices while nevertheless filling my cart.

The pages I'd written about Seth's school no longer interested me, nor did the paragraph I'd begun about Marco: *I was devastated when he left us, but I couldn't let Seth see my pain. I had to be strong for the both of us.*

It was fiction. Seth had, in fact, witnessed my weaknesses for months on end: how I didn't eat anything but cans of condensed milk and cereal; the time we went to see a private eye about tracking Marco down (without success); the time I blared Iggy Pop and refused to turn it off even after Seth's bedtime. Or how, years later, the day before Seth entered the seventh grade, I told him his grandmother had paid his father to abandon us. I tried to soften the blow by inflating the amount to $15,000.

My dear Seth had reared back, as if I'd tried to hit him.

"What an ass, right?" I said. "But watch."

I lifted my index finger as if to say, Excuse me, and then folded it back into my fist. Then I let the fist fall and shook my hand limply.

"It doesn't matter. He's dead to us, so is my mom. Shake it off."

I brought up my index finger again and this time little seventh-grader-Seth mirrored me, tucking his finger back to his fist exactly as I did. And then he was shaking his hand, but just barely, as if he couldn't be bothered. *Shake it off.*

23.

I WAS SUPPOSED TO MEET KARL FOR OUR WEEKLY DINNER—A now inaccurate term since we hadn't seen each other since Paul Feldman's. I was pretty sure I still had a salt hangover from our previous meal, and so when he emailed suggesting we meet there again, I didn't reply.

Where had Karl's imagination gone? When we were first together, he would take me and Seth on all-day adventures: sushi for lunch, then a trip to a liquor store that sold a startling assortment of sodas, followed by Chinese foot massages, and ending with a quick stop at some place he'd read about that sold marshmallows and only marshmallows by young people who were extremely devoted to the artisanal marshmallow cause. On one of our early dinner dates, just the two of us, he picked me up from work with a bag of cheeseburgers balancing on the console. We ate those burgers as he drove east on Pico, the shredded lettuce gathering on our laps, Karl waxing poetic about the Mexican party store we were headed to. He'd been right: the piñatas *were* magnificent.

When he finally called, I told him Paul Feldman's was a boring choice.

"Where would you rather go?"

I had expected my comment to offend him, and that he'd want to prove me wrong by suggesting a restaurant that graced half a dozen "best of" lists. We'd eat tiny birds, three ways, topped with tobacco-infused espuma. We'd done that once.

"Let's just do coffee. How's Monday?"

"I get it," he said. I didn't know what it was he got. "How about that place on Fairfax by Melrose?" he asked. "The one with the Dickensian baristas."

"Dickensian?"

"They wear suspenders and jaunty little caps."

I laughed.

"Maybe this living apart thing is working," he said.

"It is?"

"My jokes. They're fresher."

THE HEAVY GLASS door of the coffee bar was as fogged as a bathroom mirror. The heat had returned, but muggier this time, and the whole city had the dank funk of a teenage boy's room; Karl and I called it the "hot back" smell. I wanted to be cold so that I could drink my coffee hot; I didn't want to see Karl sweat.

He was standing by the sugar-and-cream station, sipping an espresso, wearing shorts and a golf shirt.

"Wow," I said. "Casual."

He had been leaning forward, maybe to give me a kiss on the cheek, but now he backed away. "It's a holiday. It's Labor Day."

"It is? Thank goodness Tiny Tim's isn't closed." I cocked my head at the blond guy behind the counter. "Is that a waistcoat he's wearing?"

"Did no one invite you to a barbecue? Dammit, S probably worked today, didn't she?"

"Who do you think has Devin right now? Let's pray she doesn't call her union!"

I felt the Karl twinkle: it was the physical manifestation of his pride. He practically levitated whenever I said something clever.

"God, it's hot," I said. If I was banal, he'd settle down. "Why did you order already? You couldn't wait for me?"

"I wanted some coffee before I ordered an iced herbal tisane and I didn't think you'd stay long enough for me to drink both."

"I'm not that rude, am I?"

"You didn't email me back. You're always upstairs when I pick up and drop off Dev. I texted you yesterday and it took you five hours to answer."

"Let's order first, okay?"

He shrugged and downed the rest of his drink. He didn't set down the cup carefully and I liked the brusqueness.

"Did you get invited to any barbecues?" I asked.

"A few. I'm going to Catie's later."

Catie was the hostess of the housewarming party. "I suppose she's already gone ahead and given us custody of events."

That joke got no Karl twinkle. It was probably too sad.

I insisted I pay for my own drink even though we both knew it was his money I was spending. All the tables inside were filled by youngsters and their computers, plus one older woman doing her bills. Why was there always someone doing their bills in places like this? That'd make a good tweet, I thought.

I took a deep breath as I opened the door to the outside seating area.

"At least it's a wet heat," Karl said.

"Ha. Tell Seth to tweet that."

After we were sitting, Karl said, "We never discussed S."

"I should have done the background check, I know. I'm sorry. But she went to the CPR class last Wednesday night. So that's settled. And she's really great, don't you think?"

"Even with the drinking and the rabbit?"

"The *drinking*?"

"Seth said the recycling bin is damning."

"When did he turn so Puritan? And why's he checking the trash? S and I had two bottles of sparkling wine when Devin was with you. But that was a few weekends ago."

"There's been vodka."

"That's mine," I lied. My bottle was still in the freezer, halfway full. "And even if it wasn't, I don't think it's a problem. She's of age. What's it to Seth, anyway?"

"I tried Googling Esther Fowler, couldn't find anyone that sounds like it's her."

"Boring name."

"The background check revealed nothing? No red flags?"

"Just that felony charge. Come on, you're being crazy. You know she's great." I prayed he'd drop the whole background-check thing altogether.

"Everything okay then?" he asked. "I miss you."

"I was hoping you'd wear the linen shirt today. The gray one."

He smiled. "Oh yeah?"

"I miss it."

"You can miss my shirt." He winked. "That's good enough for me." He took a sip of his iced tea. His *tisane*. "Look, Lady, Kit wants me to call your bluff and ask if you'd like me to contact a divorce lawyer."

"Call my bluff? Of course your sister is convinced I'm playing games."

"It certainly seems like you are. You ask me to move out after a single argument about Seth and his old girlfriend—"

"So you admit it—Tanya was his girlfriend!"

"I never said she wasn't."

"You said it was never serious!"

"It wasn't. They're teenagers, Lady. They weren't going to get married." He tried to reach for my hand but I pulled it away. "You're right," he said. "I should have told you they were spending time together, about their relationship. But Seth liked her, and we both knew you'd flip out."

" 'Flip out'?" I repeated. "I can just see you two, colluding. You probably reveled in it."

"Give me a break, he's my stepson!" Karl realized he'd raised his voice, and took a moment. I watched him collect himself: sip his drink, straighten his shirt.

"Do you really want to get into this here?" he asked, his voice calmer now. "Look, we had this fight, we're having it yet again. I moved out because . . . who knows why, because you really seemed to need space to think. And I can understand your anger about how I've sided with Seth on certain issues."

I tried to interject but he held up a hand and kept talking. "But you've been avoiding not only me but the whole issue of this separation, giving me the runaround, and now you're flirting like this is a first date."

"If we were on a first date, I doubt you'd suggest this place."

"I met you for the first time at a coffee shop."

"That wasn't a date."

"Is that what you want? A first date? You want me to woo you back. Fight for you. Have you ever considered that *you* might have to fight for *me*?"

"Kitty's words sure do sound awkward coming out of your mouth," I said. "Anyway, it wasn't our argument that did it."

"Now I know you're bluffing. That's what set you off, you can't hide from me, Lady. Look, Tanya is a nice girl, and her mom isn't as cracked as you think she is, she just wants to keep her daughter safe. Anyway, I don't know why this keeps coming up. I told you, Tanya and Seth broke up before Devin could even walk."

"I didn't even know they were together!" I hadn't meant to raise my voice. A woman who was as flawless as a model, but who was probably a jewelry-designer, gave her boyfriend a look like: *Check out the harridan with the latte.* I brought my voice to a whisper: "I can't believe you let them continue their little relationship even after their ridiculous sleepover, even after her mother chewed me out. And why? What for? Tanya's like Temple Grandin without the animals! What would Seth want with her?"

"Jesus, Lady. Will you listen to yourself? Tanya is different, sure. But so is Seth. They liked each other. They're teenagers, disabilities aside."

"Disabilities?"

He sighed. "Yes, disabilities. Your son has one."

"But why would you encourage them—and without telling me? While I was busy raising your son, breastfeeding him and changing his diaper, you were trying to get mine laid? What are you, a pimp?"

Karl looked like he was about to walk out on me. I needed to keep him there so that I could say every mean thing in my brain, every brutal, toxic thought. Now I knew what people meant by "let them have it." I opened my mouth, but Karl raised his palm.

"Devin's your son too."

"What?"

"You said 'raising your son' as if Devin isn't yours."

"I didn't mean it like that."

"Lady, do you want to curse me out just so you feel better? I can take one for the team. Go ahead, shoot that mouth off."

He waited. I thought about telling him that I knew he had learned at least one of the special signs. That I'd seen Seth flash him *Shake it off* when they thought I wasn't around. Like that wasn't one of our most important special signs. I had asked Karl to leave those be. They weren't made for him. I couldn't blame Seth for sharing them, he was only a kid, but Karl had no excuse for going behind my back and he knew it. But I would keep that reveal for another day when I had no more ammunition. For now, I said nothing.

"I thought Tanya was more normal than the other one," he said finally. "What's her name? The ancient Egypt fan?"

"Marisol."

"That's right, Marisol. Frankly, I'm glad she and Seth broke up soon after I came around."

"They were just buddies."

Karl looked like a condolences card made human. "They were more than that. Way more. How did you not see it?" He opened the lid of his cup and scooped out an ice cube. I watched him chew. He swallowed. "I think you need to sit down with Seth."

"I don't want to have a discussion with him about the birds and the bees!" I hadn't brought up the topic when he was younger because I wasn't sure how to. I was scared and, honestly, I didn't think he'd be able to get a date if he couldn't even speak. Maybe I hoped as much. And now—no. It would be too awkward. "I can't," I said.

"That's good because it's a little too late for that anyway."

"My God, please, that's gross. Stop it."

"It's not that. He's been asking me a lot of stuff, about Mark."

Mark was Marco. Neither Karl nor Seth knew his real name.

"Seth wants to find him," Karl said.

"Mark's dead to us."

"Maybe to you. But not to Seth. I can help, if you want."

"No."

"You can't stop it."

"Please don't get involved," I said. "This time, it's not about some girl."

"You're right, it isn't. Just, please, talk to him about it. Help him find his dad."

"He asked you to meet me to discuss this, didn't he?"

"I offered before he could ask."

He walked me to my car. He checked to see if I had any more money in the meter, and satisfied that there was still time, he opened his arms for a hug. That's when I remembered the parking ticket in my purse.

"This was on your dresser," I said. "Do you want me to pay it?"

He dropped his arms and reached for it. "I'll handle it. Thanks." He turned it over, squinting. "Looks like Seth wrote on it." He held the ticket away from him to read the words and I came to his side. This close, Karl smelled of soap and the musky smack of his sweat, and

I wished I'd accepted the hug while I still had the chance; I knew he wouldn't offer another.

The ticket read: *Santa Monica at Rexford.* An inch below were the words: *ASK HER.*

I was used to Seth's scrawl. Before the iPhone and tablet, he'd scribble in a reporter's notebook he kept in his pocket. There were still notepads and pens in drawers all over the house and in the glove compartment of my car. Just in case. I used to love coming upon one of Seth's notes. I loved imagining what might have been said in response. Whatever was spoken aloud had long disappeared, but Seth's words remained.

"What were you two talking about?" Karl asked now. "Beverly Hills City Hall?"

"Yep. City Hall." The lie was like bile and it rose in my throat. I swallowed it down. "It's a long story, not even worth telling. Sorry he wrote on that!"

24.

I WAS A HARRIDAN TURNED GRIFFIN, FLYING WEST ON MELROSE in her Jetta. When the cop pulled me over, I was also a griffin who wasn't wearing her seat belt. I must have looked sufficiently upset for him to ask if I needed help.

"My son," I said, and then my voice gave out like a bum knee. He told me I needed to put on my seat belt and he watched me as I stretched it across my body.

"You take care now," he said, but only after the buckle clicked.

Everything—everyone!—I didn't know filled the car and sucked out all the air. I could barely breathe; I was squawking.

Where to begin? That Marisol and Seth had been more than friends, supposedly fucking, perhaps as early as the seventh grade? Or that Seth had been stalking the trash like J. Edgar Hoover, looking for evidence that S wasn't a good nanny. And that he might be correct, considering the vodka consumption. Or that Seth had been in my room, writing notes to someone. The ticket wasn't that old and Devin couldn't read, which only left S and Kit. Speaking of Kit: she wanted Karl to call an attorney already. Speaking of Karl: he would never apologize for knowing about Seth and Tanya, for helping them meet in secret. He probably wouldn't be contrite about learning the special signs either. Even as I sorted through all of these problems, I knew there was one that most worried me, whether it—he—warranted my concern or not.

Mark.

I didn't want Seth to find him. Marco's last name, Green, was so nondescript that when I altered his first to Mark I had adequately hidden his true identity. And maybe the name change was a twisted homage to my mother, who *was* a coward for keeping me from her ex. Unlike Marco, my father had wanted to see his child, if rarely. Every six months is more than not at all, and my mother had made even those visits impossible.

I wasn't proud of my lie, but my shame had never overcome my desire to protect my son. I suppose I was like my own mother in that way. I'd spent half my life trying to keep Seth safe from harm. Harm being synonymous with her and Marco, though I was certain the latter would never seek us out. All phone numbers and contact information remained unlisted, all social media settings either private or pseudonymous. I needed to keep us from their poison.

I was eager to change my last name to Daniels when Karl and I got married. I wouldn't have published without its shelter. After the *Real Simple* article came out, I waited for someone from my past to come forward, or for Seth to tell me that some woman named Simone had sent him a message on Facebook, but nothing happened. I was elated when Seth too asked to be a Daniels.

Not since my last visit to the detective's had I actively tried to find Marco. Thank God Seth was too young to remember Smith Tatzko, PI, with his wood-paneled office and the giant microfiche machine on the desk behind him. His office was above a liquor store in Santa Monica, and an anchor knocker was attached to his door. The only Marco Green he could find had last been living in Alaska, but that had been six months previous. There were no other leads.

"He owe child support?" Smith Tatzko had asked.

I said no. "Marco's not Seth's father."

It could have been a joke it was so hard to believe. Seth looked just like his dad and somewhere in Smith Tatzko's office there was a photo of Marco to prove it. I had lied because I wanted Seth to know, even at his young age, that he was better than this missing man.

I paid Smith Tatzko and said I wouldn't need his services anymore. When Seth and I got home, I folded his birth certificate into a tiny square and stuffed it into a high heel I never wore. I was glad I'd given him my last name. I told myself I was trying to protect him. And I was. But there was a part of me that was keeping Marco for myself. I'd mourn him alone. He was mine.

I still had those high heels. And if I didn't, Seth could easily go order a new certificate on his own. He was new to adulthood, though; he probably didn't know what his rights were.

When I got to Sunset, I pulled in front of the Coffee Bean, the one Karl had taken Tanya to the morning after she slept in the Cottage. Had she covered her ears at the sounds of the coffee grinder and the blenders?

With the engine still running, I grabbed my phone and did what I held myself back from doing more than once a year: I opened the web browser and typed Marco Green into the search window. It had been only seven months since my last search, but this was an emergency. My finger hovered over the screen and then tapped Go.

My previous attempts were never fruitful, yielding only images of sixty-year-old executives and a string of small-town newspaper articles about a promising high school football star. But this time, a new result popped onto the screen.

Someone named Marco Green had a Twitter profile.

"My Marco?" I asked no one.

The car was sweltering. When I pulled off my seat belt the buckle grazed my shoulder and I cried out; it was hot enough to brand me.

@MarcoGreen71 was from Los Angeles, California; 1971 was Marco's birth year.

His profile photo showed a man holding up a large lizard; he was too far away for me to see his face, but his arms looked tan and ropy like Marco's had been. His bio read *Slacker turned entrepreneur. Please send Doritos.*

It looked like @MarcoGreen71 tweeted every couple of days, and none were personal. He last linked to an article about solar power lowering home utility bills.

I closed the site. Then I opened the Twitter app.

I think my son is breaking up with me.

I waited. For what? A heart? For a retweet? I refreshed the page. Nothing new, but I didn't put the phone down. Marco didn't even know of this account; no one I knew did, and yet I felt the old desperation return after years of latency; it was brushing the dust off itself and standing tall. It would get Marco to respond. It would.

I couldn't control myself. I did what I'd promised myself I wouldn't do: I would stop tweeting to myself and reach out to another person.

I searched for @MarcoGreen71. I pressed the Follow button.

"Hello," I said aloud. "Here I am."

And then I typed.

Hey @marcogreen71 this is Lady calling. Can you pick up the phone?

25.

I T'S EASY TO DEMEAN THE PAIN OF A BREAKUP, PROBABLY BEcause it's so demeaning to be dumped, but I can't gloss over what I felt when Marco left me and Seth. I can't gild the dog shit.

What I remember most is the silence. Marco didn't talk much, but he had been loud: his boots clomped; he chewed with his mouth open; his orgasms were groans he didn't attempt to muffle even with a baby in the room. And that music. He played his records at top volume, the windowpanes shaking as they absorbed the reverb. Marco's presence had a sound and when he left it was like he took all that sound with him.

Seth was either mute from birth, the disability written into his genes, or something happened to turn him that way. The silence may have been there all along, but it didn't stand out until he and I were alone. And even then, I didn't think it was a real problem until everyone else did. I was too busy nursing my anger and grieving my loss. It took years for me to stop feeling acute pain.

When your kid doesn't talk at eighteen months, it's not a big deal. When he's two, you might get a few concerned glances, a couple "You're lucky! Once they start they won't stop!" But there still isn't much concern, especially if your child is learning two languages at once, as Seth was doing at home and at Alma's. At three, someone at the supermarket might remark, "Albert Einstein didn't talk for the longest time, and look how he turned out!" A week later, the pediatrician suggests a specialist. "Head Start might not be the best preschool for a kid like Seth," he says.

That visit to the pediatrician was where my memoir should have begun, for it was the first time an expert expressed concern, thus turning Seth into a specimen. At the appointment, Dr. Herrera asked me question after question. First they were related to language acquisition: *Does he have special names for objects, even if they're gibberish to outsiders, such as ga for car? When he's upset, does he call out for you? Did he ever have latch issues? Did he need to have tongue-tie surgery at birth? Does he attempt to make noises?*

"He cries, or he's silent," I answered. "He used to vocalize more, you know, gibberish, but I feel like he only does it rarely now. I can't remember the last time. Oh, but he can laugh. Sometimes I can tell he's frustrated and wants to verbalize, but he doesn't."

As I spoke, I realized how suspicious all this sounded. How could I not have brought him in earlier? Alma never seemed concerned about Seth's silence, but maybe that was because she watched too many kids to worry about any one of them in particular. The silence in our apartment unnerved me, yes, but I was also used to it. We didn't hang out with other mothers and children, and I hadn't realized how odd it was.

Or, no, I did. I must have.

"I guess I expect him to open his mouth someday and speak in complete sentences."

Dr. Herrera scribbled something into the file. "That has been known to happen." We both looked at Seth, who was sprawled across the floor of the examination room, looking at a book about dinosaurs like any three-year-old might.

"Is he sensitive to sounds in general?" he asked.

I remembered how he used to cover his ears when Marco put on a record. But that was wise; the music was too loud for his tiny eardrums.

"My son is normal except for this one thing," I said.

Dr. Herrera's questions changed. *Does Seth show affection? Does he make eye contact?*

"You know he does. He smiled at you when you said good morning."

"I'm sorry, you're right, you're right." He held his pen aloft for a moment, like it was a model ship he was admiring. When he looked back at me, he was so serious I felt scared. "There isn't anything else I should know?" he asked.

"Like what?"

"Provided there isn't a medical reason for Seth being nonverbal, and we will be sure to check his hearing, get his blood tested—"

"What will a blood test show?"

"There are certain, very rare, diseases. Aside from all that, children often stop speaking if—"

"He never started speaking," I said. *There, there,* I think.

"True. But a child's verbal development might be affected if he has experienced trauma."

"Trauma?"

"Witnessed a violent crime, or been the victim of—"

"There's been nothing like that, thank goodness."

He looked relieved to be interrupted; he was already turning toward the exam room's computer. "Let's first get his hearing checked then. I'll get Martha to give you some referrals."

"Great," I said. "Thanks so much."

This part of the story didn't bother me. Not really. It was what happened after we left the pediatrician's office that haunted me. Another memory that wouldn't let me go.

We've returned to our apartment. I take Seth into the bedroom, where his crib lies on its side because he's outgrown it. He likes to use it as a jungle gym. We share a bed anyway, and that's where we sit.

"The doctor is concerned about you," I say. "*¿Me entiendes?*" Do you understand?

Seth nods. That and shaking his head are the primary ways he communicates. He also points and claps his hands.

"You need to start talking," I say.

You need to. I shiver. That had been my mother's favorite refrain. You need to stand up straight. You need to smile when ordering at a restaurant. You need to pause between sentences. *You need to, you need to.*

I don't even get a nod from Seth. Nor a headshake. He's got his eyes on the sideways crib and I can tell he wants to climb it. He isn't listening.

"Seth." I put my hands on his shoulders but he squirms away. I grab his arm. Even as it's happening, I know I'm being too rough. My mother never grabbed me like this. Her words may have been burred but her touch was, if not gentle, then at least neutral.

"Sit," I say. "This is important. Talking is important."

I put a hand on his jaw. He doesn't move. He's been to the dentist. He's seen a ventriloquist and his dummy. Has he witnessed a man kiss a woman? Does he remember Marco kissing me?

I pull his jaw and he opens his mouth. When I push up on his chin, he closes his mouth.

We do that for a moment. Open, closed, open.

The summer I turned fifteen, my mother had us both chewing every bite of food twenty-five times before swallowing. To aid digestion, she said. My jaws went open and closed, open and closed. That was also the summer I fainted for the first time.

"Talk," I say.

I lean in to get a better look at his open mouth. His front teeth are spaced wide apart and he doesn't have all his molars yet. His mouth smells like buttered toast; it always does, even if he hasn't eaten toast for days.

"Is your tongue merely ornamental?" I ask.

I'm sure Seth doesn't know what I mean, but my question dissipates his tolerance and he moves away.

That's when I grab for his jaw and yell, "Talk!"

The sound of my own voice startles the both of us, and with the flat of my hand against his chin I push him backward. Seth falls off the bed and onto the floor. He's bitten his tongue and there is blood on his teeth.

His whimpering, like his laughter, has a sound. If he wasn't damaged before, I think, he is now. This is the first and last time I have ever laid a hand on my son. It would make a good opening chapter for my book if I were willing to tell anyone about it.

"Hey," I whisper. "I didn't mean to hurt you. I really didn't. I love you, Seth. I'm sorry. I love you."

I rub his back until he gets up from the floor and comes to me. I swipe the blood from his teeth and put my sullied finger in my own mouth. Seth gives me a hug. He cries big, slobbery, wet tears into my shoulder until my shirt is soaked.

Children forgive too easily.

"We can talk without words," I tell him. I'm thinking of sign language, but it will be a year before Seth and I start our ASL classes. His proficiency with the language will be as swift as mine is hobbled. For now, neither of us knows anything.

I hold out my cupped hands. "This means *sorry*," I say. "Try it."

He doesn't move.

"It means more than just I'm sorry," I explain. "It means, I'm sorry *and* I love you."

Sorry Love.

I wait with my hands out like a bowl, but that first time, Seth doesn't mimic me. He isn't the sorry one.

This is the first special sign, born out of twin desires to communicate with my child and to express my guilt for hurting him. Language has two functions: to harm and to repair harm.

We never used that sign again.

ESTHER

26.

MY DAD SAID HE'D PERISH IF I DIDN'T COME UP FOR THE long weekend, but I stayed in L.A. and, hey look, he was doing A-okay. He kept texting me photos of vegetables harvested from his garden, which he called the Farm only half-facetiously and to which I replied with various produce emoticons. I wanted to say I missed him and his ridiculous gardening gloves, printed with sunflowers and fraying at the wrists, and that I wished we could gab over Arnold Palmers and avocado toasts like we used to. But I couldn't. The Katherine Mary project was growing teeth and I had to keep away any and all distractions, Dad included. Dad especially.

Because who but Steve Shapiro would figure out that something wasn't quite right with me and try to set things straight? It wasn't only my make-under and the few pounds I'd gained from drinking every night. I had changed. I could feel it in my drawings. They were so ugly and free, like nothing I'd ever done before. As much as I wanted to tell him about this project I'd gotten inside of, how I was pretending to be what I wasn't: a drinker, a mischief maker, an artist, how maybe I was those things after all, I didn't, because, if I did, the drawings would stop. Steve Shapiro would summon Esther, and I didn't want her found.

It wasn't just the art either. It was Seth. The threat and promise of him, and the trouble he'd cause if I let him. Sometimes I carried the Scrabble tiles in my pocket, just to have them near. I'd bitten into the H, hoping to leave teeth marks. I pictured returning the scarred tile to the Scrabble box for Lady to puzzle over and Seth to get off to. This was straight-up Katherine Mary thinking. Almost twenty years ago, she had paid the neighbor girl five bucks an hour to babysit me while she bagged the skateboarder. It wasn't sleeping around that she liked, but sneaking around.

I'd had my mom's bunny for just over a week when I got another idea for my project. I'd go on Craigslist to request photos of people's mothers before they became mothers: the teenage pic, the honeymoon shot, the sad candid. PHOTOS WANTED FOR ART PROJECT. I had an idea that I'd paint them. Or I'd stage the same photo, myself in their mother's place, and paint that. I'd be the whole world's mommy.

It was Monday night and I was drunk-posting the ad, the bunny nose-twitching on my lap, when the phone rang.

I picked up on the first ring, my hello loud and peppy. I must have been imagining my dad on the other end.

"Esther? Is that you?"

"Mom," I said. "I'm on Craigslist."

"Missed Connections?"

As soon as she said it, I knew she was drunk—and not Happy Kathy either. There was a drag and belligerence to her speech.

"No," I said carefully. "I'm posting a request . . . it's hard to explain. It's for something I'm working on—"

"I can't believe you took my pet."

She said something else but the sounds of traffic made it impossible to hear. Someone walked by, laughing.

"Where are you?" I asked, leaning down to put the bunny in his pen. "Call a cab when you're done, okay? Or use the app I downloaded to your phone. The charges come to me so you don't have to worry."

"Shut the fuck up," she said. "I don't care about your fucking apps!"

I didn't answer.

"You know what?" she said.

"What?"

"You should get the word 'bitch' tattooed on you. A tramp stamp. Right above your little ass crack."

"Just promise me you'll use the app," I said, and hung up.

There was a time, back when I first started college, when I would have let her talk as long as she wanted. She only called me in a mood because she was lonely, and what could I do if that loneliness had a mean streak? *You abandoned me,* she'd say. *You don't love me. You're self-ish and stuck-up. You're Daddy's girl, aren't you?* She said awful things, and they were awful because they were true. At least my mom was being honest with me. In those moments, I had unfettered access to her thoughts. In a sick way, I felt close to her. The call would come like a bill, and I would pay it.

The first time I hung up on her, she called back, bloodlust in her voice, and I hung up again. That seemed to squash it for a while, but she always fell back into the routine. Everett called it Mom Rage. My dad didn't call it anything because he had no idea.

The phone rang again.

"I seriously can't do this right now, Mom."

"You know what should be a disability? Having children. Don't ever have kids, Esther, you hear me? All they do is hurt you. They'll ruin your life."

"Good night, Mom."

After I'd posted the Craigslist ad and made sure the project's email address worked, I sat with *Women* by Kit Daniels. After the phone calls I needed a night off.

I was still thinking about the two versions of *Woman No. 17.* Kit had altered one version. But why?

I slid my body off the mattress and pulled the book down with me so that we were lying side by side on the carpet. On my back, the ceiling seemed as low as ever, like it was sagging closer and closer to the floor, and I flipped onto my stomach. I inched closer to the book and nailed it open with my chin. I slipped my hands into the waist of my jeans.

The page was matte rather than glossy. The left side of the book was blank, the number 17 printed in black ink in the lower left-hand corner, and across from it Lady stared. From this angle she was so close up I couldn't see anything except the grainy texture of the black-and-white film. Kit never shot on digital, a fanny pack of film around her hips like a cowboy and his holster.

Because it was stuffy in the Cottage, I'd left the door open a crack—*ass crack*—and I wondered now if Peter Rabbit would sniff a waft of pussy with his hyperactive nose and run scared, only to get eaten by a coyote. Or if Lady, out for a little midnight stroll, would catch me masturbating to her image. *But the book's just a pillow,* I'd tell her. *It's Seth I'm into, and he doesn't look anything like you.*

I snorted a laugh and drool slipped from my mouth, torpedoing to the page. I imagined Seth walking in on me and I squirmed off of the book and shut it with one hand, not pausing with the other.

In my sophomore year art class, a girl named Audrey videotaped herself masturbating and we'd all sat in uncomfortable silence as we watched the film. It seemed, at almost twelve minutes, unfairly long. To Audrey, I mean—she needed a more efficient technique. During crit, the professor said that her students submitted these sorts of intimate films every other year or so.

"It's derivative," she said.

"But isn't all sex?" Audrey asked.

I pushed the edge of my palm into myself and tensed everything against it. Even my teeth were gritted. I bet my face looked like the pit of a peach. I let go.

I sat up, gasping, and Peter Rabbit scrambled into his pen. The security light just beyond the door brightened the yard outside.

"Hello?" I said.

I tried to calm my breathing but it shuddered in my chest as I stood up.

I went to the door. "Lady?"

Seth was sitting on the steps of the deck. I waved and he made an *H* and then an *I* with his hand. He signed slowly enough for me to understand.

"I hope you aren't spying on me." I tried to sound casual, like my mom in most situations, but my voice came out breathier than Marilyn Monroe's and I felt my ears go hot.

He shook his head and held up a cigarette. Unlit.

"You smoke?"

He nodded.

"Your mom lets you? Out here?"

He shook his head, put a finger to his lips.

I gestured to the Cottage and he stood. I could feel him following me toward the lighted room and I wondered what exactly I was leading him to.

Thank God masturbation doesn't smell as strong as sex does. Nothing looked amiss except that Kit's book was on the floor. No indentation of my body next to it.

He threw himself across the bed and lit his cigarette by the open window. He wasn't wearing socks or shoes and his feet, narrow and hairy, dangled off the edge of the mattress. I was shocked by his brazenness until I remembered he'd lived in the Cottage before me. My bed had probably been his for a time.

"Is Lady going to fire me for this?"

He eyed the door and I closed it. The mini-fridge hummed and for a second I wished we could just chatter idiotically to distract from the fact that it was only the two of us here. I thought I could hear the sound of Seth inhaling the smoke.

"Don't ash into my sheets," I said. He smiled when I pretended to toss an empty cereal bowl like a Frisbee, one of my mom's favorite gags. I passed him the bowl, the courage rising in me, Katherine Mary waking suddenly like a dog from a nap.

With one hand Seth pulled his iPhone out of his pocket and began thumb typing. I had to sit next to him to read and the mattress tipped and settled to accommodate both of our bodies. My ears burned once more.

So whats with Kits book?

"I wondered—"

He shook his head and handed me the phone. He took another drag of his cigarette and while I typed he blew the smoke out the side of his mouth like a ventriloquist.

It was a relief not to have to say my question out loud.

Did you ever look at your mom's pic in the bk?

I pulled the book onto my lap. I opened to *Woman No. 17* and he balanced his cigarette on the lip of the bowl, leaning over the photograph. This close I could smell his Whole Foods–type shampoo, tea tree oil or eucalyptus something-or-other, which barely covered the pencil-shaving musk of his scalp. The smoke from his cigarette curled toward the ceiling. Our thighs touched. I took the phone from him.

Look close. Maybe gross for u but the nipple.

He leaned away from the book, squinting, and then shrugged.

"It's different from the one upstairs," I said. "Here it's covered. In the one upstairs, it isn't."

So what

Don't you want to know why?

Nope

He looked up and I thought he was going to kiss me but he didn't. Instead he rubbed my cheek with his index finger. I flinched but held myself back from talking.

He tapped his own cheek and grabbed the phone from me.

Theres a red mark on your cheek

It must have been from the book. "Pillow mark," I said.

My phone beeped across the room and I jumped up from the bed.

"Yes!" I couldn't help but say it. I was excited. Someone had replied to my Craigslist post.

Seth had already closed the book and was watching me. Apparently, he'd forgotten about his cigarette and its acrid smoke was filling the room like dry ice at an elementary school science fair.

"I'm doing this thing," I explained. "I want photos."

I opened the email and waited for the JPG to load. When it did, the pink mole of a cock made me yelp. I dropped the phone.

Seth picked it up and laughed when he saw what was on the screen.

"It's not funny," I said. "I want photos of people's mothers, not some sick fuck's dick pic."

I showed him the Craigslist ad on my laptop. He read it, but he was still laughing and I didn't like it. It reminded me of my mom and her drunken cackle.

"How come you can laugh but you can't talk?"

That stopped him.

"Do girls think they can cure you? Is that how you get them to fuck you?"

It was like his face was a flame that flared once and then extinguished, emitting no light.

He picked up a pencil from the counter and wrote on the back of a receipt: Lets find out if that works

"If what works?"

Take off yr clothes

"I'm no healer."

He reached for my laptop, reading the screen closely before retrieving his phone from my bed. He was typing something, his eyes darting back to the laptop once or twice as he did so.

"What are you doing?"

After a moment, he showed me the screen. It was a tweet.

Scan a pic of your mom b4 she was a mom. Email it to my pal becomingyourmother@gmail.com. It's for art!

"Thanks," I said.

He grabbed the hem of my T-shirt.

"Seth."

He opened his mouth, as if to speak, and something inside of me twisted.

"Seth," I said again, and his phone disappeared under my shirt. He dragged its corner across my midriff and opened his mouth wider. I held my breath and the phone hit my belly button and kept tracing an invisible line. His mouth was still open, and I felt my own lips part, as if to mirror him. I could hear him breathing. What was he going to say?

Seth saw the hope in my eyes and crossed his own. He let his tongue flap out of his mouth like a dog's.

I pushed him and his phone away. He was messing with me and I was stupid enough to fall for it. "You ass," I said.

Someone outside was yelling something and we turned toward the door. It was Lady, calling for Seth, probably from an upstairs window.

"You better go," I said.

27.

THE NEXT MORNING MY MIND WAS GOING SETH SETH SETH like a strip club goes GIRLS GIRLS GIRLS and I needed something to distract me. I was cradling my phone in bed, picking the sleep muck from my tear ducts, when I decided to check the new email account, just in case. Art rescues the brain from stupidity.

There was a new email waiting. I didn't recognize the address, but my heart beat fast as I read the subject: "My mother, Molly Elizabeth Murtagh, 1985." There was nothing written in the body of the email, just a photo attachment, which loaded slowly: first, a white popcorn ceiling and one of those three-tiered baskets for onions and vegetables; then, a tangle of dark brown curls against a dark window. Big brown eyes that seemed to say either *I'm a bad girl* or *This is my Halloween party face.*

The complete photo showed a woman in a blue Spandex leotard and a belt made of wide magenta-colored elastic. She held a dumbbell in her hand like a microphone. Her breasts, buoyed by the Spandex, were as big as grapefruits, and perky. Behind her on the windowsill was a framed needlepoint that read BLESS THIS MESS. It would make a good title for the shot, I thought. Unless I wanted to call her *Mother No. 2.* Happy Kathy would be the first.

I'd need to get my hands on an identical needlepoint. A curly haired wig that didn't look clownish. The wardrobe was easy, but I'd have to place upside-down bowls on my chest if I really wanted to complete the look. I'd photograph myself. I'd been into photography in high school and taken one course at Cal. Not my best medium, but the project demanded it.

And would I then paint a self-portrait, based on my photo? My heart did a little skip, imagining painting a face, my own face, but also not. (*Is this the Cindy Sherman thing,* my mom had said. The answer was yes.) I wanted to brainstorm all the possibilities, just sprawl across the floor and start taking notes in my notebook, but I had to report to the Manse in fifteen minutes for Devin duty.

Out of bed, I dressed without looking, my mind spinning away like a flicked marble. Was this how my mom had ended up wearing the talking marshmallow T-shirt, her thoughts a zillion miles away? I was more like her than I thought.

The email had come from someone named Steve Perkins. He was either one of Seth's followers or a lonely Craigslist lurker who switched from Missed Connections to free couches to the random Community section where my post lay waiting. Whoever he was, his mother was cute and silly and I wanted to depict her so bad.

I laughed out of surprise. It was something my mom said. *I want French fries so bad. I want Hillary Clinton to come over for dinner so bad.*

"Mom," I said aloud. I hoped she'd gotten home safe.

I want Seth so bad, I thought, and then I shook my head like he was water in my ears. My dad taught me to do that when I was crying over Everett. It was such a ridiculous thing to do, and yet it was effective because it always made me smile.

Through the Manse's sliding glass doors I could see Lady and Devin eating breakfast at the kitchen island. She was checking something on her phone but the steam from her coffee must have fogged the screen because she cursed soundlessly and wiped it with the crumpled paper towel next to her. Devin, in rocket-ship pajamas, was balancing milk-bloated Cheerios on the handle of his spoon, babbling to whoever was listening: that is, no one. I thought about how it might look as a photograph, and I shook the image out of my mind. Enough of Esther, I thought. My mom was always chipper in the morning, no matter how little sleep she'd gotten the night before, and harnessing the cheer was the easiest way for me to lock in to Katherine Mary.

I slid the door open. "Good morning!" I sang out.

At the sound of my voice, Lady set down her phone. Devin was sitting in his booster, but Lady was standing, bouncing slightly on the balls of her bare feet like a speed walker at a red light.

"S for Sandbox!" Devin yelled. I gave him a kiss on the top of his head.

"That's right," I said. "Sandbox does start with the letter S. You're a genius!"

"Morning," Lady said. I could tell she was trying not to look at her phone.

"Don't mind me," I said. "You can be on the Internet if you want."

"I should try to be screen-free around minors," she said.

"Minors? What exactly are you looking at on that phone?"

I thought she'd laugh at this perfect Katherine Mary joke, but instead she moved silently to her designer coffee carafe, which looked like an oversize hourglass, and began cleaning it out.

Devin started singing: *"The slippery fish, the slippery fish . . ."*

"Did you know yesterday was Labor Day?" Lady asked. Pouring coffee, her voice all business, she was doing a pretty decent impression of a homicide detective. Paging Olivia Benson.

"I did. But it's cool. I didn't have plans." It was true; I didn't want to see my mom and I didn't want to have to drive up to my dad's for the long weekend.

"I guess I should pay you time and a half," she said. To Devin she said, "Stop playing with your food and eat, kid."

"No worries," I said, though I was already calculating the money I might have earned. Photo gear wasn't going to be cheap.

She sipped her coffee and frowned.

"What's wrong?" I asked.

I thought she'd go on a tirade about the coffee, she seemed to be revving up for a rant, something harmless about the roast of the beans or the curve of her mug handle, but when I looked back at her, she looked serious. Had she seen Seth coming out of the Cottage last night?

"You're a big drinker," she said.

Devin threw a Cheerio across the kitchen. Neither of us said anything.

"What can I say? Taking care of kids makes a girl thirsty."

"I'm not kidding, S. I found multiple vodka bottles in the trash outside."

"Are you firing me?"

Lady looked stunned. "Firing you? Jesus no, should I?"

"I don't drink on duty."

"It hadn't occurred to me that you would. Should that occur to me too? Oh my God."

But she wasn't talking to or about me. Devin had overturned his bowl and milk was spreading across the countertop. It looked striking: pure white across the white-gray marble, like a still from a high-production music video. Bless this mess, I thought.

"Goddammit, Devin!" Lady yelled, pulling three feet of paper towels from the roll.

Devin began to weep.

"No use crying over *spilk milk*," I said, which was a Katherine Mary phrase. "I'll get a washcloth."

Devin sniffled as we cleaned up. Then Lady lifted him from his seat and said she'd put on the TV for him. "I just can't deal with you right now," she said. Devin called out for me from the living room, but I thought it best to ignore his pleas.

When Lady returned to the kitchen, she said, "I met up with Karl yesterday."

"Is that what's bothering you?"

She put on the kettle and placed a crisp brown coffee filter into the mouth of the carafe. She pulled down a second mug for me and I watched as she scooped fresh coffee grounds into the filter.

"The thing about rich people," Lady said suddenly, "is that they pay you for your services. But they also pay you to make them feel better. To be their friend."

She was right. The actresses my mom dressed were always hiring assistants to do more than run errands; these rich women needed besties to join them at the spa, drive them to the abortion clinic, and diagnose their bacne. Lady wasn't as rich as they were, but still.

"I know you have your own life, S, a private life. I'm not a part of it."

"That doesn't mean we can't talk. What happened with Karl yesterday?"

"Are you feeling stressed out? Am I giving you too many hours?"

"I'm fine, Lady, really. I could use the money."

"Time and a half it is then."

The kettle began to screech but she didn't immediately turn off the burner. She kept her eyes on me and let the panicked whistle fill the room.

As she poured the water, she said, "Did Seth give you directions to Beverly Hills City Hall?"

"What?" I asked.

"Did he write them on a parking ticket?"

So she had found the ticket in her closet. "I don't know what you're talking about," I said. When she didn't answer, I asked, "Did you know he smokes?"

I had no idea why I'd said it, probably from some manic need to change the subject. It was one hell of a diversion.

Or not. Lady only nodded and handed me a cup of coffee.

"I do know that, actually," she said. "How do you?"

"I saw him outside," I said. And then, "Look, I'll cut down on the vodka. I have a thing for gimlets, it's true, especially in the summer. Now, tell me what's bugging you because clearly it's got nothing to do with me."

She grinned. "You're perceptive, S for Sandbox. It's true, I really don't give a shit about the drinking. I should though, right? I should."

"Just don't tell Karl and it'll be okay."

Her face told me he already knew.

"Fuck," I said. "Am I in trouble with him?"

"Never," she said. "He considers it his duty to defend everyone except me. As long as your name isn't Lady, he'll come to your rescue: you, Seth, Devin, Kit, little autistic girls, random men he's never met . . ."

"I'm not following," I said.

She sighed and looked at the clock. "I need to shower and get writing."

Devin called my name from the living room again.

"When it's me he's yelling for, I simultaneously swoon and cringe," she said.

"Must be a mother thing."

"Seth could never do that—call for me. If he wanted my help, he had to come and yank on my shirt."

"Is it hard, to have it be so different? I bet writing has brought up a lot of memories."

"I rarely left him alone because of that. But we lived in an apartment the size of this kitchen, so, you know. Anyway, thanks for noticing that I'm . . . frayed." She glanced at her phone. I could tell that she was itching to check it. The imagined Internet is so much better than the real one.

"Come here right now!" Devin yelled.

"Do you feel it?" she asked.

"Feel *what*?"

"What I described. Like you're swooning and cringing at the same time."

"No, but I'm not his mother."

She shoveled some sugar—big brown crystals, turbinado, probably—into her coffee and took a sip. "Yesterday Karl accused me of not loving Devin."

"I'm sure you just heard it that way."

"Maybe. He definitely said that I love Seth more."

"That's bullshit."

"It is, right? It's total bullshit! Fuck Karl!"

"That's the spirit. Fuck Karl! If it makes you feel better, my mom called me a bitch last night."

"It does, sort of, which probably makes *me* the bitch. My own mother would have just said I had sandbag hips."

"Ouch. Was she into comedy roasts or something?" Lady didn't reply, not even with a laugh. "You really don't know where she is?" I asked. "You never talk? Ever?"

She shook her head. "I thought once Spanx were invented, she might find a way to reach me. You know, just to help me with the problem of my *figure*. I bet she wears them all the time, like, even to take in her garbage cans."

We both laughed.

Devin was yelling from the living room, and this time it wasn't for me. *"Seff! Seff!"*

"You better get in there before he wakes his brother," Lady said.

But it was too late because there was Seth, walking into the kitchen without a shirt on. His grubby gray sweatpants were too short and his Achilles tendons looked as thin as rubber bands, but more vulnerable. His chest hair was thicker than I remembered, a bramble of black.

"Seth, you're half-naked!" Lady cried. She looked embarrassed for him.

Seth shrugged. He didn't have his phone with him.

"You have to wear a shirt around here, okay?"

He made a fist and wrapped the other hand around it slowly. It was that sign. *Stop Drop Dead.*

Lady glanced at me. I stared into my coffee.

"Don't you dare," she muttered, I assumed to Seth.

"Seff!" Devin called again.

"I've got to get writing," Lady said then, but too loudly.

"Do it!" I raised my coffee mug. She clinked it with her own and Seth rolled his eyes.

"What?" Lady said. "I'm paying this young woman to watch your brother and be my personal writing coach. Also, we're becoming close friends, despite the age gap. Hopefully she'll do some light housekeeping." She winked at me.

Seth rolled his eyes again and on her way out of the room, Lady got on her tiptoes and kissed his shoulder. Seth leaned away from her, but in the next minute he was petting her head, exasperated and indulgent like an owner putting up with a dog who keeps begging for food. Lady laughed. There was no cringing here. Karl was onto something: she did love Seth more.

"Please get Dev dressed," Lady called behind her. She wasn't clueless enough to keep me in the kitchen with her son.

"Will do," I yelled, and stood.

I didn't want to be alone with Seth. But I did. He picked up an apple from the fruit bowl and tossed it from hand to hand. I started for the living room but my desperation to be near him overtook my relief.

"I got an email," I said.

He raised an eyebrow.

"For my project. It's a photo of someone's mother, just like I wanted. So thanks."

He smiled and took a bite of the apple. With the fruit still in his teeth, he signed something I couldn't understand but it seemed meaningless, like *Good for you!*

"I'm probably going to set up the same scene as in the picture, photograph it. Maybe paint it. We'll see. I really love to paint."

Why was I telling him all of this?

We both waited. Back in the day, boys and girls had to dance with a balloon between them. Seth and I would have to rely on a two-year-old.

He balanced the half-eaten apple on the counter and came toward me.

"Seth . . ." I said, and he held up his hand, as if to sign something else. I had the urge to grab his hand and bite it.

"I have to start work," I said.

Apple foam glistened at the corners of his mouth. A mom probably would have reached forward and wiped it off, but I wasn't his mother.

He took my hand.

"Cut it out," I said. Which is something a dad might say.

He nodded once and didn't move. Neither did I.

28.

Dad: Did you know that pterodactyls aren't dinosaurs? I learned that today. Never too late to learn something new.

Me: U r about 65 million years late actually.

Dad: ROTFL!!!!

Me: U r not rolling on the floor laughing. Poidh!

Dad: What the heck does that mean?

Dad: Hello? Are you there?

Dad: Esther?

Me: Sorry working. Means pics or it didn't happen.

Dad: I know, Maria Googled it for me. How's nannying?

Dad: The eggplant finally came in! I ate one tonight. So delish. I'll attach a photo next time I'm out in the garden. P.O.I.D.H., am I right????

Dad: Did you get the photos?

Dad: I bought a new juicer. Want me to mail you the old one?

Dad: Esther?

Dad: I just left you a voicemail. Call me when you can.

Dad: It's seven at night, I know you aren't working. Call me before I have a panic attack.

Me: Here I am sorry. Holy eggplant Batman! The juicer is 2 heavy to
        mail. Prob best to give it away.
Dad: Everything okay, Waterbug?
Me: Yeah def.
Dad: You sure?
Dad: Esther?
Me: Daddy, I'm sleeping please stop texting.
Dad: Oops! I love you!!!
Dad: Esther?

29.

B Y THE END OF THE WEEK I HAD GATHERED ALMOST EVERY-
thing I needed to photograph *Bless This Mess (Mother No. 2)*: the
leotard, the wig, the hanging basket, even the needlepoint.

More like Bless These Paychecks from Lady. Bless This Internet.

First I would do an eight-and-a-half-by-eleven painting of the
original photograph. Once I was finished, I would delete the email
with the scanned photo and then I'd stage my own photo, based on
the painting alone. Eventually the two pieces, portrait and portrait,
would hang side by side, alike and not.

I decided I wasn't going to stuff my bra for the shot because
I wanted the viewer to see what was different between me and the
mother in the painting. What I lacked. As in, tits.

I was sober for the Internet shopping and the late-night drives to
Target and the 99 Cent Store, but I painted drunk off my ass like a
freshman in her first week of college—or, not like the college freshman I had been, but like a depiction of one. This project was turning
my whole life into a *Ceci n'est pas une pipe* situation.

I was cracking myself up, my breath hot and raw with tequila, my
belly turning doughy like my mom's from too many beers with dinner
(and lunch), and I kept working. I loved the looseness of my hand as I
painted and the shocking blue color I mixed for Molly Elizabeth's leotard, chosen by Happy Kathy at the absolute zenith of my buzz. It felt

so good and intense to paint people. I'd given it up after high school, but now the feelings came back: how fun it felt to start, to wonder, *Who are you going to be?*, as I put paintbrush to canvas. It was hard to get the proportions right, but soon enough I was lost in pigment.

I was storing the empty liquor bottles in my old gym bag so Lady wouldn't find them. My dad kept texting me, but more than once I had wet paint all over my fingers and couldn't respond and pretty soon I'd forget altogether. It was exactly what Everett deemed "the ephemeral urgency of an incoming text," aka his pseudoscientific explanation for not always getting back to me. Whatever my own reasons were for not answering, my dad was getting anxious and ornery. Meanwhile, Seth had made himself scarce since the kitchen incident. I told myself it was for the best.

Now it was late-late Thursday night and I was just a couple of drinks close to passing out in my own vomit—if I could just put in the effort. I had finished painting for the night; I was pretty far gone but not so much that I didn't worry about ruining the whole portrait with one stumble. ("Why walk when you can dance?" my mom liked to say. Dance meaning stumble.) Time to clean my brushes and pass out naked.

The next three days were all mine to sleep and drink and paint. Lady had taken me off my weekly evening duty because she was still feeling guilty about making me work Labor Day. She had texted Karl about the arrangement as soon as we made it. "See," she said slowly. "I'm not a bad person," and I realized she was dictating exactly what she was typing to her husband. She looked up at me then and pretended to snarl. "It's a win-win situation, really, because now he can't force me to have dinner with him."

I tossed my brushes into the sink and my phone chimed, which meant I had a new email in my art project account. The chime kept me from checking my phone constantly, a waste of time since I'd only received two other photos since *Bless This Mess* and they'd both been dick pics. Three were enough to start a special folder in my email. After receiving the third one I posted a new Craigslist ad with slightly different wording, fingers crossed that the pit-stained pervs would find another victim.

The new email was from iammuffinbuffin@gmail.com and this time there was no subject line. The body of the email read: I can't follow instructions. Xoxo Muffin Buffin.

I took another sip of tequila and clicked open the attachment. It took forever to load and I wondered when a start-up or a think tank would invent a time unit for the Internet, those "Load, goddammit, load!" moments that made a minute feel unfairly long, or when Instagram sucked an hour of your life in what felt like ten minutes.

The picture finally loaded. Instead of a scan it was a photo of a photo, and obviously taken with a phone.

"Damn right you can't follow instructions, Muffin Buffin," I said. At least it wasn't a cock. *Ceci n'est pas un penis.*

Honestly, I was happy the photo wasn't a perfect scan. It was a little blurry, a little off-center, a little far away. Yet another degree removed! But I was also confused. This wasn't a photo of someone's mom. Or, not only. There were two people in the picture, a guy and a girl, both around my age—1990s from the look of her dark lipstick and undersized vintage shirt, which read VIRGINIA IS FOR. The word LOVERS had to be outside the frame. He was leaning against a wall and she was sort of leaning against him. The girl had her face angled to the guy, her expression serious, like she had something big to tell him. She was trying and failing to pretend she wasn't totally obsessed with him. He had his eyes on the camera, brooding or bored, a real Johnny Depp wannabe if it weren't for the Scorsese eyebrows. There was nothing in the background except the putty-colored wall. I imagined them perched on the banks of the L.A. River, waiting for a drag race. The sky was as white as the surface beyond the photo's edge.

"How the fuck will I ever stage this?" I asked.

I poured another finger of tequila into my juice glass and drank it down. Peter Rabbit seemed to sigh from his hutch. I burped and the room wobbled once.

I looked at the photo a second time. The girl wasn't wearing a bra and beneath the thin shirt I could see her silver-dollar areolae and the ski slopes of her nipples.

"Peter Rabbit," I said. "I can't handle all these pre-mom boobs." I cut open my last lime and sunk my teeth into a wedge. "Yow!" I cried.

Once I'd licked my fingers clean, I inspected the photo again. There was something familiar about this girl, and I looked closer.

I knew it, even with half her face turned away from the camera and her hair dyed auburn. I expanded the photo. I could tell by the shape of her mouth and by the mole on her neck.

It was Lady.

And the guy, I realized, looked a lot like Seth: he had that same dark hair and olive skin, the same shape of the eyes, the same nose. It had to be his dad.

Seth had sent me this photo of his parents. Why not one of Lady alone? And why from this anonymous email address? Why *xoxo* me?

It was past two a.m. and I was toasted. Everyone in the Manse had to be asleep, and even if they weren't, it's not like I could march upstairs to Seth's bedroom and ask him why he'd emailed me the photo.

I hit Reply on my phone and typed:

Thanks but what's your phone number? I have some questions. Xoxo

I deleted the *xoxo* before I pressed Send and then took another shot. I hissed off the burn like a possum in the glare of a flashlight and refreshed my email. There was no reply yet. Duh, I had sent it less than ten seconds before. I knew that in the Manse kitchen a list of pertinent phone numbers was taped to the inside of a cabinet: Lady's cell, Karl's, Kit's, the CDC in case someone swallowed some rat poison or something, Seth's old school, even 911. At the bottom, someone had written Seth's cell in red pen.

I'd sneak into the house and get his number, text him my questions. The beep of the phone would wake him.

I unlocked Peter Rabbit's pen and pulled him out. He smelled like hay and he was soft and warm as I put him inside my shirt, his heart beating against my belly button, his little claws digging into my skin.

"We're going in," I whispered, and together we headed for the Manse.

The tequila was making me feel like a ballerina assassin as I slipped into the dark house: graceful and bitchy and invincible. My scalp tingled. It was exactly why I'd switched from the vodka. My mom once told me she'd never been loyal to a specific hard liquor. She said vodka made her buzz and gin made her float and tequila made her tingle.

Bourbon made her cry. The way I felt now was so good I was ready to marry Jose Cuervo, though I'd probably question that commitment come dawn.

The house was silent except for the drone of the vintage electric clock and the exhale of the air conditioner, which was working better than ever since a repair guy had come and fixed it in less than twenty minutes. I turned on my phone's flashlight and the bunny scrabbled across my skin.

In the dark I opened the cabinet and held my breath as it squeaked. I dictated the number to myself but I must have let go of my midsection for a moment as I typed it into my phone. It was an idiot move. Peter Rabbit shot out of my shirt like a fur-covered cannonball.

"Peter!" I whispered. He went running like I was Mr. McGregor.

"Shit, shit, shit," I said under my breath. I closed the cabinet. My scalp wasn't tingling anymore, I felt dizzy. I turned off the flashlight and waited in the dark, listening.

"Peter?" I said.

He came right to my feet, a spot of white in the darkness. I bent down to pick him up but he backed away, then started hopping toward the back door.

"Come on," I said, but still I was surprised to hear him following me outside.

As soon as I got back to the Cottage, I texted Seth: Why did you send me a pic of your parents??

Three seconds.

Wut? Who dis?

S. You sent me an email of ur mom and I think ur dad.

One second.

Ill b right there

I couldn't take my eyes off my phone. I heard Peter Rabbit knocking about in his pen, it sounded like he was finally snorting up his dinner, and I kicked the door closed with my foot.

When I looked up, Seth was standing in the doorway. His hair resembled a topographical map, all ridges and dips, and the waistband of his gym shorts was rolled in on itself, like Devin's pants when he dressed himself. He was wearing his T-shirt inside out.

"You were asleep," I said.

He glanced at the tequila bottle on my desk and mock-stumbled into the room.

"Is your whole life a game of charades?" The second I said it, I worried I'd offended him. Or Happy Kathy had said it, and it was my job to experience regret because my mom sure as hell never did. But Seth didn't seem hurt, just anxious.

"Here it is," I said, and he grabbed the phone out of my hand.

He stared at the photo, zooming in and out with his fingers, again and again, and then he sat on the floor, right where he'd been standing just a minute ago.

"That's your mom, right?" I asked, kneeling next to him.

He nodded.

"And that's your dad?"

He just kept staring.

"Did you send it to me, or what?"

He didn't answer.

"Seth?" I said, but he wouldn't look away from the phone.

The fierceness of his stare told me he hadn't sent the photo. He hadn't even seen it before. Seeing it now was doing something to him, pureeing his mind into a smoothie.

"Do you know your dad?" I asked.

That made him look up. He shook his head.

"Have you ever seen—?"

Again, a shake of the head.

"You look just like him."

I handed him the tequila, because what else do you do with an eighteen-year-old who's seeing a picture of his dad for the first time? He put down the phone to grab the bottle with both hands. He took one long drink.

Then he signed something I couldn't follow.

"Sorry," I said. "I have no idea what you're signing."

He pulled his phone from his pocket.

Who sent this?

His eyes were shining, and not from the liquor.

I shrugged. "You think your dad did?"

He made a face I'd never seen on anyone before: alarm, fear, shame, desire, all mixed together. I wanted to paint that face.

I leaned forward and kissed him. I was the last thing on Seth's mind, which was maybe why I'd done it. Is it Katherine Mary who doesn't like to be ignored, or me?

He tasted stale but his lips were softer than Everett's, bigger too. I closed my eyes but the room started spinning and I had to open them.

I was just slipping my tongue into his mouth when he pulled away.

"Oh my God," I said. "I don't know what the hell I'm doing. You're right, I'm wasted."

I felt embarrassed, but then I saw his boner beneath his shorts. Boys can't fake apathy or enthusiasm, poor babies. I smiled and he pointed at my phone. He wanted to see the email, I realized. He wanted to know who had seen his tweet and sent me the photo.

"It's from Muffin Buffin—or something?"

Seth looked horrified—he recognized the email. I thought he might vomit. Hell, I was pretty sure I was going to.

"It's Lady," I said.

He was typing into his own phone.

She said there werent any pics of him. Liar.

The room began to wobble again.

"She probably had a good reason for—"

Before I could finish, Seth lunged forward and kissed me back.

LADY

30.

I WAS HAVING THE SHOPPING DREAM AGAIN. IN IT, I HAVE HUNdreds of dollars to spend at some cement-floored boutique helmed by two leggy shopgirls, but I can't find anything that fits and I am crying softly to myself in the dressing room. In this particular version, I was pulling off a too-small mohair sweater and the fabric was tickling my nose. I woke before my eyes opened and I was sure Devin was in bed with me, that he'd sleepwalked into my room sometime before dawn, as he is wont to do, in search of a cuddle and the breast milk that dried up a year ago. I thought I could smell his sleeping body and his stinky, snot-coated hands, feel the tiny furnace of him. But when I opened my eyes there was only S's bunny sitting on my chest, self-satisfied as the goddamned Cheshire Cat.

I was startled, but I didn't move. It's calming to wake to a bunny. Spas should offer them to guests. I smiled—it was a tweet waiting to happen.

I sat up and held the bunny aloft and gave him a little squeeze like he was a watermelon I was checking for ripeness.

"What are you doing here, Peter Rabbit?"

For a moment I missed Karl, who surely would've cracked a joke. Something about an awkward moment after a one-night stand. Or no—maybe he'd make an allusion to *Watership Down*. The next time we talked I would tell him about waking to Peter Rabbit, just to hear what he'd say.

I put Peter down and he snuggled into the comforter.

"Just don't shit the bed," I said, picking up my phone. Before I opened Twitter, rehearsing my phrasing—Woke next to a white bunny. Promise I'm not on drugs. #BunniesAreTheBestTherapy—I checked my email.

I'd forgotten all about sending the photo to Seth's friend until I saw the reply in the muffinbuffin account, sandwiched between emails from J.Crew and an assortment of enraged environmentalists.

Thanks but what's your phone number? I have some questions.

I wasn't going to write back. No need to engage any further.

I'd seen Seth's tweet a few days ago and last night before bed I'd finally dug out the picture of me and Marco. I snapped a photo of it with my phone and sent it off. I would call it a whim if I hadn't deliberated for days. I needed to do it. Seth finally had a friend who didn't seem off, someone from the Internet or college. Okay, an artist, but at least that meant someone normal, with a hobby if not ambition. That seemed good. And what was the danger? I barely recognized myself in the photo; I doubted anyone else would.

But if someone did recognize me and Marco—I wanted that. Seth's father hadn't responded to my tweet and I was tired of being ignored. I knew Marco, I had known him, he was real. Twenty years ago, *we* were real. This photo was proof.

Seth was looking for his dad. Well, there he was. Marco Green.

If Seth saw this photo, eventually, from his friend, it would force me to answer the questions he'd wanted answers to for so long.

This would be my first attempt to tell him, however indirectly.

I woke with a bunny on my chest. Must stop fucking magicians. Funny, but too racy for six a.m.

I had one new email in my regular account.

"Oh boy, here we go," I said, petting Peter Rabbit. "Cunt Daniels at Gmail dot com."

To: LadyDanielsWrites@gmail.com
From: Kit@kitdaniels.com
Subject: Seth

Dear Lady,

I hope you don't mind me Writing. I am worried about Seth. Do
you think he's Depressed? I feel certain Reconciliation is possible
between you and my brother, mostly because he is ready to move
back in at your say so and I know you Love him. But even if you two
resolve your Issues and he moves back in, I still think you need
to talk to Seth. I've spent a lot of time with him recently and he is
more morose than usual. He's gotten quite moody. I assume, as
Mommy, you've noticed. Last week I offered him a plantain chip
and he just shook his head at me, not even a thanks. (He knows
I know the thank you sign, as well as hello. Not a wave, the sign.
He taught it to me years ago and I always use it when we see each
other. He is also such a Polite kid so his Rudeness was a shock to
me.) Anyway, I urge you to talk to him. Or send him to someone. I
know the language barrier is an issue, but perhaps someone who
knows ASL would be a good fit? It's worth looking into.

Twin told me not to write, but you're Seth's Mommy. I had to.
This comes from a place of Love and Concern, I hope you see that.
I know we haven't always seen Eye to Eye on things, but we can
agree that we both love Seth!

Let's get lunch soon. I met the babysitter the other week. Ess?
She seems great. While she's there why don't you and I meet at
Crudo? We can eat at the bar, no reservation required. Or maybe
shabu-shabu in Little Tokyo?

All my Love,
Kit

PS I'm working a lot. I want another show—the one in Berlin
seems like it happened Centuries ago. I'm sorry you weren't able
to make it. But you must come to the next Los Angeles show,
which will probably be scheduled for next year. I'll tell you more

about the project when we meet for Lunch. Twin doesn't even
know the details, which feels Different but it's kind of Great to
have a Secret from him for once.

PPS Kisses to Nephew!

The language barrier? I kicked off the duvet. A *plantain chip*? The random capitalization wasn't even the half of it. Kit was pretentious: she had only started calling Karl "Twin" a year or so ago, and she didn't dare do it to his face. *Seth's depressed.* No, he wasn't. How could she know anything about my son? He was fine—Photographer needed to stop Meddling in Mommy's Business.

I closed my email and opened Twitter. Bunny joke, come on, bunny joke. But my mind had deleted all quips. Before I could stop myself, I typed I'm afraid I'm a bad mother and sent it into the world. It was unfunny and true and utterly scrollable.

With Peter Rabbit under my arm like I was preparing to nurse him football-style, I headed downstairs. I couldn't return the animal to S, it was her day off and it was so early that Devin wasn't even up yet. But what would I do with the bunny until then?

The dog's bed at the foot of the stairs was empty. "Milky?" I called. No answer.

"Milkshake?" I repeated, louder, but still nothing.

Was the dog sleeping somewhere else? I wondered if he'd gone into a coat closet to die in private, like a cat might. Doubtful. He was twelve years old with cysts that could turn malignant any day now, but the ferocity of his farts suggested he didn't possess the modesty required to die alone.

"Please be alive, Milky," I said.

I went to the sliding glass door. It was open a couple of inches, certainly not wide enough for a Maltese to wiggle through—or was it? I imagined Milkshake in the clutches of a coyote.

"Please God."

I ran outside with Peter Rabbit still in my arms and banged on the Cottage door.

"Hello? S? I'm sorry to wake you, but do you have Milkshake?" I knocked again. "S! I have your bunny!"

I heard a groan and something like a space heater—in the summer?—clatter to the floor.

"You okay?"

"Just a sec," she croaked. Maybe she was throwing on clothes and stowing her bong under the bed. The one I'd discovered in the Cottage during Seth's tenure was bright blue and as tall as Devin. Karl was more upset by the genre of his stepson's drug paraphernalia than by the paraphernalia itself. "A bong is just so unattractive," he'd said, shaking his head.

S finally unlocked the door and opened it just wide enough to stick her head out. She looked like hell, which is rare for a woman so young, what with all that metastasizing collagen.

"You look like hell," I said.

"Why do you have my bunny?" she asked, squinting in the sun.

"He was in my bed," I explained, handing her the animal. "Milkshake's missing."

She widened her eyes and shut the door without a word.

"S?"

A minute later, she opened the door with the dog in her arms. The relief felt like a bear hug. "Milky!" I cried.

"Switched at birth?" she said. "Sorry."

"What the fuck, S? How did this happen?"

"I don't remember."

"Were you in the house?"

"God, I don't think so. How can I not remember?"

The door was open wider now. It was dark inside the Cottage, but I could make out the empty bottle on the desk, and a paintbrush next to it.

"You're still drunk," I said.

"It's my day off."

She held out Milkshake, and I took him from her. I balanced an animal on each arm.

"Are you sure you can handle the bunny right now?"

She looked thrilled by the question. "She can! Or she thinks she can!"

"Are you speaking of yourself in the third person?"

"Sorry. Yeah, I have a pen, he'll be fine."

"Are you painting something?" I asked and gestured with my chin. "That paintbrush."

She took Peter Rabbit from me. "Too many questions."

"Are you?"

"I do landscapes sometimes. To relax."

"I'd love to see one sometime."

"Maybe."

We stood facing each other: woman to woman, animal to animal.

"Do you think Seth's depressed?" I asked.

The question surprised her. "Lady—come on." This was a plea. Probably to let her go back to bed. After a second she said, "All teenagers hate their moms."

"Seth doesn't hate me."

"You still hate your mom, and you're forty."

"I'm forty-one, actually, so thank you. Do you think Seth *hates* me, though? Because I asked Karl to move out?"

"Because you're his mom." She gave me a kind, if condescending, smile. "Good night, Lady," she said, and shut the door.

I didn't move. It was as if I'd traveled backward through time to those few months when Seth was living in the Cottage, when it felt like he'd crossed a border into a country I didn't have the proper papers to follow him into. My same face and that same door. Either he'd closed it on me or I was too afraid to knock. There was something sinister about that dank little guesthouse, or it was simply that the privacy it offered goaded its tenant to secrecy. Bad. Seth had been getting naked with girls, and high, and S was painting landscapes and drinking. Possibly snooping in my house in the middle of the night.

I turned and faced the pool, scratching behind Milkshake's ears to keep myself calm. The water was blue and still. A dead bird floated in the shallow end and I wondered if the Eavesdroppers above could see it.

31.

SETH AND I USED TO BE CLOSE. THAT'S TRUE OF MANY MOTH-ers and their young children, but our bond was stronger than most, intensified as it was by Marco's abandonment and my mother's betrayal, and by Seth's silence. We were best friends because we had no one else. According to my editor, the love between me and Seth, the maternal bond, et cetera, et cetera, would be my book's central theme and the narrative's unifying principle.

By the time Seth turned four, I had taken him to countless specialists. His hearing was perfect, the blood tests revealed nothing amiss. The first doctor recommended a second one, who recommended a speech therapist who recommended a speech pathologist, who recommended an occupational therapist, who recommended a behavioral therapist, who wanted to get Seth an expert to shadow him at day care. Alma, whose permits expired half a decade earlier, refused to allow it. Despite Seth's age, I hadn't moved him to preschool. Fuck circle time, he couldn't even say hello.

None of the appointments started when they were supposed to. The waiting rooms were dingy, and their only reading material, if it existed at all, was in Spanish or Russian. At least my insurance paid for almost everything. Key word: *almost*. A couple of doctors had suggested Seth's silence might be a problem of physiology, and I wanted Seth to get an MRI to check his throat and diaphragm, and have a doctor examine his tongue. None of that was covered. I broke down and borrowed a thousand bucks from the Actress, with whom I spoke every month or so. She felt for my predicament (her word), and gave me the money.

Turns out, aside from a few weak muscles in his tongue, Seth's body worked perfectly. Something else was broken—but what?

"The longer he doesn't speak, the harder it will be for him to do so," the doctor who reviewed the MRI told me.

I'd started writing about these visits for my book, but I couldn't get past this one. I remember thinking, *Time is running out, time is running out,* like I would die if I didn't cure Seth in time. I was hardly eating back then, I was too busy ferrying Seth from doctor to doctor before and after work, eating the dregs of his Rice Krispies and mac and cheese whenever I had a spare moment. Sleep was also hard to come by, sharing as I did a bed with a growing kid who thrashed and blanket-hogged all night long. Sometimes I put off going to sleep until four or five in the morning; night was the only time to myself, and I took it.

"Your son's window of opportunity is closing," the doctor said on that visit. "If he doesn't start to verbalize in the next two years, he most likely won't approach competence."

"You mean like those kids chained in basements?" I asked.

"Pardon?"

"You know, those neglected children who are tied up—like, in sheds—by themselves. And the ones raised by wolves? They never learn to speak."

He squinted at me like I was a mirage. "It's . . . sort of . . . like that," he said carefully. "Though feral children usually use some language, even if it's nonsense to our ears. Your son doesn't say anything at all, is that correct?"

I nodded. I left his office as soon as I could, tears burning the back of my throat.

My editor would probably like that detail, but what would she say if I admitted that when I left the doctor's office all I could think about was Marco? Two, three, even four years after he left, I expected him to seek us out. Eventually. He had to. And when he finally did, he would learn that Seth was nonverbal, that his son was *special needs*—it was the phrase teetering on every doctor's tongue, I knew it—and he wouldn't stay. Marco would leave us for the second and final time.

A few hours after that appointment, I called the Actress and told her the issue was Seth's diaphragm, that I had already scheduled the surgery, which would be minor. Her joy and relief at my lie angered me more than I expected and I never spoke to her again, let alone paid her back.

>>>

THE DOCTOR HAD recommended a behavioral specialist who was miraculously covered by my insurance. Dr. Zaire Bowen-Shultz. She decorated her office in rich jewel tones and her patience for Seth made me feel small and inadequate. Unlike me, she never got frustrated, never raised her voice. Seth liked her stash of puzzles and the thick braids that fell down her back. I would have been embarrassed when he grabbed one, wide-eyed, except Dr. Zaire Bowen-Shultz was used to kids of every race grabbing at her hair, or yelping if anyone touched their skin, or shitting in their pants, or screaming as if possessed, and so on and so on. She simply smiled and gently released her hair from his fist.

Dr. Zaire Bowen-Shultz explained Seth's mutism better than any of the previous doctors. Language is receptive and expressive, she said. "He can receive language. He understands everything that we say to him, but he can't express himself vocally. He can't take all that syntax and content in his head and turn it into sound." She passed me a tissue. "It's promising that he can gesture, though. Since that's also expressive."

"So if he can express through gestures," I asked, "why can't he talk?"

She wasn't the first to bring up an autism diagnosis, but she was the most practical about it.

I must have been making a face. "It's a spectrum," she explained. "Seth doesn't display any other characteristics of the syndrome—or not strongly. But his mutism is severe and I'm not sensing intense social anxiety." When I didn't say anything, she added, "We should definitely dialogue about it further."

She suggested a support group in addition to our meetings. She lent me two books on the subject.

"Doesn't this seem overzealous?" I asked.

"It's never a bad idea to educate yourself, right? And find community."

I tried to keep a straight face whenever she talked about community.

"Think of it like this," she said, sensing my unease. "If Seth does receive the diagnosis, the services he is eligible for will expand."

Seth looked up and smiled when he heard his name. He had dumped out all the puzzles and was raking the pieces with his fingers.

We kept going to Dr. Zaire Bowen-Shultz, but I told her I didn't want her to submit any such diagnosis. I didn't read the books. I eschewed the support group. Instead I signed us up for ASL at the Learning Annex in Carson. My son couldn't speak, okay, fine, but he could communicate.

He was four. We already had a dozen special signs like *Stop Drop Dead, Stop Honking, Ninja Mama, Afraid Afraid Afraid.* I knew when he was hungry and when he had to use the bathroom, and when he wasn't feeling well. Alma could deduce that much too, but at her house Seth preferred to sit with the babies or draw pictures or build elaborate towers with cardboard bricks—by himself. I was his only playmate and our conversations consisted of pantomime, special signs, facial expressions, nodding, head shaking, pointing. I had perfected the running monologue of a mother with an infant, except Seth hadn't been a baby in years. Other times we were silent together. Often I didn't even notice until I finally spoke and my voice cracked from lack of use.

Seth picked up ASL easily. I didn't, which I'd been told was expected for a hearing adult. But when Seth made deaf friends and entire conversations occurred between them that I couldn't follow, I started teaching him to read so that he and I could communicate via writing. Every night I wrote words on index cards and made him tape them to their corresponding objects. Then I made him pick up raisins with a pair of tweezers so that his fine motor skills would improve enough to write legibly. As soon as he could do sign language *and* write, I explained to Dr. Zaire Bowen-Shultz, the universe would be his.

"But it's his universe *now,* Lady," she said gently.

I smiled, and didn't say what I was thinking: that spending so much time with her patients had turned her delusional. She mistook difficulties for gifts.

The thing is, I didn't understand what my reading and writing lessons would mean. As soon as I realized that literacy would connect Seth not only to me, but to anyone who could read, it was too late. He could now communicate with Dr. Zaire Bowen-Shultz and Alma, also my boss and his wife, the pizza delivery guy, all adults. Eventually his peers. I let him have the universe, but now he was floating farther and farther out of my orbit.

By the time Seth was ready for kindergarten and got a scholarship to Greenhouse, he had stopped vocalizing altogether, probably because of the unwanted attention it brought, and the frustration he felt when the sounds didn't coalesce into language. I still hoped that someday he would open his mouth and talk. A sentence would fly out, as if by magic. I sometimes tried to imagine how his speech might sound, based on his laughter, and the array of possibilities shallowed my breath and made my eyes sting with tears. I pictured him whining like the kids I often overheard in the market—*"Why won't you buy me that cake?"*—and suddenly all our troubles became a faint memory: our years shuffling from one doctor's office to the next; the phone calls I had to make to confirm my deductible had been reached, that I'd be reimbursed for this or that visit; the endless hold music; the strangers who thought Seth was being rude when he didn't answer them; the kids who pretended to be deaf or retarded when they saw him signing; the times I couldn't understand what Seth wanted and yelled at him or left the room before I did something worse. It had all been challenging, but once we were safe on the other side, these years would be less painful, funny even, a moving montage in the dramedy of our astonishing lives. I was ready for the normal Seth, the real Seth, to step out of the silent visitor.

And yet, there were other days. On other days, he would roll into a ball under the covers and press his spine against my stomach, the joey to my kangaroo, and then he'd clap three times very quickly, which meant something like *I'm comfortable,* but also, *I love you,* but also, *The dark is scary but not under the covers,* but also, *I'm afraid of death but not right now,* and I know that if he had talked at that moment I would have pretended not to hear him.

32.

I GAVE MILKSHAKE A TREAT AND HE ATE IT WITH OPENMOUTHED glee as I searched the kitchen and living room for anything that looked amiss. S claimed she didn't remember coming into my house, but she must have because she had replaced one white animal with another. Karl would flip if he knew. He'd tell me to check my jewelry and the Social Security cards; I'd learned from the Actress that rich people did this regularly and that "the help" was always the first suspect. I decided right then that I wouldn't say anything to Karl. S was something, but she wasn't dangerous, and she wasn't a thief. After all, she'd given the dog back.

"Mommy!"

Devin's call was loud and persistent, but it was too confident to sound desperate. He knew I'd retrieve him in two minutes flat.

When I got to his room he was sitting up in bed with his stuffed stegosaurus on his lap.

"Hey you," I said. "You got your stegosaurus?"

"It's a dino!" he yelled and climbed out of bed, dragging the toy behind him. He tried to run past me but I grabbed him and gave his Pull-Up a squeeze. It was squishy.

"Let's change this and try the potty, okay?"

"No!"

"Dev." I was already pulling down his pants.

Once he was naked from the waist down, Devin said, "I go to potty in bathroom now."

"Good idea!" I replied.

Devin stopped at the doorway. He stood there, pulling at his tiny penis ("It's proportional!" Karl had said once). It was uncircumcised and looked like a medicine dropper.

"Come on, Dev," I said.

He didn't move. "Daddy here?"

I leaned down to kiss his cheek. "No, baby. Let's do potty now, okay?"

"Why Daddy not here?"

"Because he's staying with Aunt Kit."

"Why?"

"Because she's his sister."

"Why Kit his sister?"

"They have the same mommy. They're twins, remember?"

"Why they have the same mommy?"

"Let's go do potty now."

"Why Daddy not here?" he asked again.

"Tell you what," I said. "Today you get to have me all day, and then tonight, Daddy is coming to get you!"

Devin clapped his hands. "Yes!" he yelled. "And I can have cookie?"

"Sure," I said, leading him to the bathroom.

As I lifted him onto the toilet to pee, he said, "Where S?"

"Sleeping. It's her day off."

Devin seemed to ponder this as he peed.

"I want S," he said calmly, and then slid off the toilet.

"Not today. You have Mommy. All day!"

"Where Seth?"

"Also sleeping."

"Why everyone sleeping? It's morning time!" His voice was a whimpering whine.

"I'm not sleeping," I said. "I'm awake with you!"

He pushed his chin into my forehead. It hurt.

"Ouch," I said.

"I put you on the rug and boom!" he said, giggling.

I laughed. "Let's go get some undies for you, crazy boy."

Devin didn't move. "Where S?"

His question shouldn't have annoyed me, but it did. I wanted to say that S was hungover (*What's hungover, Mommy?*), that she probably would have to be fired if she kept up this erratic behavior (*What's fired? What's a-ratic?*), that she didn't really care about him (*Why she not care about me?*), that she only cared about her salary (*What's salary?*), that she thought Seth hated me (*Why Seth hate you? Are you a bad guy?*). Instead I told him he could watch three television episodes.

"Mommy has some writing to do," I said.

"You have email!" he yelled, and ran downstairs without his pants on.

When Seth had been Devin's age, there must have been so much he didn't understand. He couldn't ask me stuff, not like Devin, who posed questions every other minute and filed away the answers to bring up six months later. By the time Devin turned two he could chatter away about animals and trucks and traffic. It wasn't until Seth was literate that he asked me to define words, to tell him more about dinosaurs, about skyscrapers, about colors. Until then, he had subsisted almost entirely on context, impoverished. And I, without a child to interrupt me, to demand clarification and remind me that the nuances of adult speech are full of mental cul-de-sacs and thorny forests, rambled on and on, referencing a whole world of things and ideas my son couldn't possibly comprehend. We had used the sign for *why,* but, by itself, that word is only an existential cry. *Why, why, why?*

Downstairs, with Devin staring dead-eyed at the TV, pulling on his penis like it was a rubber band, I was reminded of my tweet. You bet your ass I was a bad mother! It hadn't occurred to me before, but of course it could be read as comic. Someone would think I meant it tongue-in-cheek, like so many other moms did these days: every week the Internet spat out a new article by one of these women, written as mock apologia: *I let my kids drink juice! Sometimes I even let them eat fish sticks! Sue me!* As if juice and fish sticks were signs of abuse and neglect. Their confessions were just pride dressed up as regret.

I opened the Twitter app. I decided I would delete the tweet and then unplug for the day, give Devin all of my attention like I used to give Seth.

But it was too late. Someone had already liked the tweet, and I had one more follower.

My heart hiccupped like a stalled car. Marco Green. I let out a squeal and looked up at Devin. He hadn't noticed.

I set down the phone and wiped my hand with a nearby dish towel. I took a breath. Marco. I could communicate with him. I picked up the phone and sent him a direct message.

Marco, it's Lady. I'd like to meet up and talk.

I retrieved clothes for Devin and dressed him before I let myself check my phone again.

Wow. Lady. Hi. I cant believe it.

He didn't say anything else. He didn't ask me for my number, or suggest a place to meet, or ask how his son was doing.

Just then, Seth walked downstairs. I dropped my phone on the couch. He looked tired, but he was already showered and dressed.

"Where you going?"

He signed: *C-L-A-S-S.*

"Which one?" Before he could answer, I said, "Are you depressed? Kit thinks you are."

He rolled his eyes.

"Do you hate me? S thinks you do."

I love you, Ninja Mama, he signed, but he wasn't looking at me.

"I love you too," I said. And then: "Did you play video games all night or something? Why do you look so tired?"

He started to sign something very slowly, so I could understand:

You. Reading. Me. No, not *Me,* but *My.*

And then he spelled out a word. T-W-I-T-T. He was asking if I'd read his Twitter.

"I always do. You know that."

He signed, *Stop.*

My phone rang before I could reply. I jumped. Could it be Marco—I imagined answering the call in front of Seth. How would I control my voice?

But it was only Karl.

"Karl," I said.

"You need to meet Kit for lunch."

"I got her email. She capitalizes shit randomly."

He chuckled. "She sure does fancy herself in an eighteenth-century epistolary novel, doesn't she."

"I'm not going for yaki-soba with Kit."

"Shabu-shabu—it's where you cook the meat yourself."

"Whatever, I'm not meeting her so she can tell me how to parent."

Seth was walking into the kitchen, ostensibly to grab a banana on his way out the door. He flinched when I tried to grab his arm.

I didn't hear what Karl had said and I wondered if there was a way to check my Twitter while I was talking on the phone without missing any of the conversation.

"She wants to tell you about her show," he was telling me now.

"What about it?"

The front door opened and slammed shut. Seth's version of goodbye this morning.

"I don't know," Karl said, "she's being cagey. You know how she can get about her art."

"She can't display *Woman No. 17*," I said. "You made her sign that thing, right?"

"Don't worry. She said it was new work."

"Well, I don't do nudes anymore."

"That's a shame. Isn't that a shame, Lady?"

"Karl," I said again, but I wanted him to keep going. My crotch was pawing at me like an insistent kitten.

"You like it when I talk dirty," he said. It was a reminder, not a revelation. I pictured him sitting behind his desk at work, pulling out his cock—or "kock" as I liked to think of it. Karl's Kock. No one was allowed into his office without knocking.

"I know you," he said gruffly.

"No you don't," I said.

Neither of us spoke for a moment.

"I think we should fire S," I said.

His voice changed immediately—peppy, avuncular. "Why? Because of the drinking?"

"No, I just don't think she's that nice," I said.

"Nice? Did you catch her yelling at Dev or something?"

"No, it's with me. She's . . . I don't know."

"I didn't realize she was *your* nanny."

I thought about telling him about the bunny, but he'd ask why the back door had been unlocked, and I thought the better of it.

"Dev would have a fit if she left," he said. "And you need to get your book done."

"Fine. But I'm still not writing Kit back."

When I hung up, Devin jumped on me. "Kit!"

"Yep, Kit," I said.

"I want to see Kit!"

"You will—tonight."

"Now!" he yelled.

"Really?"

"Now!"

"For lunch?"

"Yes!" He punched me in the breasts. "I want chicky nuggets."

I thought about the alternative: a listless day at the park, fighting traffic both ways, pretending to care about bad guys and trains for ten hours straight. How did S do it?

"Let me text her."

I smiled to myself. When Kit had asked me to lunch, she suggested that the babysitter—*Ess*—watch Devin. She'd be miffed if I brought a child along, but she'd be powerless to admit it.

Before I heard back from Kit, I messaged Marco. I was on a tear.

Seriously, can we meet up? Just tell me when and where.

33.

LET KIT KNOW THERE WAS NO WAY I WAS DRIVING ALL THE WAY to Little Tokyo for a meal I had to cook myself. She said that was fine; her new studio was a few blocks from Crudo and she wanted to show me what she was working on. I remembered the old warehouse she used to rent, right at the edge of Chinatown. Instead of a dark room, as I'd expected, there'd been a huge computer and high-tech printer. ("They're new," she had confessed. "I'm finally ready to dabble in digital.") That studio had been blessed with ten-foot windows overlooking the L.A. River with its attendant abandoned shopping carts and rivulets of brown water, a view Kit said she adored. Her studio-mate, who worked on the other side of the drywall, was famous for large canvases covered in small dashes. She sat on a skateboard to paint, rolling forward dash by dash.

Devin was asleep when I pulled up to the valet at Crudo. I tried to wake him and he only squirmed and whimpered.

"Come on, baby," I said. If he slept now he wouldn't nap later when it was just the two of us, and I needed time alone to wait for Marco's reply (so far there'd been nothing).

"Dev?" He didn't move; he was down for the count.

I sighed and let the valet guy—red vest, pink ticket at the ready—hold the stroller steady as I lowered my sleeping son into it.

Before Karl and I started seeing each other, I'd never been to a place like Crudo. "I like to think of it as California formal," Karl had explained. "L.A. really started the casual fine dining trend." This meant the restaurant didn't require men to wear jackets, and they didn't refold your napkin every time you got up to use the bathroom. But it was expensive and they snubbed brunch, not to mention substitutions. I knew Kit loved their mussels, and sure enough, she was already sitting at the bar with a bowl of them in front of her, along with a glass of white, probably Sancerre. Her thin white dress resembled an enormous napkin, except for the padded white belt, which looked like two maxi pads stitched end to end. She'd either purchased it in Berlin for a thousand dollars or made it in her bathroom. No lipstick, which was rare for her; without it, she looked more like Karl.

She jumped off her stool as soon as she saw us. "I didn't know Dev was coming!"

"Surprise," I whispered. "It's the nanny's day off."

She smiled at Devin, and then frowned. "A stroller? At his age?"

"I could have just dragged him in by his hair."

"I guess I thought it was an infant thing," she said. "My mistake."

"Well, the stroller has probably delayed him mentally. It's the price to pay, right?"

She laughed. "Lady, stop! Have a seat. Want wine?"

In moments she had every Central American busboy in the place rushing around us: one removing a third barstool to make room for the stroller, one pouring me water, one wiping down the bar with a washcloth, one just standing by, smiling. It wasn't yet noon and the place was almost empty. A woman as thin and blond as a giraffe sat in a corner booth with a man who was either her father, her husband, or her handler.

"Don't worry," I said to the smiling busboy, "if my kid wakes up I won't let him sit at the bar."

"They won't mind if you do," Kit said. "Isn't that right, Nate?" She grinned at the bartender, whose sculpted arms and capped white teeth told me he was an actor. They never let Latinos pour drinks or be servers. Not here, and not at Paul Feldman's either.

Nate flashed me his Clooney teeth and asked if I wanted anything stiffer than water. "Water's good," I said. I liked to abstain in front of Kit, just in case it made her feel bad.

Kit gestured for me to have some mussels and said, "Thanks for meeting me."

"Karl said it was important that I do."

"You told him about my email?"

"He brought it up first. Not the email, the lunch."

"So it was you who brought up the email first."

"Calm down, I didn't read it aloud to him or anything."

"Those plantain chips—the ones I offered Seth—were Karl's," Kit said.

"*That's* why you don't want me to read him the email? Because you ate his chips? You really have an issue taking what isn't yours, Kit."

A trio of men entered the restaurant and Kit turned to check them out. I signaled to Nate at the other end of the bar and asked for a burger.

"You have to get a side of the Romanesco," Kit said. "It's divine."

"I like divine," I said, and Nate nodded.

"So . . ." Kit began. "Seth."

"I really don't think you have anything to worry about. He's eighteen, that's a moody age. And with Karl gone, things are different—"

"It's hard for him."

"Look, he's fine. His therapist said he can go back to her whenever he needs to."

"That woman works with children. Seth is an adult."

"Ha. Barely."

"He doesn't know his father," she said.

"Why are you and Karl stuck on this?"

"Because Seth is. And he can't speak."

"Your pity doesn't help."

"It's a fact, Lady." She leaned forward. "He struggles with it. I mean, the film he made."

I had no idea what Kit was talking about, but I couldn't let her know it.

"Yeah . . ." I said.

"Don't tell me he didn't show you the video. He made it for art class."

All I could think of were the video games Seth played: World of Warcraft, Call of Duty, some annoying text-based ones that Karl had read about and introduced to Seth. "They're feminist!" he'd tried to explain to me, but I couldn't even pretend to care.

Kit knew Seth hadn't shown me any film. It was why she was telling me now; hell, it was probably her whole reason for ensnaring me into this goddamn lunch.

"He isn't taking an art class," I said. I knew this much; I'd seen his schedule, paid the tuition. "It's a film class."

"Film is art!" she said. "Seth's using the medium to express his struggles."

"That's great," I said.

"He *wants* to be able to talk," Kit said.

"Everyone wants him to talk!" I didn't mean to raise my voice, but I did, and the three assholes who had just been seated looked up from their phones in mock concern.

"I don't care if he speaks or not," Kit said. She looked deeply satisfied, as if she'd proven something about me that she'd been speculating for years. "Is that why you haven't let Devin learn sign language?"

Jesus, had Karl recounted every argument we'd ever had?

"All I said was that Dev was too young to take a class. He's still learning English."

"The earlier the better, you know that," Kit said.

"He isn't deaf!"

"But are you?" she said, and, pleased with her comeback, dipped an empty mussel into the broth and slurped it clean. From his stroller, Devin gave a little sigh, but didn't wake up.

"Let Dev and Seth communicate," she said.

"They do communicate!" I grabbed my purse and stood.

"Where are you going?"

"I have to use the bathroom. Or do you need to issue me a hall pass for that?"

I tried not to run across the restaurant. This was a fucking ambush. Figures. I'd made Karl move out and now I was the enemy. Kit never would've tried this a few years ago, when she at least put some effort into being nice to me: when we first met at Trader Joe's and she asked me to model for her; when she wanted me to date Karl; when I was Karl's lovely wife.

She'd never been friends with any of her subjects before, and if she knew anyone who was poor it was because they were starving artists, not because they were a single mother of a disabled (ugh) child and estranged from their only living relative. I was a novelty, and in the beginning, Kit wanted to bond. Or she just wanted to impart lessons, precious pearls about where to get waxed, what wine to drink, how to talk to housekeepers, how to hang art in your home, which galleries were worth anyone's time, which female artists were geniuses and which were total poseurs. She even had opinions on child-rearing, of which she had no firsthand experience. I still didn't understand how she was Karl's twin sister. He must've sucked out all the sweetness from the amniotic sac, left her to feed on only arrogance and judgment.

At least now, in the bathroom, I could check my phone.

First I texted Seth: I WANT TO SEE YOUR FILM YOU MADE FOR SCHOOL.

All-caps conveyed screaming, especially for Seth. That was the point. How dare he not show me the art he made!

I checked my Twitter account, and there, like that, was a message from Marco. Before reading it, I grabbed a white hand towel from the basket by the sink and wiped the sweat from my face.

Sure lets meet. Next week? Monday? Im in Chatsworth (dont laugh): 107 Peralta Ave.

But I did laugh. Holy shit. There was his address. I would see him next week. That was soon.

I replied, Monday works.

I was vetting him. I wouldn't let him near Seth before I saw him for myself.

On my way out of the bathroom, my phone dinged. I thought it was Seth—he'd give me enough information about his short film that I could get out of this lunch alive, and later we'd watch it together. He'd show me his pain. I knew it better than anyone.

But it was only a text from Verizon, letting me know I'd used up 75 percent of my data plan.

WHEN I RETURNED to the bar, Devin was awake, hiding under my stool in a crouch.

"Uh-oh!" I said. "Where is my child?"

Kit gave a theatrical shrug and Devin squealed. He grabbed my calf, pinching the muscle between his tiny fingers.

"Ow!" I said, and reached down to tickle him.

As Devin laughed, Kit said, "A friend of mine says tickling is torture. She'll never do it to Hildegard."

"The kid's name is Hildegard? That's torture enough." I let go of Devin and when he begged for me to keep tickling him, I raised an eyebrow at Kit.

"Let me tell you about what I'm working on," she said.

"Did you give up the real-estate project?"

Last Thanksgiving, Kit told me she'd begun scouring real-estate websites for messy interiors she might photograph. She loved to see houses just on the cusp of entropy.

"That was a hobby. Besides, too many properties are staged. Not a power cord in sight."

Devin climbed onto the stool next to me and began spinning side to side. I asked Nate to pour him a Shirley Temple, extra cherries, and I was surprised Kit didn't remark on the sugar content. Devin bounced up and down. "I love red juice," he told Nate solemnly.

"This isn't about the Women series, is it?" I asked Kit.

"God no—this is all new! Anyway, even if I were putting that up again, you're off the hook. I signed the contract, remember? Part of me wishes I hadn't. I'd love to have the original in a show someday."

"Stop."

"What? You *are* Woman Number Seventeen!"

"*Woman No. 17* is the name of a photo. I'm a person, Kit."

"Well, it's my favorite in the series. Karl's too, obviously. And look what it led to!"

"The one in the book is okay," I said.

"Not as good as the original. I can't believe I listened to Karl."

"You know S, my nanny?" I said. "She's a fan of yours. She's seen me in the book."

"Is that so? Why would she be nannying if she's so interested in art?"

I sighed. "Tell me about your new stuff."

Kit blushed, which surprised me. She was always so confident about her projects, full of bluster. But then again, I'd only heard about them after they were finished, or when they were just minor preoccupations.

"This one really matters to you," I said.

I remembered when we met, how she'd walked me to my car, squeezed into the back of Trader Joe's nightmare parking lot. She spoke in quick bursts about her vision, about how I'd be part of something honest and raw and real. She told me about her camera and her process and her background, how she'd been showing work for twenty years, how she was excited about this current project. Then she peeked into my grocery bag and saw I'd gotten the shu mai and said she loved it too. I hadn't had a friend, a real friend, in years, and Kit was this brilliant woman, more than ten years older, with vermillion lipstick and wearing what looked like a bolero made of carpet scraps, her fingernails as unkempt as her outfit was tailored, talking with infectious passion about art and truth and processed food. I didn't realize how famous she was, but perhaps I sensed it, and felt drawn to her. That day, Kit didn't have a card so she wrote down her phone number on the back page of the Fearless Flyer.

"Please call me," she'd said, and I did, two hours later.

Now she had a similar intensity in her eyes, but something sheep-ish too. The vulnerability was refreshing. Her weapons were down, for now.

Nate set the Shirley Temple in front of Devin and he immediately hooked himself to the straw. It would be gone in seconds. And then what? I doubted they had chicky nuggets.

"Personal? Cool. Are you doing self-portraits?" I asked. "S paints landscapes. I just found out."

This seemed to interest Kit, but then she put down her napkin and said forcefully, as if part of her wasn't willing to say it aloud: "Lady, I'm photographing Seth."

I thought I'd slip off my stool. "You're *what*?"

I couldn't look at her. I couldn't.

Devin was still drinking. Oh to be at the bottom of his glass instead of here next to Kit! I felt her hand on my shoulder and I leaned away.

"He loves doing it," she was saying, "of course he does or I wouldn't be photographing him."

"No," I said. "No. No. No."

"I want to show you the prints." She paused. "He's old enough."

"What are you even talking about? When did this happen? Did you wait for him to turn eighteen so you didn't have to fucking ask me? Jesus, Kit. This is low, even for you."

Just then, a busboy placed my lunch in front of me. The burger glistened with blood and grease and I thought I might vomit.

"Here's your burger, Dev," I said, but he just wrinkled his nose.

Without looking at her, I said, "He's my son, Kit. He's basically your nephew."

"That's why it's so personal. I'm interested in the perils of representation—always have been, it's what my work is about." She took a last sip of her wine. "All his life, Seth's dealt with everyone speaking *for* him."

"So why add to that?"

"The photos are humane," she said. "They're the first I've ever staged."

Now I turned to her. "Bullshit. What about *Woman No. 17*?"

She laughed. "That's you, Lady. Or it was. That was your life. Your bathroom."

"And how wonderfully depressing it was! Poor women: so real!"

I could tell she wanted to disagree, but she knew I was right.

"I think you'll really like the photos," she said. And then: "I'm surprised you're so angry."

"You knew I would be. He's my child."

"You're the one writing a book about him. That could be why it's been so hard for you to get started." She furrowed her brow and pouted at me like I was a puppy. As if I'd ever buy her performed concern.

I picked up my fork. I'd at least eat the vegetables. When I was finished I'd ask Nate for a second bowl, and keep eating.

I stopped as soon as I'd speared a bite. This wasn't a pale-green and fractal piece of Romanesco—it was just plain cauliflower, off-white and blooming like a wart.

I dropped my fork. It hit the plate with a clang.

"You okay?" Kit asked.

"This isn't Romanesco," I cried. "This is fucking bullshit cauliflower!"

Devin flinched and Nate looked up behind the bar, as did the server by the windows, who had just bent over to present the old man with his espresso in a tiny brown cup. This place served its coffee with sugar that was more uneven pebble than perfect cube. Karl loved it.

"Lady," Kit murmured. "Relax."

I turned to her. "I'm leaving. You're a traitor and I won't allow you to hurt my son." I picked up my purse and hung it on the back of the stroller.

"Lady . . ."

"And, by the way? That dress? It looks super absorbent."

I picked up Devin to put him back in the stroller. I didn't protest when he wouldn't let go of the glass of Shirley Temple. He could throw it on the floor for all I cared. We were never coming back to this horrible, elegant restaurant. He was confused we were leaving so quickly, but too excited about keeping his drink to resist the exit.

On my way out, I caught Nate's eye. "Eleven dollars for a side of cauliflower?" I said. "You deserve better, Nate." I nodded to one of the busboys. "You all do. Get out of here while you still can!"

34.

TRAFFIC ON BEVERLY WAS PRACTICALLY AT A STANDSTILL AND part of me worried Kit would overtake us on foot. Nah, no chance—Cunt Daniels was probably still at the bar, drinking a second glass of wine and joking with Nate about her insane sister-in-law.

I took some solace in knowing that I had embarrassed her, that she would have to order a dessert she didn't want just to make amends for my behavior. I was shaken, though. Seth had made a movie and kept it secret from me. He let Kit photograph him. He'd kept that a secret from me too. My hands were so clammy I could barely grip the steering wheel and my held-back tears were acid in my throat. I had to pull over.

"Why we stop?" Devin asked from the backseat once we were parked again. He was trying to scoop the ice out of his drink and I didn't bother telling him to stop.

"Mommy needs to think." I grabbed my phone and then turned up *The Jungle Book* soundtrack. *"Get mad, baby,"* sang Baloo.

First I texted Seth: Why didn't you tell me about Kit's project?

Then I texted Karl: Did you really not know about the photos???

No reply from Seth, but Karl texted back immediately: What photos? A moment later my phone rang; it was Karl. Of course he was willing to get to the bottom of this, to talk it out.

I didn't pick up. Let Kit do the explaining.

I was about to start the engine when my phone dinged four times fast, texts from Kit.

I'm so sorry I Upset you. Since you won't come to my Studio, here are a few shots of Seth. I think you will see your son's Grace and Wisdom—or come around to. They're quite a Departure for me.

I didn't want to see the images, but I couldn't help myself.

Unlike the Women series, these were in color. They'd been taken in a studio, no doubt Kit's, against a white backdrop. In all three Seth was shirtless, wearing jeans I didn't recognize. His arms were dark but he had a farmer's tan at his T-shirt line, and his chest hair swirled dark and flat as a patch of grass an animal's been sleeping in. Or like Marco's chest hair. In the first, a melancholic Seth pushed his fists into his pockets, arms straight, the waistline of his jeans stretched away from his hips. In the second, he was laughing with his arms across his chest. It was a real laugh, and I could see the fillings in his lower left molars, the ones he'd gotten when he was ten; I'd opened a new credit card to pay for them. The third was just a close-up of his back. His spine, that spine. Mine.

In their own way, these photos were sexy. Someone would definitely think so. Wouldn't they? They made Seth look vulnerable, but also, at the same time, like he was the one in control. That was their genius, I suppose: that the viewer couldn't be sure.

Either way, I wanted Seth to put his shirt back on.

I closed the images. On the CD, King Louie was still scatting as if nothing had changed in the last few seconds. Devin was kicking the back of the passenger seat. He'd dropped the empty glass, it wasn't anywhere.

I opened Twitter and re-read Marco's message. There was his address, a fruit to pluck if I were reckless enough. I checked myself out in the rearview mirror. Not bad. Despite the drama, my lip gloss had hung on. My eyelashes had kept their curl. I was wearing jeans and my favorite green T-shirt, as thin and soft as a gas-station receipt. Beneath it, my sensible but flattering nude-colored bra. My hair was okay. Whenever Marco and I drove in his car together, he used to keep one hand on the wheel and one hand on me, sliding his hand up and down my ponytail.

"We're going to visit an old friend of mine, Dev," I said, but he was too busy bobbing along to the music to care.

Before I started the engine, I texted S: Devin and I would like the yard to ourselves this afternoon. If you were planning on using the pool later on, please don't. Thanks.

Whatever happened next, I'd want to dive into that cold water without any adults watching, not even S. I'd had enough with judgment.

35.

MARCO LIVED IN A LOW-SLUNG RANCH-STYLE HOUSE WITH jagged rocks instead of a lawn. The whole effect was brown upon brown upon brown. It looked a lot like his mother's place, but in better condition. A sign out front read GREEN BUILDERS. I remembered Marco's solar energy tweet and craned my neck to get a better look at the roof. Sure enough: panels. The street was wide and Valley-flat, and the sky above was Valley-blue: cloudless and washed-out, yellowing at the edges. The heat was Valley-oppressive; it made everything in the distance tremble. No one had their windows open. The freeway hummed, close but unseen. It felt like the sound was coming from inside me, like I was secretly roaring.

I tried not to think about what I expected to happen, what I wanted to happen, what I'd say if and when Marco opened his door and saw me standing on his front porch with a little boy. Maybe for a moment his mind would hiccup and he'd mistake Devin for Seth.

I had no idea what I was doing, all I knew was that I couldn't go home. If I did, I'd just be waiting, jittery and angry, for Seth. I'd stare at Kit's photos until I got eyestrain. And when Seth finally slunk through the door I would force him to explain everything: about his art, about modeling for Kit, about all that he hoarded from me.

But now I was here. Later, in an hour or five, I could tell Seth that I had found his father. I could hand over Marco's address. I could say, "Your dad's a better man than he was when he left us." It would be my one and only card, and I wouldn't play it unless it was the truth. Seth had enough monsters in his life, he didn't need another.

Before I could lose my nerve, I got out of the car. I unbuckled Devin and carried him up the front path.

"This is Marco Green's house," I said.

"Is hot here," Devin said.

"Very hot," I said, and pointed to the doorbell so he could push it.

Even after all these years, I knew Marco, and I knew he wouldn't answer the door right away, even if he were standing a foot away from it. He made everyone wait. Or maybe just me.

Sure enough, I had to ring the bell again before I heard someone call, "Coming!" from the back of the house. It was Marco, had to be. I remembered his Valley voice, that surfer-country drone, and a cold sweat lacquered my neck. This wasn't going to be good, whatever *this* was: reunion, recon mission, confrontation, adventure, site of future regret. I almost turned around with Devin and ran back to my car.

But then he was opening the door and standing in front of us.

"Marco Green," I said, trying for gaiety. Devin waved and I hitched him higher onto my hip. I felt my T-shirt riding up but held back from pulling it down. I would seem self-possessed, even if that was the last thing I was.

Marco was shorter than I remembered, and he'd gained a little weight in the middle. Sort of a Lorax vibe, but not unappealing. He still had a full head of hair, floppy and boyish, and it was threaded through with gray, like his mother's had been. He wore brown Carhartt pants and a T-shirt that read GO GREEN WITH GREEN BUILDERS above a drawing of a house that looked just like the one I was standing in front of, except green. His arms were still a deep tan.

"Lady?" he said in a pinched, wobbly voice, and coughed.

"Hi?" I said.

"I thought I said Monday. Didn't I—"

"I know. I just . . ."

"Lady," he said again. Did he even know my last name? "And who's this?"

Devin waved again, this time more insistent. "Devin!"

Marco smiled. His teeth were tobacco-stained and plaque-ridden, and he was missing one on the bottom. This wasn't a man like Karl, who flossed twice a day and went to the dentist every six months, his appointment card propped on his dresser as a reminder.

"This is my son," I said. "My other son."

I put Devin down but held his hand tightly so that he wouldn't run off, neither into the street behind us nor into this stranger's house. Because wasn't that what Marco was, seventeen years later? I didn't know him anymore.

"I can't go home right now," I said. I knew my voice sounded high-pitched and desperate. Like I was a battered wife or an informant looking for shelter. "I need to talk to you about Seth."

Marco made a face I remembered well: a put-upon squint that accompanied any request he deemed a pain in the ass: that he get the car's oil changed, that he buy a carton of milk on his way home. It was the face he made right before he cut his toenails.

"Is this about child support?" he asked.

"If I say yes, will you slam the door in my face?"

"Why come here unannounced? What's with you?"

"It's not about child support, I swear. Fuck you, Marco."

He raised an eyebrow at me, as if he, unlike me, was a law-abiding citizen who always refrained from cursing in front of children.

"Look," he said, running a hand though his hair, "I wouldn't blame you if it was. It's expensive to raise a kid. And you did it without me. But I'll be honest. I'm broke." He laughed wryly and he seemed, suddenly, like a totally different man. His laughter had changed. It wasn't angry anymore. "I'm underwater with the house, it's not good but it isn't dire either. Once my business is on more stable ground, I'll happily pay you. In two years, I'd say."

"Two years? Seth's already eighteen!"

"Eighteen? No way." He looked proud—that was the only word for it. His son was eighteen!

"We're fine, we don't need money. We live off Sunset Plaza, with my husband. With Dev's daddy."

"My daddy," Devin said. "Daddy likes French fries."

"Hollywood Hills?" Marco said.

"Hollywood Hills—adjacent."

"Shit, I should be the one asking you for child support."

"That's not even remotely funny."

He shook his head. "Sorry, you're right. I have a daughter. Lucy. She's here one weekend a month, otherwise she stays with her mom in Claremont."

I felt like I couldn't breathe. I'd been so stupid not to assume the most obvious outcome: that this man would meet another woman, and have another child, and love her.

"Seth has a sister," I said.

"I know it sounds blockheaded of me, but I never thought of it like that. But yeah. Seth has a sister. Lucy has a brother. Wow."

Marco leaned on the doorjamb and closed his eyes as if he could only organize the facts if he concentrated deeply. So he hadn't spent the last seventeen years wondering about the son he had abandoned. He hadn't given any of it much thought at all.

"I can't believe this," I said, and again I felt my voice turning whiny and urgent.

Marco opened his eyes. "You're upset about Lucy," he said.

"I guess I am."

He actually sneered at me. "You can't just show up here, freaking out. What's the problem? I've got Lucy, you've got Dylan."

"He told you his name was Devin," I said.

Now he was smiling. "Hey, wasn't that what you wanted to name Seth?"

"I can't believe you remember that."

"I remember a lot," he said.

"You hated the name," I said.

"Nowadays, I can't summon much energy for hating things."

"I pretty much hate everyone and everything."

"No shit." He bent down and ruffled Devin's hair so effortlessly it hurt to watch. Then he stood and asked, "You guys want to come in, or what?"

It wasn't until I stepped inside and saw the hardwood floors and the piece of driftwood balanced on the mantel that I realized I'd expected a bachelor's hovel: bad carpeting and a too-large TV, bare walls and that take-out stench, stale and salty. This place was spare and masculine without being depressing. The curtains were nice.

The place smelled like Marco, like I was inside one of his T-shirts, my face deep in his neck.

"You still smoke," I said.

"Only outside. You can smell it?" He looked upset.

"I like it," I said.

Devin pulled away from me and ran toward the back of the house. Without his body weighing me down, without his little grimy hand in my own to remind me of the life I had beyond this visit, I felt afraid. If Marco sensed it, he probably thought I was just being overprotective of my kid.

"Back door's open and there's nothing he can really get into unless he finds my toolbox."

"Okay," I said.

"Lady, I . . ."

"I don't know why I'm here."

"Who cares. You're here. Man, the late '90s—the whole decade, really, until about 2002 . . . it was just . . . fuck . . . hellish for me."

I followed him to the kitchen, which was partially under construction, the counters covered with a tarp, no oven.

"Beer?" he asked, and I nodded. From the fridge he grabbed a six-pack, some IPA with a big budget for graphic design, and cracked open a bottle on the edge of the counter. I'd forgotten he could do this, open a beer anywhere, use his mouth if necessary. Explained the lost tooth.

Our fingers touched as he handed me the bottle.

"What's your husband's name?"

"Karl, like Marx."

"What does that mean?"

"It means it starts with a *K*. He moved out a few weeks ago."

"Karl with a *K* did?"

I thought of what Devin had called S—"S for Snake"—and I nodded. "It's a trial separation."

I took a sip of beer and let it fizz in my mouth.

"Mommy!" Devin beckoned from the yard. Through the window I saw him atop a huge hill of soil, arms akimbo. I felt untethered, like I was a balloon headed for some power lines. "Mommy, come!" Devin yelled.

Outside Marco and I sat on Adirondack chairs under a half-rotting gazebo while Devin played in the dirt. Marco explained that he'd recently yanked out his lawn and hadn't decided what to put in its place, and I asked if he'd gotten the tax credit. It was strange, how we could go in and out of mundane conversation, as if we hadn't been apart for seventeen years, as if he hadn't left me to raise his son a bastard. I finished my first beer and asked for another. I didn't feel angry or restless, or even uncomfortable. Devin could have been our kid, enjoying his afternoon. We had made a boy before, and we could have made this one too. Or instead.

It was as hot as the inside of a mouth, but it felt good to sweat.

"How old's Lucy?" I asked.

"Just turned twelve."

"Does she have her period?" I didn't know why I'd asked, but Marco wasn't bothered.

"Three months ago," he said, and widened his eyes in pretend horror. He loved her. He was a good dad. "She's really something."

"Seth wants to meet you," I said.

"He said that?"

"He . . ."

Of course he didn't know that Seth was nonverbal—and, yet, I'd forgotten. Or let myself forget. I didn't want to lie, but if I kept going I'd have to explain. That he wasn't a normal eighteen-year-old boy. I'd have to describe the diagnosis, the struggles, the silence that unnerved adults and annoyed kids. That the man who had left before his son's first birthday had nevertheless been present for the only word Seth had ever spoken.

"He goes to SMC," I said instead. "He just finished making a short film."

"I'd love to meet him. He sounds great—and I think . . . I think I'm finally ready. But let me tell Lucy first. She's coming in two weeks."

"Sure, okay," I said. "He thinks your name is Mark, by the way. He doesn't know anything about you."

Marco nodded, unfazed. "You were probably right to do that. Hey, you have a picture?"

I thought of Kit's portraits. "You have to see him in person."

We both watched Devin, who was now on his belly like a soldier leaning over a trench. "Lion coming!" he yelled. "And a bear!"

"Cool kid," he said. And then: "I know why you're here."

"Enlighten me."

"Because your husband moved out."

Before I could reply he took out his phone and I thought he was going to show me photos of his daughter until he said, "Let me text the neighbor girl. She's two years older than Lucy and has this big trampoline in her yard. I bet Devin would love it." He was already typing.

"But I don't want to hang out with the neighbor girl," I said.

"I know that. You're staying here." He looked up at me. "Isn't that what you want? For you and me to be alone?"

He leaned over and tapped his bottle against my calf. I thought I could feel the cold glass through my jeans.

"You always loved that I was down for you any time," he said. "I'd hate to disappoint."

THE WAY ASTRID told me her trampoline was "kidney-shaped" suggested she didn't know what a kidney was—bean or organ. She was only fourteen but she already had a tattoo of a butterfly on her wrist and the sickly and easy-to-please look of unloved girls everywhere. I had a bad feeling in my gut as she led Devin out the front door; he loved her immediately, but he was two and a half, he was an idiot. I had agreed to pay Astrid seven bucks to watch him.

"You can just Venmo me if you don't have cash," she said on their way out.

Marco's hand was on my ass as soon as the door shut.

"What are we doing?" I asked.

"This," he said, and kissed me.

I remembered his mouth, the hard and soft of it. I remembered the way he tasted, I wanted to suck it up.

He put his hands on my shoulders and nudged me gently against the wall, and once there, he unbuttoned my jeans. Both of his hands cupped me, so hard I thought he might lift me into the air.

There was no hesitation here. Marco would have me naked in less than a minute if he wanted it that way. It would be rushed and rough, as it had always been. I didn't know if he was like this with all women, but he was like this with me, and that's what mattered, that's what I wanted.

He pulled me into his bedroom and in a few efficient movements he had unzipped his pants and slid on a condom. A magic trick. He hadn't even taken off his clothes.

"Turn over," he said.

"Take off your shirt," I said.

He pulled his T-shirt over the back of his head like some men do. I deliberately looked away. Already I was imagining the sharp teeth of his zipper biting into my skin.

He pushed down my pants and underwear and before he tipped me onto the mattress, I felt his coarse chest hair scratch my back. I missed that. I waited on all fours, hands into fists against his pillows, but he wasn't moving. I was already thinking about the antiseptic slap of the condom, craving it. Karl and I never used them.

"Come on," I said.

He was making me ask for it.

"Please?" I said.

As Marco grabbed my hips, digging his thumbs into my sides, all I could think was that Marco wasn't Karl. Karl was deliberate and thorough in the bedroom, and he brought me to orgasm every time we made love. Having sex with him was like enjoying a multicourse meal that's so elevated and meticulous it makes you rethink common ingredients like bread and butter, the way they can work together to become something miraculous. Karl didn't just touch my body, he considered it, appreciated it.

Marco was done with me in fifteen minutes and he didn't make any noise. When I came it was with a sharp, shocked bark, an orgasm that doesn't so much broaden pleasure as sever it from its ache in one ruthless snap. On the wall in front of us was a calendar with a Saturday and Sunday circled in black. When Lucy would be there, I assumed.

Marco left the room to get rid of the condom; I heard a toilet flushing.

When he returned, I said, "Well."

"I'll call you once I've talked to Lucy."

"If I don't hear from you," I said, "I'll just send Seth here, uninvited."

"Do that, and I'll tell him about our little visit."

I stood up and put on my pants. "What did you spend the money on?" I asked. "The money my mom gave you?"

"I don't remember," he said.

"How could you not remember?"

"It wasn't just one thing," he said.

When I didn't reply he reached into his pocket and pulled out some cash. He handed me two five-dollar bills. "This is for Astrid."

ESTHER

36.

WHEN SETH KISSED ME, MY MIND WENT, *THIS ISN'T HAPPEN-ing, this is happening, this can't happen,* his lips biting mine like my mouth was something to gnaw. I pulled away.

"This can't happen," I said.

He didn't sign or gesture or reach for his phone, he just stood there, breathing hard. He wiped his mouth with the back of his hand. I had no idea what he was thinking, and while that should have confused or frustrated me, it didn't. Not in the least. The tequila was still smoking my bloodstream and I felt like a pistol that had just been fired. If I drank any more, Katherine Mary would have a hold on this situation. Couldn't let that happen now could I?

"You better go," I said, and, *poof,* like that, he was gone.

I didn't see him for a while after that. I began painting *Bless This Mess (Mother No. 2),* trying to make it matter as much as it had before the kiss. I opened and reopened Lady's photo, studying it. Seth looked just like his dad.

One evening, I heard Lady yell, "Why would you let her take those photos?" Lady started to cry—a keening wail. "Dammit, Seth!" she yelled.

I pictured him standing at the top of the stairs, giving nothing away. Lady would be red-faced in the foyer, the skin under her eyes a zombified gray from the weep of her mascara. I was worried they would wake Devin, but the argument stopped as abruptly as it had started, and I was left with my ear cocked like a dog's, longing for

more. It had to be Kit, she must've photographed him. I didn't dare
ask Lady about it and I didn't have the chance to ask Seth, because he
didn't give me one; he was never around. Three nights, four nights,
no visit.

On the fifth night, I finished the painting. It had come out garish
and flat, goofier than I'd intended. I could have sold it on a street corner, next to some cowhide rugs.

It was past midnight, and I was just signing the back when the Cottage doorknob twitched.

"Who's there?"

There was no answer. My insides went sharp and hot as a blade.
Seth. I placed the painting back on the easel. Part of me—no shit, the
Esther Shapiro part—knew I couldn't let him in. He was practically a
child. He was Lady's son. He didn't speak—but why did that matter?

I unlocked the door.

There he was, already inside the Cottage: his hair mussed, his feet
bare, a shy smile. I thought he might come at me with the abandon of
a toddler before a trough of ice cream, taking my tits into his hands,
nudging at my neck, but he didn't, he was waiting for me to do something.

"Please be careful of the easel," I said, and I felt less like Katherine
Mary and more like Everett Forever.

Now he was peering at the painting.

"It's one of the mothers," I said, standing close behind him. His
neck was tan and I had to hold myself back from tucking the tag back
into his shirt.

He pointed at the woman's frizzy hair, which looked even sillier
than it had in the photo, and turned to raise an eyebrow at me.

"I sort of overdid the curls. They were just really fun to paint."

He held out his phone. Something was already typed there, ready
for me to read.

Can I see the pic?

"I already deleted it. Oh—you mean the one your mom sent."

So this was why he was here, he didn't want me at all.

He held my phone close to his face, totally rapt, his eyes darting
back and forth across the screen, like he was straining to memorize

every detail. I let him look for only a minute or two before I pried it from his hands.

"Time's up," I said. "I have to work."

He raised his eyebrow again.

"I'm serious," I said. "I make art."

He made a face like, *Go on*. And also: *Prove it*. That he could express both without saying a word—that's what got me. I thought of the girl who had been in here with him, before me, the one Lady thought was too weird for her son. If the girl really didn't like to be touched, then how was Seth able to cross that line? He must have made her skin hurt, made her nerves flinch and rattle. If he liked her, he wouldn't like me.

Enough, I thought, stop thinking about that. It was Katherine Mary, hypothesizing, plotting.

But I could make him want me, for what I would let him do.

I offered him some tequila. He nodded and I poured us both drinks, imagining him watching me from behind as I dropped two ice cubes into each glass, a squeeze of lime that I let spill into the paper cut on my index finger. When we clinked glasses it was the only sound and I liked that. I thought of Kit Daniels. The politics of the body. But Seth probably hadn't read any academic articles about his aunt.

I started talking. First about how much I liked drawing and painting, and how I was really only starting to own up to that. And then, facing him on my bed, both of us with crossed legs, I told him about Everett. How if you took away his camera and pencils, the stupid Lucite boxes, the tiny spy cameras, the modes of blankity-blank discourse, the wound-up buzz he claimed to feel after a long day at the studio, he'd be a zero. A cipher.

"Art's replaced everything in his life," I said. "Even pain."

I was drunk enough that I didn't really need Seth to be listening. But he was. He laughed when I described Everett's senior show.

"Wait until I tell you what I've been working on," I said.

I described the project to Seth, how I was acting like my mom, drinking like her, and how that was influencing my art. I hadn't told anyone but Everett about Katherine Mary and her problems, and here was Seth, looking startled. He signed something quickly.

"You know I didn't follow that," I said.

On his phone he typed: Who R U?

"What do you mean? You mean, who am I, right now, with you?" He waited.

"I'm not sure," I said.

It was so honest, I knew it was Katherine Mary talking.

"I'm a liar," I said. "My mom isn't. I guess it's the one thing I admire about her. She doesn't try to be anyone else. Even when she drinks, it isn't to numb herself or escape from reality, it's to find a better one that's been there all along." I blushed. "Or that's what I've figured out since starting this project."

I kept talking because he let me, he couldn't stop me with his own words. It felt wrong and also I didn't care.

"Kiss me," I finally said.

This time, he did it without teeth, not even tongue. Just his lips, which were enough. I kissed him back. I closed my eyes and let myself fall into whatever this was. I felt him pulling off my shirt, the collar tickling my mouth, then my nose. When Seth laid his hands on either side of my bare shoulders his fingertips were warm and rough and I startled before going still. It was like he was trying to steady me. Or heal me. He kissed me again, on the neck, and then lower. With a single, gentle push, he shoved me so I was lying on my back.

When I opened my eyes we were both naked, and his body was nicer than I expected, as long as a felled tree trunk I could climb onto. How was he only eighteen? He was paying close attention to my body, touching it, looking for signs that what he was doing was working. I told him it was. Surely he'd never heard this from that other girl, and I could tell he wanted to please me. Or not me, but whoever I was now, this hybrid creature.

Afterward, we lay next to each other on our backs, the light bright and ugly. The panic was only starting to rise in me.

"I better pee or I'll get a UTI," I said.

He didn't even pat my thigh like, *Okay, baby.*

He had already left by the time I returned from the bathroom. He'd left evidence, though: At the foot of the bed lay the dirty condom, tied up like a deflated water balloon.

You could leave a used condom with a drunk—was that the argument? The drunk wouldn't mind. Made sense. That was the thing about drinking that I was beginning to understand: the list of things I didn't mind was getting longer and longer.

37.

Now, every time Seth visited, he took stock of my drinking as soon as he arrived. He was checking to see how far S had slipped into Katherine Mary before we kissed, before he let me undress him. The drunker I was, the more delighted he seemed.

Afterward, he'd ask to see the photo. I would have offered to forward it to him, but I was afraid he wouldn't come back.

One night, a week into our fucked-up affair, Seth didn't seem interested in making out. Instead he picked up my pencil and sketchpad and began writing on a blank page.

"Hey! What are you doing?"

I want to be in yr photo. I can be my dad.

"Thank you," I said, "but . . . I've decided to paint both of them, and photograph only myself." He nodded quickly, but I could tell he was disappointed. "It's to emphasize the lack, the loss, like I was telling you about." He didn't seem to be listening. "It's just my instinct," I said. "Besides, I just got another photo, of a mother and her teenage friends. I can't find models every time, you know?"

Seth was biting the edge of my sketchpad and I told him to knock it off.

"Why would you want to be in the photo? Is this another way to piss off your mom?"

He stared at me. Again, I marveled at how much he could express without words. When he came over I liked to keep the lights on and my eyes open, because he told me so much with his eyes. It embarrassed me how much I liked it, how I missed it as soon as he was gone.

"I know about Kit's photos," I said. "I heard the fight."

He was flipping through the sketchpad and wouldn't look up.

"Seth," I said, louder.

He looked up like, *What?*

Katherine Mary was revving up within me—she was always there now, especially around Seth. I would say whatever I wanted.

"Are you sleeping with me to get back at your mom?" I asked.

He looked disgusted.

"It must be exhausting," I said, my voice growing fangs, "to express all your feelings with your body."

He wasn't sure how to react, and I watched him decide not to react at all.

"Is this how it was for your mom when she was yelling at you the other night?" Here it was, the mean truth. "Do you just decide to give nothing?"

At that last word—*nothing*—he let out a little strangled squeak and I gasped. I couldn't help it. "You can make noise!" I knew it was the wrong response. "Sorry. I just didn't know you could."

He held out a fist and wrapped his other hand around it.

"Stop drop dead!" I said, louder than I intended.

He was writing something else in my sketchpad.

I make sounds but not wrds I cant

"Got it," I said. "I totally understand."

It doesnt mean Im a freak dont treat me like im retarded

"I would never," I said, but if he saw my phone's search history ("Why would someone not speak?"; "Mutism"; "Mutes + Sex") he wouldn't want to have anything to do with me.

I cant talk. The end.

"I said I got it."

Im not a metaphor

"I wish someone would mistake me for a metaphor."

He looked like what I'd said had hurt him, that I would never understand.

Im not your little toy either

So he'd caught on to me—to Katherine Mary. What we liked.

"What do you want from me?" I asked.

He dropped the sketchpad and I hoped he would kiss me so I could make a bad joke about body language and we'd never have another problem again. Instead he got his phone and typed. It was taking longer than usual. He tapped something and a robotic voice spoke:

"What do you want from ME?"

"Ugh, don't use that, it's creepy. You're not a robot."

I waited for him to type more. But he didn't because he knew what he was doing.

38.

Seth: Can I come by to see the pic again?
Me: Sorry I deleted it.
Seth: You could of forwarded it to me
Me: That's not how the project works.
Me: You there?
Me: You can come look at the portrait if you want.

39.

SETH STARED AT THE PAINTING IN THE SAME WAY HE'D STARED at the photo, devoted and searching, like it might reveal the secret to life if he would only pay it the proper attention. At least to this one person, my painting was magnetic.

We hadn't discussed what had happened the last time he'd come over, but he'd already touched my waist, held my wrist for a beat too long. He didn't want to end things either.

I was proud of the portrait. I liked how I'd captured the wall behind them, its rough texture. And the whiteness of the sky, matte and blunt. Lady's hair and the thin cliff of her collarbone. The fabric of the shirt and the lettering of the words across her chest. That bored look in Seth's dad's eyes—MARCO was the name on his shirt name tag. I'd gotten the red thread of the cursive words just right.

"Was your dad's name really Marco?" I asked. "Or is that name tag meant ironically?"

Seth looked up suddenly like there was someone yanking his neck with a string.

"Don't tell me you don't know your dad's name," I said.

Seth tossed the painting onto the bed.

"Hey, be careful with that!"

He was already picking up a pencil and my sketchpad.

His name = Mark Green

"So you do know it," I said.

Seth wrote something else. He was practically vibrating.

Marco or Mark?????

"I'm not sure what his real name is, but that's definitely what his shirt said."

But he wasn't listening, he was already slipping on his flip-flops.

"So his name is Marco," I said.

He put his phone in his back pocket.

"Now that you've solved the mystery, that's it? You're going? I get it. You were just sleeping with me to get to the photo. I told you everything about me, about my mom, and now you're over it."

He stopped at the door, preoccupied by whatever he'd figured out about his father. But there was something else showing on his face. I'd hurt his feelings.

"I mean," I said. "I like when you come visit me."

Another guy would have smiled and crossed the room to kiss me before leaving, even though I'd be out of his mind right away. At least I'd feel wanted. But Seth wasn't another guy.

40.

Seth: Youre the only reason I havent moved to Kits

Me: If that's true kiss me goodbye next time.

41.

THE SITUATION—THE AFFAIR?—WITH SETH SHOULD HAVE had me freaking out, queasy with the fear of getting caught, of at the very least him letting the cat out of the bag about my art project. His age still had the word "teen" in it, and he was still my employer's son. If Lady found out, she would kill me, and if I survived that, she would probably take me to court, claiming I'd defiled her disabled son. My dad's disappointment and shame would be matched only by my mom's pride and fucked-up satisfaction that I was as fucked up as she was. Seth knew more about me than anyone else. Everett had been the last person to hear so much about Katherine Mary, and look how that had turned out.

But I wasn't losing my shit, and that was because of the art. I couldn't remember the last time I felt this way.

Where to begin? There was the Katherine Mary project part of it, dressing like her, wearing my hair like she did when she was my age, not bothering to cover up the bags under my eyes or the pimples on my chin. There was the liquor, that longing to loosen all the screws in my body with just one drink. I was reaching across time to give her a high five. In those moments, I lost myself, forever and hallelujah, and it was like I was stepping back into the womb, tunneling farther away from that even, to before my mom had anyone but herself to fail. When I painted, she was painting too—she had never done it before, and I was showing her the way, and we were painting together. And when I let Seth pull off my clothes and get on top of me, it wasn't me, it wasn't my body he was touching. It wasn't Katherine Mary's either. It was some new person. Seth was touching someone new, someone I'd made.

And in the mornings, hungover, when I put toothpaste on my finger to brush my teeth, Katherine Mary–style, I felt the despair. She used to call it the Shadow, and now it followed me too. It was why I hugged Devin so tightly. And I guess why my mom had always held me to her chest whenever I'd been at my dad's place for the week. Unlike me, Katherine Mary didn't have art to save her from the Shadow.

Well, she did now.

I was staging the photograph of *Bless This Mess (Mother No. 2)* on the far wall of the Cottage, where Karl had installed a cheap butcher-block counter and sink. I decided I would shoot it digitally, and add an external flash to play up the glare in my painting; I was bound to mimic that light and I was into it.

I wasn't sure where I'd shoot Lady's photo, *Lovers (Mother No. 3)*, but I knew I wanted to use film. My dad's prehistoric Canon, which he'd given me in high school, would finally get some use again. I'd already ordered the shirt online, and was considering dyeing my hair red too. A wig would look silly, and unlike the first photo, this one felt sad and wistful and I had to honor that. As long as I got the right sky, I'd get away with everything else. The thought of not getting the overcast sky made me want to cry. Everett only ever cried over his work.

As soon as I was done with these two photos, I'd begin painting the new mother. It showed a teenage girl in a 1970s subdivision with her three friends. The mother looked fourteen or fifteen, and she had on an Oxford shirt that almost but not quite covered her womanly body. She was the only one looking at the camera. She had braces, and bobby pins holding back her shoulder-length hair. She looked like she was going to kick my ass. It was in black and white.

All of this took time: the painting, the staging, the shopping, the drinking, the recording. I'd hardly been sleeping. I guess that was also keeping me from thinking about what would happen if Seth and I got caught. I was too tired to worry about consequences.

The morning I overslept for work, I'd spent the night photographing *Bless This Mess (Mother No. 2)*.

Seth hadn't shown up at my door since he'd found out his dad's real name; who knows what he was doing with that precious information. I'd had three nights without him barging into the Cottage and I was starting to miss him. His Snapchat had helped, but it wasn't a replacement for actual contact. At the same time, my project was becoming something, I was inside of it, and I needed the time to work. That made me feel not like Katherine Mary but like Everett. Like a man.

Lady was knocking on my door when I came to. I sat up in bed like a vampire rising from the crypt. "Coming!" I croaked.

The curly-hair wig hung on the doorknob, its synthetic strands slippery and greasy, and it took me a second to get a good enough grip to open the door.

"Sorry, sorry," I said, opening the door just a crack. Even though the props from the photo weren't suspicious, I didn't want Lady to come inside and smell the musk of her son.

I expected her to have Devin, but she was alone.

"You okay?" she asked.

"I forgot to set my alarm," I said. "Give me fifteen minutes?"

"Come up to my room when you're ready. I have something to show you."

As I washed my face and dressed, my stomach quaked with nerves and last night's drinks. Lady hadn't brought Devin with her to check up on me, and now she wanted me to come up to her bedroom. What was she going to show me? I imagined footage of my trysts with Seth—our most recent. I was nasty, that was what Lady wanted to talk to me about.

That or Seth had told her everything about my project.

She's pretending to be someone else.

"Just face her already," Katherine Mary would say.

The Manse was quiet, which could only mean that Devin was either asleep or he wasn't home. I walked upstairs and knocked softly on Lady's bedroom door.

"Come in." Her voice sounded far away and I imagined her on the other end of her master suite, as big and cold as an ice-skating rink.

She was sitting on the bed, smiling, but she looked, as she always did lately, a little disheveled. It seemed like the news of Kit's photos, and Seth's betrayal, had broken her. A couple of times she had apologized to me—and for nothing at all.

"I'm sorry again," I said. "I haven't overslept since, like, high school."

"It's really fine."

"Where's Dev?"

"I got Seth to take him out to breakfast."

"So you guys are talking again?"

"Barely." She patted the bed next to her and I noticed she had an iPad on her lap.

"Sit," she said.

"I didn't know you had an iPad." I kicked off my shoes and climbed on the other side of the bed. The mattress groaned a little.

"It's Seth's," she said.

"Seth's?" I tried to keep my voice even.

"I got it for him when @sethconscious passed a hundred followers. Now he's got thousands. Can you believe that?" She sighed. "Of course, he asked me not to read his Twitter anymore." She laughed and tugged at a hole in her sock.

"What's funny?" I asked.

"Nothing," she replied.

I was too scared to say anything. I had no idea what was on the iPad, but all I could imagine was evidence. Exhibit A: our very first texts, before we got smart and stopped sending those. Exhibit B—holy shit, what?

"I stole this from him," she said.

"Why?"

"It's got his video on it."

"His video?" I thought of Everett wanting to film me running back to his bed stark naked.

"Sorry, I mean his . . . film," Lady said. "The one he made for school? Turns out, Karl and Kit have seen it. But I haven't. Have you?"

"No." I was relieved to be able to answer truthfully even though another part of me felt bad. All this time I'd been yakking away to Seth about my work without a clue about his.

"I found it on here. It's only, like, a minute and a half long."

"You watched it?"

She shook her head. "Not yet. We're going to watch it—you and me."

"We are? Why do I have to?"

"You don't want to?"

"It's not that—it's just, he didn't choose to share it with us."

"Please, S," she said. "I can't watch it alone."

She was already tapping the screen, and then it was playing. I leaned forward until my head touched Lady's. She smelled like jasmine.

It was a film, not a video, and it was blurry for the first few seconds. When the image came into focus, the surface was still grainy the way film is, with what looked like strands of black hair popping onto the screen and disappearing just as fast. Seth had shot it in color, but the colors were drained and milky. There was Seth, standing outside in a crowd of college students who were probably headed to class or the student union. He stood still, but they moved all around him, texting, laughing, sucking down the campus coffee–kiosk equivalent of a Frappuccino. The film was silent.

"That's SMC," Lady murmured.

"Seth goes there, right?" I said, and she nodded.

"This is a Super-8 film," I said after a moment. The image pulsed and slowed, then sped up, old-timey-like.

"Cool," Lady said.

"Yeah." I didn't tell her that every asshole film guy gets into Super-8 before switching to digital.

The camera zoomed to Seth's face and he began moving his mouth.

"Oh my God," Lady said.

"He's messing with you," I said.

She looked away from the screen. "With *me*?"

"You, as in the viewer," I said.

"How do you know?" she said. "You lied, you have seen this!"

"I haven't, I swear." I nodded at the screen. "Look at his mouth."

I was right, it opened and closed like a ventriloquist's, mouthing the words. He was a dead fish. "He doesn't know how to use his tongue," Lady said.

Sound cut in suddenly. A man's voice was saying, "Hello! I'm Seth!" Then, a woman's voice: "Hey! I'm Seth, wanna hang out?" Another man, this one with a Midwestern accent: "Can you believe that class? Bor-ing!"

The chatter continued, the voices changing. Seth kept flapping his mouth. The people moved around him, occasionally glancing at the camera and whoever was filming.

The film cut out midsentence. The end.

"Super-8 can be tricky," I said. "It's hard to tell when the film runs out."

Lady closed the iPad. "How do you know that?"

"Art history," I reminded her. "Also, my ex, Everett? He was an artist, remember? He sometimes shot film."

"It's tragic how much we pick up from the men we sleep with."

I blushed.

"What did you think of it?" I asked.

"Why didn't he show it to me?"

"No idea. Seems harmless. Pretty typical freshman-year art."

"Ouch," she said.

"Sorry."

"No, it's good to be brought back to reality, to be reminded that my kid is mediocre, just another dickhead college kid."

"That's not what I meant—"

"Don't look so upset. I'm kidding. Sort of."

"What you said—that his tongue doesn't work—"

"That's not totally true. He can eat, so obviously it functions, but even people with selective mutism can have trouble with some sounds. And unlike those people, Seth doesn't talk to anyone. Ever. Or so I assume, right?" She paused. "How did you know he was messing with the viewer?"

I couldn't tell her Seth had pulled that same trick on me. "Because Seth's always goofing off. He's making a movie about his disability because he knows the teacher will give him an A for it. Art teachers eat that shit up. But he can't help but make it a little tricky."

"You think he did it for the teacher? You don't think he *wanted* to make a movie about himself?"

"That wasn't about himself, Lady. That was about everyone else. The assumptions they put on him."

She thought about this for a moment. "His Twitter is never about how he can't talk."

"See? It's not interesting to him."

"Kit thinks the video shows how badly he wants to speak."

"As my professors used to say, that's a valid interpretation. The film's not juvenile then, because you can read it a couple of ways."

She smirked. "You're different when you talk about art, you know that, right?"

She'd caught me as Esther Shapiro and I was surprised by the pride I felt.

"How come Kit's photos bother you so much?" I asked.

The question itself was too much, it bugged her. She lay back on the pillows behind her, and a second later sat up again, all squirmy.

"In general, you mean?" she asked. "Or the ones of Seth?"

"I guess both." Now it was my turn to lean back on the pillows. I slid onto my side and propped my head on my elbows. We looked like actresses in an ad for feminine itching.

"Kit treats the people she photographs as objects, as her property."

"And Seth belongs to you," I said.

She didn't deny it. "At the time, I didn't know how it would feel to be in a famous artist's photo. I don't want Seth to experience that. It was traumatic to be in Kit's work. It wasn't me in that photograph."

"You're right, it wasn't. It was a photo of you," I said.

"You get it."

"But isn't that also what makes portraiture so powerful? You can't help but wonder what they didn't capture." I sat up. "Would you feel differently if you had been painted instead of photographed?"

She raised her eyebrows like this was a stupid question. "You do landscapes," she said. "Sunsets don't talk back. And they're not sexy."

"I don't understand."

"The pictures of Seth—he looks . . ."

"Are they sexual?" I asked. "Holy shit!"

"No, no, but someone might see them that way."

"And someone might also be turned on by a sunset. That's not my problem."

"It's never the artist's problem," she said. "Unless you're a writer. Not that I'm that either. Fuck. I need to write my horrible book." She grabbed the iPad. "I better wipe my fingerprints off this before I return it."

I followed her down the hall toward Seth's room. I felt panicked in that way you do when you're having fun but you know it's coming to an end. It had been days since I'd had a conversation with someone.

"So you're going off to write today?" I said.

"Yep." She didn't turn around.

I was thinking how to ask my next question. Katherine Mary was right at the edge of me like tears smarting my eyes.

"Did Seth kiss that girl, you think? The one whose mom freaked out?"

She turned around.

"Excuse me?"

"Sorry. I doubt you want to think about your son with a girl, but I guess I'm just wondering about the tongue thing again."

She didn't answer, just wrinkled her nose and pushed open Seth's door. I followed. The smell of his body was like a hand across my nose and mouth.

"I never thought about it," Lady finally said. "Seth's kissing, I mean."

"Bullshit."

"His dad wasn't big on kissing."

"What's his dad's name?" I asked.

"Mark. Why?"

I tried not to betray anything. "No reason. Mark didn't show affection?" I asked.

"Oh, who cares. When Seth was Devin's age—when he was twice Dev's age, three times—Seth was a marathon snuggler." She smiled. "It's one reason why he wasn't diagnosed with anything beyond the mutism. He can show affection to the people he loves."

"He has to love them?"

She shrugged me off. "He can communicate."

"That's great," I said blandly.

Lady looked triumphant. "Gestures are language too," she said.

"I know."

"Seth is basically normal."

"So what if he isn't?" I asked.

"He is."

I waited.

"Thanks for watching that film with me," she said finally. "I've been . . . fucked up."

"I can tell." When she didn't answer I said, "Anyway, thanks for chatting. I miss having conversations."

Lady raised an eyebrow and, for a second, it seemed she understood what I'd been up to. I held my breath, waiting for what she'd say next.

She stepped toward me like she might hit me, but then her arms were around my back, and we were hugging. I put my head on her shoulder like I did with my mom.

"I know," she said.

"You do?"

She rubbed my back and squeezed tighter. "Toddlers aren't the best conversationalists, are they?"

42.

SINCE SUNDOWN I'D BEEN CHASING MY BEER WITH WHISKEY, using a tiny disposable Solo shot glass for the occasion. That's what my mom did when she had a problem she couldn't solve. "A beer chaser is a young man's drink," she told me once, as if this made any sense at all. The beer made me feel bloated but carefree and the whiskey pulled me in the opposite direction where all I could think about was Seth and what Lady would do if she found out. I'd never see her again.

I wanted to cry. Brown liquor was dangerous.

I was sketching *Girl Gang (Mother No. 4)*, barely caring. On my next morning off I planned to go to the beach to stage Lady's photo. That's what mattered to me. I needed a white sky and it wasn't the right time of year for it.

"Fuck," I said to no one.

It was past midnight and there'd been no word from Seth. What if he never came back? I took a gulp of beer and belched, and startled, Peter Rabbit scurried across his pen. Someone knocked at the door.

"Come in," I said.

Once Seth was inside the Cottage he checked to see how much was left in the bottle. Then he leaned forward to smell my breath, which was no doubt hoppy with an undercurrent of gasoline.

"Very drunk," I said.

Even now, I couldn't help but expect a reply—I was just as bad as the dumbasses he had made that film for.

"I wish I would stop waiting for you to answer," I said. "It makes me hate myself." I sighed. "But what can I do? I'm a stupid speaking person. Is there any solution to self-hatred?"

He frowned. He touched his fingers to his forehead and then pushed them away and upward.

"What's that mean?"

He did it again, and then gestured for me to copy him.

"Are you teaching me how to say 'love yourself'?"

He took out his phone.

It means I dont know

"That's useful," I said.

He smiled so guilelessly that I almost said how much I'd missed him.

I remembered what Lady had said about Kit's photos, how someone would think they were sexy. But Seth was so skinny and hairy, with that big beak nose, and the black fuzz between his eyebrows. He was strange-looking. No one—not even Kit—would be able to capture his you-had-to-be-there appeal. That's what I liked about him. He wasn't a photograph.

I'm not a metaphor.

My head was fizzy from the beer, my limbs floppy from the whiskey, and already I could see what would come next, my hair in my face and there were his lips and hip bones like half-pipes and everything would be warm and slippery and here was an abandon I had always been too afraid to meet. Katherine Mary must've felt this many times; some dangers are worth it.

Except Seth didn't pull me onto the bed. Instead he showed me his phone. Always his phone. There were search results for Marco Green. Oh.

"Did you find him?" I asked. "There's a lot here."

He shook his head, and I wasn't sure if that meant that he hadn't found his dad, or that he disagreed with me.

"You think he's this soccer player? Or maybe this insurance salesman in Topeka."

Seth took the phone back. He was scrolling and flipping to the next page. Scrolling again. He tapped the screen a few times and turned it to me, his face triumphant.

It was a Twitter profile.

"You think this is him?" I asked.

The photo was too small for me to tell either way, and Seth wouldn't let me hold the phone. He pulled away to tap on @MarcoGreen71's followers. He was practically panting like a dog. *What is it, Lassie?,* I thought—or no, that was a Katherine Mary joke, stupid and mean.

When he turned the screen back to me, I saw what he was so excited about.

@muffinbuffin41, 6 followers.

"Is that your mom's Twitter?" I asked.

I took the phone and read the most recent tweets.

Aren't all mothers loose women? (Unless you had a c-section.)

I laughed.

I miss my baby when he's asleep or with The Sitter.

I read that one aloud. "Wow, she gave me a title. 'The Sitter.' You think that one's about Devin or you?"

Seth rolled his eyes.

I'm afraid I'm a bad mother.

Oh, poor Lady.

Seth took the phone back, clearly impatient. He tapped back to Marco Green and handed it to me.

"He owns his own business," I said. "That's cool."

I closed the page and gave him the phone. "Are you going to contact him?"

He signed, *I don't know.*

"What are you waiting for?"

Seth didn't respond.

"You're afraid," I said.

He still didn't respond.

"You want your mom to be the one to tell you about him?" I waited. "Seth? Hello? You could write something down. Or fuck, just sign, I don't even care if I can't understand."

I followed him outside, but I didn't call out as he crossed the yard and slipped into the darkness of the Manse, leaving me alone to be eaten by coyotes and perfumed by skunks. The winds had picked up in that last few minutes and a wood scrap was shipwrecked in the pool, probably blown in from a random construction site.

"That's me, lost and floating away," I said, or Katherine Mary did. The Hills howled and a garage or back door or car door rumbled like a drum, like my hangover come morning.

As I stepped back into the Cottage, my phone rang. My dad. I wondered if something had happened; he never called after ten thirty, which was when he and Maria put their phones in their dove-gray Heath bowl and didn't touch them again until the next morning. He called it "Steve and Maria, Unplugged."

I picked up. "What's wrong?"

"Esther, honey? Did I wake you?" I knew right away that he was fine.

"Are you trying to catch me unawares?" I asked. "You knew I'd pick up at this hour."

"What? Not at all. Maria and I were just leaving a party, one of her colleagues is moving to another firm. I'm so tired, but the fresh air feels great and I just wanted to hear your voice. It's been—what?—at least two weeks since we've spoken."

It had been longer and both of us knew it.

"That's got to be a personal record for us," he said.

"You're lucky I'm not asleep."

"Doesn't sound like it. In fact, you sound wired. And kind of mad. Maybe? What's wrong?"

"Nothing. What happened to Steve and Maria, Unplugged?"

He chuckled and I waited as he repeated what I'd said to Maria, who also laughed.

"I just love Oakland," he was saying to me now. "So vibrant, you

know what I mean? There are a lot of young people living here. First
Fridays and all that!"

"I'm not moving back up there."

"Speaking of art," he said. "You up to any of that, Waterbug?"

"Whatever Mom told you, it's not true."

"I haven't spoken to Kathy in ages. Why?"

"I—"

"Hang on," he said. A moment later he returned, "Maria says she
hopes you're painting again."

"That's just because she hated my Tevas project."

"I will neither confirm nor deny such rumors."

We both laughed.

"I'm painting a little, yeah," I said.

"You are?" I could tell by his voice that my answer had genuinely
surprised him. "I still love the one you did of the shore at Stinson,"
he said. "It's hanging in the breakfast nook now. I moved it from the
hallway."

"I'm not doing landscapes," I said. Uh-oh, this was the alcohol talking. The urge to confess. "I'm trying portraits," I said. "Of people."

"Wow. That's terrific." I heard him relay this news to Maria, but I
couldn't make out her response. "If you ever need someone to model,"
he said, "I'd love to sit for you. Come up one weekend just for that.
You know how good I am at not fidgeting."

"Thanks, Dad, but I'm painting only mothers."

Silence.

"Hello?"

"Sorry. I'm here," he said. "I suppose I should be thrilled that
you're not painting fathers. Or talking about me in therapy."

"Well, I wouldn't go that far."

He didn't laugh.

"Don't tell me you're jealous," I said. "Of my subject matter? Seriously? Dad."

I could hear Maria saying something—the words weren't clear but
her concern was. I pictured her putting her hand on my dad's arm and
saying, "Steven? Steven?"

"I was always there for you," he said.

"And you aren't anymore?" I asked.

"Gotta go, Waterbug. Love you."

"Steven Shapiro," I said sternly.

If he were Katherine Mary Fowler, he would have called me a cunt rag and hung up. Instead he sighed and said, "Stop disappearing, okay?"

"I'm not disappearing," I said.

"We haven't talked in weeks. And you return every fourth or so text. Did you get my email, with the video of me and Maria taking that trapeze lesson? You didn't write back."

"I got it," I said. "Looks like it was a lot of fun."

"I can tell you've been drinking tonight."

"How?"

"Because I was once married to your mother."

"I have to go," I said.

Now it was his turn to say my name but I wasn't as mature as he was, and not nearly as needy, and I hung up.

43.

THE NEXT MORNING LADY TOLD ME SETH HAD GONE TO KIT'S for a few days. We were in the upstairs bathroom of all places, standing over Devin as he tried to drop a deuce in the toilet.

"You need to eat more vegetables, Dev," I said. "It'll help."

"So you have no comment about Seth?" Lady asked me.

"What kind of comment would I have? He misses Karl. Don't torture yourself."

"It's still stuck!" Devin yelled and I kneeled down and placed my hands on his thighs.

"You can do this, Dev," I said. "Just push."

"Jesus, I'm having flashbacks to his birth," Lady said.

Devin let out a whimper.

"Push!" I said.

He did as he was told, and as his eyes went glassy, Lady and I cheered.

Finished, Devin climbed off the toilet and touched the floor like a stripper. His butt was so flat it turned into two sharp points when he bent over. I waited, in case Lady wanted the honors, but she didn't move. Not that I blamed her; I was getting paid to wipe.

"Why I need vegetables?" Devin asked.

"For the roughage," Lady said.

"What's roughage?" he asked.

"It's . . ." Lady began, "um . . . I have no idea." She knew this wouldn't satisfy him, so she added, "Now, flush!"

Lady wasn't writing today. She wanted to spend the day with Devin, but not alone. "Let's do something together, the three of us," she'd said over breakfast.

We decided to swim, and before Lady had told me that Seth was already gone, I'd pictured him finding the three of us in the pool, his hair matted and knotted from sleep, those same dumb basketball shorts. I'd be in my bathing suit, preferably lying across the blue raft like a French girl in a French movie about sex and secrets. Now he wouldn't see me at all. I wondered, if I had let Seth be in my photo, if I'd let him play Marco to my Lady, would he have not gone to Kit's? The hypothetical was too dangerous to ponder and so I shooed it from my brain.

Instead I found myself watching Lady closely. The tilt of her head, the side smile, which my dad would call a smirk and my mom would call the Bitch Itch. I kept thinking about the Lady in front of me versus the Lady in the photo I'd painted. Wealth had made obvious improvements: her hair had more body and her highlights were perfect. Her clothes draped just-so (her swimsuit, for starters? Designed for an heiress, built for a surfing superhero). She was exfoliated in the way that only rich people are, and her teeth were whitened though not capped (she was still down-to-earth). She looked cared-for.

But Karl and his dough couldn't smooth her edges. A part of her had shut down or fallen away since that photo was taken. She had once been younger and more hopeful. The hope wasn't here now and it wasn't in *Woman No. 17* either. Time didn't just take that away, so who did?

The next day I would stage my photo and I would bring the old Lady back to life.

Lady and I took turns catching Devin, who liked to jump off the pool steps ad nauseam. Before we got into the water, Lady had suggested I see her aesthetician for a wax.

"The razor burn, S," she began, and I swam into the water where my bikini line couldn't be critiqued.

"Why do you care?" I asked. It's what my mom would say, and had said, to me.

"Just trying to help," Lady replied, and dipped her head back to soak her hair. When she stood up straight, it took her a moment to focus on Devin and me, as if she'd momentarily forgotten that she wasn't alone. She looked like she was remembering something bad or stupid. Could've been my imagination, but she seemed more troubled than usual.

"Stop thinking about Kit," I said.

"What? Oh—if only I was thinking about that."

"I'm jumping again!" Devin cried from the edge and I moved closer to catch him. We were both saying goofy things and cheering each time he landed with a splash. He smiled so wide he gulped water with every jump.

We stayed in the water until our skin turned elderly. My eyes were burning from the chlorine and my sunscreen had for sure melted off long ago. But Devin wasn't even close to being over it, and neither was Lady; she was laughing at all the ridiculous shark games her son came up with, and she kept telling him "Kick, kick, kick!" with the pep of a swim instructor. The happiness, the innocence, was contagious. I wanted to draw it. I wanted to have it. I backstroked to Devin and told him to swim to me. Lady nodded, and pushed him into the open water. There were about four feet between us.

"Kick, kick, kick!" she cried, and Devin kicked.

"Use your arms!" I called. "Kick and paddle!"

Devin waved his arms and kept kicking.

"Look at you go!" Lady yelled.

He was moving toward me.

"Oh my God," Lady said, "he's Michael Phelps."

"You're swimming!" I cried.

"He's swimming!" Lady cried.

She was grinning at me, and I realized I must have been making the same big happy face.

I grabbed Devin and Lady came bobbing over, clapping her hands.

"I swimmed!" Devin yelled. "I swimmed!" He pushed off me to do it again.

The two of us watched him paddle toward the edge of the pool.

"He's swimming," Lady said. "I can't believe it. Not even three and he's really swimming."

"That was the best," I said, and we high-fived.

After some enforced string-cheese eating at the pool steps, Devin swam by himself in the shallow end while Lady and I sat at the edge, dipping into the water whenever we got hot. She confessed that Seth had learned to swim only a couple of years ago, when they moved into this house; I told her about the outdoor pool in Berkeley that my dad preferred, icy cold even on summer mornings; we laughed at Devin trying to swim and pick his nose at the same time. At noon Lady ordered Brazilian food for lunch, which we ate on the chaise lounges under the umbrella; I lured Devin out of the water with French fries and apple juice.

"How are the landscapes?" Lady asked me once we were all settled into our food.

"Uh . . . they're okay . . . I guess. It's just a hobby."

"It's still important to you."

"I want to do one with an overcast sky. Which is hard, considering . . ." I gestured at the blue sky above us.

"So you don't paint what you see?"

"Not necessarily. Sometimes it's in my head. What I remember." I didn't dare look at her. "Or the past."

"I hope you'll show me one someday," she said.

I didn't answer, and we both turned to watch Devin, who had returned to the pool.

"This has been so fun," Lady said.

"It has."

At five, we'd been inside for a while, tired and pink from the sun. We were watching a marathon of *Yo Gabba Gabba!* and Devin was nodding off between us. He'd swum instead of napped.

"Is it too early to put him down?" Lady asked.

I shrugged. "You're the mom. I guess he might get up at five a.m. tomorrow, but maybe that's a price you're willing to pay."

"I'll put him to bed and then make us some omelets," she said. "Unless . . . you have plans?"

"Nope," I said. Not unless Seth comes home, I thought.

"I can pay you overtime," she said.

"Shut up," I said.

Devin didn't even protest when I turned off the TV and Lady lifted him from the couch, more tenderly than I had ever seen. This day had helped her.

While they were upstairs I got out the eggs, milk, and cheese. I'd started to make a salad when Lady returned. She was wearing jersey sweatpants and a thin white T-shirt.

"Nice loungewear," I said.

"Karl told me it's eclipsing the jeans market." She put the cheese back in the fridge. "A classic omelet is just eggs. But we can add chives. Let's put persimmon in the salad. That okay?"

"I have zero opinions about persimmon in salad," I said and she laughed.

"How do you feel about French 75s? I know you drink like a fish, but do you drink well?"

I tried to act like what she'd said hadn't fazed me. "What are French 75s?"

"My sweet grasshopper, you have so much to learn."

It was a cocktail, the kind Maria might order on someone's birthday. Gin plus Champagne, lemon juice, and simple syrup, which I watched Lady make on the stove. It was just water with sugar melted into it.

"Where'd you learn all this?" I asked.

"Some of it you'll pick up in your thirties. I didn't—because, well, my thirties were complicated. But you will." She was cutting the pith from a lemon. "Most of it I learned from Karl. And, okay, Kit. She gave me a few pointers early on." She dropped a curl of lemon rind into a filled glass and handed it to me. "This is one of Kit's."

I sipped. It was as fizzy as every other drink Lady had ever served me, but it was slightly sweet and bright from the sugar and lemon. The gin kept it under control, gave it some gravitas.

"It's good," I said.

"Dangerously good," she said. "Tomorrow you'll be happy you have the day off."

A classic omelet looks like a pair of Meryl Streep's underwear and tastes like eating air. Or not—I don't trust myself because by the time we were eating I was on my third French 75 and even the salad tasted like packing peanuts compared to the carbonated tartness of the cocktail. I could drink it forever.

"Do you think this would taste the same in, like, a plastic cup?"

"Honey, nothing tastes the same in a plastic cup," Lady said.

She didn't seem drunk until she carried our plates to the sink, and I saw she was swaying a little and humming the *Yo Gabba Gabba!* theme song.

"I have an idea!" she said, turning suddenly. "Let's pour one more round—just one more—and then creep upstairs to Dev's room. He's so cute when he's sleeping."

"It's when he's awake that he's a little shit," I said, like Katherine Mary might, and downed my drink.

She cackled. "Thank God you're funny," she said, and grabbed a new bottle of Champagne from the fridge.

"How many of these do you have in there?" I asked.

"Just enough to reach oblivion."

But she said it like someone who never drinks that much.

Upstairs it was quiet and dark, and when Lady spilled some of her drink in the hallway she laughed in openmouthed silence before refilling her glass with the bottle of Champagne in her other hand.

The room glowed blue from Devin's nightlight, like we'd entered mid–alien abduction.

"It's creepy in here," I whispered.

Lady brought an index finger to her lips and gestured to the bed.

Devin had kicked off his sheet and flung his arms across the pillow so that he was posed like a pinup model. His hair stuck straight out from his head, his lips were the pinkest I'd ever seen them, and he snored slightly, like Milkshake sometimes did. He did look cute.

Lady was leaning over the bed and I could tell she wanted to touch him.

"Here," I whispered. "Let me." I took her glass from her.

With her free hand Lady bent over to pet Devin's hair and pull his covers to his chin. She sighed before leaning closer. She held her lips to his cheeks until he flinched.

"Run!" she whispered, and we hustled out of the room before he could wake up.

In the hallway she said, "He's so precious when he's like that, it kills me."

I remembered what Karl had told me long ago, about not playing favorites, so I didn't agree or disagree. Instead I said, "I'll probably pass out pretty good after I finish this drink," and handed her glass back.

I waited for Lady to agree. When she didn't answer I could tell she'd turned down Melancholy Avenue and was either reviewing some old shame or rehearsing a future one. I didn't expect it with gin, but Katherine Mary didn't touch Champagne so what did I know?

I snapped my fingers twice. "Don't lose me now, Lady," I said.

"Sorry." And then: "Do you want to see the original?"

I thought she'd been thinking about Devin, which meant she was talking about Seth.

"Seth?" I asked slowly.

"No! The photo. It's in my closet."

I had to play dumb because she didn't know I'd been in her bedroom closet. I waited for her to say more.

"Woman No. 17," she hissed.

All I had to do was nod.

She pushed open her bedroom door with her shoulder. The lights were on, and her dirty clothes were flung all over the floor and the reading chair, which probably hadn't seen a book since Karl had moved out.

The closet door was open, its lights on too, and I stood where I was as Lady sailed into it.

"Come on," she said. "It's like a whole other room in here."

I complied, trying to keep my eyes off the wall where the photo hung. I finished the rest of my drink and was about to burp into the crook of my elbow when Lady poured me some Champagne. I let out a big mean belch and she smiled wickedly.

"Excuse me," I said, and she said I was excused.

Lady was nodding at the photo, which hung above the dresser just like I remembered. "Karl will get it in the divorce. It's his."

"Are you actually going to divorce him?" I asked.

"I don't want to. But maybe I do. Who knows? I should, now that I've . . ." Her voice trailed off as she turned to face me. The closet was big but it was still a closet and I could smell the stale spiked Champagne on her breath and steaming from her pores (and mine).

Lady finished her drink and refilled her glass, then rested the bottle on the dresser.

"You can get closer," she said, "if you want a better look."

I did. Lady moved aside, slumping against the dresser and then sliding to the floor to sit.

"You okay down there?" I asked, but my eyes were already on the photo. I was leaning forward, the drawer hitting my rib cage.

"You sure can hold your liquor," Lady was saying. I didn't answer.

I'd been studying the photo in Kit's monograph for a couple of weeks now, and here was the original, so close I could reach out and pet it with my grubby fingers if I wanted to. Almost everything about the picture was the same. There was the paisley shower curtain hanging on plastic rings; midway across, the curtain had ripped away from a ring and it sagged open. There were the threadbare Sea World towels and the edge of a window, propped open with what looked like a can of instant coffee. There was the overhead light fixture. There was the black cord that I assumed led to a hair dryer just beyond the frame.

I hadn't noticed before how the wall of the bathroom was oddly rippled—bubbled with what I guessed was moisture trapped under the paint. Had this been changed for Kit's book? I doubted it. Whenever

I saw a painting or photograph in real life after studying it for a class, I was always amazed by the tiny details I had missed. Sure I could get the *Mona Lisa* on a coffee mug but the real *Mona Lisa,* the painted one I mean, would find a way to escape reproduction, I don't care what all the fancy-pants French theorists argue. A work of art has an energy to it: not just a painting or a sculpture, but a photo too, even if the photographer made more than one print. It was like I could smell the darkroom chemicals coming off this one.

On the floor at my feet, Lady was singing the *Yo Gabba Gabba!* theme song again, but she wasn't telling me to hurry up, she wasn't asking me why I was so obsessed with Kit's work, so I went back to the photo, finally looking at Lady. I'd been waiting to do it last. Her hair, pulled into a careless bun at the top of her head. The scratch on her arm, healed to a scab. Her stockings, with the meekest run in them, right at the shin.

And there was the one change: the nipple peeking out. It altered the entire tone of the scene. She looked so pathetic in this shot.

"Lady?"

She stopped singing and stood, teetering a little.

"The picture I have? In the book? It looks different."

"You can tell, huh?"

"I mean . . ." I began. "It's not obvious at first, but . . ." I pointed to the photo, to her body. "Well, I hate to break it to you, but your boob isn't showing in the version in Kit's book."

She nodded. She seemed relieved I'd noticed.

"You've been looking at Kit's book a lot?"

"I guess I—"

"And that's what you see here?"

"Why did you change it?"

"That's just a distraction," she said.

"Your nipple?"

She sighed and picked up the Champagne bottle, taking a long swig. She handed it to me and I hesitated. My head was starting to hurt, like my brain was a river and it was drying up, the soil in the beds cracking, but I also wasn't as drunk as Lady, and I needed to be or she wouldn't tell me anything. I put the bottle to my lips and drank.

Then I drank some more. I was realizing now that you had to keep going with Champagne or everything sucked.

When I handed the bottle back to her, she said, "Kit changed something else. I had Karl ask her—no, he told her to do it. She's all about her artistic integrity but I guess not when her brother needs a favor." She paused. "No one could see this version."

"Why not? It's not that porny."

She raised an eyebrow.

"So why is it even hanging up here?" I asked.

"Good question. I don't have an answer. Maybe it's because Karl likes the truth?"

She rolled her eyes and pointed to the photo.

"What?" I asked.

Now her finger was touching the glass. It slid across it, leaving a smear, and I was going to protest but something stopped me. She was passing the image of herself and moving toward the image of the window. Next to the coffee can, mostly out of the frame, was a plastic bottle. For vitamins, maybe. I hadn't thought much of it before. Was it not in the book version? I leaned forward. I could just make out two cut-off words: PREG ESS.

"Is that edited out? That vitamin bottle?" Suddenly I felt very drunk. "I'm confused."

"Pregnancy Essentials," she said. "Prenatals are the size of horse pills and they taste like salmon."

"I don't understand."

She rolled her eyes for the second time and I could tell she was annoyed that I wasn't catching on quickly enough. Here she was, letting me in on a giant secret, and I was too dense or wasted to get it.

"I was pregnant when the photo was taken," she said.

She pushed me aside and opened Karl's top drawer, pulling out a Ziploc bag of what looked like the Vitamin E pills my dad takes: yellow and translucent, with a clear liquid inside.

"Are those prenatal vitamins?" I asked.

She laughed. "No, stupid. They're GoldCaps. Pot? You swallow one and it gives you the best high—mellow, mild until it isn't. Karl has a prescription." She opened the bag and handed me a pill. "Take it."

My mom never mixed anything with her alcohol except carbs and spray cheese.

"I'm not sure I—"

"Do it," she said, and I swallowed the pill without water or even Champagne. The bottle was empty anyway.

"So you don't want anyone to know you got an abortion," I said.

She shook her head and gave me a pitying glance.

"I don't get it," I said.

"I had the baby."

"Dev?" I said, and looked back at the photo.

"Karl's not his father," Lady said, "not his biological one anyway. I don't need anyone knowing that."

"Except me."

"And Kit and Karl. Seth didn't know I was pregnant. It was very early. Even as I was taking those horrible pills, I was considering not going through with it. Did I really want to be a single mother of two? I'd already fucked up one child."

"What made you change your mind?" I asked.

She shrugged. "I met Karl."

Suddenly it was weird to be standing in the closet, an empty bottle of Champagne and two empty glasses between us. I fished out my curl of lemon rind, gone soggy and slick at the bottom of my glass, and gave it a lick before flinging it back.

"I've got more gin downstairs than a juniper forest," Lady said in a squeaky noir voice. I probably gave her an odd look because she said, "If that sounds like a Karl joke, that's because it is."

We hurtled downstairs with a speed that shocked me. We were drunk off our asses but not drunk enough to forget what we wanted, which was to drink more and more until her confession or my unspoken one, ourselves or each other, were wiped out, deleted. I imagined pouring the gin straight into my eyeballs, lubricating them and letting the poison drip to my brain, into every little gray, wormy crevice. Now I knew something about Lady that Seth didn't, and I wanted to unknow it. Of all the things I needed in this world, another opportunity to betray a person I cared about was at the bottom of the list.

Lady had these tiny metal shot glasses, painted a bright blue and flecked with white, the mouth of the cup curled over into a delicate tube.

"Cool glasses," I said.

"I'm wearing contacts," she replied, and we cracked up as we drank.

The gin, or the weed, or the combination of the two, had turned us loopy. Lady put on a record of some cheesy 1970s band that Karl loved and I swayed to it as she stepped onto the couch and surfed its cushions. It was my first time hearing a record, and when I told her how cool the crackling sounded at the beginning of the first song, Lady had said, "You're so young I want to vomit," and we cracked up again.

A second bottle of gin, or was it still the first, emerged from a teak cabinet, as did some tonic water, and we kept drinking. Milkshake trotted over to me and I began dancing with him, somehow the record had changed, it was Joni Mitchell now, and I rubbed my face into Milkshake's warm silky neck, felt his tiny cold leathery nose, and let the singing go higher and higher; when would it stop, I didn't want it to.

"This is some real *Ladies of the Canyon* shit right here," I said.

Lady was across the room, sucking down one of Devin's applesauce squeeze pouches, and she flashed me a goofy thumbs-up. I laughed and laughed. The whole house was lit up gold and I wondered how Devin could sleep in that halo, why he would ever want to.

"Let's go visit the Eavesdroppers," Lady said then. The baby monitor had materialized, and she clutched it in her fist.

She was outside before I could ask whom she was talking about.

THE NIGHT WAS cooler and darker than I expected, the moon above as slender as a fingernail clipping, Joni still crooning from the open back doors. Lady danced to the edge of the yard and flicked a switch. Suddenly the pool glowed like a ghost.

"Now we can start the show," she stage-whispered. She had wrapped a serape over her and it fell off her shoulders as she pointed to the houses in the hills above us. "The Eavesdroppers."

"Why, hello!" I called. Milkshake was jumping around at my feet, scratching my knees with his tiny talons. "Doggy! Go back inside or you'll get eaten by a coyote!"

"Coyote food! Coyote food!" Lady started yelling, and I pointed at the monitor on the table nearby and hushed her.

Lady snorted, then handed me the bottle of gin and a small jar. "Eat something or you'll die," she said.

It was a jar of baby hot dogs. For toddlers, to be enjoyed cold; Devin loved them. I'd tried one before out of curiosity. They tasted like sucking on my own finger: salty skin.

"Yuck," I said, but then I thought, Siggy! I grabbed three.

"One at a time," Lady instructed.

"My own mom eats like this and she's so skinny."

"Ah yes, as my own mother would say: she's one of the lucky ones. Simone also liked to announce, 'A minute on the lips, a decade on the hips.'"

"Clearly," I said, and did my dance again.

Lady hooted and now we were dancing together at the edge of the pool. The serape was in a pile at our feet. She grabbed my hand, and dipped me.

"Who was the guy?" I asked, my head hanging behind me. I imagined it detaching and plopping into the water.

"What guy?"

"Devin's biological—"

She pulled me to standing and we broke away like two cells dividing. She started dancing circles around me. She was good at it, she wanted to be watched. Her hips swayed side to side like a ringing bell, her arms lifted, a soft, dreamy look in her eyes.

"A patient at the doctor's office I managed," she said. "It was a one-time thing, a stress reliever for both of us. I would never want him to know. He never mattered—in a good way, I mean." She stopped dancing. She looked so sad. "I hate when sex matters. Don't you?"

I reached down for the bottle of gin, which she'd set on the first pool step. I took a long glug, praying that she'd forget this subject by the time I was done.

When I offered her the bottle, she asked, "Did I tell you that Karl and Seth do the special signs?"

I was too drunk to remember if I was supposed to know what the special signs even were. *Stop Drop Dead*.

"Those were ours and Karl knew it."

Lady took a sip from the bottle and I put a hand on her cheek.

"Let's swim," I whispered. As far as I was concerned, my head was already sailing across the deep end.

It wasn't long before Lady was down to a nude bra and underwear, tasteful and sheer at the same time. I was still fully clothed.

"Let me get my suit," I said, already skipping to the Cottage.

I opened the door a crack before Lady called out, "Wait! Here's one." She tossed me the suit she'd been wearing earlier and looked at me expectantly.

"Turn around," I said.

She pshawed and dove into the pool.

The suit was damp and it stuck to my skin as I tried to pull it up my thighs. I heard Lady splashing in the water, and then she was standing next to me, dripping wet. Her pubic hair was a prim dark line.

"Let me help you." She paused. "Wow, you have great tits."

"I do?"

"The Eavesdroppers love your hips the best, though!"

She yanked the suit up my body, nearly pulling me to the ground in the process.

"Gentle!" I said, laughing. "You're gonna hurt me! Is this how Mommy Simone used to dress you or something?"

"Probably," she said.

"No way."

"I don't remember." There, again, was that ghostly sadness.

Her head was at my midsection as she kept tugging on the suit. Careful not to lose my balance, I bent down until my mouth was inches away from her ear—pale and delicate. In the glow of the pool light, it was as iridescent as a pearl.

"Why do you keep the photo?" I whispered.

She didn't move. "It's how we met, why we met. He loves it."

"Do you?"

She pulled at the strap and I stood.

"Some things are hard to let go of," she said.

Once I had the suit all the way on, it was clear that it was too small. "You better give me a raise for this."

We both laughed and it was a real thing, the purest joy, a swim after dark. It wasn't the drinks talking, or the weed, and it wasn't the anger we had for everyone else, it wasn't the secrets, they didn't exist. It was us. Only us.

44.

I WOKE ON THE CHAISE LOUNGE. A TOWEL WAS FLUNG ACROSS my chest and another was caught up in my legs. They weren't the swim towels either, but the beige ones from the downstairs guest bathroom, and now they were covered with dew. I had to peel myself from the plastic chair—I could just picture the red welts puckering my back—and when I did I saw that I was still wearing Lady's bathing suit. Now it was dawn, birds everywhere. It felt like a dentist had gone into my brain and sucked everything out with that little rubber sucking tube. I turned and threw up on the pavement.

"Lady?" I croaked, but I knew I was alone out here.

What had happened? But I knew. A blackout had happened, the one I'd been too chickenshit (or too smart) to meet before now. What I remembered from last night: Lady's secret, the gin, the tiny cups, the dancing, the dog, the swim. I vaguely recalled, as if from a movie I'd seen half of on cable once, how we'd done handstands in the shallow end, and then I'd floated on my back with her palms under me, both of us chanting, *Light as a feather, stiff as a board.* It all collapsed after that.

I stood. My mouth was sharp and sour with the taste of vomit. I needed water. I dragged myself to the hose, and when I put my mouth to the nozzle and turned it on I was surprised by how warm the water was, still heated through by yesterday's sun. It was like drinking stale tea and I retched again.

I stood and looked out at the pool. That's another thing rich people get that the rest of us don't: pools at dawn.

Something white bobbed up and down in the deep end.

"Fuck," I said. "Milkshake? Please let that be a T-shirt."

I rushed to the other side of the pool to get a better look, the dread rising up to my throat.

It wasn't a T-shirt. Or the dog. It was Peter Rabbit. He was dead, floating like a pool toy.

I put my hand over my mouth so I wouldn't scream or cry out or throw up again. I looked away from his bloated body, to the sky. It was so white.

45.

I SHOULD HAVE SCOOPED THE POOR THING OUT WITH THE POOL skimmer, but the sky was perfect and it wouldn't last for long. I could go shoot the portrait and be back before Lady woke up. She wouldn't want to take Devin outside anyway; if her hangover was anything like mine she'd plop him in front of the TV while she went searching for an Alka-Seltzer and a breakfast sandwich.

That's what I did. Or not at first. First, I peed for approximately ten Mississippis, the urine in the toilet a problematic shade of fluorescent yellow. And then I packed my camera and tripod, and threw on the shirt I'd purchased, along with a new tube of burgundy lipstick. My hair wasn't the right color, but I'd decided it never would be, even if I'd managed to buy the exact same shade of Manic Panic that Lady had been into twenty or so years ago. At least my hair was knotted and crusty from my night of debauchery, which looked closer to Lady's textured wave than it ever did clean. I took one long look at my portrait of Lady and Marco before locking up the Cottage behind me.

I avoided the pool on my way out—I just couldn't face it. I'd taken Peter Rabbit from my mom for his own protection, and look what had happened.

When I got down the hill I headed first to Astro Burger, one of

Katherine Mary's great loves. How fitting that it was right across the street from where I was headed. Sausage-and-egg sandwich in my hand, a medium fountain Coke between my thighs, I parked on Melrose. The heat was coming so I ate fast with the car still running. Within twenty minutes the sky would be blue and cloudless and I had to be quick.

For all I knew, Lady had told me last night where she'd taken the photo with Marco. That, or the white sky had handed me a vision this morning: I would need to get away from the coast because the ocean air would look too viscous and misty on film. What I needed was a wall like the one Lady and Marco were leaning against. And I had that white sky. Or I did for a little while longer. I didn't deserve it, I didn't deserve anything, not even a bunny, but I wasn't about to turn my back on the opportunity either.

After all that grease and sugar my stomach was still sour. My head might explode into brain dust before I finished the shoot. I took one last look at myself in the car's side mirror, adjusted my hair and applied the lipstick, and headed toward Paramount.

The outside studio walls were a lighter shade of beige than the one in Lady's photo, but it was a decent approximation and at this hour no one was around to tell me to move along, little girl. Down the block, the studio's tall, rounded gates presided like the entrance to heaven, but here there was just an empty sidewalk and the smell of Astro's fries wafting across Gower.

I set up the camera on my tripod, right at the edge of the building. Above me, posters the size of billboards advertised whatever new shit show would get canceled midway through the season. Like the word LOVERS, they wouldn't fit in the shot.

"I love L.A.," I said to myself in my best Randy Newman impression. Either I was still drunk or there was too much Katherine Mary in me. Or both. I needed to shove off enough of the goof to focus on the photo.

I used the pink chalk I'd stolen from Devin to mark where to stand, and then I focused on the spot in the viewfinder. Once I had it, I righted the camera to frame the shot. It was a bitch photographing yourself—I'd never done it, not seriously at least. If I were going for authenticity, I'd use my old point-and-shoot from middle school, but I wasn't trying to duplicate. I was interpreting. It was my failure to duplicate that was interesting. At least I wasn't shooting digital.

I wondered who had taken the photo of Lady and Marco. Seth and I had never discussed it, but he must have tortured himself with that question. If someday Devin found out that Karl wasn't his real dad, would he obsess over the truth like Seth was doing now? Seth would do it for him.

I set the timer and stepped to my mark like I was a stage actor ready for the curtain to rise. I was standing in the right place, but the camera clicked before I'd really thought about who I was. I closed my eyes and thought of the portrait. The way some of the paint had gummed up at the sleeve of Lady's shirt; how I'd gotten the rosacea on her arm just right. The sad light—it was so obviously miles away from any ocean, any breeze, how could I have thought that would have worked? The devotion in her eyes. Her goddamned fear that it would end too soon. That's what desire is.

Lady had kept this one photo, despite the fact that it was evidence of who Seth's dad was. Or because of it. And she'd even sent it into this project. Unlike Kit's photo, she wanted to share it. She hadn't just invited me to make art out of it, she needed me to.

I reset the timer and stepped to my mark. I imagined Seth's dad—Marco, Mark, whoever he was—and I looked at that empty space where he was supposed to be. He was already gone. I was Lady, it was a long, long time ago, and my hope and desire and fear stretched like an invisible line from my head all the way to the unreadable sky. I didn't see or hear the shutter open, but I felt it and let it capture me, again and again. I'm here, I'm here.

I took a few more shots before my phone started dinging. Text after text. Finally I stopped to see who it was.

Seth: You been hanging out with my mom?

Seth: Shes your boss not your friend

Seth: Answer me. I know your phone is on even when your sleeping.

"What the fuck?" I said to no one.

Me: Sorry I was working. WTF?

Seth: Check her Twitter

Me: What does it say? Just tell me.

He didn't answer. I could tell he wasn't giving me anything more.

I wasn't on stupid Twitter but I'd seen Seth look up the account the other night. @muffinbuffin41. I scrolled down and read up from the bottom:

I'm totally wasted with The Sitter.

The Sitter might be 20 years younger but I look better in my own bathing suit.

I'm snacking on tiny hot dogs while The Sitter times how long she can stay underwater.

Now The Sitter wants to swim with the dog. I told her to get the bunny.

Yep The Sitter has a bunny.

How do you clean vomit off an iPhone? #AskingForAFriend

The Sitter is my best friend.

The last tweet, her most recent, made me smile.

LADY

46.

I WAS SPRAWLED ACROSS THE LOVE SEAT, SIPPING MY HEADACHE away with a Bloody Mary, when the land line rang. It was seven thirty in the morning, which meant it was either an East Coast telemarketer or someone with limited English frantically trying to reach Jose or Vlad. But nevertheless, there I was, at the receiver, saying, "Daniels Residence," my voice hoarse and phlegmy, the drained Bloody Mary still in my hand.

"Hello?" the voice, a man's, said. "I'm not sure I have the right number, but I'm looking for Pearl Daniels, née Kegan?"

"This is she," I said.

"And you go by Lady? Is that correct? You're the daughter of Simone Kegan?"

I thought I might vomit, and it wasn't from the hangover. "Who is this?"

He told me his name was Douglas McDonald of Holler, Banerjee and Vebber.

"I represent your mother's estate."

"What? I don't follow."

"Is this a good time for you to talk?"

"Please just tell me what's going on."

"I'm sorry to let you know that your mother—she passed." He cleared his throat. "Simone's will lists you as the sole beneficiary."

"I see," was all I could manage as he continued, his tone business-like, capable. Thankfully I had enough wits about me to put down my glass before it slipped from my hand and shattered across the floor. I was sweating—the rank stink of fear—and every part of me felt slick and clammy. My mother was gone. I tried to fish the rest of a pickle nub out of my glass, but I couldn't reach it, and my fingers came up sticky. My mother was dead.

"In some respects," Douglas McDonald continued, "there isn't much, though there is the house on Monte Mar . . ."

She hadn't moved, not once. She had stayed put. I could have just driven over. All these years, she'd been there: vicious and gorgeous, the same always. Not anymore.

". . . which in this market, the land alone could go for—"

"Excuse me," I said. "Excuse. Me."

I knew I was nearly screeching. Devin looked away from the TV for the first time in two hours.

"Are you all right, Mrs. Daniels?" the lawyer asked.

"Am I all right? Did you just ask me that? What do you think? Is it a habit of yours to call people before eight in the morning to tell them so coldly that their *mommies* have died?"

Silence.

"Please forgive me, Mrs. Daniels."

"Call me Lady."

"I apologize, Lady. Sincerely. I didn't realize . . . well, it's my understanding that you and your mother hadn't spoken in almost twenty years."

I was crying, and I knew he could hear it.

"When's the funeral?" I asked.

He didn't answer.

"When is it? What, am I not allowed to come?"

"It was a couple of weeks ago," he said gently.

This news hurt me in a way I didn't expect and I began to cry harder, great anguished heaves hiccupping in my chest. I'd missed my mother's funeral. I'd been stupid enough to believe that because I hated her I didn't also love her.

When I came up for air, I asked, "How . . . how did she die?"

"Car accident. But she'd recently been diagnosed with pancreatic cancer." He sounded almost pleased to relay this information. "A few weeks prior," he explained, "she and I met at my office. After the diagnosis, she wanted to make sure everything regarding her estate and assets was in order. She always planned to give you everything, Mrs. . . . Lady."

I could hardly speak. Douglas McDonald must have sensed my shock, and didn't seem to expect a response as he went on to explain the will. I was barely listening.

After I'd hung up, I flung myself back on the love seat. I was still crying, and my nose wouldn't stop running.

"Mommy," Devin said, finally tearing himself away from the screen. "You done with your dog hair?"

I laughed and wiped my face with my sleeve. "Hair of the dog, baby. And, yes, I finished it. Go back to watching your show now. Mommy's all right. Mommy . . ." I started to cry again, and Devin—either charitably or cruelly, how could you tell with a toddler?—went right back to watching his show.

My cell was lodged between the cushions and I dug it out immediately, though I wasn't sure whom I would call. The only person who had known my mother was Marco, and I certainly wouldn't get what I needed from him.

We'd seen each other four times now, always in the middle of the day, always at his house in Chatsworth, and we hardly spoke at all, at least not about anything personal. The sex was never as brutal and quick as it had been the first time—we kissed, we laughed, we occasionally verged on tenderness—but still it felt like there was something worthless about it, just something for two damaged people to share, if "share" could even describe a transaction so physical. For me, our meetings were making everything worse; they were exacerbating all of my problems, and yet I needed them. Now I could never let Seth meet Marco. Our trysts were beginning to feel like the Bloody Mary I'd finished: a drink to distract from the pain of the other drinks, merely more of a bad thing. Dog hair.

Marco had been the true confession I'd wanted to make to S the night before. Somehow I'd told her about the photograph and my pregnancy instead. Again I'd betrayed Karl.

I called S, but the phone rang four times before going to voicemail.

I didn't leave a message. Obviously she wouldn't pick up; she was sleeping it off in the low cave of the Cottage. Lucky girl.

47.

I WAS DRIFTING OFF TO THE DULCET TONES OF *GO, DIEGO, GO!* when my cell phone rang. It was Karl calling, and I'd never been so happy to see his face light up my screen. He and I hadn't spoken since I'd started with Marco. Even after Seth had decamped for Kit's, I could only bear to text or email. If Karl heard my voice he'd surely intuit that I'd been denigrating myself. Now, though, none of that mattered. I needed his comfort and his wisdom, his jokes.

"Thank God it's you," I said.

"Lady? What's wrong? Is it Dev?"

"My mother died."

I started crying again. I was wailing, I couldn't help myself, it was the loss of my mother and also every secret I'd saddled myself with. Because Karl was Karl, he let me cry. He didn't say anything, he just waited until I was finished. Devin was watching TV as if his life depended on it.

Finally, I blew my nose and said, "Sorry. I'm sorry."

I explained that the lawyer had called. "It only took him a couple days to find me," I said.

"Your mom could have done it," he said. "She could have found you, if she had tried."

"And now," I began to cry again, "she never will. I can't believe she's dead. My mother . . ."

"This is probably insensitive of me, Lady, but can I ask why you feel so sad? I thought you were okay with not having her in your life."

"I guess in the back of my mind I assumed I'd see her again. She'd ask me to forgive her, I'd take her hand . . ."

He chuckled. "Ah yes, the fantasy of the bedside vigil. Kit wanted that with our mother, and I guess she sort of got it in the hospital.

They had a moment. It was the only one in the history of their relationship where Mom wasn't mean to her."

"My mother didn't even get a bedside! The bitch had cancer but it
was a car accident that killed her. The bizarre part is that she left me
everything. Can you believe it? The house in Beverlywood? It's mine."

Now he was silent.

"What?" I asked.

"How long were you going to wait?"

"Wait for what?"

"When can I expect the papers?" His voice had gotten very tight
and strained.

"Karl, I'm a mess right now, please stop with the code words."

"Well, now that you own a house in Beverlywood, there's no reason to stay in ours."

"I love this house, you know that."

"What about me—do you love me?"

"I—" I wanted to tell him that I missed him and his wit, his smell,
the pasta he made on Sunday nights, and that every time I left Marco's
I felt tainted. Karl could lick me clean like the mother cat he was. I
remembered last night, in the closet. I'd told S the one thing I made
Karl promise never to confess to another human being, and all it had
taken was a little gin.

I began to cry.

"Are you crying about your mother or me?" he asked.

"I don't know."

"Something's up with Seth," he said after a moment. "He's angry,
clomping around, doing the brooding thing. He brought up his father
again. He asked me if you still knew his dad. Ridiculous, I know, but
you need to talk to him."

"I would if he ever came back. Seth's left me." I was crying again.

"How about I bring him with me tonight, when I come to pick up
Dev? You two can discuss it."

"I need to see you first. Just you. As soon as possible. Let's meet
at my mother's house—I need to be there. The lawyer guy said he'd
meet me at ten."

Karl agreed, but he hung up before I did. I was done weeping. For now. My headache had returned, a crying-induced one, dehydration caused not by liquor but by my own body, in service of my body. It was a noble pain.

48.

IT WASN'T LOST ON ME THAT I WAS YET AGAIN DRAGGING DEVIN along to see a man with whom I had a complicated relationship. This time, at least, the man was his father, or the person he assumed was his father. It wasn't much of an assumption; I had seen Devin's real father only twice in my life, whereas Karl had rubbed a can of cold Diet Coke against my lower back while I was in labor, signed the birth certificate, gone out to buy the diapers, and worn the baby carrier. He wasn't Devin's father, okay, but he was his daddy, and no one could take that away. I'd have to tell S that.

As I pulled onto Monte Mar, Devin announced from the backseat, "You have a mommy!" I had been explaining the situation with my mother all morning, and I'd had to repeat the information on the drive over. It was a lot for a little kid to process: this new and dead grandmother, this house we owned, but not for long, what a will was.

"Everyone has a mommy," I said. "I just didn't see mine."

"Why you not see her?"

"Because she wasn't nice. I loved her, but she wasn't nice."

"Why?"

"It's hard to explain, honey. Lots of people have complicated relationships with their mothers and they need to sever communication with them in order to lead healthy lives."

He was quiet. Sometimes, if I answered his big questions with adult language, it short-circuited his brain.

I pointed out the window. "That's the house!"

It looked the same. Better, even. The glossy black door, the bright green hedges, what I assumed was a new roof. I wasn't surprised. My mother's property was an extension of herself, and she would never,

ever, let herself go. She might have died in a car accident, but at least on her last day of life her cancer hadn't yet ravaged her. At the moment of impact, she'd been pretty, and that must have brought her peace.

I was about to cry when I saw a man was already waiting on the porch. I pulled myself together. It had to be Douglas McDonald: he was tiny and middle-aged, with two cell phones clipped to his belt, a set of keys in one hand and a manila envelope in the other. He waved with the hand that held the keys.

"I'm sorry again for your loss," he began as soon as we were face-to-face. I said thank you.

He was meeting me so soon after our phone call because he knew he'd botched that conversation. He needed to prove he was human, that he had feelings.

I kept it short because I wanted him gone by the time Karl arrived. I assured him I would come to his office first thing Monday morning to review and sign all the paperwork.

"I'm only going to walk through the house now," I said.

"Spend all the time you need." He handed me the manila envelope and explained that a copy of the will was inside. "For your perusal," he said, as if it were a wine list.

After he had driven off, Devin and I waited on the front lawn because I couldn't bear the idea of going inside just yet. Devin wasn't much older than Seth had been the last time I'd walked into this house, and out of it, and I needed to change the choreography. I needed a man.

Karl pulled up a few minutes later and as soon as he saw Devin, he rushed out of the car with a big floppy grin on his face. He walked toward Devin like a gorilla, hunched over with bent legs, his arms outward, reaching for a hug.

"Daddy!" Devin roared, and the two of them pawed at each other as I looked on.

Karl wasn't making eye contact with me, or that's what it felt like.

When they finally disengaged, I said, "Hey. Thanks for coming."

Karl touched my elbow and I leaned in to him. "Please hug me," I said, and he did. It took all of me not to stick my face into the crook of his neck and inhale.

"I had to lie to Seth and Kit about coming here," he whispered into my ear. "They think I'm meeting an old friend from SC."

"You could've told them the truth," I said. "Or am I enemy numero uno over there?"

He didn't answer because Devin had crawled between us. "Mommy and Daddy! Time to go in the house!"

Karl stepped back to pick him up, and I turned to unlock the door.

Inside, it smelled like it always had: the chemical lemon of wood polish, combined with reduced-fat everything—that had a sour spunk, didn't it? My father had lived here until I was almost four and after that brief tenure it had been just my mother and me, and the only men who set foot into the house were the ones delivering packages or hired to fix something. It was almost exhilarating to know Karl was standing right behind me, taking in this space, violating it by his mere presence. I didn't feel so sad anymore.

I flipped on the light. The credenza remained by the front door, but the vase was bereft of flowers. I felt a pang of despair for my mother, and then triumph.

"You'll have to figure out what to do with all of this," Karl said, gesturing first to the credenza and then to the umbrella stand. Devin was squirming in his arms. "You're the sole successor, correct?"

"I think so." I waved the envelope and then tossed it onto the table. "But I don't want to get into it today."

"I go play now?" Devin asked.

"No," Karl said.

"Let him," I said. "It's just a house."

Karl sighed, releasing Devin from his arms. The boy ran to the living room and immediately climbed onto the couch, dismantling it, pillow by pillow. I watched Karl watch him, his eyes crinkling with pride.

"Come with me," I said, putting out my hand. He didn't take it.

I showed him my old room, which had long ago been redesigned for guests, replete with a Hollywood Regency bedside table, and on it, a mirrored tissue-box holder and a tray with a carafe and glass, ostensibly for water.

I sat down on the bed. I knew without looking that there was no sheet under the coverlet; my mother didn't like to sully linens unnecessarily.

"Looks like a guest room," Karl said.

I was sure in the closet we would find the shoe hotels my mother used to house her impressive collection of footwear. Her own closet wasn't large enough to accommodate them.

"Check this out," I said, pulling open the closet door.

There they were: her shoes, the compartments for them piled high and orderly. The pairs I didn't recognize gutted me as much as the ones I did.

"Lots of shoes," Karl said. He seemed impatient—or no, nervous.

"This way," I said.

In my mother's room, the four-poster bed and the large vanity remained, though the latter was covered not only with makeup and eye creams as I expected, but with prescription bottles, and ointments as well. The paraphernalia of the sick and infirm. The room itself had a different smell from what I was used to: medicinal and cloying, and also powdery, like a piece of cheap milk chocolate. An old-lady smell.

"Someone must have come in here and tidied up," Karl said, bending down to check out a bottle of pills. They were lined up in neat clusters.

"Nope. This was my mother. She was very clean."

"Look." Karl held up a silver picture frame, certainly purchased at Tiffany's or Neiman's, billed as an heirloom piece. I imagined it heavy in his hand. "Is this Seth?" he asked.

The photo was a little blurry. In it, Seth stood in the crib my mother had bought for him. The picture had been taken mid-blink and his eyes were only partially open.

"Must've been the only photo she had of him," I said. I was crying again. "How could she be dead?"

"You regret pushing her away."

It wasn't a question, and he didn't say it gently either. This time, he was the one to leave the room first. I followed him.

In my mother's office, I was relieved there was no evidence of Seth.

This was where the crib had been set up all those years before, though now the room was filled with other furniture, most of it imported from Asia, with the occasional midcentury end table.

"What's all this?" Karl asked.

"Her business. She sold furniture—I'm surprised she was still at it, though."

Karl abruptly craned his neck into the hallway and yelled, "Dev, we're back here! You okay?"

Devin yelled something unintelligible but didn't come running.

"Stop avoiding me," I said.

"We're the only two people standing in a room choked with Saran-wrapped furniture," he said. "How is that avoiding you?"

"You wish Devin were in here with us right now, so we wouldn't have to talk."

"I miss my kid, okay? Weekends just aren't enough with him."

"I'm sorry."

"Are you?" His tone was mean, bitter. "Are you really?"

"I said I was, so I am, okay?"

He sighed. "I got a place. An apartment. In Park La Brea. Two bed-rooms."

"Park La Brea? In one of those Eastern Bloc high rises?"

"That's all you have to say?"

"Who's going to live there?"

"I can't stay at Kitty's forever, and I can't handle this limbo state any longer."

"If I asked you to come home, would you?"

I thought Karl would say, *Yes, of course,* without hesitation, which is why I'd asked the question at all.

But he didn't. "I'm not sure, to be honest. You push people away, Lady. That's what you do. You have no reason to be angry with me, and yet—"

"I know about the special signs," I said.

"That's what this is about? Seth and I sharing a few of your made-up hand gestures?"

"Don't say it like that. You have no idea how much they've meant to us."

"We can stop if it's truly an issue. They're not that useful."

"It's not about useful!" I said. "Those signs were between me and Seth. I told you that."

"You're the only one who wants to keep them special." Karl's voice was kind, but only because he knew what he was about to say would hurt me. "Seth isn't your possession."

"I didn't say he was."

"It's how you behave. You won't let me parent him. And I'm tired of hiding out at my sister's place like an escaped convict. This situation is real, Lady." He started waving his hands around and I had to step back. "Do you get it? It's real! This isn't some game we're playing! This isn't a little thought experiment!"

"I know it isn't."

"I can't believe you had the nerve to ask if I'd come home. You don't even mean it, you just want me to assure you that I'll do anything you wish at the drop of a hat."

"Are you done lecturing me in my dead mother's house?"

Karl looked like he might walk out. "Please. You hated your mother and what you're feeling now isn't grief. It's guilt. You're probably relieved too, because now Seth will never know his grandmother. That's one less person to get in between the two of you."

"Wow, that's low. Especially when that son isn't choosing to be with me after a lifetime of raising him."

"Now you know how your mother felt."

I didn't say anything. My heart was pounding sloppily: *ka-thunk, ka-thunk*.

"I saw Kit's photos," he said finally. "The new ones. They're wonderful. And Seth enjoyed doing them with her. She's his aunt for all intents and purposes."

"She isn't—"

"Why won't you let him be happy?"

"Why are you saying all of this to me?" The tears were tightening my throat. "Why are you being so mean?" What I wanted to say was, *Why are you being like Marco? Why are you being like my mother?*

That seemed to break the spell. Karl sighed and leaned against a dresser. He said my name again, but he was looking away, as if he expected someone else to answer. To him I was a sad, fragile little woman. And I was. Even when we met, when I was poor and angry and lonely—and pregnant—I hadn't been this wretched. I could tell he was trying to decide if I was the same woman he'd married. Or if he'd been mistaken all along. Had he ever truly loved the real Lady? The discrepancies were painful, for both of us.

"Don't make it easy for me to push you away," I said. "Don't be like everyone else."

"I'm not." He was nearly whispering. "I'm not."

"Why do you keep it?" I asked.

"Keep what?"

"The photo of me. Kit's photo."

"It's in the closet, no one can see it."

"No one but us."

"Don't you think that's important?" he asked. "Just you and me."

"That's what you always said, and I loved it. I just don't want Devin to ever think you aren't his. I want him to be happy."

"He is happy. Look at him. And so is Seth—happy for a teenage boy, at least. You're a wonderful mother. You just need to figure out what you're doing. What you want. Do you want to be my wife?"

Just then, Devin ran into the room.

"There's my boy!" Karl cried, and with such false cheer I almost laughed.

"Ready to leave with Daddy?" I said.

Devin shook his head. "Let's go see Marco!" he said.

"Who's Marco?" Karl asked, laughing.

I forced out a guffaw. "I have no idea!"

Devin looked at me, confused. "Marco! Your friend!"

"You okay?" Karl asked me.

I nodded, but I wasn't. I felt panicked, not to mention sick.

"You all right?" Karl asked. "Lady, did you eat anything this morning?"

I pointed to my bag on the end table behind me. "There's a bar in my—" I began, but the room was already going black, I was already falling to the floor.

ESTHER

49.

I DROVE WEST WITH ALL MY GEAR TOSSED ACROSS THE PASSEN-ger seat like a couple of salt-stiff beach towels. There were two rolls to develop and I planned to arrive at the lab right when it opened. The place had been around for decades, and I guess there were enough photo nerds in L.A. to keep it alive. Mornings the guy with the gimp arm worked the counter, and if I flirted with him and said my name was Diane Arbus, wink-wink, he might shave a couple bucks off the order. I would call Lady back while I waited, I didn't care if there was one of those signs on the wall with a crossed-out cell phone, I was a paying customer, I was Diane fucking Arbus, dammit, back from the dead with a headache the size of the Inland Empire.

Lady had called over an hour ago without leaving a message. She was probably wondering how I was feeling (like an old plastic bag filled with battery acid, thanks for asking), and why I wasn't sleeping it off in the Cottage. Was that actually my bunny floating dead in the deep end of her swimming pool? Seth had texted me twice more about his mom's tweets, and he might have confronted her too. If he had, well, shit, then her questions were going to be a lot scarier.

Stopped at a red arrow, I finally replied to Seth.

Saw the tweets. I didn't realize I wasn't allowed to hang with your mom.

For the rest of the drive I waited for my phone to light up with his reply, but it didn't, and it wasn't until after I'd paid the lab (no Gimp Arm today, so no discount) that I heard back from him. He wanted

to know what I was doing. With one hand I pushed the lab's big glass
doors open, the watery Culver City sunlight simultaneously assault-
ing and purifying me, and answered:

What am I doing existentially, on this planet, with this life? Or right now?

My phone dinged immediately. Right now

I'm at a lab off la cienega waiting for pics to develop. Old school style.

This time, there was no answer. I wasn't going to wait for one.

Why . . . ?

Still nothing.

I know you've got your phone in your hands or by your balls. Answer.

I waited.

Fuck this. At least yr mom doesn't send mixed signals.

I thought for sure that would do the trick, but alas.

I'm getting a drink.

50.

THERE WAS ONE DIVE BAR NEARBY, ITS WINDOWLESS BRICK
exterior painted dark gray, and I was willing to bet that the gallery
snobs hadn't yet ruined it with Marcona almonds and atonal music. It
shouldered a mini-mall on Venice, which meant I could also do my
laundry or fill a plastic jug with potable water. The bar was called Bills,
and I was never sure if it meant bills, as in cash, or if Bill had simply
left out the apostrophe. Though every time I'd passed it the wide dark
door was closed and unmanned by a bouncer, I knew the place would
be open during the day because, years ago, driving by on my way to
school, I'd witnessed a man going in as if drinking were his job.

At least my mom had never been a barfly like that. She was a func-
tional alcoholic. She wasn't classy, but she had dignity, she had coworkers and health insurance, she had a daughter to support half the
time, emotionally if not financially. She occasionally went out drinking, but mostly she liked to drink alone, at nights or on the weekends,
in front of the TV, thank you very much.

Anyway, I knew it wasn't Katherine Mary who longed for a vodka soda, but me. I could already anticipate the drink's fizz and burn, the acid of the lime. The way the vodka would ice my veins. Here I was, walking down Venice Boulevard in a fake-vintage shirt without a bra, burgundy lipstick crumbing the corners of my mouth, and nobody but me wanted what I wanted. I dialed Lady's number.

She didn't answer, which was probably for the best since I wanted to tell her that I was walking into a scary bar when most people my age were going for brunch with their buds. *The Sitter is my best friend.* It could be true; I had no one else but her. I couldn't wait to get the photos back, to see what I'd made.

The door was heavy, its inside padded with burgundy Naugahyde. The nearest wall announced that patrons needed to be over twenty-one, and that the management retained the right to refuse service to anyone. Beneath these a handwritten note announced NO PERSONAL CHECKS, EFFECTIVE 8/3/2009. I'd pictured myself entering a dim and mysterious cave of a room, a few sad sacks huddled over shots at the far end of the bar, but this place was bright with halogen-powered lights, the kind that people with "environmental sensitivities" sue their bosses to replace. The floor was carpeted. The bar was a mass of thick gray plastic that reminded me of a Jacuzzi, and no one was drinking at its edge. Ranchera music played softly from a speaker in the corner.

"*Hola,*" the bartender said. Bill? He didn't look up from his phone.

"This is the craziest bar I have ever seen," I said, and pulled myself onto a stool.

"*Sí.*"

"Vodka and soda, please," I said. I dug through my bag for my ID, but the guy was already reaching for the vodka.

He served it to me in a plastic cup and said, "*Seis.*"

"Do you have ice?"

He shook his head.

I pulled out a five. "*Cinco* then."

He took the money without complaint.

The drink was lukewarm and flat, but I finished it in a few big gulps anyway. The clenched feeling at the center of my head began to go slack.

"*Uno mas,*" I said, and the guy complied.

I was midway through the second when a clot of men in work clothes entered and began speaking in quick Spanish to the bartender, who had finally put down his phone to attend to their needs. A couple of the dudes looked over at me, but only for a second, as if properly acknowledging my presence would mess up whatever Elk Club vibe they had nurtured. A minute later, a middle-aged white guy in Carhartts came in and held up a wad of cash to grunts of gratitude. El Jefe.

My phone dinged and I sat up straighter. But it wasn't Seth, it was my dad.

Dad: Happy Day Off, Waterbug! What are you doing?

I sighed. Poor Steven Shapiro.

Me: I'm curing a vicious hangover. On my second vodka tonic at a dive bar in Culver City surrounded by manual laborers.

Dad: LOL!

Dad: Esther?

Dad: Really, what are you doing?

Dad: Honey?

I was having a little fun, letting him sweat, when the white guy was suddenly by my side, grinning. His teeth were nicer and straighter than I expected.

"Can I buy you a drink . . ."—he looked at my shirt—"Virginia?"

"No, *gracias,*" I said.

"What are you doing here?" he asked.

"Drinking. Is this a private club or something?"

He scratched his cheek, which was tan but acne-pitted, and leaned away from me. "I didn't mean it like that, Your Highness."

I didn't know what to say, so I went back to staring at my phone.

"You don't have to be a bitch about it," he said. "I was just trying to make conversation."

Now the other men were looking at us. I lifted my cup and drank the rest of it as fast as I could. If there'd been ice it would have avalanched down the side of the plastic, smashing into my lips, making me look like an idiot. Sometimes there is a God.

I slid off the stool as gracefully as I could. The room was brighter than ever, the vodka's doing. Not that I'd let that show.

If you counted the shadows of my nipples beneath my shirt, I had four eyes. I pointed them all at El Jefe. Lady at my age: she's a beast.

I made sure everyone could hear me. "When the rent goes up here—and, believe me, it will—you guys will be priced out. They'll shut this place down and you'll have nowhere to go. Nowhere."

Vaccinated with vodka, I glided to the exit.

51.

BEING DRUNK WAS THE BEST! I COULDN'T WAIT TO SEE THE photos! I was young and hot, and all the sleazy men of the world would starve to death while they dreamed of going down on me. Strutting back into the lab *Saturday Night Fever*–style, I felt so invincible that I didn't see anything in front of me. Or anyone.

Someone was calling my name and I turned.

It took me a second to recognize the woman speaking. She was in her fifties, and she had her hair up in a tight, headache-inducing ponytail.

"Kit Daniels," she said.

Kit Flippin' Daniels!

"Oh! Kit! Mrs.—Ms. Daniels!"

"Please. Kit."

"Kit! Sorry, I just didn't expect you to be here . . . you know . . . out of context!" I let out a big, high-pitched laugh, more hyena that human. "But duh! This is a photo lab, so why should I be surprised?"

She bestowed a kind smile upon me and smoothed the front of her dress, an ankle-length kaftan deal with billowy sleeves and a deep V-neck. In gray. Who else but Kit Daniels would own a kaftan in such an understated color? She wore no jewelry, as if to let her décolletage do the talking. I wanted to bow before her, ask if she needed her studio swept, her hair braided, anything.

"Seth is feeding the meter," she said.

"Seth's with you?"

"When he said you were at a lab off La Cienega," she said, "I knew just the place. It's the only one left in Southern California. For professionals, I mean. I met the owner at jury duty, if you can believe it. He said the mail-order business was skyrocketing. People all over the country are sending in their rolls of film. Seems sad, doesn't it? Or inspiring. You pick."

The woman behind the counter obviously recognized Kit because she was ogling. I glared at her and she did a one-eighty into the back room.

"Do you need to pick up some prints?" I asked when we were alone.

She waved her hand like there was a gnat in her way. "I shoot almost entirely digital these days, or I develop myself, at my studio," she said. "But you're picking up, right?"

I said nothing.

"It's funny," she continued, "because the other day, when I had lunch with Lady, she told me you were a painter."

"I am. I mean . . . I also paint."

"Also?" Kit said. "Very impressive."

"I'm either multitalented or a dilettante."

"You're funny," she said without laughing. "And this look you've got going." She was nodding at my shirt.

"Business casual," I said.

"If you're willing, I'd love to see the prints."

"You would?" A private crit with Kit Daniels! But no, I couldn't—if Lady found out. What exactly had Seth told his aunt?

Just then, he came through the door wearing blue basketball shorts and his TALK WITH THE HAND T-shirt. On his feet were shower sandals and tube socks. Obviously, he and Kit weren't related by blood.

Kit signed, *Hello,* as if she hadn't seen him two minutes ago.

"Seth," I said. He immediately realized what I was wearing and he had to suppress a laugh. "What are you guys doing here, anyway?" I asked.

"Seth was . . . concerned," Kit said.

I made my best bimbo face. "Concerned? Why?"

"You've been drinking," Kit said, and I knew Seth had mentioned my text.

Seth signed, *Sorry.*

"I just had a beer. It's so hot already, and I have a headache."

Kit crossed her arms; Seth was gazing at his shower shoes.

"It's not even noon," Kit said.

"But what's that saying? It's five p.m. somewhere! And who cares how early it is? It was just a beer, I'm of age. I'm not taking care of Dev. I don't see what the big deal is. If I smoked cigarettes, no one would care."

Kit unfolded her arms and put a hand on my shoulder. "I would care. Cigarettes tar your lungs, they're nasty. And, I know, drinking is completely legal. But what about last night, with Lady?"

I saw me and Lady, outside at night, and before that, standing in her closet, the empty Champagne bottle, the secret, Lady's secret, spilling out as we looked at the photograph. By Kit. Who was now in front of me. She had no idea that I knew.

"Lady isn't in a good place right now," Kit said.

I pretended she hadn't said that, and turned to Seth. "Does she know about Muffin Buffin?"

"What's that?" Kit asked.

I tried to telegraph to Seth a billion questions with only my eyes, starting with, *Did you really think confiding in your mother's nemesis would help matters?* but he wouldn't look at me.

"Guys?" Kit said, and then shook her head. "Never mind. Seth was worried you'd drink and drive."

I leaned in until Seth was forced to look up. "Seriously? That's why you're here with your aunt? You were afraid for my safety? Yeah right."

Seth signed, *Stop Drop Dead.*

Kit let out a little whinny. "She knows the private signs? I don't even know them!"

I shook my head. "I have no idea what that means," I lied.

"I can't believe I didn't realize it sooner," Kit said, and Seth yanked his head up like one of those wind puppets.

"Realize what?" I asked.

"You two."

Seth recovered faster than I did. His face was a mask of surprise and disgust—no, worse than disgust. It was repulsion he was expressing: that the idea of sleeping with me would be like eating the bloated worm at the bottom of the tequila bottle. *Gee, thanks, Seth.* It was such a convincing reaction that my blood went as cold as the vodka I'd been craving when I'd walked into Bills. How had I not seen it sooner? Seth was a skilled liar. Dangerous, even.

Well, so was I.

"We're friends," I said. "That's it. Maybe that's unusual, Kit, but it shouldn't be. We're both into art."

Kit didn't say anything for a moment, but then she was all at once disarmed. "My goodness. I'm sorry for jumping to conclusions. I suppose it's only your connection I'm sensing. You're both artists. That's wonderful! Have you seen his film? You should! Don't be shy, Seth." She laughed, embarrassed now. "I apologize. It's just that Lady is blind to so much, I wouldn't have been surprised if you guys were, you know, pursuing a relationship."

Seth was typing something on his phone. He handed it to Kit, and I leaned over to read it.

Stop kit. Thats totally gross

"Yeah," I said. "Totally gross. I mean, Seth only just graduated from high school. And he's a mute, for God's sake! Like, he can't speak up for himself!" I was afraid to look at him, so instead I walked to the counter and rang the bell for the clerk to return. "Still want to see my photos?"

52.

THEY FOLLOWED ME OUTSIDE. KIT SAID I COULD LAY THE prints on the hood of her car (late 1970s Volvo, pristine, red). Was this how she did it with all her cohorts? She'd already put on her reading glasses (seafoam green, and so extreme they were architectural), and from her glove compartment she'd retrieved a bunch of magnets, shaped like tiny hockey pucks. I didn't understand what they were for until she explained, "To stick the photos to the car, so they don't blow away." I couldn't believe this was really a thing.

I'd never before seen my photos at the same time that I was sharing them. It felt like a violation, like getting a pap smear while masturbating, but if the dread was magnified, so was the thrill. I hadn't received feedback on my work since Everett. He'd line up my paintings and step forward, and then back, then forward again, so close to the canvases I thought he might taste one with the tip of his tongue. The feeling of him looking closely at something I'd made, not saying anything, thinking. I'd forgotten how much it mattered that someone cared.

At least the whole process distracted me from Seth, who was glowering like a villain behind Kit. He'd been stung by my comment, just as I'd been by his. There was truth to what we'd proclaimed. It was too easy: the disgust we'd declared so publicly would wreck what we had shared privately.

I slowly took out the first packet of photos. I'd ordered a contact sheet as well as the negatives, and I'd had every shot printed individually too. They were four by six, like regular point-and-shoot prints, to mimic Lady's original picture.

"I might pick one to print larger," I explained. "But for now, I wanted to see them like this."

Kit didn't ask me why and I wondered again what she already knew about the project. Then the photos were on the hood, and I was magnetizing them to it, and the metal was so hot from the sun I worried the prints might melt a little. Cars whizzed by. Someone honked, probably at us.

There I was. And again, and again—ten, fifteen, twenty, twenty-five versions of me. I looked so defenseless and fake, like a teenager trying to take a selfie with her new camera's timer. Nothing like Lady. The confidence I'd been carrying all morning collapsed. At least I'd gotten the sky right, and the blank space where Seth's dad was supposed to be felt exactly as it should: like an absence, like a loss.

Kit was carefully assessing each one, her lips pursed. If Lady could see us. The shame made me want to slam my hand against the car, sweep the photos to the ground. But now Seth was leaning in to get a look. He shook his head once, and I knew what it meant. His mother wasn't there, not even a little. I'd failed. I wanted to ask, *But what about Marco? You see that, right?*

"You sort of have to know the project," I said when Kit was finished looking. "I'm not sure what Seth has told you."

"I know nothing."

"I'm staging photos of other people's mothers, before their children were born."

"Do you have the original photo here with you?" Kit asked. "Can I see it?"

"I paint a portrait, based on the photo I receive. My photo's based on the painting."

"I see," she said.

"It's multiple layers of remove," I said.

"You don't need to explain the joke."

"I'm not—"

She began to remove the magnets from all the photos except for one. It was the first shot I'd taken, before I'd been ready. My body was a little blurry, my mouth open and stupid with surprise. It wasn't at all like Lady's pose.

"This one is interesting," she said.

"It is?" I asked.

"Francesca Woodman, Cindy Sherman, Sophie Calle."

I wasn't sure where this list was going. "All my idols," I said. "I love their work."

"I can tell. Those artists already exist," she said. "And so do I, not to bring myself into this."

"I love your stuff so much. The Women—"

"The Women came two decades after other, more groundbreaking work." She looked up, as if suddenly remembering something. "Seth did tell me something about you."

"You did?" I said to him. He looked freaked out.

"He said you were trying to get people to send photos, but that you kept receiving pictures of penises."

"I only got three!" I said. "Did you write that on your phone to her?" Seth couldn't help but grin, and I socked him.

"Three is enough," Kit said.

"Enough for what?" I asked.

"For something new," she said.

LADY

53.

AFTER I CAME TO, KARL SAT ME DOWN AT MY MOTHER'S kitchen table and watched as I ate my energy bar and downed three glasses of water. He was worried about me but I could tell he didn't want to send mixed signals; when he felt my pulse, he was as impersonal as a doctor. "You guys can go," I said finally. "I'm fine." That was all the permission Karl needed. He kissed me once on the forehead and told me to be careful. To eat some chicken. I hugged Devin, said I already missed him, and a moment later Karl carried him out of the house and I was alone.

At least my fainting had kept us from discussing Marco. The perils of a child who can speak your secrets aloud are manifold. I could only hope that Devin would forget about Mommy's friend, and that Karl would assume Marco was a character in an insipid kid's movie and never ask follow-up questions. If Karl was right, and I did favor Seth, it was only because Seth had never before ratted me out. Devin, like most toddlers, was a snitch.

Karl was correct about one thing: I needed protein. I hadn't eaten a real meal since last night's omelet. I needed a burger. More than that, I needed a cold beer.

I knew perfectly well that wanting a beer meant I wanted to see Marco. I wanted Marco.

When I went to text him, I saw that I had a missed call from S. No voicemail. I wished, again, that I'd told her about Marco and not about the photograph. Until I had turned it into a confession, that old secret had almost lost its power.

If I had told S about Marco, that would have made that mistake real. I wouldn't be texting him now: Okay if I come by?

My phone chimed a minute later. Ill be there in ten.

I fled my childhood home like it was on fire.

54.

THIS WAS MY FIFTH VISIT TO MARCO, AND BY NOW I ALREADY knew which days were street-sweeping days (Tuesday and Wednesday mornings), and which freeway exit was closest.

Marco was just pulling into the driveway when I parked. He emerged from his truck with a bag of groceries.

"I thought you said you were only ten minutes away," I said as I crossed the street from my car. "That was half an hour ago at least."

He held up the bag. "I needed provisions. Lucy will be here at three."

"So if I wait long enough, I can meet her?"

"You never stay more than an hour," he reminded me as he led me inside. "And I've got some panels that need cleaning."

The house was dark and cool and I thought of the Cottage. Marco tossed his baseball cap across the living room. His hair was matted with sweat that I could smell. It might make me faint again.

"Solar panels need to be cleaned?" I asked.

"Everything needs to be cleaned. It's part of the business model." He was walking down the hall to the kitchen. "Upkeep pays a lot of our bills."

"My mother died," I said.

He turned. "Really?"

"Really."

"Shit, Lady. You okay?"

"I need a beer. And do you have anything to eat in that grocery bag?"

He poached me two eggs, like old times. If he knew the meal was transporting us to our days of yore, he didn't mention it. He sat across the kitchen table, drinking his own beer, as I punctured the pristine white globes with my fork tines.

"I'm hungover," I said as the viscous yolks colored my plate yellow.

"Well, you're grieving," he said.

"I was hungover before I found out she was dead."

I took a big, slippery bite of egg and Marco said, "I used to love watching you eat."

"You did?"

"It was the only time you weren't mad at me. That, and when we fucked."

"Nothing has changed." I leaned toward him with my beer bottle, as if to clang it against his, but he looked taken aback.

"We're good though now, aren't we?" he asked.

"These eggs are good," I said.

"And the sex?"

"I'm afraid my marriage is really over. Karl's getting his own place, like for real."

"Don't blame me for that," he said. He got up and began to put the groceries away. There was a carton of milk. Blueberries. Frosted Flakes.

"Will you tell Lucy about Seth this weekend?" I said, taking a last bite, slick and salty. I swallowed. "You need to meet him."

He had the canvas bag balled up in his fist. "This isn't going to turn into a Brady Bunch story, Lady."

"Who said I wanted it to?"

"I can tell."

"I want Karl," I said. "I'm just fucking you."

I pushed the plate away and stood up. I hoped the remaining yolk would congeal to the plate so that later Marco would have to scrub it clean, use a little elbow grease as he thought of me.

"Are you really that into this?" Marco asked. He was coming toward me.

"Honestly?" I said. He nodded. "Seeing you makes me feel like shit. And the longer we keep this up, the harder it will be to tell Seth that you exist."

He grabbed my waist, as if we were slow dancing, and like that, the pulse in my groin began to *tat-tat-tat,* a song my body played for Marco alone.

"Finally, some real talk from Lady," he said. He kissed my neck.

"What about you? Are you into it?" I asked.

"It feels good, yeah," he mumbled against my skin. The heat was spreading across my belly.

Marco backed away for a moment, so that we were facing each other. "But I've got a lot less at stake than you do." He smiled sadly, then kissed my neck once more. He put his hands on my tits. As if on reflex, my nipples turned hard under his palms.

"If I tell Lucy," he said, still kissing me, "and then you tell Seth, you probably won't come over anymore, will you? Not like this."

He was unbuttoning my jeans. He was kneeling down so that his face was at my crotch. I remembered the old Stooges song he used to play so loudly the neighbors would bang on the walls. "I Wanna Be Your Dog." But I'd always been the subservient one, the one begging for treats. Had something changed?

"You don't know that," I said. "I might decide to come back."

His tongue was sliding up and down my underwear, lapping me slowly. He wouldn't remove them until I fell to my knees too. I could already smell myself; I was filling the kitchen.

He stopped. "But you want Karl."

I didn't reply. He slipped a finger beneath my underwear. "And once Seth knows about me," he said, watching me squirm. "You'll have to behave. You'll have to be a mom again."

"What the hell am I right now?" I said, but I could barely get the words out.

ESTHER

55.

KIT DROVE OFF, LEAVING IT TO ME TO CHAUFFEUR SETH WHER-ever he wished. "You don't mind, do you?" she had asked as she started her engine, not caring what my answer was. "I've got a meeting in Venice." Seth had stood apart like we were his divorced parents and this was a low-grade custody argument. I wondered why he'd surrendered his independence and asked her to drive. Now his car was stuck at Kit's.

She merged onto La Cienega and sped away with a backward wave out her window. I felt relieved, actually, because now the lump of tears in my throat could explode. I would cry like the little brat I was, the kind who didn't understand the value of constructive criticism. Jesus, it wasn't every day that your idol tells you that you're unoriginal. What a gift. At least those dick pics had potential.

Seth's hand was on my shoulder.

"I know. I'm being a baby." I wiped the snot from my face and kept myself turned away from him. "The photos definitely aren't great, but I don't think she really got the project either. I mean, she hasn't seen all of it: the paintings, for starters. And what about the notebooks about my mom? My drinking?" He raised an eyebrow. "It's more than that, though. The whole becoming her, you know. It's got a performative element too."

He thrust his phone in front of my face. I had to blink away the tears to read what he'd written.

Her gallery guy doesnt like the pics of me

"Really?" I turned.

He typed something else.

Thats prob why she said that stuff. Passing the shit along u know?

"You think?" I asked.

We all do it

"Thanks," I said.

He shoved his phone back into his pocket and I said, "I didn't mean what I said to Kit. About you being disabled."

He signed something, and when I didn't follow he signed again, slower this time.

I A-M.

"You are. Right. And so I guess I really am repulsive to you?"

He made a face like, *Maybe you are, Maybe you aren't,* and when I pretended to protest, he pointed at my shirt. I laughed. "Oops, I totally forgot I'm dressed like 1990s Chloë Sevigny."

I could tell from Seth's face that he had no idea who that was.

"I mean, I'm dressed like your mother."

He winced.

"My clothes are in my car. Come on."

He followed me to the alley behind the lab, and when we reached my car, he went to the passenger side, as if to get in.

"You aren't going to stand guard outside while I change?"

Seth shook the door handle in reply and I unlocked the car. We both got in, he in the front and I in the back. Once I'd changed into my own shirt, I climbed up front.

"It's hot as hell in here," I said.

I was about to roll down the window when Seth touched my arm.

"Seth," I said. "We can't . . . not here."

But I was already reaching for him. I ran a hand through his curls, which today were wild around his head. I touched his earlobe.

"Hi," I said.

He didn't do anything.

"This has to be the last time," I said. "If your mom finds out—"

He pulled away and I couldn't read what he was feeling.

"Were you not about to kiss me?"

Nothing.

"Are you upset?"

Still nothing.

"What's going on with you? Why did you bring Kit here?"

He spelled a word: A-R-T.

"My art? You wanted her to know I'm a genius, is that it? Bullshit."

Seth had his phone in his hand now, like he might write me something. He didn't.

"You were mad at me just an hour ago," I said. "About me and your mom. Remember? But, like, why can't I be friends with her? She's cool. You can't expect this—you and me—to go on forever."

Seth was edging toward the passenger-side door, away from me.

"So now you're leaving—yet again?" I asked. "Go ahead, call an Uber, take the bus."

But instead of opening the door, he had his hand on his crotch, rubbing himself.

"What are you doing?"

He plunged a hand down his pants and pulled out his dick. It was as hard as a baton, and its head was pink and throbbing; it was like a single salivary gland, a shot from a surgery documentary. Even though I couldn't see it, I could picture the mass of black hair at its shaft, thicketed and rough, a nasty bird's nest.

With the other hand, Seth picked up his phone.

"Stop," I said just as a light blinked. The flash. It would make the photograph bright and sad, like he was taking it indoors at night, alone; it was even sadder that he wasn't.

"Stop!" I said again, even though it was too late.

I got out of the car and waited for my own phone to alert me that the photo had arrived. When it did, I didn't look. I wouldn't. I heard the other door open and shut, and Seth's shoes crunching the gravelly cement as he approached me.

"I hate you," I said.

He took out his phone.

Something to remember me by?

He hadn't even wanted to be with me one last time.

"That was wrong. I said stop."

Wrong? Think about what youve done. Im barely legal.

"Are you blackmailing me?"

No its called a joke

I sighed. "It isn't funny."

Seth was looking at his phone again. Now he was tapping the screen. He handed it to me. It was a Yelp page.

"Green Builders?" I said, reading. And then, I understood. "This is your dad. Marco."

He grabbed the phone and typed.

Its a home address. Take me there.

"After that performance?" I said, nodding to the car.

If you take Kits advice you can use it for ur big solo show

"So now you think I should listen to her?"

I cant meet him alone

How long had he been meaning to ask me this favor? It could have been the real reason he'd sent me the angry texts this morning, and why he'd brought Kit to tear me down, and why he'd left me at his mercy, without a car of his own.

Please S

LADY

56.

I DON'T REMEMBER WHEN WE HAD MOVED TO THE LIVING ROOM, but that's where we were now, the morning light seeping between the blinds and pleating the floor. I was naked from the waist down and straddling Marco on the cracked leather couch, my face in his curls. Some things don't change. He was whispering something I couldn't hear into my ear, circling my wrists with his fingers. He'd lost his combative edge, and so had I. It had taken some work, but I'd found sweet Marco, here he was.

"I think I might want you after all," I whispered.

"I'm okay with that," he said. He kept on whispering, so quiet and rushed I couldn't make out the words.

This was probably just pillow talk, in-the-moment lies. But then again, he had continued to let me into his house, and he had asked me earlier if *we* were good—as if we were a unit, two against the world. He wanted me to keep coming back.

Marco was the father of my child. At least right now he wanted me for who I was, defects and all.

57.

WHAT WERE YOU WHISPERING IN MY EAR?" I ASKED AS WE put our clothes back on. We always dressed right after.

"You really want to know? Now?"

"Was it that dirty?"

He tossed me my jeans. "Not at all, actually."

"Really?"

"I . . . I'm liking this." He pointed at himself and then at me. *This,* meaning us.

His smile shocked me, it was so sincere. "You want to, I don't know, have dinner sometime?"

"With your superior cooking skills? What would be the point?"

"I'm serious," he said. He stood at the other end of the couch fully clothed except for his bare feet. He still did that thing where he stood with his toes spread apart, as if to better grasp the earth beneath him. "I want to. Do you?"

"Is it because I have money?" I asked finally.

"Is what because you have money?"

"You're underwater with the house, right?" I said.

He didn't look away. This was new: a Marco who didn't evade, didn't feint and dodge. "Karl's the one with the money, isn't he?" he asked.

"I just inherited my mother's estate."

He looked so surprised I thought he might slip into taking offense. "I never thought you'd rescue me," he said. "Is that what you think? I never thought about you at all."

"So you've already implied."

"Until recently I mean. You got under my skin, Lady. And now what? Now here we are."

He was kissing me when the doorbell rang.

"Who the fuck is that?" Marco said.

"Lucy?"

"This early? No way." He was already leaving the living room. "Stay here. It's probably some Jehovah's Witnesses. I'll be right back."

I lay down on the couch. My hangover had returned, a headache beating like a metronome at the front of my skull. I closed my eyes. When Marco came back, I would either get up and leave, like I always did, or I'd stay. If I stayed, our illicit meetings would become sanctioned, nothing to be ashamed of. No Karl. How could I not know what I wanted?

I strained to hear what was going on at the front door. I couldn't understand what Marco was saying, but from the tone of his voice, confused rather than officious, I knew he couldn't be talking to a solicitor, religious or otherwise. I sat up. Now I heard another voice, a young woman's.

I recognized it—she sounded like S. I suddenly felt drunk instead of hungover. Like I had last night, holding S up in the water.

The woman who sounded like S spoke again. Was it really S? Was that possible? She had figured out my secret and I didn't even have to tell her myself. She knew I'd end up here.

The Sitter is now The Soothsayer, I thought.

Without thinking, I left the room and headed toward the voice.

"But you're definitely Marco Green?" she was saying.

"I am indeed," Marco said. "Why?"

"S?" I tried.

Marco turned toward me, and in doing so, moved from the partially opened door. There was S—my ears hadn't fooled me. Except this S didn't look like herself, she wasn't wearing a bra and her hair was a tangled mess around her face. It reminded me of something, but I couldn't place it. I felt a charge of something, a current of static electricity, and then it disappeared.

"S?" I said again.

When she saw me, she startled as if I were a poltergeist coming toward her.

I'd been wrong: S hadn't foreseen this—me—at all.

Next to her stood Seth. He was wearing the blue basketball shorts I'd bought for him over two years ago. The ones with the unraveling waistband. He never let me throw anything away.

"Seth," I said now. I was announcing people like a butler, stating the obvious. I couldn't manage anything more.

He'd seen me before S had, and now he was breathing heavily. It was the sound he made when he was angry, when he wanted to yell, but couldn't. What agony, I thought.

"Seth," I said again. I made my hands into a bowl, even though I knew he wouldn't remember. *Sorry Love.*

He backed away and S steadied him so he wouldn't fall off the steps.

"Seth," Marco said. He was just standing there, staring at his son. I could tell he was shaken. Seth looked exactly like him—nearly twenty years ago. Marco had been sucked back in time.

"What are you doing here?" I asked.

"We're—" S glanced at Seth as if to confirm that she should adhere to the script they'd previously agreed upon. "We're looking for Seth's father. Mark Green."

"That's me," Marco said, stepping onto the porch. "But I'm Marco, not Mark."

Seth began signing furiously. I caught a few words. *Name. Mom. Liar. Fuck you.*

"Hey, hey," S said in a soothing voice. "Let's get the whole story."

"Yes, let's," I said. "How did you end up here? Why are you together?"

Seth signed something else. I think it was *Helping me.*

"Goddammit with the ASL, Seth, use your phone," I said.

"From your Twitter," S said, the words modulated so that everyone might keep calm and obey her. It was the voice she used to get Devin to put on his shoes. "Muffin Buffin."

Seth signed something else, deliberately fast, and I deliberately caught none of it.

Marco was watching Seth with a furrowed brow. "Are you deaf?" he asked.

He turned to me. "Is he deaf?"

Marco began to twiddle his fingers in a sorry approximation of ASL. Seth had hung with enough hearing-impaired kids to be offended, but when I turned to him, he wasn't sneering. He was staring. This was his dad, and he couldn't look away.

"Stop," S said to Marco. "He isn't deaf."

"It's called selective mutism," I said. "He doesn't speak," I continued. "He never has."

Seth had turned to me. Now it was hard to tell exactly what he was angry about, but his breathing was getting heavier, and I thought he might pick up one of Marco's large planters and throw it across the front yard in a rage. I remembered the old tantrums, the way his inability to express something as simple as *I don't want apple juice* made him fling himself across a restaurant floor, or bite my arm, the body tearing itself apart as if to dislodge the language inside of it.

"He autistic?" Marco said. He was speaking like Seth was, in fact, deaf.

"No," I said. "And he isn't an eccentric genius either."

S raised an eyebrow—I must have used a similar line on her. She was reading something else on my face, something between me and Marco. Smart girl.

"Have you guys been in touch for a long time?" S asked.

"Only a few weeks," Marco said. He was looking at Seth, still trying to take in the fact of him. "She came to tell me about Seth. How he wanted to meet."

"Seth is right in front of you," I said. "He can't speak, but he can hear you perfectly."

I turned to Seth, who was practically vibrating. When I reached out to try to calm him, he flung himself away. S stepped in and gave me a look that suggested I stop, for my own good.

"Why didn't you tell him?" she asked.

"I was going to tell you, Sethy," I said. "I swear. Marco wanted me to wait."

"Now, hold on," Marco said, "there's a good reason for that. I do want to know you, man. I just have some business to attend to first."

"That's not what I meant," S said.

She looked at Seth, as if trying to understand what he might want to say, what he might be feeling. And she was getting it; she was reading something on his face, in his body: all that was illegible to me.

"You didn't tell him," S repeated, and this time she nodded at Marco.

For a moment Seth's body calmed.

"Tell him what?" I began, but now I understood. I had told Marco about Seth, about what Seth wanted—a father, to know his father—but I'd withheld the other thing, the central thing, the problem everyone was forced to orbit around.

I hadn't told him what was wrong with my son, our son.

"I didn't know how," I said weakly.

Seth let out a little whimper. He placed a middle finger at each temple and waited. It was a special sign that he'd made up at fifteen, one I'd banned because it was cruel, the equivalent of a kid saying, *I hate you.*

Then he carefully spelled out K-A-R-L. Karl. The father who knew everything about Seth and loved him.

"What's he saying?" Marco said, like the buffoon he was. I ignored him.

"What is there to tell Karl?" I asked, and everyone looked away, as if sorry for me and my caravan of secrets.

Seth pulled out his phone. I didn't know if he was going to text his stepfather right then, or maybe type something for us to read. God, I longed for the latter. There it was: the old, deep-seated pain of wanting to communicate with Seth. *What's wrong? Just tell me why you're crying! How can I make it better?* Every mother begs like this in the first days of a child's life, but I hadn't ever been able to stop. This was my relentless plea.

Once Seth had typed something, he put his phone in his pocket. I would never know.

A moment later, his keys were in his fist and he had directed them across the street. My car blinked on.

"Don't you dare leave," I said, but he was already at the sidewalk, already headed across the street.

"Lady's right," Marco called. "Come inside, let's talk. I mean, not talk, but—"

"Just shut up," I said.

Seth signed *Thank you* to S, and she nodded. Again, that sharp, fleeting current of understanding.

"Please," I called out, but he wasn't going to turn around, and we all knew it.

58.

Seth was driving away when I started asking the questions I already knew the answers to: "How do you know about my Twitter? Why are you dressed like that?"

"The photo you sent," she said. "The one of you and Marco. You emailed it to me."

Marco had already gone inside, saying he needed to piss, and he'd left the door open. As if all three of us were going to hang out.

"What did you do with the photo?" I asked. "Why did you want it?"

"It was for an art thing. But is that really what matters right now?" S asked. "I mean, what's Seth going to do now? Are you and Marco . . . ?"

"That's none of your business."

"I didn't tell Seth anything you told me. I swear."

"So you're good at keeping secrets, so what? I assume you kept all of Seth's too."

"He and I are friends."

"Good for you. I haven't had a friend in almost nineteen years. Did you know that? Not a real one. Not since Seth was born—or probably earlier. When I got with Marco, none of my girlfriends liked him. I guess you could say Karl and I were friends, but you can't count your husband, can you?" I was surprised by my tears. "I guess you can't count your kid's nanny either. That's even more lame."

"The Sitter, you mean," she said. "I don't even care about that. What I do care about is the fact that Marco is a jackass. You can't be serious, Lady. That guy? Seth is better off not knowing him."

"How easy for you to say," I said. "You've got a dad who loves you."

"So does Seth."

"I was talking about myself." I wiped my tears. "God, I am such a fuck-up."

"At least you haven't killed a bunny."

"What?"

"You didn't see him? In the pool."

"It's my fault," I said. "I told you not to swim with Milkshake."

"Good thing, or he'd be the dead one." She shook her head so she wouldn't cry, like a dog shaking off water. "I'll drive you home," she said. "Tell me where your purse is. I'll go inside and get it."

"It's your day off," I said.

"Consider it pro bono work," she said, and this time I did laugh, for a second. I told her where my purse was.

A few minutes later she emerged with it in her arms.

"Marco says bye and sorry."

Bye and Sorry. There was no sign for that.

ESTHER

59.

MY FATHER CALLED AS WE WERE GETTING INTO THE CAR. I didn't answer. I had bigger problems than his questions about my health, my "self-care" as he called it, and I didn't give a shit about his and Maria's garden right now, or a salad recipe with tarragon I just had to try. Not now, Steven Shapiro, not now.

Marco lived in one of those neighborhoods where all human activity occurred inside, as if a curfew had just been announced, or a smog warning. Every car was parked, no one had a dog to walk, and I hardly checked my side mirrors as I pulled from the curb. We were on the freeway within a minute, and every time I merged into another lane, Lady, like my echo, checked the traffic too, as if she were the one driving.

"I won't kill us," I said. "I'm hungover, not drunk."

My buzz from Bills had been sucked away like water in a tide pool. Nothing is more sobering than being found out. Although, so far, it was Lady, not me, who was in trouble. Marco was an idiot, and Lady was worse for sleeping with him instead of introducing him to Seth. Lady had chosen Marco over everyone else.

"Is it strange to say that I wish you'd told me about Marco?" I asked.

I glanced in the rearview to make sure the guy behind me wasn't still on my ass, and on instinct, Lady peered over her own shoulder. My camera was in the backseat, along with the packages from the lab.

"You were taking pictures," she said.

"I'm an artist," I said.

"Let me guess," she said. "Seth was your subject."

"Wrong," I said. "But you could say you were."

"I guess I asked for it, sending you the photo."

"You had no idea it was going to me, your employee. Not that it matters. The whole thing is dead anyway. It sucks. It's derivative."

"You sound just like Cunt Daniels," she said. "I guess that means you must be talented."

"Cunt Daniels thinks I'm a hack."

"Oh who fucking cares about her right now," Lady said. "I don't want to hear anything about her. I cannot handle it. Please just get me home."

The heat in the car was dry and soupy at once. I rolled down my window and the wind was so forceful and loud my eyes watered. I closed it.

"Sorry about the AC," I said.

Lady was staring straight ahead. If she was hot, she didn't show it.

"What's really going on between you and Seth?" she asked, and turned to me.

I kept my gaze on the road.

"Be honest," she said. "You owe me that."

Here it was, the moment I'd been dreading, the inevitable walk to the gallows. I just didn't think it would come when she and I were alone in my Camry, going 75 on the 170, the heat like a weight we had to wear, like a heavy X-ray apron. Any second now she might reach over and grab the wheel, kill us both, take out a few other drivers too.

I hadn't answered yet, and I realized she was nervous, her hand cranking her window open and closed. Noises—engines, a helicopter, the wind—flew into the space between us, then were shut out, then returned.

She went on: "In the past, I wouldn't have asked. I wouldn't have even known to ask! But he's an adult. I get it. And you two are fairly close in age." I could tell she was counting the years between us.

She leaned over and put a hand on my leg. "Why wouldn't you fall in love with him?" She sat back, removed her hand. "He's so unusual and funny. He's smart."

"But not a genius, remember?"

"So I'm right. You love him."

"No," I said. "I don't." This was the truth, and I was happy to announce it.

"You aren't together?" she asked.

Of course the questions wouldn't stop. This wasn't just anyone we were talking about, it was Seth: her baby, her boy. He was like a wild animal, rarely seen and barely understood. Lady thought I'd caught him.

"No." That was true—we'd never been together.

"So nothing happened between you two?"

Here was the real question, and here it, my lie, would be.

"Never," I said. "Lady, I would never do that to you."

I'd lied, I was a liar, but I'd also saved this, I'd saved us.

60.

LADY HAD TURNED ON THE RADIO, AND ASIDE FROM AN OCCA-sional remark about NPR or the traffic, we were quiet, and it wasn't until we were finally on familiar ground, driving through Studio City on Laurel Canyon, that our silence felt right and companionable. I rolled my window all the way down and let the warm breeze flutter across me. I couldn't believe she'd let it rest.

My phone rang again; this time it was my mom.

"Anyone I know?" Lady asked.

"For some reason, both my parents are bugging me this morning."

"Maybe they're conspiring against you."

"I think the only time that's ever happened was the moment I was conceived."

"No wonder Seth wants to be your friend. You're horrible."

"I'm serious! My mom and dad don't talk—at least, not since I turned eighteen."

I turned onto Mulholland and Lady took out her phone.

"How can you check it right now?" I asked. "With this view?"

The canyon below was cloaked in haze but the sandy mountainside to our right was craggy and spotted with cacti. The land seemed wild despite the mansions sitting just a private drive away. I could never look away.

"Bah," she said. "I see it all the time."

"Please. You're addicted to Twitter," I said. "You don't have to hide it."

"Maybe. But I haven't stopped being ashamed." She meant it as a joke, but she wasn't lying either.

"It'll turn out fine," I said.

"Karl and I are over."

"You were separated. You don't have to tell him."

"It doesn't have anything to do with that. Karl doesn't even know about Marco, or he didn't when he decided he couldn't wait any longer for me to get my act together. I think I was just testing him when I asked him to move out . . . and he failed that test, he didn't keep fighting for me. He's getting his own apartment, he's moving on. It only took him a couple of months to shake me off. How messed up am I, for believing that's what I wanted?" An ugly sob dropped out of her. "God, what have I done?"

I tried to soothe her with a hush, the same technique I used for putting Devin down to sleep. I hoped she wouldn't notice the similarities. Lady was wiping her eyes with a napkin she'd found in the console.

"I always cry into Starbucks napkins too," I said. She actually smiled.

We had descended into Laurel Canyon, the newer part, no bohemians here, the part my father liked because the roads were wider and paved better, but it was still the Canyon if you squinted your eyes. Eucalyptus trees and dust. It was funny how Lady's part of the hill was close to all of this, but so different. Where she lived, there was no community, only money.

"What if Seth wants to live with Karl?" Lady was saying now. "Custody for Dev will definitely be fifty-fifty. I'll move. I have to. I can't stay in that big house by myself." She let out another little cry, and hiccupped.

She turned to me. "But you'll still work for both of us. Right?"

Once Devin had asked Lady if he could eat an entire cake himself on his birthday. She'd said yes because that was months away, he would never remember her promise, and it was easier than saying no.

"Sure," I said.

Lady tossed the balled-up napkin into her purse and went back to fiddling on her phone.

A few more turns and we were out of Laurel Canyon and into the Hills. There were work trucks congesting the narrow roads, and women speed walking in yoga pants. They all looked my age—at least from the back. At the corner of Sunset Plaza: a clusterfuck of Open House signs. Around the corner: yet another mansion was having its 1990s glass blocks removed. I was about to point it out when suddenly Lady leaned forward, her seat belt straining against her chest. Her phone was still in her hand but away from her face, like it was alive and rotting.

"What is it?" I asked.

Lady reached out as if to punch me, or strangle me, and I almost slammed into a Land Rover barreling toward us.

LADY

61.

@sethconscious:
Hey, @muffinbuffin41, guess what? Im fucking The Sitter.

ESTHER

62.

You're going to kill us!" I yelled, and pulled the car to the shoulder where the road turned to rocks. A ficus hedge blocked Lady's window and filtered the car greenish, the whites of her eyes gone gray like an overboiled egg yolk.

"What the hell is wrong with you?" I asked. "I almost hit that car back there."

Lady still had her phone out and she was holding it inches from me, shoving it in my face.

"You and Seth . . ." She stopped, like she was struggling to trudge on. "You *fucked*?" That was the word she'd read, I realized. "He wrote"—here she finally pulled back and read the screen—" 'I'm fucking The Sitter.' "

The edges of my vision flickered. "Asshole."

"He is not!" And then, "Is it true?"

"Do you guys call me The Sitter all the time, or just online?"

"So it is true."

"No—he isn't *fucking The Sitter*. Well, in a way he is, with that." I flung my hands at her stupid phone. "It's over between us and he knows that. Why would he tell you? And like that?"

Lady mewed like a wounded animal and I realized I had confessed.

"It's true," she repeated. "How could it be true? You just told me—"

I knew I was supposed to be tender and kind, and that I should acknowledge my lie, but I was too angry at Seth.

"Your son slept with me just so he could tell you about it," I said.

She slapped me with her free hand and I heard myself cry out as if it weren't my own voice. My mom had been the last person to slap me. Five years ago. We'd been in the parking lot of the apartment complex we were living in. I had just told her that I'd decided to go to Berkeley instead of UCLA. She had hit me and said, "Leave me then. Just go. Go have your perfect life." My face felt the same way now: raw and stinging, brittle-edged. At least Lady hadn't used her phone.

I thought I heard her crying. She had her hands to her face and I looked back to the windshield as if that could give her privacy.

"Today I found out that my mom died," she said.

I turned to her. "She did? Why didn't you say anything earlier?"

Her face was red and puffy, uglier than I'd thought possible. "This hurts."

"I swear, I didn't want to hurt you." I paused. "But I think Seth did."

"You're kidding, right? This isn't some elaborate revenge scheme," she said. She laughed. "Besides, he already has one in motion."

"He does?"

"By not speaking," she replied.

LADY

63.

SEEKING BABYSITTER FOR PRECOCIOUS TODDLER—
Hollywood

Looking for a new babysitter for my smart and chatty
toddler, effective immediately. 2–3 days a week, live-in
option to be considered after a 6-week probation period.

Requirements:
   5+ years of experience working with kids
   References from previous childcare positions
   Driver's license and full background check

Also, I have another son who is (barely) an adult. He suffers
from selective mutism. If you're unlucky enough to meet
him, I ask that you refrain from getting involved in his mind
games.

If you're an artist of any kind, please look elsewhere. I've had
enough of you for one lifetime.

64.

REPLIED TO SETH'S TWEET WITH A LINK TO MY NEW CRAIGS-
list ad, and afterward I lay on my bed face-first like a corpse in a

river. The sheets smelled of no one. Devin—good little toddler—never got out of his bed, and Karl's scent had been laundered away weeks ago. The futon I'd shared with Seth for so many years had been smaller, queen-sized, with a slight dip in the center, no headboard.

I could still conjure his innocuous kid musk, how his sweat would stain the pillowcases and the pillows beneath too, how he would wake with his curls matted to his neck as if we slept not in L.A. but a humid jungle with bugs the size of scissors. If he woke from a nightmare he might grab my arm and pull hard, yanking me from my dreams. "What is it," I'd say to the dark, and when he was younger he would curl into me, a heated little coil of a boy. When he was older, he simply wouldn't let go of my arm.

Karl—perfect Karl—had changed all that. He moved me into his California king and set up Seth with his own Tempur-Pedic. It was for the better. But now Karl was leaving me and so was Seth, and by tomorrow S would be gone too. I'd have partial custody of Devin and the rest of the time I'd wander this big house like a ghost, smelling only myself. That must have been my mother's lot, alone unless you counted her collection of high heels, her flowers, her beauty.

Stuck like this, rolling across my huge bed, I would even start missing Marco. I'd long for him again, at least to keep the stink of solitude off me. He was an idiot, yes, but he hadn't lied to me, from the very start he'd shown me what he lacked, what he was incapable of.

I could have told him about Seth, that he couldn't speak. I should have said that there was no medical reason for him not to. That all the doctors, the specialists, and the therapists had explained as much to me over the years in their benign, condescending tones. If nothing was wrong, it had to be something else. What had happened to him?

I happened. I was the trauma, I am the trauma. Whatever I did to him I keep doing it.

I got off the bed and stood in the center of the room, surveying its contents as bloodlessly as I could. There was no way I was staying in this house if everyone else was leaving. It was haunted, most of all by me. I knew if I looked out the window to the pool below, I'd glimpse the dead rabbit there like a single cloud in a blue sky.

I went to the window to confirm my suspicions, and when I saw S below, I stepped away from the glass abruptly, surprised. I didn't want her to see me, but I also wanted, badly, to see her.

Warily, I returned to my perch and watched as she got on her hands and knees at the edge of the pool, a pair of blue dishwashing gloves on her hands. Her Lady costume had been replaced with cut-off jean shorts and a black tank top, the hem of which was getting wet as she leaned into the pool with her arm stretched toward Peter Rabbit. Now she was scooping him out of the water, and she was doing it slowly, tenderly. I couldn't see her face well enough, but I was sure she wasn't wrinkling her nose or closing her eyes against the sight of the bloated animal. Even now I couldn't hate her.

She dropped the rabbit into a plastic bag and whispered something to herself—a prayer or an apology—before tying it closed. Then she dropped the bag on one of the chaise lounges, presumably to dispose of it the next time she walked to the garbage cans. Now she was running a toe through the water. Could she be contemplating a swim?

I had enjoyed slapping her. I didn't regret it, and I probably never would. That didn't mean I wouldn't miss her though.

As if she could feel me watching her from above, she looked up. Someone was knocking at the door.

65.

I RAN MY FINGERS THROUGH MY HAIR BEFORE I WENT DOWN-stairs because I couldn't fathom who might be waiting for me. The Sparkletts man had come two days ago. I hadn't ordered anything on-line. "One minute," I called out.

When I got to the door I peered through the peephole. A man and a woman, maybe ten years older than I was, stood outside. The woman was doing a little soft-shoe dance and the man was smiling straight ahead, as if he were getting his photo taken at the DMV. I realized he must be posing for me.

I opened the door. "Can I help you?"

The woman was already trying to peer around me, as if casing the joint. She and the man didn't fit together. Judging by his white teeth, his tidy gray hair, and his sunglasses with their Transitions lenses (already turning less dark in the shade of the porch), the man was well-off. The woman, on the other hand, her face showed traces of long-ago beauty, but she was beginning to prune, and there was a hardness to her face that revealed a life of not-enough, be it sleep or money or maybe even love. And too much of something else: sun, drink, risk, misery. She wore a T-shirt that read STOP INTERRUPTING ME WHILE I'M TRYING TO ANNOY YOU!

The man spoke, his voice a little too loud, a little too practiced: "You must be Lady."

"And you are?" I asked.

"We're looking for Esther," the woman said. She had an appealing voice: deep and raspy, with just a twang of nasal to it. She had no idea she possessed such a gift, which made it even better. "Esther Shapiro," she said.

The man nodded, and I wondered if he too heard what was magical in the voice.

"Who?" I asked.

"The young woman who's taking care of your son," he said.

"You mean S? Her last name is Fowler."

"That's my name," the woman said.

Now I was really confused. "Okay . . . ?"

"S Fowler," the man said, and clapped his hands together.

"S Fowler?" the woman repeated with an eyebrow raised.

"That's her current nom de plume, Kathy," the man explained.

So there it was. "You must be the parents," I said. "Please, come in."

The woman, Kathy, stepped in first, and then S's father.

"Steve Shapiro," he said, and put out his hand. His shake was vigorous; on his wrist was an elaborate waterproof watch. "It's so wonderful to meet you!" he said. "This is Katherine."

"Kathy," she said as she moved across the foyer, her eyes upward, taking in first the sweep of the living room, then the staircase, then the sliding glass doors to the yard. She reminded me of S on her first interview: the unabashed nosiness, a comfort in her own body.

"Is S—Esther—expecting you?" I asked. "She's in the back packing up."

"Packing up?" Steve echoed. He shot a worried glance at Kathy, but she didn't return the look. "She didn't tell us."

"Tell you what?" I asked. "That I fired her?" Steve looked at me, stunned, and I had to admit, this was a little fun.

Kathy started to laugh, and Steve said, "Kathy."

"I'm sorry," she replied. "It's just that I was also fired from my first nanny position."

"What a shock," Steve replied drily.

"Her plan worked out beautifully then. That's my girl," Kathy said, but more to herself, and because Steve didn't ask her to elaborate, I didn't either.

"You're probably wondering why we're here," Steve said.

"I guess I am, yes."

"We're worried about Esther."

"You, not we," Kathy said and hitchhiked a thumb in the direction of her ex. "The guy hopped on a flight first thing this morning!"

"Esther hasn't been texting me back with her usual alacrity," he explained. "She's been drinking."

"Is that why you canned her?" Kathy asked.

I shook my head. "She does drink a lot. But that's not why I fired her. I fired her because she's a liar."

"My daughter is the most honest person I've ever met," Steve said, and for once he and his ex-wife seemed to agree on something, because she was nodding.

"Children are different with their parents," I said.

"What did she lie to you about?" Steve asked.

"Well, her last name, for starters."

I was about to lay it all out for them, what the hell, why shouldn't I get S in trouble with her parents, when I heard the sliding glass door slurp open behind me.

"Mom? Dad?" I heard S say.

We all turned at once.

She stood in front of the open door with the bagged dead bunny in one hand. She must have been on her way to throw it out and seen us through the glass. Milkshake trotted up to her from the kitchen and jumped onto her legs, trying to sniff the corpse. She kicked him off and then stood with her feet together, almost coy and feminine, in a way I'd never seen her before.

"What are you doing here?"

"I was explaining to your parents, Esther Shapiro, that you've been fired," I said.

"I was going to quit."

"Waterbug," Steve said softly.

"Why didn't you tell me you were coming down?" she asked him.

"I was so worried," he explained. "It was sort of a split-second decision. Clearly, my fears weren't unfounded." He looked her up and down. "Why is your hair cut like that? And you look so . . . tired. Are you all right?"

Kathy hushed Steve. "She looks tired because she's not wearing any makeup, genius."

"She never wears makeup," I said, and Steve looked at me like I was nuts.

Kathy skipped toward her daughter and almost immediately S dropped the bag and sunk into her mother's arms, limp-limbed, her head kneading into her mother's chest like a baby goat at a petting zoo. The comfort and familiarity between them wasn't what I expected.

"I thought you had mom rage," I said as Milkshake inspected the dead animal on the floor.

I was struck by how different S—Esther—seemed around her parents. Even her body language had shifted to some other register, one she had never shown me. Her limbs were loose and relaxed, but there was something more self-conscious in her facial expression. She cared about what she looked like.

"Does anyone outside this house call you S?" I asked.

"It's a new thing she's trying out," Steve said when his daughter didn't answer. She was still hanging on her mother.

"That's Peter Rabbit in there," I said to Kathy, and nodded at the plastic bag on the floor.

Kathy pushed away from S to get a better look.

Steve leaned forward. "Who's Peter—?"

Kathy gasped. "What? He's dead?"

"He drowned. I'm so sorry."

Kathy kneeled by the bag for a moment, but it was as if it was too much to see, and she quickly stood. "Say what you will about me, Esther, but I would have never killed my own pet."

S swept her index fingers under her eyes, as if she were wiping away mascara that wasn't there. "I know, Mom. I know."

"You think I'd do that?"

"I don't! I never should have taken him."

Steve was watching them. "Esther, your hair," he said loudly. Either he was obsessed with how she looked, or he was trying to defuse the conflict between mother and daughter. "And those shorts," he added. I wasn't certain what he meant, but the shorts looked terrible on S; they wrinkled and rode up at her inner thighs as if the fat there were munching on the material.

"I gather this is a costume of some kind," Steve said finally.

"Daddy," S said. She was begging him to stop.

"Is this a . . . performance?" he said.

"Earlier today she was dressed like me," I said. "Or me circa 1997. I hope whoever she's pretending to be now looked better in those shorts."

"Hey," Steve snapped at me.

"I've never hurt anything in my life," Kathy said now. When Steve snorted, she said. "You're a man, Steve, not a bunny."

She had walked away from S, she wasn't even looking at her, and I could tell she wanted to process this news sitting down: my couch maybe, a bed. "You think . . . hurting things . . . that's part of being me?" she asked S, finally turning to her.

"No," S said; she was practically crying.

"You're dressed as Kathy," Steve said.

"You are?" I asked.

"I see it now," he said.

"That's how she always looks," I said.

"No, it isn't," Kathy said.

"It isn't?" I turned to S. "Who are you?" I asked.

"She definitely isn't me," Kathy said, and I watched S's face crumple for a moment, and then rally to regain its composure.

"She's an artist," Steve said.

"Stop making excuses for her," Kathy said. She kneeled down and picked up the bag, trembling. "I need a fucking drink."

"Of course you do," Steve said.

"Go prance back to Maria and stay out of it," Kathy said. She was headed to the front door. I recognized S in her once more: the entitlement and passion, and the swagger. All of that had been part of S's act and she had nailed it. I had fallen for a fraud.

"Come back with me to Berkeley, Waterbug," Steve said gently. "We just changed the sheets in the guest room. We can just chill out for a few weeks."

"I want you out by tonight," I said. "Whoever you are."

S just nodded—at me, or at her father, I didn't know. A flicker of pain crossed her face as she glanced at her mother, who was standing at the door, her hand on the knob.

"I'll be outside," Kathy said.

The front door clicked behind her. Another mother, gone.

"Can I just—" she began.

"Can you just what?" I asked. "And to think *you* were the one to call Seth a manipulative asshole."

Steve was holding up his two fingers like a tourist in Paris asking for the check.

"What?" I said.

"I understand why you're upset, Ms. Daniels, but I think we all need to take a deep breath and calm down. I can assure you Esther has never done anything like this before."

"You can 'assure me'? How can you really know what your adult child is up to?"

"Well, I—"

"You can't," I said. "No parent can."

S stopped us. "Can I go up to Dev's room, Lady? Just for a minute? I need to, like, say goodbye."

"He isn't here, remember? Not that I'd let you see him if he were."

"Just please say I can. I need a minute. I was myself with him."

"Sure you were," I said.

ESTHER

66.

LADY TOLD US SHE WAS GOING UP TO HER BEDROOM TO TAKE A shower, and that whatever stupid *ujjayi* breath I planned to do in Dev's room better be completed by the time she was done. My father told her he'd help me move out as swiftly as possible.

"Leave your address on the counter," she said to him. "I'll mail her last paycheck there." Apparently, Lady was beyond talking to me directly.

When we were alone, my dad sighed.

"You think Mom already left?" I asked.

"I'll see if she's out there."

"I hurt her."

"What happened here, Waterbug? You're dressing up like Kathy, like your boss . . . ?"

"It's over, Dad. Don't worry. It was really, really stupid."

"Don't sell yourself short. It didn't turn out as you'd planned, but it probably wasn't stupid."

"Just stop it!" I said. "You don't have to think everything I do is great. I fucked up, and the only one I can blame is myself."

"Well, you're taking responsibility," he said, nodding. "That's good. You're growing up. You're a good girl."

"I am?"

"Of course you are."

He had meant it to be nice, but it hurt.

"Give that boy's room one last look," he said. "You loved him, I see that. Say goodbye and let's get out of here. Let's go home and forget about all of this."

His words were a balm, as they always were, even when they were more fantasy than truth. I watched him head outside and then I mounted the staircase, already thinking about how little I had to pack to get out of here. My dad would insist we drive up Highway 1, stop at Nepenthe for a glass of wine and a dazzling view of the ocean. Ten-plus hours later, we'd get to the East Bay. Berkeley, with its fog and its coeds and scowling retirees, would be exactly as I'd left it. I'd sleep like the dead in the guest bedroom, its window overlooking the backyard's wise, sad redwood tree, its trunk thick as a freeway pillar, the thing just lucky it hadn't been chopped down to make toothbrushes during the Gold Rush. The next morning I would put on makeup, try to fix my hair right, and then I'd walk down to Philz for a coffee. Later I'd wait in some stupid breadline with Maria. I'd look for a job that very day, probably apply to grad school in psychology. Maybe I could work at a preschool, get an apartment in Oakland. If I visited my mom, it would be for a weekend here or there, but that would be it.

At the top of the stairs I looked down at the first floor. My dad had already left the house; I was alone. To my left was Seth's room, his door shut, to my right, Devin's, the door wide open and welcoming to visitors, to intruders, the sweet smell of pink baby lotion and cloying Ikea particleboard furniture already drifting toward me, as if pulling me closer. I'd miss that guy.

The thing Lady didn't get, or the thing she'd forgotten, was that being a child was painful too. She was so wrapped up in losing Seth, in the treacheries of him growing up, that she couldn't remember what it felt like to be the one on the other side. The burden of that. Sure, Seth had left her womb and never returned, but he was the one who had to do the leaving.

I dragged my fingers across Seth's door and gave Devin's room a little hello and goodbye with a nod of my head. See you, old pal.

Lady's room was at the end of the hallway, her door shut like a mouth. I told myself I wanted to see if it was locked as I headed toward it.

The door opened with the softest click. The light from the bedroom, her blinds drawn all the way up, poured into the darkened hallway. I stepped in.

Lady was in the shower, as she'd claimed she would be. I heard the water running on the other side of the bathroom door, could imagine the room filled with steam, even the pounding of water on my own back. Even now I couldn't be in my own body.

I only had a few minutes. I walked to the closet and shut myself inside of it, my heart like a hand opening and closing into a fist. I turned on the light. There was the photograph, waiting for me. In it, the white of the tub's porcelain was startling and stark, especially against the softness of Lady's body, her dark pupils.

I don't know why I wanted it, but I did. I'd take it. Either Lady would see it as revenge, the collateral I'd extracted from her. A threat that persisted. Or she'd know I was protecting her sons from finding out the truth. I was removing the evidence for her: as a favor, as a friend. Maybe now Karl could come back.

I slipped the photo off the wall and hurried out of the closet, out of the room. I galloped down the stairs and outside to the Cottage. No one had witnessed my theft.

I imagined, someday, Lady might try to get the photograph back. She'd have to come find me.

LADY

8 Months Later

WHEN THE GLOSSY POSTCARD SHOWED UP IN MY MAILBOX, I initially assumed it was an ad for a sample sale, or a reminder from the dentist. But when I saw that it was an invitation to an art show at Seth's school, my hands shook. My legs went weak. I hadn't seen or heard from him in months, not since the day he fled Marco's house and moved in with Karl full-time. The show was called *Seven Films for the End of Days* and Seth's name was listed alphabetically with six others. "Yes!" I said. My exuberance embarrassed me, even though no one was around to see it.

I missed Seth. I wrote him letters. They were written by hand because we had both, wisely, vanished from the Internet. *Dear Seth,* one of them began, *I hate the small plates restaurant trend. I'm hungry, dammit!* He never answered and I didn't blame him. I kept writing the letters. *How come everyone thinks ladybugs are so cute when in fact they're insects like all the others? They've got the best publicist in town.*

I inspected the postcard once more, turned it over in my hands like it might contain some deeper secret if I looked at it closely enough, and then tucked it into my purse. I couldn't help but think of S. I wondered what she'd say about this show, about my son making art. I wanted to describe to her my dreams: Seth and me out to breakfast, Seth and me swimming in the pool. Once, we were at Office Depot, buying highlighters. Everything in them could have happened, but hadn't. That's what made them cruel. S would get it.

I headed for the elevator. I was already thinking what I would wear. What I would say. What I would see. His film.

My new living room overlooked the Beverly Center, the mall like a cruise ship sailing into San Vicente, and from my bedroom, Milkshake and I could watch the goings-on at Cedars: the dutiful cancer patients arriving for their chemotherapy, the hopeful family members with their wan bouquets, ambulances like blinking toy trucks. Devin's room was as narrow as a supermarket aisle, and he had only one tiny window, but it was shaped like an egg and he liked that best. All you can see through it was sky, and that was a relief too.

I had sold my mother's house. The money sat in my checking account, waiting for me to decide what to do with it. Groceries, preschool tuition for Devin, rent: rinse and repeat until it was gone. Or that was what I told myself before I began working at the Wellness Center and started adding to the pile of cash. There I answered the phone, processed insurance claims, and poured spa water for clients. The acupuncture was free for employees and I got my treatments every Wednesday after work. To Seth I wrote: *When Dr. Melinda places the needles into my ear and on the insides of my ankles and tells me I'll sleep well tonight, I want to believe her. The Center's slogan is "Practice Hope." I'm trying!*

Karl wanted me to invest the money; he kept forwarding me emails about financial planning webinars, and he even offered to pay for an adviser to meet with me. I demurred. We hadn't even drawn up divorce papers. Nothing needed to be decided. Nothing.

KARL SAW SETH's postcard when he was over for our ASL lesson. I had hired the private tutor not long after moving in. It was the three of us: me, Karl, and Devin, sitting in the living room as Liv patiently reviewed the vocab, the emphasis of each word or phrase. Dev quickly surpassed me in skill, his hands fluttering like Seth's, so natural I wondered if his older brother had started teaching him a while ago. If he did, that would make me smile. This was a language we could all learn.

The postcard was attached to the freezer door, next to a fringe of old Bed Bath & Beyond coupons I always forget to use even though the place is right across the street from here. Karl and I had just put Devin to bed, and he was on his way out when his eyes caught the postcard.

"Are you going to be there?" he asked.

"He was the one to send it, right? This wasn't your doing?"

"I honestly didn't know he mailed you one until just now."

I smiled.

"Can we go together?" he asked.

"Sure," I said.

This was different. For months, Karl and I had avoided being alone together. On the evenings we met with Liv, Karl left as soon as Devin was in bed. He dutifully told me about Seth's classes, and what they made for dinner. Things a mother should know. We were careful to be chaste. And care was required, because there was a frisson between us, I could feel it growing.

"I'll ask Kit if she can watch Devin," I said. I waited for Karl to say that his sister would want to go to the show too, but he didn't.

Instead he said, "It's a date."

THE NIGHT OF Seth's show, I put on a black skirt and tights, and the pink top I knew Karl liked. I waited outside for him to pick me up. It was a little chilly for spring. The jacarandas were tacky with purple.

"Jack . . . Aranda," I said, when I was in the car. "I think he's your lawyer, right?"

Karl grinned and tapped the steering wheel. "My, how far you have fallen, Lady."

I nestled into the car's leather seat like a ball in a glove. "You dragged me down to your level," I said. "What was I to do?"

Karl told me he liked my outfit. "You're wearing stockings," he said.

"Well, you did call this a date, didn't you?"

I was flirting and so was he. I wondered if we would talk about the photo tonight. Or ever. If he noticed that *Woman No. 17* was missing, he hadn't yet mentioned it. I knew S had stolen it, probably the night we got drunk. It might be hanging in her father's dining room, for everyone to ooh and aah over, or it might be buried under a stack of stolen *Us Weekly*s at her mother's. The truth was, I was relieved it was gone. It was someone else's problem now, one less secret I had to keep.

Now Karl asked if I was nervous.

"I haven't eaten all day, if that gives you any idea. What will I say to him?"

"Don't worry about that. Just being there, that's what matters."

We were on the 10. The traffic going the other direction was bad, and I felt relief, followed by guilt as Karl accelerated past them, toward the ocean.

I didn't tell him about the book until we'd passed the 405.

"But what did your editor say?" Karl asked. He'd rolled the window down an inch or two, as he always did on the freeway. His white hair fluttered in the breeze.

"She said no one's ever done that to her. She thinks it must be really bad for me to pull it. Erin"—that was my agent—"is pissed."

"Well, that's because you went ahead and offered to return the money."

"What else could I do? I can't write it. It's not my story to tell."

Karl nodded. "Say that," he said. "Say that when you see Seth."

THE SCREENING WAS held in a lecture-style classroom, with tiered seating. The periodic table of elements hung on the wall to my right and I pretended to study it intently before the event began. In the hallway outside someone had set up a table with sparkling water and a plastic liter of Pepsi, a tray of sweating cheese cubes. That's where most people were milling around until the screening began, but I told Karl I felt light-headed and needed to sit. I kept wondering when I'd see Seth, and what I would do, what he would do.

Karl placed a napkin loaded with cheese in front of me and sat down. Then he nudged me and said, "There's the man of the hour."

There he was. Seth. He stood at the podium behind a laptop—presumably it would play the movies that projected on the screen behind him. He was in deep concentration, probably troubleshooting some annoying computer error that no one else in this group of artsy kids could figure out. He leaned closer to the screen, and then away.

He had on a new T-shirt: plain and black like a stagehand's, no pockets, clearly expensive. So this event mattered to him. A lot. I imagined Karl lending him his credit card, and Seth at the mall, trying on the shirt, wondering if it looked okay. He'd never gone shopping for clothes without me.

Karl had told me that Seth had recently begun using a program on his iPad that spoke his written text in a robotic voice. I wondered if I'd hear it tonight. I didn't want to.

Seth looked older. Had he gotten taller? He had grown out his hair to his cheekbones, and it looked good this way—like a skateboarder might wear it. That made me think of S's mom and the stupid guy she'd left her husband for. I didn't want to think about that.

I'm trying to think more about my mom these days, I had written Seth, a week or so ago. *What movies she liked, what kind of stuff she cooked.* I didn't mention S and her project, but maybe that was implicit. *I'd love to tell you more about her, when we see each other next.*

Seth looked up at the crowd, expectant. I waited for him to see me, frozen in my seat, my pink top already wrinkling at the waist. The glistening pile of cheese Karl had placed in front of me.

"Seth!" I heard Karl call out, and I winced.

When Seth saw us, all I could think to do was smile and wave.

He waved back.

Hello. Hello.

A moment later the lights in the room dimmed.

"Well, that went well," Karl whispered and I laughed because he was right. I stuffed a cube of cheese into my mouth as the first movie started.

I'd been so nervous that I'd forgotten we'd come here to see Seth's film.

I'm looking forward to watching it, I'd written him. But the truth was that I hadn't given it much thought. I was too afraid to.

The first two movies were amateurish but amusing, occasionally pretty. There was one where a ballet dancer leapt across a parking lot as a zombie lurked behind a pickup truck. In another, two guys plotted to lose their virginity before the world ended, and then got too stoned to remember their plan. Between each one, the audience clapped and hooted.

Unlike the others, Seth's movie didn't open with a title. Just his name in dark-blue letters, floating there before it disappeared. People cheered and I smiled—he had a crowd.

On the screen now: a table, or something else made of wood. It was shot up close so that you couldn't tell what it was. The hurrahs from the audience dwindled away, as if everyone had agreed to be quiet in order to hear the movie. But there was no sound. Of course there wasn't, I thought. There was only the plane of wood. The occasional wobble of the camera.

And then: a hand. Seth's. I recognized those nail beds. He held a medicine dropper and he began to drip water onto the wood. Tiny drops of water, freckling the surface, fleck, fleck, fleck.

This went on for a minute. Then another.

People began to shift in their seats. Someone coughed. It reminded me of the movies they had in museums, playing on a loop in a small dark room. How people would peek their heads in for a second before turning away. Those rooms were almost always empty.

On the screen, Seth's hand kept dropping the water.

A door opened and shut somewhere. Someone else coughed. The kid in the row in front of us moved around in his seat, obviously bored. I wanted to turn to Karl, to see what he thought, but I forced myself to keep my eyes on the screen.

Did the water feel exploited, I imagined writing to Seth.

I kept watching. His hand moved out of the frame and reemerged with another dropperful of water. The water formed into a tiny puddle, and then a larger one. And larger.

I realized I was holding my breath.

Plink, plink went the water. Seth's hand moved out of frame once more. When he returned with a white cloth instead of the medicine dropper, I exhaled. I watched as he wiped the water away, all of it. There wasn't even a streak remaining. And then the film went black. The end.

Karl leaned over and whispered into my ear, "What did that mean, you think?"

I had no idea. I felt hollowed out and elated. It didn't have to mean anything. It wasn't my movie. It didn't matter what I thought.

SETH HAD DUCKED out of the screening before it was over and we couldn't find him anywhere. I was worried, but Karl wasn't. "He's simply playing up the enigmatic artiste thing."

"What if his feelings were hurt?" I said. "By how people had fidgeted during his film?"

"That was the whole point! It was boring! Wait—wasn't it?"

He had me laughing, and in the car, outside my building, he kissed me, only once, but slowly, and then he pulled away. He said he'd like to take me out again soon. I agreed.

An hour later, I was drinking wine, in my pajamas, watching the ambulances down below.

"Mommy?"

Devin stood at the lip of the hallway, his hair mussed from sleep. He reminded me of Seth. Not how he looked, but the fact of him. I would give him everything I had. I would rescue him from every dark place. It still wouldn't be enough. I would do it anyway.

"What's the matter, honey?" I asked.

"I'm scared."

"There's nothing to be afraid of," I said.

As he listed why I was wrong—ghosts, thunder, monsters—I picked him up and carried him back to his room, his legs circling my waist, his arms around my neck.

I can admit, now, that my own mother used to carry me like this, I imagined writing to Seth. *Just because I don't remember doesn't mean she didn't.*

"It's all right," I said, talking over Devin as he continued to list all that was unsafe in the world. "I'm here. I won't let anything hurt you."

ARTFORUM

Critics' Picks [online]
Esther Shapiro
Gavin Brown's Enterprise

For all its promises to democratize and disrupt, the Internet is often as oppressive as it is liberating, particularly for women and other marginalized voices. Feminist artists have been interrogating this contradiction for at least a decade, from Ann Hirsch's tongue-in-cheek experimentation with the inevitable sexualizing of any female who dares to set up her own YouTube channel, to Kit Daniels's recent series of photographs of teenage girls she met through a "questionable" (Daniels's word) open casting call on Craigslist. Into this spirited discourse steps Esther Shapiro with her first solo show, *Dick Picks* at Gavin Brown's Enterprise, a set of fifteen photographs of male genitalia that were initially emailed or texted to the artist herself. By enlarging these images to 40 by 50 inches and displaying them without frames, Shapiro emphasizes their amateurish nature. These were obviously shot and sent with cell phones, and without much forethought. Such carelessness reminds one, by contrast, of the coiffed and studied selfies that young women post to social media every day, either as an act of self-empowering image control, or as a surrender to the male gaze and porn culture—or both. *Dick Picks* calls to mind Thomas Ruff's nudes, likewise culled from the web, as well as the work of Richard Prince, particularly his appropriation of strangers' Instagram shots, including those of Suicide Girls. The difference is that Shapiro is a woman and her subjects are not. Though certainly sensational, her adaptation of these male self-portraits manages to transcend labels like scandalous or pornographic because the artist was the very person—the woman—to receive these images, often against her will; she was compelled to witness them whether she wanted to or not. And now so are we. When viewed from this feminist perspective, many of these photos take on a violent, even gruesome, tone, while others, enlarged to the point of being blurry, are abstract and painterly, their sexual bite rendered harmless and tender. Of course, this is Shapiro's doing, and she and the viewer both know it. Herein lies this young artist's gift.

—Pauline Deck

Acknowledgments

Erin Hosier, my fierce and funny agent, believed in this book from the very start. Thank you, Erin, for meeting me in the rain in Beverly Hills all those years ago, and for being not only my advocate but my friend too. Thanks are due to everyone at Dunow, Carlson & Lerner, especially Arielle Datz, and to the wonderful Amy Schiffman at Intellectual Property Group.

Everyone at Hogarth/Crown: you are a joy to work with! I am deeply grateful to my editor, Lindsay Sagnette, whose passion for this novel inspired and motivated me (and sometimes caused me to cackle with delight), and whose insights and line edits made this a better book. Lindsay, you get it, you get me, and it has been a privilege learning from you. Special thanks as well to Molly Stern, Rachel Rokicki, Kevin Callahan, Lisa Erickson, and the (already) legendary Rose Fox. Thank you all for making me feel at home.

I would like to thank the Ucross Foundation for the time, space, and community it provides artists and writers. It's heavenly.

I'm not a visual artist, but I'm lucky to know so many brilliant ones in real life. Thank you to the following painters and photographers for their guidance: Charlie White, Tei Blow, Christine Frerichs, and Tanya Hartman.

Lyssa Rome was generous with her time and knowledge about speech development. Thanks, Lyssa. This novel was also informed by Andrew Solomon's compassionate and profound book *Far from the Tree: Parents, Children, and the Search for Identity;* the parents Solomon writes about are patient, accepting, and tenacious, and reading their stories was what first made me imagine a fictional mother who doesn't possess those qualities.

No one else has a better writing group than I do. The Hugging Party—Yael Goldstein Love, Kate Milliken, Lydia Kiesling, Kara Levy, and member emeritus Lisa Srisuro—thank you for reading sections of this book and asking the tough questions. You're all so smart and sexy, I can't stand it.

Thanks to my fellow staff writers at *The Millions,* and to my students and colleagues at Writing Workshops Los Angeles, especially director Chris Daley, who works harder than anyone I know. And a shout-out to my former classmate Tom McAllister (@t_mcallister) for the Titans tweet!

Mike Reynolds, Madeline McDonnell, Kristen Daniels, and Susan Straight all offered wise and encouraging feedback on this manuscript—thank you (and I owe you). For their friendship I'd also like to thank Diana Samardzic, Kathleen Potthoff, Molly McDonald, Douglas Diesenhaus, Rachel Fershleiser, Carrie Neill, Allison Hill, Paria Kooklan, Julia Whicker, Josh Yocum, Deena Drewis, Umbreen Bhatti, Ryan Miller, Tali Horowitz, Heather Lambirth, Anna Solomon, Neelanjana Banerjee, Darcy Vebber, Ann Holler, Catie Disabato, Cecil Castellucci, Meaghan O'Connell, Rumaan Alam, and Tess Taylor.

People often ask me how I'm able to write with two young children. My answer is this: childcare. Thank you to the people who cared for my kids so I could write: André Julien and Anna Baldwin at Greenhouse Childcare; all the teachers at Hearts Leap North Preschool, most especially Adriana DeVost and Andi Roncajolo; and Miriam Herrera. Miry, thanks for taking such loving care of my gnome.

I love getting the chance to publicly thank my family, because, well, I have the best family in the whole wide world. Thank you to Bob Lepucki (aka my personal location manager), Keitha Lowrance, Margaret Guzik, Mitchell Guzik, Lauren Lepucki Tatzko, Heidi Cascardo, Sarah Guzik (aka my personal Millennial reader), Asher Guzik (aka my personal plants expert), Kam Brown, and Art Brown.

Finally, I want to thank my husband, Patrick Brown, and our two beautiful children, Dixon Bean Brown and Ginger Dean Brown. Patty, thanks for reading and re-reading this book, and for everything you do for me and our family. It's a pleasure being your dog.

About the Author

EDAN LEPUCKI is the *New York Times* bestselling author of the novel *California*, as well as the novella *If You're Not Yet Like Me*. A contributing editor and staff writer at *The Millions*, she has also published fiction and nonfiction in *McSweeney's*, the *Los Angeles Times*, the *New York Times*, *The Cut*, and elsewhere. She is the founder of Writing Workshops Los Angeles.